Dear Mystery Lover:

No one writes about Cleveland, Ohio, with the power and passion of Les Roberts. This outstanding writer is enamored of his adopted home, and city residents clearly return this affection. When Roberts walks down Cleveland's streets, he's greeted like a celebrity.

But this is no naive love affair; Roberts understands the many facets of this diverse Midwestern town. While it may be the sophisticated home of one of this country's great symphony orchestras, it has a dark, troubled side. (Few will forget when its Cuyahoga River actually caught on fire.) In this fine novel, Roberts writes about ethnic hatreds that divide: bitter conflicts from the past that explode into a present-day murder.

This is the first of the Milan Jacovich mysteries in DEAD LETTER. The author's other wry Cleveland books will soon be available in paperback. Our exciting DEAD LETTER publishing plans for this writer go something like this: More Roberts!

Enjoy.

Yours in M

Dan

Dana Edwi
Senior Editor
St. Martin's DEAD LETTER Paperback Mysteries

Other titles from St. Martin's
Dead Letter Mysteries

PRAISE FOR LES ROBERTS AND THE MILAN JACOVICH NOVELS

The Cleveland Connection

"Roberts' most ambitious work thus far...A potent plot... A brave, satisfying story."

—*Publishers Weekly*

"An intriguing and ingratiating hero... An intriguing case to solve."

—*San Diego Union*

"There's an affection for Cleveland and its ethnic, working-class life that gives vividness to the detection."

—*Washington Post Book World*

"Roberts' best effort yet. The plot has all the right ingredients—danger, suspense, intrigue, action—in all the right amounts; Milan Jacovich is the kind of guy we want on our side when the chips are down... Don't miss this one."

—*Booklist* (starred review)

"Very good, and very tough...Les Roberts has written an extremely good novel that is well worth reading by all, not just mystery lovers."

—*Armchair Detective*

"The dialogue sparkles, the scenes are taut, and the humor is as dry as a proper martini...very, very good indeed."

—*Flint Journal* (MI)

By the same author:

THE CLEVELAND CONNECTION

A MILAN JACOVICH MYSTERY

LES ROBERTS

St. Martin's Paperbacks

All characters in this book are fictional, and any resemblance to persons living or dead is purely coincidental.

THE CLEVELAND CONNECTION

ISBN: 0-312-96218-5

Printed in the United States of America

St. Martin's Press hardcover edition published in 1993
St. Martin's Paperbacks edition/June 1997

10 9 8 7 6 5 4 3 2 1

To Danny and Pat Pavlovitch—
for the laughter.

ONE

You could have knocked me over with a feather.

Joe Bradac was the last guy I'd expect to see standing on the threshold of my apartment at nine o'clock on a Monday morning. A cop at the door wouldn't have surprised me; I was once a cop myself, so not only do I have a load of friends on the force, but since becoming a private investigator and security specialist my interests and those of the police department occasionally dovetail—or clash—and Cleveland's boys in blue visit me more often than I'd like. It could have been my landlord knocking—I try to pay my rent by the fifth of the month, but occasionally I forget. Maybe a Jehovah's Witness waving a religious tract at me; in Cleveland Heights, where I have my office in my apartment, they are as ubiquitous as the gray squirrel. Once in a while even a dissatisfied client shows up at the door—things happen, after all. But not Joe Bradac.

Joe Bradac lives with my ex-wife.

Lila and I have one of those amicable divorces that seem to work out better than the marriage ever did. She got the house and car and we split everything else, including custody of my two sons, Milan Junior and Stephen, who are now sixteen and twelve years old respectively. Although they live under her roof, there's rarely a problem when I want to see them.

It wasn't always so; when we first split up Lila could get pretty sticky if I wanted to be with the boys more often than my court-mandated every other weekend. But now she and I talk a few times a week on the phone, we see each other occasionally, and though she's grown more prickly than ever with me, we get along about as well as can be expected. After four years of separation, we aren't in love anymore—time is a thief of love—but when you've cared about somebody for more than half your life, the caring doesn't end just because a piece of paper says it should. I took the divorce hard for a while—especially the part about not living with my kids—and I took Joe pretty hard, too. But finally I've let go and moved on to the rest of my life.

Even so, Joe Bradac and I aren't pals. We never have been, not in high school and not since, and his moving in with Lila and playing resident daddy to my boys hasn't done anything to further the friendship. So when I opened my door and saw him in the hallway, his fists shoved into the pockets of that blue jacket of his, the fake fur collar pulled up around his rather prominent ears, you could have knocked me over with a feather.

Joe walks softly when he's around me; he never knows how I'm going to react to him, and this time his approach was to make a pretty pitiful attempt at a smile, which came out looking like the grimace of a baby with a gas pain. But then Joe's attempts at just about anything are pitiful. He's one of those guys who kind of tiptoes through life trying not to wake anybody up. I've never understood why Lila is attracted to him. She can be a real buccaneer when she wants to, and there are times when she gives Joe a pretty rough time. Maybe it's because he lets her.

The end of his nose was red from the cold, and a sprinkle of snowflakes was only half melted on his shoulders. "Whattaya say, Milan?"

"Joe," I said. That's about as cordial as I get with Joe. I didn't offer to shake hands because I had the sports section of the paper in one hand and a cup of coffee in the other. And I didn't want to shake his hand anyway.

"Can I come in for a minute?"

His manner was hesitant, as always. Nevertheless, his

visit was so unexpected and so out of character that a cold finger of alarm jabbed me in the back. "Nothing's wrong, is there, Joe? With Lila or the boys?"

He shook his head. "Everybody's fine," he said. "Stephen had a little cough last week but he's okay now. And Milan Junior's doing real good in school. He had to write a paper on something for history—the Civil War, I think it was—and he got a B plus."

Relief flooded over me like a sudden rainstorm, even as it galled me having to hear news of my own children from Joe Bradac, and my attitude softened a little. I stood aside and let him walk past me into my front room, which I use as my office. My desk is in there, and a cracked leather sofa and a couple of not too comfortable chairs I keep for the rare client who comes to see me. I do my real living in a little parlor off the big one, where I have my TV and my easy chair and all my books and magazines. Joe could damn well sit in one of the client's chairs and keep it impersonal. He had nothing to do with where I lived.

He plopped down where I pointed, a passive man in word and deed. I went behind my desk. I didn't offer him any coffee; what I was drinking was the last of the pot and I wasn't about to make more just for him. His body language is as unaggressive and meek as he is, and he sat there like a pile of dirty clothes waiting to be put in the washing machine.

"I hope you don't mind my just coming over like this," he said. "I was afraid if I called you wouldn't see me."

He had that right. I sat down. "It is kind of a surprise."

He wiggled his butt in the seat, a princess on a pea. "I wouldn't've if it wasn't important. I need your advice."

I leaned back a little too hard in my chair and fought for balance for a second. Emotional balance too. The guy had nerve, give him that. "Have you tried Dear Abby?"

The rest of his face turned as red as his nose. "Not *that* kind of advice. Jeez, I wouldn't insult you. . . ."

"What is it, then, Joe?" Thirty seconds with Joe Bradac was enough to make anyone's eyes cross with boredom and

3

impatience. I don't know how Lila puts up with him. Or manages to stay awake.

He took a breath. "You mind if I smoke?"

"Where do you think you are, church?"

He extracted a pack of Luckies from his jacket and lit one, tossing the dead match into my already-full ashtray.

"What's your trouble?"

"It's not mine, exactly. It's a mutual friend."

"You and I don't have any mutual friends," I said.

"Well, old acquaintance, then. You remember Walter Paich? Skinny guy, his father worked the iron mills? He was two years behind us in high school."

I dug into my memory, but though the name tinkled a distant bell my vision of Walter Paich was vague, and more than twenty years out of date. "What about him?"

"I ran into his sister Danica last night." He pronounced it the old-world way, *Danitza.* "I'd gone for a beer with a couple of guys from my bowling league, and she was at a table with some other girls, and I went over to say hello and we got to talking. You probably don't remember her, she was just a kid. She must be, oh, eight or nine years younger than us, like seven years younger than Walter, so I didn't know her real well, just to see around, you know."

"Get to the point, Joe, all right?"

"Sure, Milan," he said, jerking nervously. I played football in high school and college, nose guard, and probably outweigh Joe by sixty pounds, and since he got together with Lila, whenever he sees me he worries I'm going to tear him apart. I admit the thought has occurred to me more than once, but not recently. I enjoy his discomfort, though. Deep down I truly enjoy it.

"Anyways, we got to talking, you know, about old times and how's the family, the way you do with somebody you didn't see in a long time, and I could tell something was bothering her."

"How?"

"Huh?"

"How could you tell?"

4

His eyes roamed the room as though there'd be an answer up near the ceiling. "I just could. She was nervous, had kind of a sad look. So I asked if everything was okay."

"What a caring guy you are, Joe."

He chose to ignore that one. "Well, the thing of it is, see, she's real worried about her grandpa."

"Why?"

"He's been missing for a week."

"Missing?"

"He just disappeared, and they haven't seen or heard from him since."

I lit a cigarette of my own, a Winston. It was my first of the day and tasted terrible, as usual. "There's a real neat organization called the police department to help people with things like that. You may have heard of them."

"She called the cops four days ago, but she can't get them to take her serious," Joe said.

"Why not?"

"The old man's disappeared before, just taken off on his own for a few days at a crack, and the minute they heard that they put it on the bottom of the pile."

"I don't blame them."

"Danica thinks it's different this time."

"Why?"

"I dunno. Gut feeling, I guess."

He sat there with that earnest, nerdy look of his, and I realized how much I wanted him to go away. "I'm still not sure I know why you're here, Joe."

He squirmed some more and blew out a lungful of smoke, which merged with mine to create a fog over my desk. "I told her about you. I mean, she asked me what was new with me and, well, your name came up." He'd rather have cut off a finger than say that, so he hurried on. "She remembers you real good, because of the football. She asked how you were, and I told about your being an investigator and all. Anyway, she wants to hire you."

I sighed. "Nice of you to drum up business for me, but mostly I do industrial security—you know that. Missing per-

5

sons just isn't my line. But I could recommend someone for her."

He tapped the ash off the end of his cigarette. "See, the grandfather's from the old country. All his friends, too. I think the family'd be more comfortable with another Slav."

"These're Serbs, right?"

He kind of stuck out his chin, which I took to mean yes.

I shook my head. I'm Slovenian; my people come from a different part of Yugoslavia. The Serbs and the Slovenes haven't really gotten along for five hundred years, and I have a busted marriage to prove it. They share a language but use different alphabets, and they go to different churches, which sounds on the face of it like New York City, but the reality is something else again. At the moment the two republics are engaged in a mutual economic boycott, including the nonpayment of debts, and their armies are snarling across the border. They don't have much use for each other, but that's nothing compared to the enmity between the Serbs and the Croatians, whose factional differences make the petty sniping between our own Southerners and Yankees seem like a neighborhood dispute over mowing the lawn. It's hard for someone who isn't a Slav to understand—hell, it's hard for *me* to understand. But just because we all share geographic roots doesn't mean we like each other. Serbia and Croatia and Slovenia were all separate countries not too long ago, and at the end of 1990 Slovenia voted to be independent again. The republic of Serbia didn't like that too much, and the Slavs who live in Cleveland are every bit as militant, one way or another, as those back in the old country.

Joe, like Lila, is a Serb. He must have somehow divined what I was thinking, or maybe it had occurred to him too, because he gave an apologetic shrug and raised his hands in front of him. I guess for his purposes and those of Danica Paich, a Slovenian was better than nothing.

"What's your angle in this, Joe?"

He looked confused, par for Joe's course. "I got no angle, Milan."

"I mean, you meet this girl in a bar after twenty years and she spills her guts to you. Why are you getting involved?"

"Just trying to help an old friend."

"You stepping out on Lila with this Danica Paich?"

His face got redder, and he put his hand over his heart; any minute I expected him to recite the Pledge of Allegiance. "Come on, you know me better than that. Hey, Walter was a good guy, I'm just doing his sister a little favor. Him and me were pretty good friends back in the old days."

Sure. Joe was such a dweeb none of us wanted much to do with him, so he hung out with the younger kids, who were less demanding. Now his life was so dull and uninteresting he was probably jumping at the chance to get in on some excitement, even though it was only secondhand. I checked the appointment calendar tacked on the corkboard behind my desk. It had little cartoon Ninja Turtles all over it, and was hardly what you'd expect in a private investigator's office, but it was my Christmas gift from my younger son Stephen, and I didn't much give a damn if it was appropriate or not. Other than my appointment with a prospective client that afternoon and a scheduled Wednesday morning court appearance as a prosecution witness, I didn't have too much on my docket.

"I suppose it wouldn't hurt to talk with her," I said.

Joe almost deflated with relief. "Great. Maybe we could all get together for dinner?"

Presume not too much on my good nature, Cassius. No client, no case, and no old friendship was worth having to break bread with Joe Bradac. "Is there any particular reason why you should be there?"

He looked crestfallen. "Gee, Milan, it was my idea in the first place. . . . "

I began to think my initial suspicions were correct, that Joe was somehow enchanted with this Danica Paich and was using her grandfather's problems as a way to get close to her. And by producing me, a genuine private detective, he'd look like a hero, or at the very least, a concerned and caring friend.

Of course that might have been my own paranoia working overtime. And there *was* an old man missing. It would rub at my conscience if I didn't at least have an initial meeting with the granddaughter. "I think Danica might feel more free to talk with fewer people around," I added.

He still looked hurt at being excluded; clearly it hadn't been part of his game plan.

"Whatever you think is right," he said.

Fuck him.

After the first blizzard of winter, the efficient clearance crews in Cleveland salt all the streets and push whatever snow is left up against the curbs or the sides of buildings to allow traffic to function on the roads. The piles just sit there and diminish a bit every day until the next snowfall, getting a little dirtier and sadder-looking until they melt away in March or April.

It was that kind of evening as I drove downtown, the tail end of the bad-weather season, with the city eagerly anticipating the benediction of spring. Joe had called Danica Paich from my office and then handed me the phone, and after some chat we'd decided to meet at six at a restaurant in the lobby of the building where she worked, the British Petroleum Building, most often referred to as "the BP," on the east side of Public Square.

The restaurant is called Gershwin's. Replete with tasteful maroon awnings outside, within there are three levels, and on one of the upper ones a piano player performs songs by the place's namesake and such other composers as Kern, Porter, Rodgers, and Harold Arlen, giving the lie to Cleveland's false and unfortunate blue-collar image as a town where bowling is about as cultural as it gets. No one ever talks about our world-class symphony orchestra, the jazz clubs, the terrific restaurants serving food of every stripe and ethnicity, the museums and galleries, the superb library system, the great repertory theaters, and the free concerts. Its richly varied cultural life is the little secret Cleveland keeps from the rest of the world.

I arrived a bit early, as I'd had a meeting with an old client to review his small manufacturing plant's security system. His office was in Richmond Heights, and by the time I got out of there most of the traffic was heading out of downtown and I had a clear shot all the way down Euclid to Public Square. I parked in a garage a block away, walked through the down-slanting mist that you can't really call rain but gets you pretty wet anyway, and had a beer at the bar while I waited. Through the interior window the lush greenery of the building's atrium lobby cheered things up a lot, rather like a tropical jungle in the middle of Cleveland.

Gershwin's affords an unusually good people-watching opportunity. This was an upwardly mobile crowd; the only blue collars in evidence were buttoned down over bright-hued paisley ties. They used to call this little hunk of time at the end of the workday the cocktail hour, but with increased sensibilities about the perils of drinking and driving it came to be known in more recent times as happy hour. The trend makers, feeling that that was still too frivolous, have rechristened the after-work ritual "attitude adjustment." In the old neighborhood, when someone's attitude needed adjusting you took him down to the cellar and bounced him off the wall a few times. Now you buy him an overpriced mineral water and fix him a plate of hot hors d'oeuvres.

I observed the middle-management mating dance for a while. Everyone was talking louder than necessary in an almost desperate effort to be noticed in the look-alike crowd. The women all contrived to dress the fine line between professionally correct and sensually alluring, what I call the mixed-message wardrobe, very starchy and businesslike but with tight-fitting skirts and lots of sleek, nyloned leg showing. Some of the younger men, rainmakers-in-training, had removed their suit jackets to display patterned designer suspenders, and I watched one guy with wide pink-and-gray jobbies bust a move on a brittle blonde at the end of the bar. My father used to wear suspenders—utilitarian black ones, and he wore them to keep his pants up, unlike these successful young guys on the rise who use them to flaunt their own individuality in defiance of corporate uniformity, reminding me somehow of conservative businessmen who furtively wear ladies' panties beneath their gray flannel suits.

I had on a tweed jacket, a plaid shirt, and a blue knit tie, and nobody paid much attention to me because my clothes said I was neither an attorney, a stockbroker, nor the head of a department. I do share one thing with such corporate types, though: I admit feeling silly about it, but I have a beeper.

I always thought—I still think, to tell the truth—that unless you're a heart surgeon, wearing a beeper on your belt is presumptious and pompous, a sign of the deluded self-importance that afflicts many people these days. They all labor under the firm conviction that if they aren't able to make instant contact with everyone they've ever met, the earth will fly off its axis and go careening out into space, signaling the end of civilization as we know it. But in my business, it's easier to carry a little device on my belt than to jump up and check my answering machine twice an hour. I still haven't gotten over feeling like a horse's ass when the beeper goes off in public, though, and every eye in the place is suddenly on me.

After a while I sensed someone at my elbow and turned to look down at a petite young woman with dark brown hair in a soft cut that framed her face, bright blue eyes, very red lipstick, and the broad planes of her Slavic ancestry flattening her prominent cheekbones. "Hello, Milan," she said.

I got off my stool as clumsily as a trained bear. I towered over her by more than a foot. "Danica?"

She nodded, smiling. "I'd recognize you anywhere. From high school. You haven't changed."

I sucked in my gut and ran a hand through my rapidly thinning hair. "Not much," I said. I peered at her, trying to recall that face at ten years old, but the memory wouldn't kick in, even though she looked a good five years younger than she was. She had obviously improved with age—if she'd looked anything like that I would have remembered her. She wasn't flashy or even beautiful, but she was pretty in a way that would just get better the older she got.

"That's okay," she said, reading my thoughts. "I didn't expect you to remember me. I was just a little kid." She unbuttoned her gray wool coat and I helped her shrug it from her shoulders. The skirt of her dark blue suit was slit up the

10

side to mid-thigh, and a beautiful white cameo adorned the neck of her ivory-colored blouse.

"How've you been, Milan? God, it must be twenty years since I've seen you."

"At least," I agreed. "I'm fine."

"Joe says you have your own business now. That's wonderful." She flashed an uncertain smile. "And you married Lila Coso."

"Wooed, won, and lost," I said. "Now she's Joe's lady. I suppose he told you that too."

She had the class to pass that one over. "Whatever made you become a detective? Was that a longtime dream of yours?"

"Hardly. I got a B.A. in business administration at Kent State and took my master's in psychology. The agency kind of happened. But I don't consider myself a detective. I'm an industrial security specialist, and that makes up ninety percent of my business. Every once in a while I get involved in something else, though, like for a friend."

Her face lit up from within, and she blushed. Danica Paich was a woman whose moods were reflected on her face like sunlight hitting the ripples on the face of Lake Erie, ever constant, yet changing all the time. "I'm glad you think of me as a friend after all these years," she said. "I appreciate your coming. This must be pretty small potatoes for you."

"Not at all. And speaking of potatoes, should we get a table?"

"Someplace where we can talk," she agreed.

The hostess led us to a quiet booth in a room away from the bar, although we could still hear and enjoy the music. I'm an oddball among my friends: I like Gershwin and Irving Berlin while most of them are into either seventies rock or tambouritza orchestras. Danica declined a drink, so I didn't have one either. After all, she was the client and was paying for all this.

"You were telling me your life story."

I smiled. "I hope I wasn't being that pompous. Let's see; after college I wound up in Vietnam. With the MPs. Going

11

into the army wasn't the thing to do back then, especially for a guy from Kent, but I felt pretty strongly about it at the time." I smiled. "Funny how things change."

"And then you came back and decided to go into industrial security?"

"No, I became a cop. Remember Marko Meglich?"

She crinkled up her eyes for a moment. "Wasn't he on the football team too?"

I nodded. "Wide receiver. He'd always been my best friend, and he decided he wanted to be a cop and talked me into it too. But after four years or so the politics and the bureaucracy got to me, so I quit and opened my own store. Marko's still on the force—only he calls himself Mark now, and he's a lieutenant."

The waiter arrived and we ordered dinner. She chose some sort of fish with dill sauce and I went for a steak, medium. I have the palate of a peasant. I can't help it, that's how I am.

"How about you?" I said. "Fill me in."

"I was a business major too, at Cleveland State. I put myself through by waitressing. I really got interested in computers in school, so I concentrated on that, and I guess it paid off, because now I run a department." She nodded at the ceiling. "Right upstairs, here. I've been there almost seven years. Most people around the office call me Diana, in case you have to phone and ask for me."

I frowned. It was typical of big corporate thinking. They tend to Anglicize anything they can't turn into an acronym. "I think I like Danica better."

"I do too," she said.

"I'll call you Danica, then." I paused. There was no ring on her left hand—single guys tend to notice those things—but I figured I'd ask anyway. "Married?"

She shook her head. "Too busy carving out a career. My biological clock isn't ticking too loudly yet, so for the time being it's okay."

"And your brother Walter? How's he?"

Something happened to her pretty face that turned down

the corners of her eyes. "He works for Deming Steel, on the floor somewhere. Third generation of our family. I don't see him much."

It was more than pleasant sitting there with an attractive woman, listening to music and enjoying a good meal. I hadn't done that in quite a while, and I had to remind myself that this dinner wasn't really social. After our salad plates were cleared I asked about her grandfather.

She dabbed at her mouth with a napkin, but it was due more to nervousness than necessity. "I'm very worried about him. He just took off one afternoon and never came back."

"What afternoon?"

"Monday. A week ago today."

I didn't say anything, just nodded. She'd tell me what she had to in her own good time. Keeping one's mouth shut often yields greater results than asking a million questions.

"He's too old to be running around somewhere all by himself."

"How old is he?"

"Seventy-six. He's done this before, for a day or two, but he's always called my mother to let her know he was all right."

"What do you mean, he's done it before?"

"He has a Ford van, an old one he's had since when my grandmother was alive. He'll just take off in it without telling anybody and drive to Cincinnati or Pittsburgh or Toledo, or someplace nobody's ever heard of, some little town. He wanders around, talks to people, finds the Serbian social club if there is one or a Serbian bar if there isn't, and then comes back when he's good and ready."

"But he always calls?"

She nodded, her eyebrows knitting. "At first it made us crazy, but now we're used to it, so for the first few days we didn't think much about it. But more than a week without a word—that's never happened. I'm worried sick."

"When he left the house last Monday did he say anything?"

"I wasn't there, but my mother said he just waved and

13

walked out the door like he always does." Her smile was rueful. "Grandpa never does say much."

I understood. My grandfather never said much either. He'd just glare at you if you sat in his favorite chair and make a quick, chopping motion with his hand to get you out of it. After dinner he'd usually wipe his mouth, grunt "Good," and go in and watch TV. He was a face pincher, though; he'd grab a handful of tender grandchild cheek and squeeze until the tears came, and even though it hurt I never complained, because I knew it was his way of showing love.

"And he didn't take anything with him?"

"Like what?"

"I don't know," I said. "A suitcase, a gym bag, a paper sack."

"No, there was nothing unusual, Mama said. He just left like he does every day. Except he didn't come back."

I held my next question until our dinners were in front of us and the waiter had retreated. "Do you know if your grandpa was upset about anything? Was something bothering him?"

"He doesn't have much to be upset about, ever. He's been retired for ten years or so; all he does is hang out with his pals."

"Where?"

"Where what?"

"Where does he hang out?"

"A little bar on St. Clair. Janko's, I think it's called. He goes there almost every day."

I knew the place, a Serbian bar a few blocks to the west of where I was born. I cut into my steak.

Her eyes opened wide, and I noticed there were darker rings around the blue. "Find him," she said.

TWO

Danica and I made our necessary business arrangements, and she signed a contract I'd brought along and gave me a check as a retainer. I felt funny about charging her to help out in a family crisis, but I worked through it. After all, I hadn't seen her in twenty years. And it is what I do for a living.

We drove to Pasnow Avenue, where her mother and grandfather lived, with her leading the way in her new Camry and me following along in my Pontiac Sunbird. I'd been driving it for nine months, and was just now getting used to it, being more accustomed to something bigger and heavier. My previous car, a Chevy Caprice wagon, had come to an untimely end. There were times, in deep snow or on ice-slick streets, when the Pontiac barely got the job done, but all in all I felt okay about it.

That particular stretch of Pasnow Avenue is in Slavic Town, not far from where I'd grown up. The house had white-painted aluminum siding, with stone steps going up to the front porch. The original wooden porch railings had been removed and replaced with ugly wrought iron ones, and the shutters and roof were painted gray, although the trim color of preference on Pasnow Street was predominantly green. There was a second-floor porch, added on after the original construction, which I imagine was a fine, cool place to sit on a summer evening with a can of Stroh's, listening to the Indians game on a portable radio. There are a lot more black families in the area now than when I'd lived there, but the character of the neighborhood has remained unchanged: honest, blue-collar, and proud, with places called Bosko's Bar and Cubelic's Polka Village. I felt comfortable here.

I was comfortable in Tootsie Paich's living room, too. She'd see to it that I was or know the reason why. Tootsie was a plump, sweet-looking woman in her late fifties, and when I looked at her I could see the genes she had passed on to Danica, the bright blue eyes and the broad facial planes, the olive skin and dark brown hair. She was bustling around, an apron covering her gray skirt and white blouse, forcing coffee and pastry on me, which, on top of the steak dinner I'd just eaten, I did not need, and pouring a strong Yugoslavian wine called *zelavka,* which always gives me a headache. Her living room was a small neat square, done in dark varnished woods, busy flowered upholstery, and a medium green wall-to-wall shag carpet, with a print of a still life of a fruit platter hanging over the sofa in a too ornate frame. Danica had only given her mother half an hour's notice that we were coming, so I knew the spotless condition of her home was not just for company.

"I think I remember you, Milan," she said, literally pushing a wineglass into my hand and curling my fingers around the stem. "Didn't you used to come over here with Walter?"

"No, ma'am. I don't think so. Walter's a little younger than me. That makes a lot of difference in high school."

"Oh, well," she said, her hands fluttering, primping at her hair and at the collar of her blouse. She spoke with the barest of accents; probably only another Slav would notice it.

Danica sat on the edge of the chintz easy chair, knees pressed together, not much at ease. "Mama, Milan is going to help us find Grandpa," she said. She'd surely explained it on the phone, but I got the idea Tootsie tended to ramble, and Danica was trying to keep her on track.

"Yes, that's very nice of you," Tootsie said, and rolled her eyes toward the ceiling. "And when you find him, you can keep him. That man, I don't know what I'm going to do with him. The older he gets, the more trouble."

I smiled. "Our parents look after us when we're growing up, and then we have to take care of them."

"I have to say that I think Danica's making more of this than is necessary," Tootsie said. "It's not the kind of thing a detective . . . I don't mean to offend you, Milan, but . . ."

"Your father's been missing a week, Mrs. Paich. Aren't you the least little bit worried?"

"Yes, but this isn't something new." She sighed. "He's always going off somewhere, getting himself into trouble."

"What kind of trouble?"

"Tavern trouble," she said. "Hangs out in the bars. It seems I spend my life worrying about him. And Walter."

"Walter?"

Danica said, "Mama, Milan doesn't have all night."

The two women looked at each other, and then Mrs. Paich glanced away. "Well, how can I help you?" she asked.

"I'll need a photograph, if you have one. And whatever you can tell me about him."

"The picture is easy," she said. She rose and went into the postage-stamp dining room, fumbled in the drawer of a built-in highboy, and came back with an old-fashioned album, the kind with black pages and pasteboard covers with a thin layer of leather glued onto them. It was dog-eared and tattered, and about a foot thick with the pages that had been added through the years. I would have bought a second album to accommodate the extra photos, but then that's just me.

She sat down next to me on the sofa and spread the book open across both our laps.

"This is my parents' wedding picture," she said, pointing to the faded sepia enlargement on the first page. The groom, Bogdan Zdrale, wore the uniform of a corporal in the National Resistance Army and sat on an ornate love seat with one hand on his thigh, back erect and eyes eagle-fierce. The bride, in white, stood behind him, touching his shoulder. It was an uneasy, formal pose, typical of the times. Obviously the females in the family passed their looks along, because the resemblance between Danica, her mother, and her grand-mother was startling. Bogdan, even in his early twenties, had

17

the craggy, rough-hewn features one can see on a St. Clair Avenue street corner today. The couple didn't look like young people in love, but back then marriage was a different proposition, and it may have been that they hardly knew each other yet.

"Your father was a soldier, Mrs. Paich?"

"He trained as a machinist. He might have made the army his career if not for the Second World War," she said. "But he spent a few years in a German prison camp, and he lost his taste for soldiering, I think. Then he came over here, and—"

"Do you have a more recent picture?"

She paged through the album quickly, so I got a sense of a family growing up at an accelerated pace. Most of the photos had been fitted into those little gummed corners, and several were in danger of falling out. It was a very old album.

"Here's Walter and Danica when they were children," she said, looking lovingly at the picture. Walter was a sullen boy of twelve in a suit he obviously hated to wear, and seeing his likeness I remembered him, if not with perfect clarity, as a sullen teenager who never smiled. Danica was a tousled imp in her going-to-church dress, about five years old and grinning at the camera, much more at ease and more outgoing than her brother, who seemed to be nursing a grudge against the world. I suppose everyone has a childhood picture in which they're frowning, grumping, or ready to cry, but this one reminded me of the way Walter Paich had looked every time I'd seen him.

"Mama," Danica said, "Milan doesn't want to look at that." She was blushing. Prettily.

Tootsie lingered over the photo of her children for a moment longer, her eyes soft and moist, then resumed her search until she found what she was looking for. "This was taken about two years ago," she said, pointing to the color snapshot.

Bogdan again, now an old man, thin and gnarled and hickory hard. His brown eyes were still fierce. His hair was still thick, although now iron gray, and standing up straight.

18

I could tell it was a candid shot, because the subject was turning to look at the camera, startled and belligerent, like an angry ostrich. The setting was parklike, the sun hot and bright, and Bogdan wore a polyester suit and a tan shirt that was not quite ironed, with a wide patterned tie knotted too tightly around his neck. I suppressed a grin of embarrassment; most of the ties I own look like that. Now they're coming back into style.

"This was at the christening of Walter's little girl Constance," Danica explained. "Grandpa hates having his picture taken."

"Is that why there are so few of him in the album?"

"He always says no and turns his face away," Tootsie said, as though her father's camera shyness was another burden for her. She indicated the other photos on the page—herself, Danica, a grown-up Walter looking as uncomfortable in a suit as he had when he was twelve, and a thin, hollow-eyed younger woman in a blue satiny suit holding a pretty baby in a christening dress.

"May I have that?" I said, pointing to Bogdan's photo.

Tootsie made a supplicating face. "It's the only recent picture I have," she said.

"I'll have it copied and return it to you."

Her hand fluttered over the album page; then she lowered it and her fingers picked at the gummed corners that held the photograph. "I guess that'd be all right."

"Your father is retired, Mrs. Paich?"

"Oh, yes. For about ten years now."

"What does he do with his days?"

She closed the album and put it beside her on the sofa, keeping one protective hand on it just in case I might be inclined to snatch it and run. "Not much. He watches TV." She laughed. "He likes the soap operas. *Days of Our Lives*. Then after that he goes down to Janko's and sits around until dinnertime."

"Does he drink heavily?"

"No," Danica said, "not at all anymore. He was getting headaches, and the doctor told him to stop, so now he just drinks lots of coffee. I imagine they think he's a pain in the neck at Janko's, but they humor him."

"Who are his friends?" I said. "Anyone he sees a lot?"

"Elmo Laketa," Tootsie answered. "They've been friends for sixty years, since the old country. They worked for Deming Steel together until my father retired. Elmo left a few months later." She lowered her voice as if talking about an eccentric uncle who waves his penis at passersby from an attic window. "Elmo isn't well."

I wrote Elmo's name down in my notebook. "Where does he live?"

"I don't even know," Danica said, "but you can always find him at Janko's."

"Okay," I said. "What about Walter?"

The two women exchanged glances again. Walter seemed to be a delicate subject. Tootsie said, "Why you want to bother with him? He doesn't even see his grandpa five times a year."

"Walter pretty much keeps to himself," Danica added.

"I may want to talk to him anyway. You never know."

She hesitated for a moment and then gave me Walter's address and phone number. I wrote them in my notebook. "Good luck catching him at home," she said.

"Why?"

She waved a hand in front of her face as if to wipe her words off an invisible chalkboard. "No, nothing—he's hard to reach sometimes. Just keep trying him."

I wondered about a guy with a wife and small baby being hard to reach at home but filed the thought away for future reference and put Bogdan's photo in my jacket pocket, with the contract and Danica's check.

"I hope you can find Papa," Tootsie said. "I don't know why, but I've got a funny feeling about this, way down here." She touched a spot just below her breastbone.

I didn't tell her so, but I had a funny feeling about it too.

It was late, past midnight when I finally got home. I had a slight buzz from Tootsie's zelavka, but I sat at my desk, switched on the lamp with the green glass shade that my ex-girlfriend Mary had given me, and reviewed what Tootsie had told me about her father.

Bogdan Zdrale. Born January 11, 1917, in Žagreb. Joined the Yugoslavian army in 1939, attained the rank of corporal. Spent 1943 through 1945 in a German concentration camp in a suburb of Belgrade. Maybe that was why he always looked angry. That would do it for me, I figured.

Reunited with his wife Marija and daughter Tootsie after the war, he emigrated to New York, then quickly to Cleveland. Went to work as a puddler at the Deming Steel plant in 1948. Marija active in Saint Theodosius Parish, Bogdan reluctantly attending church only at Easter and Christmas. Grandchildren Walter Paich, born in 1952, and Danica Paich, born 1959. Great grandchild Constance Paich, born 1990. No hobbies, and since he gave up drinking, no vices other than cigarettes. Marija died in 1971, Bogdan retired from Deming Steel with full pension in 1982. Lived with his widowed daughter on Pasnow Avenue. In good health except for a chronic bad back and recurrent headaches, which lessened after he went on the wagon. Watched daytime TV at home and drank coffee at Janko's Tavern. Disappeared for a day or two at a time to visit Serbian bars in nearby cities, then came home.

And that was all.

Seventy-five years squished into a single page of notes. A few words, facts without essence. I wondered if, at the end, it would take much more than that to sum up my life. Born Cleveland, Ohio. Kent State. Vietnam. The police force. Private security agency. Smoked Winstons, drank Stroh's. Married, two children, divorced, retired, died. It was a sobering thought. I don't kid myself that I'm changing the world during my brief tenure here, but I'd like to believe I'm at least making a little dent. I think we all nurture a secret terror that our living and dying will go unremarked, unmourned, that unlike Jimmy Stewart in that perennial Christmas movie, our life won't make a damn bit of difference to anyone.

I transferred the information about Bogdan Zdrale from

21

my notebook onto three-by-five cards. I prefer working that way, moving the cards around on my desktop until they began to make sense. Of course, I was a long way from making any sense of the old man's disappearance, but I had only just begun. Somehow it was more important to me than a simple task performed for a client. Perhaps there was something about Danica's big blue eyes that touched me. Or perhaps it was simple curiosity, an old occupational affliction of mine that has gotten me into a good bit of trouble over the years.

Or maybe it was what I like to call the Cleveland connection.

There are more people of Slavic heritage in the Greater Cleveland area than anywhere else in the world outside Europe itself, which gives us a sense of belonging that's becoming increasingly rare in these times of upward mobility and corporate relocation. St. Clair Avenue and the town of Euclid along the lake and Parma on the West side are all ethnic enclaves that have retained their ethnic character in the face of the postwar baby boom, the Eisenhower era, the Vietnam years, the great flower-power epoch of the sixties, and the conspicuous consumption of the eighties. I had grown up among people whose roots I shared, gone to school with them, socialized with them, fought with and loved them. Even at Kent State the Slavs managed to find each other, banding together for friendship and support. We followed the doings of the Cold War as if it was happening down on East Fifty-fifth Street instead of across the ocean, because even though we became Americanized and in some cases, like Mark Meglich, had Anglicized our names, we still felt a part of a small, tight community. To this day most of my close friends share an Eastern European heritage—Matt Baznik and Alex Cerne and Rudy Dolsak and Marko Meglich, all natives of Cleveland, all bound in some way to one another by custom or through friends or relatives in the old country. It's an unconscious thing, but we all sense the connection. It's common to any immigrant culture; I'm sure the Germans of Chicago and the Poles of Detroit and the Vietnamese of Southern California feel the same way.

Bogdan Zdrale, in his shiny suit and tight collar and too-wide tie, reminded me of my own grandfather and father and Uncle Anton, now gone, and my Auntie Branka who still lives just off Lake Shore Boulevard and 185th Street, wears a black dress every day, and cooks huge meals for anyone who happens by. And in an almost metaphysical way, of myself. Bogdan Zdrale, Serbian or not, was part of me, of my heritage. Part of the Cleveland connection.

I got out a file folder, marked it ZDRALE, and put the signed contract and the index cards in it.

I studied the picture before I put it away in the file. Even though the photographer had taken him unawares and he looked startled and irritated, there was still a remnant of that hawklike ferocity I had noticed in his wedding portrait, an anger that went beyond mere annoyance at a candid snapshot.

There had to be more to Bogdan Zdrale than a short chronology of birth, marriage, fatherhood, the same job for thirty-five years, and retirement. I figured I'd find out what it was before I was through.

The first thing I did the next morning was to call Spanish John Hanratty at the hot-car division down at police headquarters. John and I went through our rookie training together and had worked the streets on the same shift for more than a year, until he got a call to investigate a neighbor's complaint of domestic violence and walked in on a redneck whaling the tar out of his wife with a silver-studded cowboy belt. Both husband and wife turned on him when he tried to break it up, and he caught a bullet in the kneecap for his trouble. They gave him a commendation and an extra stripe and stuck him behind a desk, where his now permanent limp wouldn't get in the way of his work, and the street lost a good cop.

They call him Spanish John because his mother was Puerto Rican, and with his dusky brown complexion, black hair, and piercing brown eyes he doesn't look much like a guy named Hanratty. But the Hispanic blood in his veins was enough to make him an affirmative action baby, a "gimme," in

23

police parlance, hired on specifically as a part of the department's active outreaching to the minority communities. His limp may have curtailed his police activities but it didn't hurt his love life much. Spanish John's list of conquests would fill a large notebook.

"John, can you put the word out about a missing car for me?"

"Somebody rip off your wheels?"

"It isn't my car, and it isn't exactly stolen," I said.

He paused for a second. I could envision him with his ever-present red pencil hovering over the complaint sheet. "Whose car is it, and what is it, exactly, if it isn't stolen?"

I explained it to him.

"Sounds like you should be talking to missing persons."

"They aren't real interested, John, because this isn't the first time the old guy has pulled a vanishing act."

"Where do you fit?"

"The family hired me to find him."

"I see, said the blind man as he fell in the brook," Spanish John said. "Okay, I'll put it on the sheet. You got the license?"

I gave it to him, along with a description of the light green 1982 Ford van.

"And what do I do when somebody finds it?"

"Call me," I said.

I didn't even get my morning coffee finished before Joe Bradac was on the line. My contact with Joe was normally limited to four times a year or so, and usually by accident, as I tried not to go to Lila's house while he was there and made a point of only calling when I knew he'd be at work. Twice in two days was making me dizzy.

"Whattaya say, Milan?"

I like my first name. It's very ethnic, and lots of people mispronounce it—it's MY-lan, not MEE-lan or Mih-LAHN or any other way you can think of to mangle it—but it's kind of distinctive and I guess it's who I am. But when Joe says it, even correctly, it puts my teeth on edge.

"How'd your meeting with Danica go?" he said. In the background I heard the ambient noises of the machine shop he co-owns, clanking tools, male voices shouting and questioning, and Majic 105, the golden oldies station, playing on a cheap radio. It was a masculine, big-shouldered kind of sound that didn't fit Joe Bradac at all.

"Fine," I said.

He waited for a bit. Then, "That's all? Just 'fine'?"

"What do you want from me, Joe?"

His voice was thin and reedy, with a whine in it that made my nose crinkle up. "I just thought since I set this job up for you, the least you can do is give me a hint on what's going on."

"The least I can do is respect the confidentiality of my client," I said. "Ask Danica; whatever she wants you to know is her business. I'm sure Lila will tell you that in all the time we were married I never much discussed my cases with her. And I'm sure as hell not going to tell you what I wouldn't tell my wife." I hit the last word hard. The emphasis was not lost on him. He's pretty quick sometimes, Joe.

"Aw," he said. "Aw, okay, then. I was just asking, Milan."

It was not an auspicious beginning to the morning. I finished my coffee and a fast perusal of the newspaper and went down to my car to begin the day's festivities. The light snow had stopped sometime during the night and what had fallen had melted, leaving the streets wet and slick but navigable. The Lanigan and Webster and Malone show on the radio made the gray morning a little brighter. Real loony tunes, Lanigan and Webster and Malone, but irreverent and funny. I don't know how they get away with some of their stuff sometimes.

Cuyahoga Heights is almost due south of downtown Cleveland, hugging the east bank of the Cuyahoga River. It's a nice-sounding name, Cuyahoga Heights, conjuring up visions of gentle slopes, freshly painted houses with a river view, and probably an upscale shopping mall on the main street. It isn't exactly like that. U.S. Steel makes its home

25

there, and LTV Steel and the Southern Sewage Plant, and along Harvard Avenue are small iron forges that have been owned and run by the same families for generations. The Deming Steel plant and its corporate headquarters take up a lot of space in the Heights, too. It's that kind of neighborhood. Not many people live there; most who do work at one of the mills or plants within shouting distance. The air is heavy with the smell of smoke and machinery, a metallic odor that gets into your sinuses and stays there no matter how many times you blow your nose. But because of the enormous tax base created by the heavy industries, the school system has more money to spend per pupil than nearly any other district in the state. Sometimes God plays fair.

The Deming Steel plant looked a lot like a federal prison, an intimidating, sprawling edifice of dirty stone, the long stretch of wall broken up by tiny-paned windows so grimed over they probably didn't admit much light anyway. A dizzying maze of girders and pipelines and metal catwalks criss-crossed the structure and ran along its roofline. There were a couple of smaller buildings off to one side, presumably where people worked who don't get dirty doing it, but the office buildings were as grim as the plant itself. The compound was surrounded by steel wire fences, with the employee parking lot outside, and I thought about what it must be like to toil in the mill all day and then have to walk a quarter of a mile through the snow to your car. Four tall smokestacks were silhouetted against the gray sky, belching unspeakable pollution into the air. They've cleaned the smoke up some in the last few years, but it's still pretty ugly. We pay a heavy price for progress.

A low menacing hum pervaded the atmosphere—not loud, but enough to get into your brain after a while and make you want to bang yourself on the side of the ear. A guard was at the gate. I don't know why, probably to keep people from wandering in and swiping a steel girder. At least the position gave gainful employment to the officious little guy in his fifties who wore his belt beneath his belly, and he took his job very seriously, which I suppose is what kept him sane, sitting in a little cubicle the size of a telephone booth with the thrum of the working mill in his head all day. When I asked him for directions he seemed to resent my taking him from his more important functions, and with graceless resignation he pointed me to the personnel department in one of the smaller buildings on the east side of the complex and sternly admonished me not to park in the numbered spaces. It might've been interesting to find out what would happen to me if I did.

Most of the vehicles in the administration building's lot were American sedans in the compact or midsize range. People who worked at Deming weren't the flashy-sports-car type, neither by income or inclination, and were encouraged to buy American. After all, it's the domestic car companies that buy the product that keeps their mortgages paid up. Rather like the food chain, I thought. A sign read NUMBERED SPACES FOR PERMITTEES ONLY. I wonder who made up that word, *permittees,* and whether or not he's been properly punished.

Another middle-aged guy in a guard uniform was tootling around the lot in a golf cart, keeping a gimlet eye on those who parked in numbered spaces to make certain they were permittees, as if the safety and security of the republic depended on him.

How was work today, dear? Oh, pretty good, Mabel. Some son of a buck who isn't a permittee tried to put his car in a numbered space, but I straightened him out pretty quick. He'll park someplace without a number next time, believe you me! Good for you, dear. Here, have a beer.

I managed to find a legal parking spot and entered through the door marked PERSONNEL, my leather briefcase in my hand. There was nothing in it but a couple of pens, a spare notebook, a pad of yellow paper, and a printed schedule of the Cavaliers home games, but a briefcase looks official and lends authority to the one who carries it, and that comes in handy sometimes. Inside, the building was clean if impersonal, with waxed floors and lots of offices with windows onto the corridor. There were no outside windows, presumably to keep the employees from gazing across at the scenic delights of the smoke-belching mill itself and dreaming bucolic daydreams.

The woman at the desk in the personnel office didn't even raise her eyes when I came in but told me to fill out a yellow application. When I informed her that I wanted to see Walter Paich, she took off her glasses in an unmistakable get-serious fashion and even deigned to look at me before telling me it would be impossible during business hours.

"This isn't a social club," she told me. A damn good thing, too; they'd have quite a time recruiting members to willfully spend time in a place with all the charm and ambience of San Quentin.

"I'm an attorney," I lied, and gave her one of the phony MILAN JACOVICH, ATTORNEY-AT-LAW cards I had printed up years ago to get me into places I couldn't go otherwise. People are awed by lawyers—or more specifically, "attorneys." I can't think why. "I won't take but a minute of his time," I said, "I just have some documents for him to sign."

Another word calculated to bring people up short. A document is a different proposition than a paper or a form. You don't fool around when it comes to documents. A document is important stuff.

It only impressed her a little bit. "What kind of documents?"

"I'm afraid that's confidential," I said.

I'm surprised that more people haven't tipped to the wondrous power of language. *Confidential,* for instance, is another intimidating word, conjuring up visions either of matters pertaining to national security or gossip about the arcane sexual practices of movie stars and millionaires. It's also much more effective than "None of your damn business."

The dragon at the personnel desk sniffed. I didn't think she had a cold; it was more of an editorial comment on my confidential documents. She probably compartmentalized her workday into neat little ten-minute segments, and I was throwing her off schedule. Finally she said, "Very well," and pulled out a plastic-covered company directory about the size of the Akron phone book. She put her glasses back on and thumbed through it as carefully as if it were a Judith Krantz novel she hadn't read yet, then picked up the phone and punched out four numbers. After waiting briefly, she asked for Walter Paich, listened, then said, "I see," and put the phone down.

"Paich called in sick this morning," she said, "for the third day in a row." The way she said it, I got the idea she was taking his absenteeism as a personal affront.

Euclid is an incorporated bedroom community hugging the shoreline of Lake Erie on the east side of what is known as Greater Cleveland, home to a lot of families of Eastern European extraction, mostly Slavs, Poles, and Lithuanians, with a sprinkling of Hungarians, Germans, Ukrainians, and Russians. The address I was looking for was just off Lake Shore Boulevard, Euclid's main drag, hard by Kenneth J. Sims Park at 230th Street, and turned out to be a square brick Georgian of the type they overbuilt just after the Second World War, with no front porch, a lawn that needed tending, and louvered windows with a couple of glass slats broken. Over the doorbell, which was plastic and had a dim light behind it, was a slot for a name card, but whatever had been written there in ballpoint had faded long ago.

I pushed the button and heard a buzzing inside. After a moment the door opened and a woman about Danica's age gave me a scared-rabbit look. Euclid is still the kind of neighborhood where you open the door without asking who it is. Not a good idea anywhere, certainly not in the larger cities, but there are a few places left in the world where the ring of a doorbell doesn't necessarily signal the arrival of an armed robber, a rapist, or a religious fanatic wanting to sell you a Bible.

"Yes?" she said. I recognized her from the pictures in Tootsie's family album. She was thin almost to the point of anorexia, with her hair pulled back into a ponytail held by a rubber band from which a few lank wisps escaped. There was a slight bump on the bridge of her nose. She was wearing a pair of run-down house slippers, green polyester pants, and a pink acrylic sweater. Her sharp collar bones were visible above the neckline. A huge-eyed little girl of about two was wrapped around her thigh, holding on for dear life. A pretty kid, but then all little girls are pretty.

"Mrs. Paich? Vera Paich?"

She had to give it some thought. "Uh-huh."

"My name is Milan Jacovich. I'm an old friend of Walter's. From high school."

"Oh." I don't think she believed me, but it didn't matter to her.

"May I come in?"

She started as if I'd awakened her. "Walter's not here now."

"Well, I'm also a friend of your sister-in-law's," I said, and then I added, "Danica," because the entire concept of a sister-in-law seemed alien to her. "I'd like to talk to you for just a minute."

Her eyes got as big as the kid's.

"I'm not selling anything," I said. "It has to do with Walter's grandfather."

She blinked, bobbed her head, and opened the door wide enough for me to squeeze through.

There were no family pictures on the mantle, just a vase with fake flowers and a ceramic pot that once might have held a house plant but now seemed to serve no purpose at all. The bilious cabbage roses on the fading wallpaper would have overwhelmed any real plant anyway. The living room was furnished in discount modern, all synthetics and aluminum tubing and pressed wood with veneer that was chipped at the edges. A protective sheet of plastic covering the sofa crackled when Vera Paich sat down on it. The child clambered up next to her and clung to her like a baby monkey, looking up at me through her long lashes, her huge blue eyes uncertain.

"Mrs. Paich—may I call you Vera?"

I didn't think that was such a tough question, but it took her several seconds to decide before nodding permission.

"Do you know Mr. Zdrale has been missing over a week?"

"Uh-huh," she said. She gathered the little girl closer to her. "Danica called me."

"She called me, too. I'm a private investigator."

She allowed herself the tiniest smile, as though there was a finite number allotted each person and she didn't want to waste one. "Like on TV?"

"Sort of," I said. It's a question I get asked a lot, and I rarely bother to set people straight. People will have their fantasies, and it's often cruel to disabuse them. "Danica has asked me to find her grandfather. Have you heard from him?"

"Me?"

"You or Walter."

She shook her head.

"When's the last time you saw him?"

"Me?" She pondered that one for a long time. The questions were getting harder. "I don't know," she said finally. "A long time ago."

"A week? A month?"

She chewed off what little lipstick she'd been wearing. The child crawled onto her mother's lap and threw her arms around her neck, looking over her shoulder at me as though I were the monster of her worst nightmare. "A couple of months, I guess."

I found that peculiar. The concept of the family unit is strong among the peoples of Eastern Europe, which is why so many of them settled in one place, and the idea of more than a day or two going by without everyone contacting everyone else seemed preposterous to me. "That's a long time," I said.

"We don't see the family much. Walter's family. I mean, they all live down in town, and we're out here in Euclid."

I didn't point out to her that it wasn't much more than a fifteen-minute drive. "You wouldn't have any idea where he might have gone, would you?"

"Me?"

That was one "Me?" too many, but I tightened my stomach muscles and gritted my teeth to keep from saying something I'd be sorry for later. This was, after all, important. "Yes," I said.

She shook her head again, gravely this time. "Nuh-uh."

"Do you think Walter might?"

She lifted her bony shoulders as though it hurt her to do so.

"Where is Walter now?"

"At work."

"At work? You mean at the Deming plant? In Cuyahoga Heights?"

This was clearly a particularly thorny riddle demanding some more of her deep consideration. She studied the two green mounds that were her polyester-covered knees, her brows low over her eyes as she thought about it.

"Uh-huh," she said at last.

THREE

Janko's Tavern, which catered to the many Serbs of Cleveland's Slavic Town, was a classic example of the neighborhood ethnic saloon that you still find all over the East and Midwest, in spite of the creeping homogenization of America that has given us the fern bar and the sports bar with the big-screen TV and the cocktail lounge attached to an upscale restaurant. It differed little from my old hangout, Vuk's, a Slovenian tavern about six blocks west on St. Clair Avenue. Against a wall near the rest rooms was one of those machines where you put in fifty cents and try to snag a stuffed toy with a metallic claw. The patron currently working it was on the dark side of fifty, wearing a T-shirt and overalls over an enormous potbelly. An unfiltered Camel dangled from his lower lip. Lined up on top of the machine were four cheap stuffed animals he'd already won. What he was going to do with them was anybody's guess.

Janko's had a video game in the corner, a bow to the temper of the times that Vuk disdained, and its buzzes and beeps nearly drowned out the sound from the TV that played over the bar from the time the place opened early in the morning until last call at night. Unless there was a ball game on—any kind of ball game, any size or shape ball—nobody would pay much attention to the television, but it was on anyway, permanent background music. At the moment a daytime talk show was running its dreary course, peopled with

33

attention pigs who would confess to the most revolting behavior just to be on national television. A stunning black woman was talking into the camera, her voice husky with emotion. Across her chest was superimposed SEDUCED HER STEPSON.

Otherwise Janko's was the same as any other tavern of its ilk—a de facto social club with a permanent haze of blue smoke, the friendly smell of beer, and a clientele of working guys from the neighborhood who'd all known each other since grammar school. An unpretentious drinking parlor where a guy could have a brew and talk about cars and sports and women, where the barkeep would cut you off if you had too much, lie to your wife that you hadn't been in, and listen to your problems as if he hadn't heard your story a million times before. The kind of joint where you could relax, knowing you couldn't possibly get into any trouble.

Unless you were looking for it.

It was three o'clock in the afternoon. I didn't know if Janko's served sandwiches like Vuk's did, klobasa sausage fried in olive oil with green peppers and onions, but whatever lunch crowd they attracted had cleared out, and the wave of after-work drinkers hadn't arrived yet, so there were only a few people at the bar, mostly older men who might have been retired or simply unemployed. A guy in his thirties played the video game with the deadly seriousness of an addict, slamming the flat of his hand down on the button to shoot down enemy spaceships or zap attacking Ninja warriors, from where I stood I couldn't tell which. Over at a table an obese old man with a portable oxygen tank on a wheeled cart and a plastic mask hanging from a cord around his neck was lighting up a cigarette. I hoped he wouldn't ignite the oxygen and blow us all to hell, but I didn't have much faith.

Not a mixed drink or a highball anywhere, although a variety of liquor bottles was arrayed behind the bar against a smoked-glass mirror. This was largely a beer crowd, Stroh's and Bud, no fancy imports. There was bourbon and vodka to be had, but guys who used the hard stuff were generally perceived as having an alcohol problem and often did their

34

drinking in places where the other customers didn't know their wives or parents personally.

I sat down at the bar, one stool away from my nearest neighbor, a man in his sixties with a three-day growth of gray stubble. On his head was the generic peaked cap with a C.A.T. patch. The bartender was not much younger, needed a shave almost as badly, and was wearing a Cavs sweatshirt.

"Yeah?" the bartender said. He wasn't hostile, but he wasn't friendly either. I didn't imagine they got much drop-in business here, and he probably thought I was lost.

"Stroh's. No glass."

"No glass," he said mildly. "Tough guy, eh?" He slapped the bottle onto the bar in front of me. "Two dollars."

I didn't imagine that was what he charged the regulars, but I put three dollars next to the bottle, and he snatched two up and put them in the register without ringing up a sale. I left the other where it was.

"Are you Janko, by any chance?"

" 'S right."

"Hiya." I toasted him with my Stroh's and took a slug, then lit up a Winston. He started down to the other end of the bar when I said, "You happen to know a guy named Elmo Laketa?"

He stopped and gave me a hard look. He'd probably spent his life behind a bar, and all his looks were hard, but he put some extra effort into this one. "No."

"You sure?"

"What kind of question's that?"

"I heard he comes in here."

"You hear lotsa things. I once heard the world was gonna come to an end, but I'm still around, right?"

"I don't know. Are you?" I can do the hard look myself when I put my mind to it. "If you never heard of Elmo Laketa, maybe you're not."

Janko put his hands down beneath the level of the bar. I knew my pal Vuk kept a sawed-off baseball bat just out of sight under the bar to handle tough customers, a Reggie Jackson model. Maybe Janko had the more up-to-date Cecil

Fielder. In any case, I figured he had something down there that could cause some damage, and that he wasn't shy about using it. The guy one stool down shifted uneasily, leaning slightly away from me. He probably didn't want to get blood splattered all over his plaid flannel shirt.

"Don't get excited," I said.

Janko's eyes were as flat as a snake's. "I never get excited."

I could believe that. "I just want to talk to Laketa. No trouble."

"Yeah, well like I said, I don't know him." He gave me the level look of a really good poker player who's just bumped the pot and dared you to call him.

There isn't much you can do when someone is lying to you. I knew it, he knew I knew it, and that was going to have to be the end of it. I don't wear a badge anymore, and I don't have the means of persuasion available to the official minions of the law. I had the idea that slipping him a few dollars would not only fail to produce results but would get him angry. And until I found out what he had stashed beneath the bar, I didn't want to get him angry. Could be a scattergun.

"Hey, big man," a hoarse voice called. At the table near the corner, the fat old guy with the oxygen tank was beckoning to me. I guessed it was to me; I am a pretty big man, and he'd put the emphasis on the word *big*, as though there were a little man in the vicinity, too, and he didn't want to cause confusion.

"You," he said. "Big man. Come over here."

I glanced at Janko, but he'd suddenly developed a profound disinterest in whatever I did and was making a point of watching Phil Donahue imploring the stepson seducer, "How could such a terrible thing have happened?"

I put out my cigarette and took my beer and went over to the old man.

"Sit," he ordered.

I pulled out a chair and sat across from him. Eyeglasses had left two purple indentations on either side of his flat nose, but he wasn't wearing them now. His checkered work shirt

36

was buttoned all the way to the top, and the heavy flesh of his neck spilled out over the collar. A full ashtray and an empty Bud bottle was in front of him, and a half full glass of what looked like very flat beer. His breathing was labored, with an alarming rattle. It didn't take a medical degree to recognize an advanced case of emphysema. Every puff of his cigarette pushed him closer to his grave—but then I suppose that's true for all of us who smoke.

A mass of fat covered what had once been a powerful frame. He had wide shoulders and a deep, broad chest. Thick, solid wrists and forearms, and scarred hands that looked as if they'd been hewn from granite, roughened by sixty years of manual labor, with gnarled, broken fingernails. He had a broad forehead with eyebrows that, in his old age, had sprouted wildly into upswept gray wings over shrewd and knowing eyes.

"You police?" he said.

"No."

"You look like a police."

"I'm not. I used to be, but not anymore."

He took a moment to decide whether or not he believed me. "Why you want Elmo Laketa?"

"I just want to talk to him."

"What for?"

"I'm trying to help a friend of his."

He studied me carefully, his rheumy eyes flicking from the top of my head to my face. "Serb?"

I sighed. "Slovenian."

He nodded, as if he'd thought so all along, and it seemed to disappoint him. I gave him a business card, one of the genuine ones that said MILAN SECURITY. He fumbled in his shirt pocket for a pair of steel-rimmed specs and held them in front of his face with the earpieces still folded over. He read my card, carefully examined the blank obverse for reasons I couldn't fathom, and put it in his pocket along with the glasses.

"You Jacovich?" He pronounced it correctly, the *J* sounding like a *Y*, something I couldn't always count on with non-Slavs. I nodded.

"I'm Laketa," he said.

Bogdan Zdrale's best friend for a lifetime. Tall buggy-whip-thin Bogdan; Laketa broad and round—when they stood side by side they must look like the number 10. I shook his hand, which seemed to surprise him. He looked pointedly at his beer glass. "You buy?"

I turned and waved at Janko to bring us two more. Elmo Laketa didn't say anything until the fresh beers were on the table and he'd poured his glass full and then drained it. "So," he said, exhaling noisily and wiping off a mustache of foam. "What you want with me, big man?"

I lit another Winston. If he was going to smoke in his condition, I didn't see why I should deprive myself. Nevertheless I made sure to blow the smoke away from him. "I'm looking for your friend Bogdan Zdrale."

"How you know Bogdan?"

"I don't," I admitted.

"So what you want with him?"

"His family has asked me to find him. His daughter and granddaughter. They're very worried. They haven't seen or heard from him for eight days now."

"So?"

"They tell me you're his best friend."

"So?"

"I thought maybe you'd have an idea of where he went."

He shook his large head from side to side, the plastic oxygen mask bobbing. "He don't tell me nothing," he said. "I know Bogdan sixty years already. More. We grow up one mile away from each other. After the war I help him to come here with family. I get him the job at the mill. We work together thirty years. Now every day we come in here, Bogdan sit right where you are now. He drink coffee, we talk, we watch the TV." He refilled his glass, and when the head threatened to boil over he stuck a thick, nicotine-stained finger into the rising foam to tame it. Then he licked the finger. Waste not, want not.

"You know his family then?" I said.

"Sure. His Tootsie and my Sophie grow up together."

"And Tootsie's kids? Danica and Walter?"

"Danica, sure. Pretty girl."

"And Walter?"

He made a face. "Walter, he's a bum."

"Why?"

"Why's anybody a bum? Just is."

I decided to let it go for the time being, because I wasn't sure it mattered. "When's the last time you saw Bogdan?"

"I can't remember."

"Within the last few days?"

He crinkled his brow, thinking about it. "A week ago, maybe. A week Sunday. I don't worry about it, though. Sometimes he don't come in."

"Why not?"

He swatted his hand at me, missing my face by about three feet. "Bogdan, sometimes he get crazy. Worries too much."

"About what?"

"How the hell I know?" Laketa said. "He worries, he don't talk to nobody. Take off in his truck, drive someplace. Toledo maybe, or Pittsburgh, two, three days. Then he come back."

"But this time he didn't come back."

He nodded once, emphatically.

"Do you know who he sees in Pittsburgh?"

He shook his huge head. "Just go, look around a little, come back. He don't know nobody there, or Toledo. He just go. Crazy sometimes."

He chugalugged the rest of his beer, slammed the glass on the table, and started to say something, but his breath caught deep in his chest and he began to cough and wheeze. He waited for the spasm to stop, but it didn't, and all at once his eyes widened and I could see real terror behind them. He put one hand to his chest, and with the other he motioned frantically to me to put out my cigarette. After I crushed it in the tin ashtray he placed the plastic mask over his nose and

39

mouth and turned a valve on the oxygen tank with trembling hands. Janko came out from behind the bar and stood off to one side, shaking his head sadly, looking concerned.

The gas hissed as Elmo Laketa sucked it into his sickly lungs, finally getting his tortured breathing under control. After about a minute he took the mask away and switched the tank off again. Tears streamed down his grizzled cheeks for a while, and the mask dangled beneath his chin. Then he gulped and shook his head, wiping his eyes with the napkin from under his beer glass.

"Dovno!" he gasped with what little breath he had left. *Shit* in Serbo-Croatian.

"Are you all right, Mr. Laketa?"

He nodded, his chest heaving.

"You're killing yourself with those cigarettes."

"You too," he croaked. He picked up my beer bottle, which was still almost full, and put the cold wet glass against his forehead and rolled it around for a moment, slumping back in his chair with his eyes closed and his mouth open, a great ruined mountain of a man, struggling for air.

Then he opened his eyes, peeking around the bottle at me. "So, big man?"

"So," I said. "If you hear from Bogdan Zdrale, or hear anything about him, will you let me know?"

"How I hear anything?" he said. Speaking was still very difficult for him, so he waved his hands around to indicate that he hardly ever left Janko's.

"If you do. Anything. Just give me a call. You've got my number there on the card."

I shook his hand again and stood up, preparing to go. He said my last name so softly I almost didn't hear it over the drone of the television and the beeping of the video game. I leaned in close, smelling the beer and tobacco on his breath. Smelling death, too. He put his forehead against mine.

"Zdrale my friend," he whispered. "Best friend. Find him, okay?"

I squeezed his shoulder. "Okay," I said.

I was almost at the door when I felt a hand on my arm. It was Janko.

"Hey," he said, pulling the bottom of his sweatshirt down over his hard little paunch, "I didn't mean to get in your face before. I don't know you, see, and these are good people come in here. I try to protect them when strangers come around."

"It's okay, I understand."

"Listen, you looking for Bogdan, I'll help you if I can. He's a nice old guy. I don't make a nickel off him with his coffee drinking, but I like him."

"He comes in here every day?"

"Just about. Sometimes not, but mostly yes."

"Did he seem . . . different, lately?"

"How do you mean?"

"I don't know," I said. "Maybe like something was bothering him?"

He gave me what passed for a smile. "It'd be hard to tell. He never says much, even on his good days."

"You know Walter Paich?"

"The grandson?" He wrinkled his nose. "Yeah, he comes in sometimes."

"Has he been in lately?"

"I don't exactly keep track," Janko said. "I don't think I've seen him around, though. I'm not sure I'd remember anyway; it's not exactly a big event in my life, Walter coming in. But I don't think so."

"You don't like Walter?"

He sighed patiently. "I don't even think about Walter. Look, there's people come in here to drink, they're my regulars, but they're my friends, too. We talk, we tell jokes, we play horse at the bar, once in a while we get a little bet down on a game, you know, when the Cavs are goin' good. We talk about our kids, our grandkids. Sometimes on a football Sunday they come in here with their wives and eat potato chips and watch the Brownies. Friends, you know what I'm saying?" He wiped his hands on his sweatshirt. "Other people, they're customers is all. I don't know nothing about them and

I don't care. All I know is, this one's a shot and a beer, that one's a Bud Light, the other one's something else. That's how bartenders remember people. Take you, f'rinstance. You could tell me your name fifty times, to me you're still a Stroh's, no glass."

"And Walter?"

He didn't even have to think. "Shot and a beer."

I took out another one of my cards. "If you hear of anything, give me a bell, okay?"

"What you oughta do," Janko said, taking it, "is you oughta talk to Lazo Samarzic."

"Who's he?"

"He's kind of the head guy around here."

"Head guy?"

Janko looked heavenward for assistance. "Jeez, I gotta spell it out for you? He's like the unofficial mayor of the community. Like back in the old country they'd have the elder, y'know? Not that he's old, I mean not like . . ." He tossed his head back in the direction of Elmo Laketa. "But he's tough and he's smart, and if you're part of the group—I mean, like from the neighborhood and a Serbian—Mr. Samarzic takes care of people's problems, he kicks a little butt when he has to, and usually he's up on what's goin' on."

I wrote Lazo Samarzic's name in my notebook. "Will he be in tonight?"

"Naw," Janko said. "Just on weekends with his wife. You want him, him and his brother Mirko got a vegetable stand down to the West Side Market. Samarzic Brothers."

"Will he be there tomorrow?"

He shrugged. "Maybe," he said.

Walter Paich was home when I stopped by his house at seven o'clock. He opened the door and stood there, thin to the point of haggard, his eyes haunted, a half-smoked cigarette between his fingers. His sallow skin hung loosely on his face the way your clothes do after you lose a lot of weight. He was a few years younger than I am but looked ten years older. I wouldn't have recognized him from the high school kid I'd known. I could hear a TV set on somewhere inside, a dull murmur of voices whose words I couldn't make out.

"Hello, Walter," I said. "It's Milan Jacovich. Remember me?"

He moistened dry lips with his tongue. He was the kind of guy who spent a lot of time breathing through his mouth. Smoker's breath.

"Yeah, sure. High school."

"Right. It's been a long time."

He made no effort to shake hands, so I didn't either. Nor did he move out of the doorway. He had the dull-faced, impotent look of a guy who'd been angry all his life and was never able to do anything about it. He was wearing a dingy black suit a few sizes too large for him with a slightly frayed white shirt and a paisley tie that was knotted too tight around his stringy neck. I thought the only person who wore a suit in his own house in the evening was Ward Cleaver. Walter was tall and pale, with three days' growth of beard, black hair receding on the sides and slicked back into a short ponytail. Blackheads clogged the large pores on his nose, and his eyes were rimmed with red, like those of someone taking a breather from an extended drunk.

"What are you doing here?" he said. Apparently Walter wasn't much on the social graces.

"I wanted to talk to you for a few minutes."

Behind him I saw his wife creep into the living room on tiptoes, baby Constance in her arms. She was wearing the same clothes she'd had on that afternoon, and the same scared-rabbit expression.

"What about? You selling insurance? I don't need no insurance."

"I'd like to talk to you about your grandfather."

His eyes narrowed, and he stood up a little straighter. "What for?"

I explained about Danica, and he listened woodenly, chewing at the inside of his cheek as if it were a hunk of Dubble Bubble, Vera almost cowering behind him. He made no move to invite me inside, which was unfortunate, because it was damn cold standing there on the small stone stoop.

"I don't know nothing about that," he said when I'd finished. "I don't see him much."

"That's what your wife told me this afternoon," I said.

His eyes moved quickly to his wife, who moved back a step and looked away. "You was here before?"

"I went to the plant, too, but I couldn't reach you." If he'd told his wife he was at work I wasn't going to be the one to blow the whistle. Not that she'd do much about it. She was one of those people who was afraid of everything and everyone, but from the way he looked at her I had the feeling that when it came to her husband, she had reason. Walter had a mean mouth, thin and pulled down at the corners, and eyes that squinted from too much smoking. The sullen teenager had become a sullen adult. Maybe it was too many years on the floor at Deming Steel, where the sun never reached to warm or brighten, or maybe it was something else. There was a sour smell about him, an aura of thinly repressed subcutaneous rage.

"Whattaya think, my grandfather's here?"

"No," I said.

"If he was here we wouldn't need you looking for him, right? Well, he's not here, so you're wasting your time."

"He's been gone eight days. I'd think you'd be a little concerned."

He shrugged. "He's a big boy. What he does is his business." He looked at his wife again, and she seemed to be trying to shrink down as small as the baby, or even to turn into one of the cabbage roses on the wallpaper. "Look, I got nothing to say about my grandfather. It's family. Danica had no business taking it outside the family. You take a hike, all right?"

He moved slightly toward me, his chin jutting out like the prow of a minesweeper. I hoped he wasn't going to get belligerent. I could have broken him in half with one hand, but I didn't want to. It wouldn't solve anything; it would just complicate matters. Besides, he was Danica's brother. But I wasn't going to be run off like an encyclopedia salesman. "Any idea where he might have gone, Walter?"

He shifted position and put his hand on the edge of the door as if he was about to close it. "How the fuck should I know?" he said.

FOUR

I slept in fits and spurts, troubled by the stone walls I had run into all that day. Old widowers like Bogdan Zdrale don't just disappear. They don't abscond to Costa Rica with their secretaries, they don't plunder their partner's till, they don't suddenly become spies or go into the government's witness protection program. Mostly what they do is play golf if they're affluent, cards if they aren't, or watch soap operas and drink coffee in their neighborhood tavern all day. Which meant that perhaps he was out there somewhere sick or dying, and the longer he stayed away from his house and his family, the slimmer the chances of finding him alive.

I arose earlier than usual because I didn't see the percentage in lying in bed staring at my ceiling. It was still dark out. Ohio is at the western edge of the eastern time zone; sunrise reaches us about forty-five minutes later than it does the folks on the east coast. I've lived here all my life, but I'll never get used to it staying dark so late in the mornings.

I made a pot of coffee and a few pieces of rye toast and spent an hour on the phone, mostly with the highway patrol, ours as well as those of Pennsylvania, Indiana, and Michigan, trying to cajole them into keeping an eye out for Zdrale's Ford van even though it hadn't been reported stolen. I skipped West Virginia and Kentucky, which also share borders with Ohio, because I didn't figure they were places he'd go. Bodgan didn't seem the bluegrass-and-mint-julep type. He was the

47

kind of man who would likely seek out his own people, those who had immigrated here from Eastern Europe after the Second World War, who shared his background and experience as well as his heritage, language, and customs. There aren't many Serbian communities in Kentucky.

My index cards needed updating, and when I was done I stared at them for a while. They didn't magically spell out any answers for me. Except for Danica, nobody in the family seemed very concerned about Bogdan's disappearance, even though his friends at Janko's were. Maybe Tootsie was more relieved than worried that, for a few days, she wouldn't have to deal with her father, cook for him and clean up after him and worry whether he was dressed warmly enough. But Walter Paich's hostility and his unexplained absence from work niggled at the back of my brain, so perhaps it was something more after all.

This was to be the day I had to go to court, but on the way downtown I stopped off at police headquarters on Payne Avenue and East Twenty-first Street. It's a huge, intimidating building of rough sandstone that looks like a place you'd want to give a wide berth. There are a lot of beautiful old buildings downtown, but this isn't one of them.

Lieutenant Mark Meglich, né Marko, was in his second-floor office, wearing the vest and trousers of a brown suit, a white shirt that looked as though he'd taken it out of the package new three minutes before, and a gold tie. The jacket was neatly hung up behind the door on a padded contoured hanger that wouldn't alter the tailored shape. Marko was my boyhood chum and high school and college football teammate, my rabbi in the police department during my few short years there, and is now the number-two man in the homicide division. His hair is thinning, though not quite as noticeably as mine, and he's bulked up some from his football weight. He's also grown pompous and self-important and sports a brushy mustache to prove it, but if a friend of twenty-five years can't make allowances for a little thing like hair on the upper lip, then what's friendship worth?

"What are you all dolled up for?" he said, noting my gray

suit and blue oxford-cloth shirt. "You on your way to court? It's too early in the morning for a hot date."

"Good guess, Mark."

He smiled. He always smiles when I called him Mark instead of Marko. He's been trying to break me of the old habit for fifteen years now, and whenever he thinks he's succeeding it brings him a lot of pleasure. I can play him like a button-box accordion, depending on how I address him. "What brings you down this way?" he said. "It couldn't be to ask for your badge back, could it?"

"Maybe," I said. "What's the current temperature in hell?"

That was a sore spot with Marko, my quitting the force and going private. He's never forgiven me for it. He certainly never lets me forget it. He filled his lungs with stale station-house air and let it come out slowly and sadly. "You're a real disappointment to me, Milan."

"You're a big person; deal with it."

I sat down and he moved a foot-high pile of manila file folders to another spot on his desk so he could see me. I guessed that they represented his current case load. "You remember Walter Paich, Mark? From high school?"

He thought about it. "Not really. The name sounds familiar."

"Skinny guy, about two years behind us."

He dismissed the idea out of hand. "I never bothered to get to know the littler kids. Why, is he dead or something?"

"Not unless he bought it since last night. What makes you ask?"

He raised a satanic eyebrow at me. "This *is* the homicide store."

"No, he's not dead, but his sister's a client of mine."

"His sister." Marko smirked. "Somethin' going on there, Milan?" He was always trying to fix me up with women. He and I had gotten our divorces at about the same time, and while I'd kept a low profile for almost a year before embarking on a long and just-ended relationship, Marko had gone in search of his lost youth in the arms of a succession of twenty-year-old ditzoids who, despite their obvious charms, were unable to carry on an intelligent conversation while in the vertical position.

I explained about Joe Bradac and the Paiches and Bogdan Zdrale. When I'd finished he said, "You must've taken the wrong turn in the hallway. Missing persons is on the other side of the building."

"I know, but they aren't interested. I thought maybe you could flash your gold shield at somebody over there and get them off their duffs."

He scribbled something on a yellow pad. "I can mention it, but not much more. Everybody's pretty funny about guarding his own patch in this place. Remember what happened with Lieutenant Ingeldinger on that crack business last year."

"Marko," I said, forgetting his sensitivity to his old name, "an old man is missing, maybe hurt, maybe worse. Don't tell me about territorial imperatives. Aren't you guys here to help the people in this community? Isn't that the job?"

He sighed. "You're so damn naive, Milan. I wonder how you made it to your age without buying the Brooklyn Bridge, or a swamp in Florida."

"Does the name Lazo Samarzic mean anything to you?"

"Should it?"

I shrugged. "He's got a stall at the West Side Market, but the way I hear, he's kind of the Serbian godfather in the old neighborhood."

"You mean godfather like watching over his godchildren and seeing they don't come to harm, or godfather like a horse's head in your bed?"

"That's what I'm asking you."

He wrote Samarzic's name down on the pad. "I'll check if he's got a sheet."

"He probably doesn't, but if you can find out what his deal is, it might be helpful."

"Sure, no problem," he said. "I don't have much else to do here." He waved a hand at the thick pile of still-open cases. "Anything else you'd like?"

"Yeah, now that you mention it. Check if Walter Paich has a sheet, too."

He rested an elbow on the desk and leaned his chin in his hand, a tolerant smile he might bestow on an incorrigible but basically good kid who keeps running away from Boys Town on his lips. "Stay as sweet as you are, Milan," he said.

It was only a few minutes' drive from the police station to the courthouse, and even counting the time it took to park the Sunbird I arrived at the courtroom some five minutes ahead of my scheduled appearance. Dan Cooper, the smart young black attorney who was trying the case for the prosecutor's office, was on one of the uncomfortable wooden benches in the corridor. He rose to meet me, looking more than a bit frazzled.

"Damn, Milan, I'm sorry. I tried to call you," he said, shifting his briefcase from one hand to another so he could shake mine. "The defense has asked for a continuance."

"Does that mean you don't need me this morning?"

He nodded. "They gave us a date two weeks from now."

I fiddled with my lapel. "You mean I put my court suit on for nothing?"

"Blame it on the judge," he said. "I hope we can count on you two weeks from today."

I nodded, but I must have looked pissed off. This wasn't the first time this had happened to me. It was aggravating to have my time wasted. Time is the only thing we spend that we can't get more of.

"Look," Cooper said, "let me make it up to you, buy you lunch or something."

"It's only eleven o'clock, Dan. Give me a rain check."

He pumped my hand again. "You got it. I'll be in touch when this thing gets into gear again."

I ransomed my car from the parking lot, tucking the receipt into my shirt pocket so I could add it to Cooper's bill. Actually I hadn't had breakfast, and his offer of lunch had stirred my stomach a bit. What I really wanted was to head out to Pacers, a great rib joint I know out in Euclid, enjoy some good barbecue and the company of Linda, one of their waitresses, a pretty brown-eyed brunette with a smile that promised and a figure that intrigued. But that's another story.

Unfortunately it isn't mine.

It could have worked out worse. The West Side Market, one of Cleveland's most colorful spots, is open on Mondays, Wednesdays, Fridays, and Saturdays, and this would be an excellent opportunity to go and chat with Lazo Samarzic.

I headed down Carnegie Avenue and across the Hope Memorial Bridge, lately renamed in honor of Bob Hope's father. It used to be called the Lorain-Carnegie Bridge and is one of my favorite city landmarks. On each bank of the river there are four huge stone statues flanking the highway, resembling figures from a Masters of the Universe cartoon. There have been times I was slogging through a particularly difficult or dangerous situation when I felt like asking for their assistance.

Despite the misconceptions movies and TV have fostered in people like Vera Paich, private investigators are not superheros. We're just ordinary guys, often blue-collar, like myself, just trying to get a job done, like tool-and-die makers or house painters. If along the way we can do somebody some good, all the better. But it isn't what you'd call a glamour job, and sometimes it's dangerous enough that I wish I could call on those He-Man statues to come to life and give me a hand.

I don't get west of the river that much; people who live on the East side frequently don't, and vice versa. It isn't quite the heated rivalry that exists between Serbs and Croatians, but for most native Clevelanders the twain ne'er meet. People who live in Lakewood or Rocky River often say, "The West side's the best side; the East side's the least side." East siders have sayings even less polite. I'm not sure if one part of town is better than the other; it's all a matter of what you're used to. I was born and raised on the East side, so that colors my thinking, but I have to admit there are a lot of neat things on the West side, not the least of which is the West Side Market.

It sprawls at the northeast corner of West Twenty-fifth Street and Lorain Avenue, an orange-colored brick building with an enormous pointed clock tower on the top. It's not really tall if you compare it to Terminal Tower, which is visible right across the river, but it's the kind of building you can somehow see from a long way off, one of those places that says Cleveland in capital letters. The neighborhood has gone through many transitions over the years. At the moment it's tilting toward Hispanic, with lots of little bodegas and *carnicerías*, but the architecture is pure early-twentieth-century quasi-European.

Inside, the West Side Market is one huge room with a vaulted tile roof curving overhead like a giant tunnel, packed almost elbow to elbow with butcher's stalls. Strings of klobasa sausages hang from hooks, bright pink lamb chops and standing rib roasts nestle in glass cases next to chubby liverwursts and Thuringers and blood sausages. Some of the stalls feature more esoteric items like hogs' heads, which smile up at you from beds of ice. There's no accounting for taste, I guess—lots of otherwise normal people think beef tongue is yummy. The city and surrounding area is such a melting pot that there's someone within hailing distance who'll eat practically anything. Interspersed with the butchers are bakery counters, and specialty stalls that sell spices and mustards and exotic bottled sauces with which to enhance the meat.

Most of the shoppers were women, dressed in slacks and short jackets of fake leather or polyester fill, all carrying shopping bags made of net or canvas. Some had preschool toddlers with them, some had come in pairs to make a companionable morning out of shopping for dinner. Quite a few were elderly, and even though it might be a hardship to get to the market, it was worth it to them to patronize the same people with whom they had done business for forty years or more.

What always strikes me at the market is that the vendors in the individual stalls resemble one another. Standing three across behind a meat counter are a grizzled man of fifty years, a twenty-five-year-old woman, and an apple-cheeked post-adolescent, all wearing butcher's aprons, all with the same swoop of nose, plane of cheek, high forehead and water blue eyes, their movements, the set of their shoulders, their carriages the same, because these food businesses are invariably family run and family owned, as attested to by the number of signs over the stalls reading *and Sons*, or *Brothers*. So it is that products of the same gene pool man the front lines, occasionally bumping elbows as they wait on the customers but mostly working within a well-established rhythm that keeps them out of one another's way. There is a genial din inside the building, as everyone is talking—merchants to customers, fathers to sons, brothers to brothers, mothers to daughters, questioning, cajoling, coaxing, selling, bargaining, *hondeling*. Down at one end of the building up on the white-tiled wall is a huge mural, a colorful mosaic of fruits and vegetables.

Outside, just to the north and east of the main structure in a long open-air shed in the shape of a huge L are the produce merchants, in two long lines on either side of a central aisle. Canvas flaps at the sides can be lowered on cold or rainy days to protect the food as well as the vendors and customers, but on this particular day, with the temperature hovering in the mid fifties and not much wind, the shed was open. I hurried under the protective jut of the roof and began walking the main aisle, flanked by displays of fruits and vegetables so vivid in color that they were startling to the eye. It didn't look much like the produce usually found in supermarkets. It was more visually appealing, and you sensed that each apple, each tomato had been lovingly selected by hand, one at a time. The reds were deep and bright, the greens crisp and cool, the yellows like light from the sun. I breathed in deeply, almost tasting the fresh, clean smell.

On either side of me the vendors worked the crowd. "Look, I got great peppers here!" "Whaddya like, pears? Look at these here pears here." I'm an easy sell so I avoided making eye contact with any of them for fear I'd wind up with bags full of food, beyond what I could possibly eat.

Shoppers and merchants alike gave me a strange look; most people don't visit the market wearing a suit and tie. But I pretended not to notice as I ran their gauntlet, my eyes raised to see the signs over the stalls. Like the meat sellers inside, the produce dealers almost all had concerns named for their families. Finally I found the one I was looking for: SAMARZIC BROTHERS.

Two men and a woman worked behind the counter, keeping up a running patter with their customers and any passerby whose attention they caught. The two men were not quite twins; the younger one was bigger and meaner-looking, with a nose that had been broken more than once. Just from the body language it was obvious that the older of the two was the boss. He worked much closer to the woman, and when they touched in their rapid choreography behind the counter, the easy intimacy between them was apparent. Though they didn't look alike in the way of siblings, there was between them the kind of resemblance that comes not only from a shared ethnic heritage but from many years of living in the same house, watching the same TV shows, and sleeping in the same bed.

She was dark-haired, about five foot nine, dressed in a rough-knit cardigan sweater over a flannel shirt and a white T-shirt beneath it. Her shoulders were broad, and there was a merry sweetness in her bright blue eyes. Her work-roughened hands attested to many cold mornings like this on the front line at the West Side Market. I guessed she was about fifty, but it was hard to tell for sure.

The two men were both a few years older. The one I took to be her husband was about six foot three. What was left of his hair started well up on the crown of his head. Heavy black brows met in the middle of his forehead, and a bristling mustache peeked out from between a nose like a new potato and a thin, knife wound of a mouth. He had shoulders like a minivan, and the forearms and wrists emerging from the sleeves of his wool pullover were as thick as a man's calf, covered with coiled wires of coarse black hair. His rough complexion tattled of teenage skin problems. There wasn't much warmth behind his eyes.

"Mr. Samarzic?" I said.

Both men looked up, but then the younger one quickly looked away. Obviously when anyone said "Mr. Samarzic" they wanted his brother.

The other man hardly glanced at me. "Lookit here, I got spring tomatoes," he said. "Juicy, you won't believe it."

They did look good.

"Whaddya need, fruit? Delicious apples I got, from Washington state, just picked 'em up this morning." Like Tootsie Paich's, his Slavic accent was just a ghost; it was more the cadence of his speech than his pronunciation that made me decide he hadn't been born in the United States.

"Are you Lazo Samarzic?"

He nodded curtly. "Yeah, whattaya need?"

"My name is Milan Jacovich."

"So whattaya need?"

"I'm a private investigator."

His wife looked over at me quickly while she bagged a pound of potatoes for another customer, her heavy brows two pyramids of concern over her eyes. Mentioning my profession usually either scares people or intrigues them, but nobody ever says uh-huh and lets it go at that. It's one of those jobs that gets your attention.

But it hardly slowed Samarzic down at all. "I sell vegetables and fruit," he said. "That's how I pay the rent. You here to buy something or what?"

"I'd like to talk to you, if you've got a few minutes."

His eyes met mine angrily, his blunt sausage fingers a blur, arranging produce on the sloping stand with the fussy artistry of a symphony conductor. Then he glanced up and down the aisle at the press of customers. "Do I look to you like I got a few minutes?"

"It's about Bogdan Zdrale."

The fingers flying over the peppers and tomatoes slowed from rapid to simply quick. I wouldn't have noticed it at all if I hadn't been looking for it. "What?" he said, glancing away.

"Bogdan Zdrale. You know him?"

"I know him," he said.

"He's disappeared."

"Yeah?"

"Yeah."

"Too bad. But it's not my business."

"No, it's mine," I said. "Look, it'll just take a minute or two, I'd really like to talk to you."

His hands stopped moving over the produce, and I saw the tendons in his forearms swell as he clenched his fingers. His ears were red, whether from the cold in the shed or from something else, I didn't know. "You don't talk English? I said I got no time—"

"Lazo," his wife said quietly.

He looked over at her, and immediately the hard gleam in his eyes got softer and warmer. "What?" he said gruffly, but it was the mock gruffness of a playful lover. He was a big, tough-looking man, but it was plain he adored his wife unconditionally.

"You go on," she said. "Mirko and I can take care here." Her voice was husky, strong.

He pressed his thin lips together tightly and an incongruous dimple formed in his cheek, but it would take more than that to make him cute. He finally nodded at her, then at me, and came out from behind the vegetable displays, wiping his hands on his apron.

"Come," he said. "We'll walk."

We headed down toward the end of the shed, past the riot of multihued produce, and emerged onto West Twenty-fifth Street. The cold bit at our cheeks, but it felt refreshing. We both took out crumpled packs of Winstons at almost the same time, like a reflex.

"Here, have one of mine," I said. He considered it for longer than was polite and finally decided that accepting a smoke wouldn't obligate him. He made sure we used his lighter for both cigarettes, though, as if that would make it even.

"Where'd you hear my name?" He put the lighter in his pocket.

"Around."

"Around where?"

"Just around."

"You're a cagey guy, Jacovich."

"I don't remember where I heard about you the first

time," I lied. "You're a pretty well-known man, Mr. Samarzic."

His broad chest inflated like a pouter pigeon's, and his full mustache twitched with pleasure. It was obvious he enjoyed his notoriety, liked hearing it confirmed even more. "So what's this?" He made a stirring motion with his free hand. "What's this about Zdrale?"

"He's been gone for ten days," I said, "and his family is worried about him."

He nodded, his eyelids fluttering in the slight mist that was falling. "They're right to worry. An old man like that, got no damn sense."

"I thought you might have an idea where he is."

"Me? Why should I?"

"He's your friend."

"I got lots of friends don't tell me every move they make, every place they go, every time they go to shit."

"But you're a leader in the Serbian community. You know what's going on with all the people."

He stared at me from under the heavy brows. "You Serb?"

"Slovene," I said.

His look wasn't quite contemptuous, but it was close enough. He took a deep drag on his cigarette and blew the smoke out through clenched teeth, which I'm sure isn't approved by the American Dental Association. "Why would Zdrale tell me what he don't tell his family?"

"He might confide in you, when he wouldn't with somebody else. If he were in trouble. Or scared."

"In trouble!" he scoffed. "What, maybe he knocked up some woman? At his age that's not trouble—that's to celebrate!"

"Scared, then?"

"An old man like that, what could scare him?" Samarzic walked toward the corner, hands in his pockets and the cigarette balanced on his lower lip, his shoulders lifted to protect his ears from the wind. "He gets up every morning and the bones hurt. He worries whether or not he can go to the toilet.

He's too old for women, bored, nothing to do, all his friends are dead, and his family thinks he's a pain in the ass. What's to be scared of? Dying?" His laugh, dismissing the idea, sounded like a single pistol shot. "When you live like that, death is a favor."

"Easy for you to say. Old men's bones ache, sure. But they can still watch the sun come up and hear the birds, and see their great grandchildren play. Their old friends might be gone, but they make new ones, because they're not a threat to anybody anymore, they aren't looking to climb over anybody's face. They've made their big play and now it's time to relax and enjoy. Old men are as scared of death as young ones. More, even, because they know it's right around the corner."

He made a derisive sound, sucking hungrily on his cigarette. I pulled the knot of my tie down and unbuttoned the collar of my shirt. "When you were a little kid and they wanted you to go to bed, did you ever beg them, 'Just a few more minutes'?"

"Every kid says that."

"Old people, too. They want just a few more minutes."

We got to the corner, where a young man with the round face, slanted eyes, and slack mouth of Down's syndrome sat in a doorway with a glass bowl full of money. Samarzic slowed down and tossed a wadded-up dollar bill into the bowl with the easy familiarity of a ritual, and the young man grinned up at him and nodded thanks. Samarzic walked on a few steps, then flipped his cigarette into the street. It made a high arc as it flew, and the sparks scattered when it hit. "Zdrale don't tell me anything," he said, shaking his head. "He's just an old man I say hello to. He's old enough to be my father, Christ sake! We don't hang around. He don't talk to me about nothing important."

"When's the last time you saw him?"

He stopped, turning to face me. He looked wide and hard and tough. "You accusing me of something, Jacovich?"

"No. Hell, why would I do that? I'm just trying to track him down, talking to everybody he knows."

He massaged his fleshy nose as if it were hurting him. "I got a lawyer, you know."

"You don't need a lawyer, and you don't even have to talk to me. I'm not a cop. I'm just looking for an old man who's turned up missing. You know he sometimes takes off for days at a time and his family doesn't know where to find him."

He nodded. "It's America. He got a right."

"Know where he goes?"

He hugged his elbows against himself to ward off the chill. "Do I? Nah, he don't tell me. Some Serb bar in Toledo or Pittsburgh or someplace. He hangs out, plays cards, talks. Talks his old man silliness about how it was in Europe in the old days."

"You know of a specific place?"

He took his hands out of his pants pockets and flailed them in a gesture of frustration. "There's a place in Toledo on Monroe Street, lots of Serbs go in. I think sometimes Old Zdrale might go there."

"You know the name?"

He started to say something, then changed in mid-thought. "I never go to Toledo," is all he said.

"Never?"

He shook his head vehemently. "Toledo's no big deal. What's the big deal about Toledo?"

"Nothing, I guess."

"You goddamn right!" he said.

FIVE

These days Wednesday is my poker night. It wasn't always. As a matter of fact, I was never much of a player, being more interested in my wife and sons than in sitting around a table with a bunch of guys drinking beer and losing money. But after the trauma of a divorce, and then an intense eighteen-month relationship which eventually crashed and burned, the loneliness of a midweek evening seems almost insupportable. What do you do with alone when for so long there's been together? When there's been someone who's a part of your life, a part of who you are? Books are great, but after a while you run the risk of becoming a well-read recluse. I'm not a TV watcher unless it's an old movie or a ball game—besides, you fall asleep in a chair in front of *Nightline* and then wake up in the middle of the night with a stiff neck just so many times before you start looking for other things to do.

You don't even think about going out to a bar, because in a place where nobody knows you, you're more alone than in your living room, and if you go to a neighborhood joint where your friends hang out they know you're in a bad way and they all look at you with pity and buy you a beer, which is more painful than the loneliness. Worse still is sitting in your own house and drinking by yourself, because that can get to be an ugly habit, and the next thing you know you're at a smoky meeting in a church basement standing up in front of a bunch of hollow-eyed strangers who yell "Hi, Milan!" in unison. So you go through the motions of doing your life, you fill up your days and hope they're busy enough for you to fall right asleep at night and not dream of the warm body that isn't next to you, that might be next to somebody else, that isn't part of you anymore.

It doesn't always work.

It hardly ever works.

And there are those nights when the solitude chomps down hard with weasel teeth, when all you want to do is pick up the phone and call that person who became a part of you and then ripped herself away, taking with her bits of flesh and gristle, exposing nerve endings to the cold. But you've done all that already, and it didn't do any good. So you look for other alternatives.

I found one in my pal Ed Stahl's Wednesday night game. It's low-stakes, friendly poker where if you walk away more than a ten-buck loser it's a big calamity that's talked about for weeks after. When Mary and I stopped seeing each other, I asked Ed if I could come around once in a while and sit in. Gambling isn't one of my vices—unless you count buying a couple of Super Lotto tickets every week from the Ohio Lottery—but one night a week I can fend off the weasel's bite, and all it costs is whatever I lose plus my contribution of two bags of pretzel twists. Once in a while turned into every week because I can't think of a single reason not to go, except I'm a lousy poker player. I draw to inside straights, I think two pair is a big deal, and when I bluff nobody ever believes me.

It's warm and friendly in Ed's big old house near the Coventry Library in Cleveland Heights. The place used to be a sort of mansion until it fell into disrepair, and Ed picked up the foreclosure for pocket change. There's always enough beer, decent sandwiches, and a newspaper and media crowd that keeps the wisecracks popping. Nobody ever asks me how I'm feeling, how I'm holding up, how I'm doing alone, or am I seeing anybody. All they want to know is am I in or out.

Ed Stahl writes a daily column for the *Plain Dealer* and is probably Cleveland's biggest and most vocal cheerleader, but the Pulitzer Prize he won several years ago but never talks about is proof that his writing is a lot more than hometown boosterism. He can get pretty tough uncovering things certain people would rather keep buried, and his probing investigations have punctured more than one shady scheme to bilk the good folk of this town out of their hard-earned tax dollars. A confirmed bachelor who dates only occasionally and runs for cover at the mere mention of wedding bells, even someone else's, Ed smokes a malodorous pipe and drinks a little too much, living up to the hard-bitten newshound stereotype. But he blows that image by listening to classical music and Gregorian chants, having his clothes tailored at the most exclusive shops in town, and driving an Acura Integra that he keeps as pristine as an operating room. He's constantly romanced by the city's rich and powerful, as a cushion against a time when they may need him, or need him to shut up. They think everybody has a price; they don't know Ed Stahl isn't for sale.

I met Ed back when I was a rookie cop and he was a reporter who counted himself lucky to get a byline. We'd exchanged a few professional favors, and what began as a mutual back scratch evolved into a friendship that has weathered a lot of years and seen a lot of water flow under the bridge. Sometimes he listens to me kvetch about my life and my kids and my lonely nights, and once in a while I drive him home when he's gotten shit-faced. We've been lunch buddies and ballgame buddies and one-phone-call-every-two-weeks buddies, and now we're poker cronies as well, but whatever it is, we don't label it, we just enjoy and cherish it.

There wasn't much I could do about Bogdan until the next day, and with the cast of characters that often shows up at the game, there was a chance I could pick up a nugget of information.

The players vary from week to week, although not very much. If you're serious about playing poker, the stakes at Ed's table are way too low, which winnows out the heavy-duty gamblers. If you're a two-fisted drinker the beer is too tame, if you're a swinger the company is too male, and if you're married it's one of those nights out with the boys that're likely to cause more friction than they're worth. That leaves a fairly narrow window.

On hand this particular evening were Ed, looking dour as always in a black and white cardigan and a white shirt, and his fellow ink-stained wretch from the *Plain Dealer,* Frank Randazzo, who covers the sports scene at Cleveland State and Kent State and dresses the way a sportswriter is supposed to, i.e., horribly. On this occasion he wore fuzzy yellow socks, black penny loafers, wine-colored pants, and a conservative blue dress shirt with a white tab collar. Spanish John Hanratty, who has become Ed Stahl's ear on the force since I went private, was making one of his increasingly rare appearances at the poker table, having decided that chasing a pair of tens wasn't as much fun as chasing women. Joining us too was an old high school pal of mine, Alex Cerne, whom I had recommended to Ed as the best dentist in town, just the man to straighten out Ed's considerable overbite. Alex is, like me, of Slovenian descent, but he gets around more than I do in the Slavic community, and I planned to ask if he might have some poop on Lazo Samarzic I hadn't heard.

The sixth player was a young television director from Channel 16, Tim Archambault, with whom Ed has engaged in so many arguments about the relative merits of print journalism versus the electronic media that they have become friends, even though Tim dresses right out of the Banana Republic catalogue and therefore often looks like Jungle Jim on safari.

We said hello all around and spent the obligatory ten minutes talking sports, which gave Frank Randazzo the opportunity to step forward and be the insider, and when all chat of trades and acquisitions and draft picks and the Final Four had been exhausted, we took our accustomed places at the table. Once we started to play, the only sounds were the crinkle of cheese puff bags, the chink of poker chips, beer cans hissing open, murmured bets, and the sibilant shuffling of cards.

Ed's dining room has windows on three sides, overlooking a garden that is more like a jungle, with hanging willow branches, creeping ivy, large-leafed exotics that wouldn't last past the first Ohio frost in anyone else's garden, and grass which Ed allowed to run wild. The vegetation was fairly skimpy now in the last throes of the cold weather, but I remembered warmer days when all you could see was green with an occasional flash of yellow flowers or the bright scarlet wing of a cardinal. The round dining table was antique, heavy oak with huge claw feet, and Ed covered it with a thick pad and a green felt cloth for the poker game. Each of us took our seat with ecclesiastic solemnity, placing our beer cans carefully to the right of our five dollars' worth of red, white, and blue chips.

It was determined by the turn of the high card that Spanish John would deal the first hand. "Jacks or better," he announced. Just about the only games we ever play are jacks or better, straight five- or seven-card stud, or five-card draw. Those who favor more arcane forms of poker like toad-in-the-hole, Mrs. Peabody, do-si-do or any game in which there are wild cards, which Ed dismisses as better suited for the Ladies' Aid Society's annual Las Vegas Night, are never invited back.

I was to Spanish John's left. My hand was nothing to brag about, so I passed, as did Ed. Alex opened for a dime. Randazzo bumped him, and Archambault and I threw our cards in.

"Dealer stays," John said, and those who hung in asked for new cards. Alex took the modest pot with three tens, and it was my deal.

"Straight seven," I announced. Ed was stuffing his pipe with tobacco as I shuffled and lit up as I began to deal. A noxious cloud spread across the table.

"Jesus," Alex said, fanning the smoke away. "You have to smoke that smelly goddamn thing in my face?"

Ed fixed him with a stare that could paralyze a charging rhino.

"It's bad for your teeth," Alex said lamely, but you could tell his heart wasn't in it.

"So are you," Ed parried.

"It smells like burning upholstery." Alex waved his hand again to clear the air.

"This is a poker game," Ed said. "You don't expect to have somebody wussing around about smoking at a poker game. You drink beer and belch and scratch your ass if you want. And you smoke. That's why we don't invite girls."

Archambault smiled. "Women," he said.

"What?"

"Women, not girls. They get pissed if you call anyone older than twelve a girl."

"Who gets pissed?"

"Women. If you ever got laid once in a while you'd know that. You'd also know that most of them hate smoking."

"Fuck you, too, Mr. Cuisinart, Mr. BMW, Mr. state-of-the-art camcorder," Ed said.

Ed is often cranky—it's one of his most endearing qualities—but he never goes for the jugular except in print. Tim Archambault's sensitivity about being a thirty-something yuppie is well known, and he bends over backwards to convince people he isn't one, despite his ownership of those glitzy toys. I sensed bite behind Ed's banter. His prominent ears were redder than usual, and he bit down on his pipestem as though it was the pin in a hand grenade.

I dealt the third card up to everyone, glad to see Ed was high with a queen. If he had to bet it might take his mind off whatever it was that was troubling him and defuse the tension in the room. Alex Cerne was wearing that narrow-eyed expression of annoyance I'd known since high school, and Tim Archambault seemed ready to cry.

"First queen bets," I said, but Ed wasn't paying attention. He was studying Archambault and puffing his pipe with the defiance of Nathan Hale on the gibbet. The air in the dining room was turning a grayish blue.

"Up to you, Ed," I said, raising my voice enough to penetrate. It worked; Ed shifted slightly in his chair and tossed a white chip into the middle of the table without even looking at his hole cards.

Everyone else made their bets and I passed out the fourth

card, up. Ed got a jack and was still high. He tossed in two more white chips.

"Don't you want to look at your cards, Ed?" I said.

"Play your own fucking hand, Milan." It wasn't said with quite the antagonism he'd displayed toward Alex and Tim, but it was still out of character for him, and he was sending out Apache war signals with every puff of his pipe. Alex kept gazing up at the smoke haze, his mouth twisting, and Tim locked his eyes on the tabletop as if he were trying to memorize it. We played out the rest of the hand, and Frank Randazzo won it with a medium straight, raking the chips toward him with both hands and wearing a smile only slightly to the east of smug.

I was aware of the sound of Ed's breathing. He was obviously upset about something, and I didn't think it was because Alex disliked his smelly pipe. I stood up. "I'm hungry," I said. "Deal me out and I'll make sandwiches. Come with me, Ed, and show me where the mustard is."

He squinted up at me as though I'd taken leave of my faculties. "It's in the refrigerator. Where do you keep *your* mustard, in a cedar chest in the attic?"

"Come anyway," I said, staring him down.

He's usually a lot quicker than that, but finally he got it. "I'm out, too," he said.

Ed has one of those huge country kitchens designed to feed the entire Italian army; it's wasted on a bachelor who eats out a lot. I got out a loaf of the pumpernickel for which Cleveland is justly famous, a head of lettuce, a tomato, the mayonnaise, and the prepackaged sliced ham and sliced bologna Ed had supplied for us, along with that great mustard they serve at the stadium during Browns and Indians games, and set to building sandwiches. He sat on a stool near the counter and watched me work, sulking because he knew he'd been out of line. I didn't speak to him.

Finally he said, "So what do you want me to do, sleep in the living room?"

I just shrugged.

"I suppose I owe everyone an apology."

"It's your house. But aren't you a little uptight tonight?"

He scowled. Ed is a master scowler. "You'd be uptight too if you got death threats on the telephone."

I was in the midst of slicing the tomato and nearly took my thumb off. "Death threats?"

There was a heavy red ceramic ashtray on the counter, and he knocked his pipe against it noisily. The charred tobacco came out in a lump and smoldered there, sending a plume of stinky smoke up toward the ceiling. "They've wagged their fingers in my face before," he said, "but not like this."

"Who's they?"

He shrugged. "Whoever it is I've managed to piss off," he said, "including the mayor, the governor, the chief of police, several different city councilmen, every other local politician in northern Ohio, the Mafia, the blacks, the Poles, the Ku Klux Klan, the National Organization for Women, the NRA, the Gay and Lesbian Alliance, and some outraged Browns fans who wanted to lynch me from the Soldiers and Sailors Monument after the 1990 season when I said Art Modell ought to back up the truck and dump the whole team." He tapped his pipestem on his front teeth, and it made a little clicking sound. "But nobody ever called my house before."

I put the knife down. "Who called you?"

He snickered. "You think he gave his name? The phone rang here about an hour ago and when I picked up, somebody just said, 'You're a walking-around dead guy, Ed,' and hung up."

"That's all he said?"

"That was it."

"Any ideas? Hints?"

"As I say, a few people might not like me."

Frank Randazzo stuck his head around the doorjamb. "You guys in or out or what?" he said.

"Five minutes, Frank," I told him, and he threw me a look and withdrew. He knew something was going on, but he was cool enough to butt out when he was asked.

"Have you been to the police about this, Ed?"

He shook his head gravely.

"Maybe you could talk to Spanish John," I suggested.

"Spanish John does grand theft auto. If they steal my car, I'll talk to him. My guess is that it's got something to do with this morning's column. Did you read it?"

"No," I said.

He gave me a guilt-inducing smile. "Why the hell not? It's your responsibility as a friend to read me every morning, Milan. It's how I make my living." He went and picked up the second section of the morning paper from the kitchen table, folding it open to his column, and shoved it at me.

I began reading. I didn't have my reading glasses with me, so I had to hold the paper away from my face. The distance gets a little greater every year. Pretty soon my arms won't be long enough.

AROMARAMA
by Ed Stahl

The single largest municipal services contract in the city is the one for hauling away our trash. I don't know why we have so much garbage. Maybe it's all those losing Ohio Lottery slips we crumple up and throw away each week, or the Browns Super Bowl tickets we never get to use. Hope dies hard in Cleveland. Maybe it's just that everyone reads the newspaper—which should make our circulation manager a happy man—and then throws it in the trash instead of recycling it. In any event, our garbage is worth a small fortune to the guy who gets to take it away.

Now, no one goes through grammar school dreaming of becoming a garbage collector. It's not like being a doctor or a nurse or a linebacker or a fireman. But one would think there'd be a block-long line of eager-eyed hopefuls wanting to become Trash Hauler to the North Coast anyway, because the remuneration is sweet.

Yet this year when contract renewal time came around, there was only one bidder—Dosti & Son of the west side. Yes, the same Dosti & Son who've been hauling your trash away in their familiar green trucks for the last eight years, clanging can lids and waking you up early in the morning.

All right. There's something to be said for continuity, even in trash removal, and to tell the truth, the Dostis have been doing a pretty good job.

But the law requires that a successful bidder submit an acceptable bid guarantee and contract bond. Dosti & Son did no such thing. They didn't have to do much more than show up. Yet they were awarded the contract.

How come?

Doesn't the law apply to the Dostis? Are they somehow immune from the rules and regulations that the rest of us have to live with by virtue of some divine right we haven't heard about? Heaven forbid, has money changed hands under the table? Or is it because company president, James Dosti, whom you might know better by his nickname, Jimmy Sweets, is the first cousin of Giancarlo D'Allessandro, who has been under more local and federal indictments than Pete Rose, for violation of the RICO statutes, and who might have a few of our elected officials in his hip pocket?

I know—this is America, guilt by association is un-American, and an indictment isn't a conviction. But something about this contract award stinks, the way it does when the Dosti truck hasn't come by for three weeks and your garbage is sitting out in the sun. And those good people we have voted into public office to serve our interests ought to be asking some pretty hard questions on our behalf before the smell gets worse.

By the time I'd read the whole column Ed had finished constructing the ham sandwich I'd started and was carefully bisecting it with the knife. He glanced over his glasses, his eyebrows arching up near where his hairline used to be. He looked proud, as he usually does where his work is concerned, but there was a fluttering of uncertainty there too. And something else that might have been fear.

"You're swinging a big stick, Ed."

"I don't know how to do it any other way."

"There are those who'd say it's not your business."

"It *is* my business. It's exactly what my business is."

"You're saying the phone call was from Jimmy Sweets?"

"I hardly think he'd call. They have people to do things

like that." He put half of the sandwich on a paper plate and passed it over to me. The other half he attacked without much enjoyment. "I don't know, Milan," he sighed around a large mouthful. "I dig deep, try to stick to facts, maybe make this a better place to live, and what it all boils down to is people train their puppies to shit on my column every day. They don't care about Jimmy Dosti or who's screwing who, or what high muckamuck is on the pad. Now someone's calling up here saying lousy things to me on the phone. What's the point?"

"You know the point as well as I do," I said. "If somebody doesn't notice when something is wrong and point it out so someone else can fix it, pretty soon the slime buckets will run the whole show, and then where'll the rest of us be?"

I bit into the sandwich and made a face. "Who puts *mayonnaise* on a ham sandwich?"

"I do. What about it?"

"It's those German genes," I said.

"What do Slovenians put on it?"

In answer I opened my sandwich, scraped the mayo off the bread with the edge of the knife, unscrewed the cap of the Stadium Mustard, and showed him what Slovenians put on a sandwich.

"So what are you saying, Milan? That I'm like the lady in the skimpy costume who points to the magician every time he does a trick?"

I pictured Ed in spangled drag; it was the most fun I'd had in a month. "Not exactly. But you kind of keep track."

"Big deal," he said, chewing morosely.

"It can be," I said. "Look at all the help you've given me over the years."

"That's because with you there's always something. You've always got a name to check out, and you think I know everybody in town."

"Don't you?"

"Not everybody. Agnes J. Marnell, who teaches third grade out in Berea. I don't know her."

Alex Cerne came through the door from the dining room.

"Are we playing poker or are you two gonna post the banns?"

"Hang on, Alex," I said. "Either one of you ever hear of a guy named Lazo Samarzic?"

"You're the Slavs, why are you asking me?" Ed said, and then something kicked in and he snapped his fingers. "Wait a minute, wait—yeah. Lazo Samarzic."

Alex said, "I think he runs some kind of Serbian national organization over on the east side."

Ed Stahl picked up his sandwich. "Right," he said, "I remember now. It's not a formal organization, exactly. I don't believe they have a charter or even a name. But they're Serbian and very militant."

"About what?"

"Who knows with you guys," he said. "It all dates back to the Battle of Kosovo. The Serbs hate the Croatians because they traditionally side with the Armenians in their territorial disputes. And the Slovenians were more pro-Tito than the Serbians. That's really what the current fighting is all about. Now, as I understand it, nobody really hates you Slovenians, but historically you've been closer to the Croatians, which means the Serbians aren't that crazy about you, either."

"I know all that, Ed, and the Battle of Kosovo was six hundred years ago. I've got a case working—I want to know what's going on *now.*"

"With Lazo Samarzic?" Ed said. "Hell, I don't know. I probably have a few notes on him, but they're at the office. It wouldn't be much in any case, certainly not enough for a story."

Alex put in, "He's a real ass-kicker."

"How do you mean?"

"Kind of a guardian angel of the Slavic Town Serbs. Anyone tries to fuck over his people, he steps in."

"Violently?"

Ed polished off his half of the sandwich and immediately started stuffing his pipe again. I hurried to finish my half so I wouldn't be eating while he was smoking.

"It's possible," Ed said. "Every living soul is capable of violence, Milan. You, me, Alex, Mother Teresa if she gets pissed off enough, even our little yuppie puppy in there. It all depends on the button you push. I guess that's what's bothering me about the phone call."

"I'll look around, Ed."

"No," he said. "Don't. Don't bother with it. It's probably nothing, and if it's something I'll handle it myself. Forget about it, Milan." He waved his pipe under Alex's nose. "Let's play poker." He walked out into the dining room, loudly asking whose deal it was. Sometimes living up to an image, such as that of the fearless investigative reporter, can take its toll.

Alex leaned against the counter, one hand in the hip pocket of his Dockers. He glanced from me to the door. "Everything okay?"

"Sure," I said.

"Where do you know Lazo Samarzic from?"

"I bought some green peppers from him this morning."

"I hope that's all you do."

"Why?"

He ran his tongue over his front teeth as if checking for plaque. "I've never had the pleasure, but there's no one more lethal than a zealot. You know those guys. And I hear Samarzic is a pretty tough customer when he's crossed."

"I'll try not to cross him." I said. "Even if the peppers are no good, I won't ask for my money back."

Alex Cerne rubbed his hands together as if he were washing them. As a dentist he probably washes his hands fifty times a day and the habit is ingrained. He shook his head sadly. "You're some friend, you know that? You said you were going to make sandwiches. Then you only make one and you eat it yourself. What about the rest of us?"

I grabbed his chin in my hand as I passed him and gave it a grandmotherly squeeze. "Bad for your teeth," I said.

Six

Official, badge-carrying policemen are public servants; by definition, a private detective like me is not. Therefore, I have a couple of advantages over my blue-clad brethren down on Payne Avenue.

For one thing, there aren't so many regulations.

I don't worry about warrants or Miranda or all the other regulations that protect the rights of criminals but handcuff the police as surely as if they were locked in their own steel bracelets.

Oh, I have my own set of rules. All of us do; we have to. Otherwise there'd be anarchy, chaos in the streets, raping and pillaging, a death trap on the highways, and the best seats at the Browns games would go to the biggest, strongest, and best-armed instead of just the wealthiest, as they do now. But my rules are mine, self-imposed and carefully constructed to give me the maximum advantages as I move through my life.

The police can get your cooperation by thundering at you about civic duty, or they can put on the squeeze about business licenses or building violations or even about a busted taillight. Private detectives get what they need by wheedling, begging, and carrying around bogus business cards and empty briefcases, and speaking in somber tones about "confidentiality" and "documents." The cop on the street has to answer to his superiors, who answer to theirs, and it goes right on up the line to the commissioner or the mayor or the governor or wherever the buck might stop. I can develop an investigation any way I want to, without having to check in with the lieutenant, worry about following accepted procedures, or violating some scumbag's constitutional rights. As a private citizen and small businessman I only need answer to my own conscience and the IRS.

However, a distinct disadvantage of not carrying a buzzer is that when I call out-of-town information in a place like Toledo and ask the operator to give me the names and numbers of every bar on Monroe Street, she tells me to go to hell.

So I got up early the next morning, and while the coffee was brewing I took the two dollars and thirty cents I had won at poker the night before to the Lax and Mandel Bakery on Taylor Road to buy and take home a dobish torte, which was both delicious and bad for me. It even made my lousy coffee taste good. After breakfast I went over to the public library on Lee Road to peruse the Toledo Yellow Pages.

I suppose it would have been just as simple to go to Toledo, a matter of approximately two hours on the turnpike, and cruise the bars on Monroe Street. But the road between Cleveland and Toledo in February is one of the dullest in the world, a drive-by sensory deprivation center, with nothing to look at except an occasional farmhouse or the silhouette of a denuded tree, and I figured I could use my time to much better advantage. I found phone numbers for twelve saloons on Monroe, and I jotted them down in my notebook and went back home to call them.

I decided to save LeRoy's Taverne, Leroy Johnson, proprietor, until last. Somewhere, there might very well be a Serbian named LeRoy Johnson, but I doubted he'd own anything called a Taverne in Toledo. I started with a Rudy's Bar, but had no luck; it catered to a German clientele, not Serbian, and they'd never heard of anyone named Bogdan Zdrale. Then on to the Dew Drop Inn, the Tip Toe Inn, and the Teddy Bear Lounge, with similar negative results. The names of the establishments gave me a pretty good idea as to what kind of ambience was offered up on Monroe Street in Toledo.

My fifth call finally netted me something—not much, but

at least something. I knew I was on the right track when I called Ray's Place at eleven o'clock in the morning and heard polka music in the background.

"Yeah, Bogdan," the guy on the phone said. From his voice I figured him to be considerably younger than Janko, so maybe he wasn't the owner but just the bartender. "Old guy, lives in Cleveland someplace, comes in here every six, eight weeks or so, drinks coffee and goes home again. Sure I know him. I mean, I don't know him real good, but I know him from when he comes in. Nice old guy. He do something wrong?"

I felt a rush of adrenaline. At least they knew him at Ray's. "Not at all. But he's been missing for more than a week and his family's worried. When's the last time he came in, do you remember?"

He thought it over. From the sound of his breathing I figured his nose had been broken a long time ago and set by someone who didn't know what they were doing. "Maybe a month," he said finally.

"Not more recently?"

"Naw. It was snowing out, I remember that—snowing bad. I asks him why he don't stay around a while and drive back when the weather got a little nicer, but that old guy, he don't listen to nobody."

The last time the weather could have been described as "snowing bad" was about five weeks earlier, in the middle of January. But then Cleveland gets snow, especially on the east side, that frequently misses Toledo. In any event, it hadn't snowed anywhere in Ohio for ten days, hadn't really stormed for nearly a month, so Ray or whoever this was probably had the time frame right. Wherever Bogdan had gone, it probably wasn't to Toledo. Unless the guy was lying, and I couldn't imagine why he'd want to do that. He sounded truthful, anyway. I thanked him, hung up, and spent the next half hour wondering about it.

I never did get around to calling LeRoy's Taverne.

It's an occupation hazard, mistrusting everyone. I don't like myself when I do it, but I've been lied to so often by so many people, mistrust is automatic. I had no reason to doubt the man who answered at Ray's, or to mistrust Lazo Samarzic and Walter Paich. Then again, I didn't have a good reason to believe them, either.

I dialed Ed Stahl's direct line at the *Plain Dealer*.

"Just wanted to see how you were doing," I said.

"Why?" I heard him smacking his lips on the pipestem and could imagine the purple cloud hovering over his head. "I only lost four bucks last night. Was I that pissy about it?"

"Any more phone calls?"

I waited a beat or two. "Are you going to call every five minutes and check on me?" he asked.

"Better than your winding up in Lake Erie with cement galoshes."

He laughed. "Milan, the outfit doesn't do cement galoshes anymore. They're into gambling, loan sharking, money laundering, extortion, and whores. They're legit."

"Ed, why don't you give Mark Meglich a call?"

I heard him puff some more. "Because he hates my guts, because sometimes I make him and his whole department look bad. Of course, they don't notice the other times, when I praise them. It's the knocks they remember."

"Call him anyway. Just to be on the record."

"My whole life is on the record. Five days a week. Section two, front page."

I called the Deming Steel plant and asked to speak to Walter Paich, only to be told he'd called in sick that morning. That made four days in a row. I didn't know if Walter thought the union would cover his ass for him or if he just didn't give a damn about his job anymore.

Something about Walter didn't sit right with me. Maybe it was just his crappy attitude, but there were guys like that in Vuk's Tavern every night of the week, antagonistic, hostile men who have never made life's cut and are doing a lousy job of eating their anger. It could have been the way he treated his wife, or maybe that he bugged out of work when he wasn't supposed to. Probably a combination of all of that added to his seeming indifference to his grandfather's well-being. Whatever, Walter was a burr under my saddle.

I don't much operate on hunches. My MP and police training is too ingrained to go after somebody on a gut feeling. But there are such things as "vibes," as they used to say in the sixties. And I'd rarely gotten such negative ones from anybody as I did from Walter Paich. He was all sullen resentment, like a knotted fist, exuding the noxious gas of anger.

I was annoyed with myself. In two days I'd managed to find out that Bogdan Zdrale hadn't gone to Ray's Bar in Toledo, that the highway patrols in three states hadn't seen his van, and that Walter Paich malingered on the job. Not much here to go into the highlight film.

I was going to call Marko, but the sun was trying to bust out, the sky threatened spring snow, and my left ear was feeling hot and cauliflowered from all the phone work, so I decided to drive down and see him instead.

He was wearing a blue pinstripe today, three pieces, and a patterned yellow power tie. I don't own a power tie. I've always figured that if you're really secure about yourself you don't have to drape yourself with symbols of power and authority. That's probably why Marko always comes across poised and elegant and I look like somebody's old running shoes.

I installed myself in his visitor's chair and poured a cup of bitter coffee. He should have had a plate of Tums sitting out like homemade cookies. "Did you run those names for me, Marko?"

"Gee, Milan, I didn't," he said in a voice that could freeze meat. "I've been so busy with all the murders we're supposed to solve down here it just slipped my mind. Give me a minute, will you?"

The cold tone didn't surprise me. I think he'd envisioned a career-long partnership of Meglich and Jacovich, two boyhood pals grown to heroic manhood, ranging the nighttime streets and making Cleveland safe for the good guys, rather like a modern-day Earp and Holliday, or more realistically, a Slovenian tag team. When I quit the department he was forced to switch dreams, and there is a certain residual bitterness, which usually shows its head when I ask for a favor.

He excused himself for a few minutes and went down the hall, and I sat there by myself, looking around his office. On the desk was a ceramic mug with his name and shield and the logo of the Cleveland Police Department on it. He'd purchased it a year earlier when he decided he ranked too high in the departmental hierarchy to have to drink from plastic cups. He had his framed degree from Kent State on the wall, as though he were a doctor or a lawyer, and next to it was a photograph of him with the mayor of Cleveland. A few years ago there had been a different picture in that spot, one with the former mayor, but Marko was far too canny a political animal to leave that one up there in full sight. Commendations, awards, the memorabilia of an eighteen-year police career culminating in a lieutenancy shoved into a ten-by-twelve cubicle painted drab gray and furnished with utilitarian metal chairs and a desk scarred with heel marks and cigarette burns and coffee spills. On a file cabinet were several thick volumes of the state penal code, all dog-eared and obviously well used. If I'd stayed in uniform all this could have been mine.

Marko came back with a few sheets of computer printout and tossed them onto the desk before he sat down. "Well, that was a big waste of time," he said.

"Why?"

From the top drawer he took a pair of rectangular glasses like a grandmother might wear, perched them on his nose, and consulted the printout. "Nothing on Bogdan Zdrale," he said. "The computer never heard of him." He peered over the glasses at me. "And the computer knows all and sees all."

"Okay."

"Very little on Lazo Samarzic."

"What does that mean, very little?"

"About four years ago there was a shooting in West Allis, Wisconsin. A Serbian farmer named Mele Malinkovich, found shot in the head in a public park at about two o'clock in the morning. Samarzic had been to see him three or four days before his death, so the local guys drove over here to talk him up. He was alibied, so nothing ever came of it." He pushed the glasses back up his nose with a forefinger. "If you're interested, West Allis never cleared the Malinkovich case."

I jotted the information down in my notebook and verified the spelling of Malinkovich. "It might mean nothing," I said.

"Might." He shuffled the printouts. "Now we come to our old school chum Walter Paich."

The hairs on the back of my neck stood up, and I leaned forward in the chair as Marko read the computer print.

" 'March 1989,' " he recited. " 'DUI; driver's license suspended for six months. February 1990, domestic disturbance. No charges filed.' "

"Domestic disturbance?"

Marko looked up at me. "A polite way of saying he was smacking his old lady around."

"And she wouldn't file charges?"

He took the glasses off and laid them atop the paper. "You know how many of those squeals ever see the inside of a courtroom? The woman usually changes her mind, the husband walks, and we're the Gestapo. So in cases like that the investigating officer's objective is to calm things down and keep anyone from getting badly hurt, not clog up the courts with petty shit."

"Beating up your wife is petty shit?"

Marko shrugged. He didn't invent the system, I knew, but he still couldn't look me in the eye. That didn't make it any better. For him or for me. Or for the Vera Paiches of the world.

"Anything else?"

He consulted the sheet again. " 'November 1990, drunk and disorderly,' which means—ah, here it is—a fistfight outside a bar called Janko's."

"I know the place."

He grinned. "You better stay out of those Serbian saloons, Milan. They find out you're Slovenian they'll send you home in an ice truck."

"What happened with his D and D?"

He shook his head. "Nothing. No charges filed."

"What was the fight about?"

"It doesn't say. What's the difference, anyway? A bar fight doesn't have to be about anything, you know that. You've got two guys, mad at the world, mad that they're sitting in a shitty tavern drinking cheap booze and not on a yacht in the Caribbean with Michelle Pfeiffer. They start talking, not because they want to but because the loneliness and the isolation and the hopelessness of it all starts pressing in on them and they crave human contact with *somebody,* even the barfly on the next stool. One says he's a die-hard Browns fan, the other one likes the Steelers and ba-da-bing, ba-da-boom! you've got a D and D."

"Is it really that easy?"

He folded his glasses and put them back in the drawer. "Why do you have a hard-on for Walter Paich?"

"I don't. I don't like guys that hit their wives, but outside of that I have no problem with him."

Marko nodded.

"Unless he's lying to me," I said.

Gray midday light was shouldering its way into Gershwin's through the windows that looked out on Superior Avenue. It was snowing, certainly nothing you'd categorize as a blizzard; it was probably too late in the season for that. It was the kind of snow that would stick, though, the kind I used to have to shovel out of my driveway, back when I had a driveway, and a house to go with it. Milan Junior and I would go at it, and little Stephen, who couldn't have been much more than six, would be out there too, wrapped up like a mummy to ward off the brutal cold, flailing away with his toy shovel and making things worse instead of better. Shoveling snow with the boys had been fun, even though it occasionally played hell with my lower back. Now that I live in an apartment, someone else is paid to do that sort of thing, and at my house I assumed Joe would be bending his back over the walkway and the front steps. It gave me a small satisfaction that the boys were old enough to dream up all sorts of reasons not to help, and even if they did it wouldn't be much fun for Joe. Small favors.

The lunch crowd wasn't quite as noisy as the attitude-adjustment hour brunch. They had to go back to the office and at least give the appearance of working, so they were drinking white wine or mineral water in place of the heavy-duty bourbon or vodka they'd switch to later in the day. The ambient music was canned instead of live, and the lunch prices were a few dollars lower and the portions a few ounces smaller, but otherwise the atmosphere was pretty much the same. Today Danica Paich chose a chef's salad and I ordered a chopped steak with mushrooms, first cousin to a hamburger. She was wearing a gray wool dress that hugged her body with respect and affection, set off by a bright blue and red silk scarf. It was a tribute to her own sense of style that the ensemble didn't look like that of a flight attendant. She was clearly the best-looking woman in the place, despite the lines of worry that were tugging at her eyes. She didn't look as though she'd been getting very much sleep.

"I was surprised that you called me for lunch, Milan."

"Why? Didn't you figure you'd get a progress report?"

"You could have done that over the phone, though."

I shrugged. "I had to eat anyway."

She smiled at me, a tired smile but a warm one. "You never knew what a crush I had on you in school, did you?"

"You're kidding," I said. Not exactly a quick, snappy retort, nor an appropriate one. But it was the best I could do on the spur of the moment. I never said I was Cary Grant.

She lowered her head and looked up at me. "You didn't know I was alive. But I used to go to the football games, and down to the McDonald's where you guys hung out all the time. You were always smiling, Milan, smiling at us little kids like we were real people. And you were just so big!" She looked away. "Sure I had a crush on you. I was nine years old, and it was heavy."

"Everything is heavy when you're nine. When you get older you're fussier about what costs you sleep."

I filled her in on what little I'd been able to glean about

83

her grandfather. I was no closer to finding him than I'd been three days earlier, and we both knew it. She was too nice to bitch about it, but I sensed she was deeply disappointed.

"So," I said finally, "let's go over it again. Maybe you know more than you think you do."

"I don't understand," she said.

"I just want to get you talking some more, and I'll listen very closely and maybe I can pick up something I missed the first time around. Sometimes we can get too close to a situation and not really focus on it. Could be there are things you didn't tell me just because it never occurred to you to bring them up."

"For instance?"

I put my hand on hers. It made her jump. "For instance, Walter."

"I told you about Walter."

She said it a little too hard for comfort, and I took my hand away. She fiddled with her spoon, holding it in both hands, playing with it. I just looked at her, trying to keep everything off my face, all my cynicism about Walter, all my uneasiness. I figured if I kept quiet long enough she'd tell something I wanted to hear.

I was right.

"I don't know what I can add to what you already know," she said at last. "Walter's . . . not very nice. He never has been. You probably don't remember him that much, from when he was a kid, but he's got a mean streak. I don't know why." She took her lower lip between her teeth for a second, then released it. "It wasn't easy being his little sister. He used to do some things to me that were so awful I can't even tell you. I don't know if he likes to make people miserable, or if it's just the only thing he knows how to do. He moved out as soon as he was nineteen, and he doesn't have much contact with the family anymore. The only reason he had us all at Constance's christening is so we'd have to buy presents. That's why I didn't say much about him. He hardly ever saw Grandpa, so he's not a good one to ask."

I drummed my fingers on the tablecloth. I should have

been writing all this down in my notebook, but I didn't want to inhibit her. It bothered me, though, that Walter was so isolated from the rest of his family. Slavs just aren't like that. Even if they don't get along, family is family, especially on holidays. A Serb who hardly ever sees his grandfather is a rare bird indeed.

"Why is Walter such a loner?" I said.

"He's always been that way, mad at the world, and he takes it out on anyone smaller and weaker than he is. I guess it's the only thing that makes him feel good about himself. So he doesn't have much to do with the rest of us." She looked away, ashamed of what she was about to say. "And that's just fine with us, too. He's very difficult to be around."

"Did you know that he's been taking a lot of time off from work?"

She shook her head. "It doesn't surprise me. He's a classic underachiever. It's the way he was in school too. He does enough to get by and not a speck more. That's why he's got just about the same job he did when he was nineteen."

"And he's bitter about it?"

"Sure," she said. "Watching all the guys he started out with getting promoted, making more money, having more . . . status. Having his little sister who he used to tie up and stick with pins grow up and go to college and make more money in a year than he makes in five."

"He used to tie you up and stick you with pins?"

She tried to toss it off, but there were shadows behind her blue eyes. "What else do you do on a cold winter afternoon when you're fifteen?"

I tried not to show my shock. "It sounds like Walter is waiting around for someone to give him something and resenting it that they don't."

"And they never will, because there's nothing about him that makes anyone want to help. Walter's a bastard!" When Danica spoke about her brother a cynical edge hardened her voice and gave a nasty downward turn to her mouth. It wasn't attractive.

"Let's change the subject a minute, Danica. Do you know Lazo Samarzic?"

"Everybody knows Lazo Samarzic."

"I didn't."

"You aren't a Serb."

"People keep pointing that out."

"Why do you ask about Mr. Samarzic?"

"If you know him, you must know that nothing goes on in the neighborhood that he isn't part of."

She shook her head. "No, it isn't like that. He's a community leader, that's all. He likes helping people. He doesn't do it for personal profit."

I could believe that. If Lazo Samarzic were making a lot of money as a racketeer he probably wouldn't spend his days hawking fruits and vegetables at the West Side Market.

"Does Walter know him?"

"Oh, yes. I don't know if they're actually friends, but Walter sucks around him a lot. He runs errands and things. Why? What does Lazo Samarzic have to do with Grandpa?"

"Did you ever hear your grandfather mention him?"

"I don't think so. As I said, everyone knows Mr. Samarzic, but I'd be surprised to learn that he knew Grandpa."

"Life's full of surprises," I said. I was about to elaborate, but one of those little surprises got me sidetracked.

My beeper went off.

It was a soft, shirring sound, but it sounded like the peal of a cathedral bell in my head. I felt as if everyone had heard the noise coming from the vicinity of my belt and was looking at me with barely disguised amusement. It was obvious from my mode of dress that I wasn't a dedicated power luncher; how dare I wear a beeper above my station in life?

I excused myself and went to the pay phone and tapped out the number that had appeared on the readout. I knew it by heart, anyway. It was Spanish John Hanratty's private line at the stolen-car office, and when he answered he told me that Bogdan Zdrale's Ford van had been found.

"Where, John?"

"Out in a shopping mall in Wickliffe. It's been there for

several days now, nobody's quite sure how long. Finally one of the local merchants called in a complaint to the Lake County Sheriff's Office, and they saw the license on our sheet and called us."

"Where is the van now?"

"Right where somebody left it," he said.

I had to bring Danica along. I couldn't not bring her; she wouldn't put up with it. Once she heard they'd found Bogdan's van, there was no keeping her away, and I didn't want to argue with her in a crowded restaurant. She'd seemed soft at first, but they don't give executive positions to soft and indecisive people. So I gave in without much of a fight. We decided to take my car.

The freeway trip took longer than usual because of the weather, but this particular stretch of asphalt wasn't as heavily traveled as the ones closer in to downtown, so it was only about forty-five minutes later that I wheeled the Sunbird into the Shoregate Shopping Center parking area.

The van was easy to spot, even through the falling veil of white. It was square and boxy, built in the days before the proliferation of sleek, low, aerodynamic minivans, and was higher than most of the vehicles around it. It had been left along the perimeter of the parking lot, about sixty feet from a hamburger restaurant, out of the main stream of traffic and away from the buildings so as not to attract nighttime attention. Its nose faced a row of winter-naked bushes, almost touching them. Beneath it was black pavement while around it the snow was sticking. Parked on the left was a Lake County sheriff's vehicle and on the right a car I recognized as belonging to Spanish John Hanratty. It's hard to miss a bright yellow Corvette in Cleveland.

The Lake County deputy was a man named Irv Hofstra, whose lower lip protruded in a permanent pout, making him look like a middle-aged Gerber baby. Whether his face was red from the cold, from anger, or it always looked that way I didn't know. He clearly didn't have much use for private detectives and seemed distinctly annoyed that someone from the Cleveland police had involved him in what was obviously a Cuyahoga County affair and gotten him out of a warm office and away from the daytime soaps, but he was polite enough, especially with Danica there.

Spanish John took one look at Danica Paich and really turned on the charm. I use the term advisedly; it was as if someone had thrown an interior switch. He walked her off into the lot, away from the van, with his hand gently touching her elbow, assuring her with his white-toothed smile that everything was all right and not to worry. Sincerity and concern leaked out of him like milk through a defective carton. Their footprints in the snow were very close together, almost overlapping. I'd seen him operate with attractive women before, and only our long friendship stopped me from stepping in between them and telling him to go chase his own tail.

"Listen, Danica," I heard him say before they got out of earshot, "we've got the van—that's a big step. It gives us something to go on."

I didn't contradict him, but he knew better. Finding the van in this fairly remote spot, at least remote from the usual haunts of Bogdan Zdrale, boded no good at all. The fact that it had been there for several days wasn't a very good sign either. But I didn't want to tell Danica that. There was no point in making her unhappy until I had to, and I was starting to believe that I would have to, eventually.

They talked for about five minutes—rather, John talked and Danica listened. And I ground my teeth. After he'd made all the points with her that he was going to, John seemed to remember that I was the reason he was out there. He came back and took me aside. Talking to me he wasn't quite so charming.

"I've called for a tow. We'll take it downtown and check it out, but from what I can see the steering wheel and the door handles have been wiped down. Same with the rear panel. I'd be surprised if we find a print anyplace."

"How do you read it?"

"I think somebody swiped Grandpa, put him in the pond, and dumped his van as far away as they could conveniently get." He blew his breath out, which quickly turned to vapor, and hunched his shoulders up around his ears, not so much as protection from the elements, it seemed, but almost as a hedge against committing himself. Hang around a major police department long enough, as he had, and you learn not to make rash statements that later might come back to haunt you. But when we locked eyeballs I could see we thought along the same lines.

Danica stared straight ahead as we retraced the drive back to Cleveland on I-90. She was feigning toughness, I could tell, and the effort was taking its toll on her.

"It's all right to cry, Danica."

She turned to face me head on. "Whatever makes you think I'm going to cry?" she said.

SEVEN

I was beginning to accumulate quite a collection of index cards to shuffle around on my desk. Unfortunately they didn't make any more sense than before.

Spanish John was right; he called me first thing in the morning to confirm that the steering wheel and door handles of the old Ford van had been wiped clean of fingerprints, both inside and out. There were a few partials on the vinyl seat backs in the rear, smudged and inconclusive, but they were probably Bogdan Zdrale's anyway. John told me that on one of the door handles and on the gearshift knob they'd found fibers from a terry-cloth towel, further proof that the lack of prints was deliberate.

It wasn't too much of a leap of imagination to put the pieces together and arrive at a conclusion: person or persons unknown had spirited Bogdan Zdrale away, had perhaps killed him, and had abandoned his van as far from the scene as they could conveniently get, first eradicating all traces of themselves.

What I couldn't come up with was a reason. Simple robbery didn't quite fit the picture. Almost anyone could have easily robbed a seventy-five-year-old man with a minimum of violence, however tough a nut he may have been in his younger days. An elderly pensioner was an unlikely robbery victim anyway, although these days the feral night people that make up our drug subculture will kill you for your pocket change. And the abandonment of the van more than thirty miles from where Zdrale habitually hung out didn't fit that scenario; old and battered as it was, it would have brought a few dollars from a chop shop or even a legitimate parts dealer.

Someone had taken pains to get the van out of the way so it wouldn't be noticed for a while. And they'd taken the time to wipe off the fingerprints. None of that squared with drug craziness on the street level, which is at its most circumspect a hit-and-run proposition.

Elmo Laketa had lived for the past thirty years in the old neighborhood in a square gray three-bedroom frame bungalow on Marquette Street just north of St. Clair Avenue near the Kirtland Pumping Station. He'd probably paid it off within three or four years of buying it, because the old-timers hate being in hock to anyone. Hardworking stiffs like Laketa and Zdrale, seeking a new life in the United States after war and the vagaries of international politics had savaged their homeland, paid their own way and asked for very little in return. A roof over their heads, enough to eat for their families, an occasional bottle, and eventually a smidgin of respect for their gray hairs.

When I called Elmo he cheerfully told me to come on over, even though I doubted whether my name even registered with him. It probably didn't matter who I was or what I wanted. Old men like the company; they crave someone to talk to and break the monotony of their dotage, even if they don't know whoever it is personally, because unlike China, where elders are revered, in our fast-lane, me-first society where money and position are the methods by which we keep score, the old are practically invisible. And sadly, disposable.

I was impressed with the house; Elmo Laketa lived alone and certainly couldn't afford maid service, but everything was neat, dusted, polished and in order, with doilies and antimacassars on virtually every piece of furniture. It made me ashamed of the genial disarray of my own apartment, with a week's worth of old newspapers lying around and a sinkful of dishes that were rinsed but not washed. Perhaps his daughter

Sophie came over and cleaned for him, but I tended to think that the old fellow worked at his housekeeping. He didn't have much else to occupy his time.

We sat in his living room on a sagging sofa of cracked beige leather, sipping coffee strong enough to stand a pencil in upright. That's the only kind anyone in Cleveland ever drinks. It's a black coffee–spicy sausage–pumpernickel kind of town. It's a cigarette kind of town, too. Laketa smoked as furiously as ever, even though it was not yet ten o'clock in the morning. The oxygen tank on its rolling dolly stood in the corner at the ready. The way he lit one cigarette from the end of another, he'd probably need the thing before long.

"Bogdan don't know nobody in Wickliffe," he was saying. He had trouble pronouncing the name of the town.

"Can you be sure of that?"

He regarded me like the simpleton I was for even asking the question. "I never hear him say Wickliffe, all these years. He don't ever go there. Why he'd leave car?" He ran his hand over his face, the stubble on his chin rasping against the calluses on his fingertips. "Nah—is trouble. Trouble, big man." He chanted it like his own personal mantra.

I nodded. "That's why I need your help, Mr. Laketa. To find out what kind of trouble."

"Always trouble, Bogdan," he said. "For long time he drink too much. Marija die. Walter . . ." His nose crinkled as if he'd smelled something bad.

"What about Walter, Mr. Laketa?"

He obviously didn't want to talk about it. "Not a nice man. Not Bogdan's fault, Walter." He shook his head and sighed. "Bogdan his whole life have lots of trouble."

"Everybody has troubles."

"Yah, sure. But him, it eat him up inside. In his guts. Make him a sad man." His massive shoulders rose and fell. "Lots of things, you know? When we was kids, was okay. But when he grow up . . . in the war. Ever since war, Bogdan a sad man. Mad, too."

"He was mad about the war?"

He gave that one-bark laugh again, then coughed a few

times to clear his throat. "Everyone in Europe mad about war. It was bad time. Bad time for Serbs, for everybody."

Before putting my cup down on the coffee table I gave the matter some serious consideration. There wasn't a single smudge on its glass top, as if it had been Windexed that morning. Finally I rested the cup on a newspaper, last week's *Ameriska Domovina*, the Serb paper. "What happened during the war?"

The leather cushion crackled and popped a complaint as he leaned his bulk back against it. His eyes were turned inward to somewhere long ago and far away. "People died," he said simply. "What war is about—dying. Bogdan, he kill some." He looked up at me. "Me too."

"He spent two years in a German prison camp, didn't he?"

He nodded. "Till war was over."

"Is that what he's mad about?"

"Sure, mad!" The words exploded from him, and the effort made him gasp. He struggled for a breath, his shoulders shaking, and he flicked a look over at the oxygen tank, but he got himself under control before he had to use it.

"The war was a long time ago, Mr. Laketa."

He pulled on his fleshy nose. "You ever been in a war?"

"Vietnam," I told him.

"Then you know," he said, moving a bit closer to me and lowering his voice to a quieter and more intimate level. Those who have faced the guns of their country's enemies are forever brothers. "Don't matter how long, some things you don't forget."

That was true. I saw things in Southeast Asia that still make me wake up sweat-drenched and shaking in the middle of the night, horrors the dim bulbs who make slasher movies couldn't even conceive of. It didn't much matter what war, or what uniform. Desert Storm, Cam Rahn Bay, the Cho-san Reservoir, Iwo Jima or Gettysburg—even if you manage to come through combat with your skin relatively intact, you're never quite the same person again. The pop psychologists who currently talk about executive stress would suffer circuit overload and burst like a water balloon just thinking about it.

I don't much dwell on my war, and I talk about it even less; it's something I had to do at the time, and I've tried to put it behind me. But Elmo Laketa was right, there are some things, some horrors, that stick with you like a stubborn allergy that just won't go away.

Still, fifty years is a long time to walk around with a hard-on.

"Now, Mr. Laketa? Does he have troubles now?"

"He's old," he said. "Like me, old. That's troubles. You wait. You'll find out."

"Troubles with other people, though." He looked puzzled. "Gambling, for instance. Does he bet on the horses, or on football?"

He allowed himself the ghost of a smile. "Bogdan, he's one cheap sum of a bitch. He don't waste money like that."

"How about drugs?"

The look he gave me could have withered an elm tree. I didn't ask whether Mr. Zdrale might be entangled with any women. Apparently both possibilities were too silly even to contemplate.

"Politics, then?"

"What politics?"

"I don't know. Local? Or Serbian politics, maybe?"

His chest heaved, and the air in his ravaged lungs whistled. He glared at me from beneath his fierce eyebrows. "Politics for rich people. Bogdan always been poor. Poor men don't give shit for politics. Too busy trying to live."

"Is he involved with Lazo Samarzic?"

His eyes flickered away for just a moment, long enough for me to know I'd hit a nerve. "How you mean, involved?" The way he pronounced the word, I could tell it wasn't in his everyday vocabulary. "He know him. Everybody know Samarzic."

"How about Walter? He know Samarzic too?"

"Listen, big man," Elmo Laketa said, leaning forward in his chair, broad stomach resting on heavy thighs. "You waste your time. My time, too. All this shit don't mean nothing about Bogdan. He just go off someplace, like always. Why you make so much of it? You *look* for trouble?"

I sighed. "No, Mr. Laketa. It just finds me."

Dinner at home was a klobasa sausage sandwich with fried onions and horseradish and a plate of sauerkraut on the side, washed down with a couple of Stroh's. The Cavs were playing the Detroit Pistons at the Coliseum, but it was being carried on the SportsChannel. It didn't hold my interest very much. So I grabbed a pop-mystery novel I'd bought a few weeks before but hadn't gotten around to reading, settled down with another beer, and left the game on as background. Big swinging bachelor Friday night, but I was getting used to it.

Again.

Maybe I'm tougher than I give myself credit for. It takes a strong mind-set to be single, I think. You have to be pretty content with your own company and snug in your own skin to spend most of your nights alone. I'm not sure how well I do it, but it's where I am, and my options are limited. So I've found things to occupy myself that don't require the presence of another person. Right now suffering the solitude just seems easier than trying to do anything about it.

Just after eleven I started getting sleepy, more from boredom than anything else. I was ready to pack it in as another of my less memorable Friday evenings when the phone rang at my elbow. At that time of night I didn't think it could be good news. When I answered and heard Marko Meglich's voice I knew it wasn't.

"I'm sending a car for you," he said, using his official homicide-cop manner. "Be downstairs in fifteen minutes, all right?"

"What's up?"

"I think we found that old man you've been looking for."

My dinner turned to a pound of lead in my stomach. "Bogdan Zdrale?"

"I don't know for sure. That's what I want you to tell me. I know it's late, but d'you mind?"

"Fifteen minutes," I said. I hung up, pulled on a warm

sweater and changed from fleece-lined bedroom slippers to a pair of street shoes. The hair on the back of my neck was standing up straight. It didn't take a rocket scientist to divine that if Marko was sending a car for me, he needed me to identify the old man he'd found. That meant that the old man was unable to identify himself.

Before going downstairs, I went to my file drawer in the front room, took out the photo Tootsie Paich had given me, and stuck it in the pocket of my jacket, hoping I wouldn't have to take it out again.

The officer who picked me up was an old acquaintance, Jimmy Scully, a cop who'd been on the job for about sixteen years. He'd been a uniform back when I was signing in on the roster every morning, but now he was plainclothes and one of Marko's homicide hotshots. He was driving a Plymouth with a few kids' toys and a coloring book in the back seat, so I figured it was his own car. On the way to wherever it was we were going we caught up on old times and old friends, playing "whatever happened to?" and generally passing the time of night. We'd not done much more than say hello when we'd been on the force together, and we really didn't have much to say to one another. In his eyes I was a defector, a backslid cop, which made me half human, some sort of alien who happened to look like everybody else and speak English. Like most badge wearers he couldn't understand anyone voluntarily choosing to quit. He was cordial but cool, as he probably was to all civilians. I couldn't get any information out of him regarding what had happened, where we were heading, or what we'd find when we got there.

"Better save your questions for the lou," was all he'd say. Idle chat was one thing, but Scully was not about to divulge any information that might possibly be deemed important or official.

It only took about ten minutes to get from my place on the crest of Cedar Hill to our destination. One of the nice things about living in Cleveland Heights is that it's relatively close to downtown but far enough away to miss out on some of Cleveland's inner-city problems.

We turned south on East Fifty-fifth Street, not too far from the Kingsbury Run area, where in the thirties a series of gruesome mutilation murders were discovered. The crimes are still unsolved, despite the efforts of Eliot Ness, who was Cleveland's director of public safety at the time. The murders are one of those things like the Cuyahoga River catching fire that people remember about Cleveland while ignoring all the many good things, the beautiful architecture and the proud and colorful history.

The Deming Steel plant was about another two miles south. At night the white smoke belching out of the stacks was like a moving curtain drawn across the night, full of fire, tinging the cloud cover above us with orange. On either side were desolate stretches of vacant land, strewn with enormous discarded truck tires and noxious-smelling slag heaps. At this hour it was a barren moonscape, no traffic and no people on the streets—certainly not if they knew what was good for them. Deming Steel is sandwiched between one of Cleveland's black ghettos and an old-time Polish neighborhood to the south, which differs little from Slavic Town except for the language spoken. It's all part of the American dream.

We wound up on Thirty-seventh Street about half a mile south of Woodland Avenue near the aptly named Iron Court, hard by the concrete ribbon of Interstate 77, which knifes southward from downtown through the barren stretches of heavy industry and wholesale produce warehouses. Just beyond the Northern Ohio Food Terminal, the place where fresh fruits and vegetables are delivered and then distributed to the grocery stores and restaurants of Cleveland, the surface is pitted and broken as the road swoops down into a deep gully. On either side of the roadway there are steep embankments, where the good burghers of Cleveland have seen fit to abandon their old furniture and packing crates. Burned skeletons of sofas and mattresses stand mute sentry. The kids from the poverty pockets nearby make these refuse-choked embankments their winter sports field during snow season, often using a garbage can lid in lieu of a sled.

At the very bottom of the gully, dark as the inside of a subterranean cave, the street snakes under a viaduct, the walls of which are marked with unreadable graffiti. There are no sidewalks, and on the surface of the pavement water from the recent snows had collected in dank puddles.

Our headlights picked out Marko as we pulled up beneath the viaduct. He was wearing a black parka with the white fur hood back, his gold ID shield hanging from the breast pocket. A white turtleneck sweater showed above the collar. Already the police had stretched yellow tape across the street, marking off the crime scene. There were four black-and-whites, two unmarked cars, and Marko's tan Volvo. And the meat wagon, the coroner's tour bus, with two bored-looking attendants leaning against the side of it. One of them was drinking light beer out of a can. Portable floodlamps illuminated the whole scene with stark white light, making a ghastly tableau even more ghastly. I climbed out of Scully's car on shaky legs.

The dirt on either side of the roadway under the viaduct was piled knee-high with refuse, and the body of a man who had fallen forward from his knees lay against the bank of litter. His face was half buried in trash, and in the back of his head was a small bullet hole. Blood and brain matter had caked around the wound to turn his iron gray hair a rusty brown. His clothes were torn in several places. The cloying stink of decayed flesh cut through the cold air, and I had to take several deep breaths through my mouth to keep my dinner from reappearing. A police photographer was busy using up several rolls of film, his flash bouncing off the graffiti-covered walls, his motor-driven camera whirring and clicking.

There's something about violent death that is achingly lonesome. A brisk lake wind was sending dust and newspapers skittering across the pavement and cops both in uniform and in mufti milled around with their collars turned up, blowing on their hands to keep warm. The victim was the only thing not moving in the midst of all the activity.

Marko walked over and shook my hand. Old friends who see each other frequently usually dispense with the ritual of a handshake, but somehow in the sobering presence of a human life lost there was reassurance in the touch of another. "Couple of black kids found him," Marko said. "They'd come down here to make out, I guess. Not exactly a spot where I'd come to get laid, but . . ." He shook his head and looked over at the crime lab technicians. "We'll be through here in a second and you can take a look," he said. "It ain't pretty. He's been here quite a while."

The frail, crumpled body at my feet was bloated now and misshapen. The sudden flaring of the camera's flash made it look even more grotesque, almost surreal. A light mist was falling, the photographic strobes turning the drops into a nearly opaque curtain.

"What a lousy place to die," I said.

Marko rubbed his hands together and then stuck them in the pockets of his parka. "Why do these things always happen in the middle of the night?" he said. "Why can't murderers keep regular hours, like bankers and insurance brokers?"

I stared at the body. "One bullet hole?"

"We won't be sure until we get him on a table, but my guess is a twenty-two, what I can see from here. In the back of the head. Looks like they made him kneel down and then did him." He stuck a cigarette in the corner of his mouth.

The photographer finally stepped back and nodded to us. Marko barked out some orders and the coroner's men came forward, hands encased in rubber gloves and faces protected by surgical masks, which they'd probably soaked with perfume or after-shave. They rolled the body over, and some of the trapped gases escaped with an audible hiss. Marko and I turned our heads away from the stench, and he lit his cigarette quickly and blew the smoke through his nose.

"It never gets any easier," he said tightly.

"Any ID?"

"His wallet's missing. And he only had change in his pocket, less than a buck."

I looked over my shoulder at the corpse's face, or what was left of it. Decomposition had begun, the rats had been at him, and the remaining features were distorted, whether by the rictus of death or in terror I couldn't know. There was no doubt in my mind that I had found Bogdan Zdrale. The facial planes, the bristly gray hair, the angular frame; it all fit the puzzle. The knowledge that I was going to have to break the news to Danica and Tootsie weighed heavily on me, and already I was rehearsing what I'd say—and what I'd leave out. By law the police are not obligated to notify the next of kin, although it's traditional that they do so. But I knew Marko. He was going to lay the sad chore off on me. I'd sooner have taken a flogging.

He looked at the body, and then turned away and looked up at the streaks of flame in the sky. "Shit," he said softly.

"Yeah."

"Any ideas?"

"Not a glimmer."

"How come? You've been looking for him for a week."

"There were a lot of things happening in his life, but I didn't run into anyone who'd want to hurt him. He was an old man and he minded his own business."

"This is a bad area of town," Marko said. "An old white man running around here, anything liable to happen to him."

"If he was running around. But his van turned up out in Wickliffe, wiped down and abandoned. More likely he was brought here."

"Who by?"

"The one who killed him."

I walked around for a minute, trying not to look at the wasted corpse but unable to keep my eyes away. "Does the condition of the body suggest anything to you? The position?"

"What?"

"It's too neat. A small-caliber bullet in the back of a kneeling man's head. More like an execution."

"Or a hit," he said. "That occurred to me, too. In the old

101

days they'd have dumped him in one of those culverts out on Mayfield Road." A gust of wind ruffled his hair. "Now they don't have any more culverts on Mayfield. Progress."

"It doesn't make any sense."

"Murder never does."

"Yeah, but this especially."

"What?"

"Whacking an old retired Serbian mill worker." I shivered, suddenly chilled far beyond what might have been caused by the cold wind. "It has all the earmarks of the outfit."

"I like the way you think, Milan," Marko said.

EIGHT

Sleep didn't come easy. I was too wired, for one thing, and the sight of Bogdan Zdrale seemed to have been tattooed on the insides of my eyelids; each time I closed my eyes he was there, crumpled and broken under the viaduct in the detritus of East Thirty-seventh Street. Finally after tossing around enough to dislodge all the bedclothes, I got out of bed and went into the den with a blanket, turned on a terrible old movie about Hugh O'Brian as a cowboy in the African bush, and nodded off in my chair. Hugh O'Brian works better than Sominex.

I awoke at six A.M. with my back sore and my neck stiff. I'm too old to sleep sitting up all night. And I still had a disagreeable task facing me.

I drank a whole pot of my own lousy coffee to kill some time, and when it was a decent hour I called Danica at home and arranged to meet her at Tootsie's house. It was a ten-minute drive down the hill to Slavic Town, but that morning it seemed like a cross-country trek. It was a bright chilly day, and when I started the Sunbird up billows of white belched from the tailpipe as if even my car couldn't quite warm up to the occasion.

Confronting the Paich women was every bit as unpleasant as I'd thought it would be. There are times when all of us become socially inept, and breaking the news about Zdrale to his daughter and granddaughter was high up on my own personal worst list. There is no socially acceptable method of reporting the death of a family member, no way to cushion the shock or lessen the pain. No easy way. "I'm sorry to have to tell you this . . ." was the best I was able to dredge up, and it sounded pretty lame as it came out of my mouth.

We all deal with family tragedy at one time or another, but facing up to the murder of a loved one is a nightmare for anyone. Danica cried into her hands and wondered aloud who could have done such a terrible thing. Tootsie sat stoically with her fingers tightly interlaced in her lap, staring straight ahead, her mouth a finely drawn incision across her face. It would be a long time before these two would think of father and grandfather and find any peace, if they ever could.

I felt as awkward as a dancing elephant. I had been engaged in a professional capacity; it wasn't my place to offer a comforting arm or shoulder. Yet I felt connected to this family who had been on the periphery of my growing up. I sat on Tootsie Paich's sofa, helpless to give support or succor, listening to the ornate china clock ticking on the mantel. It had probably come from the old country, perhaps had even been packed lovingly in Marija Zdrale's worn carpetbag and somehow survived a customs search.

I assured them that death had come quickly, and after the initial shock wore off, Danica took charge, figuring I suppose that somebody had to. She was going to call the rest of the family right away, but I asked her not to notify Walter. I volunteered to tell him myself, and she seemed relieved that she wouldn't have to talk to him. It was another unpleasant task that really wasn't my place to perform, but I dealt myself in anyway. I wanted to see his face when he found out.

Danica walked me to the door and came out onto the front steps with me. The sun was trying to make a day of it, struggling through the clouds. She put her hand on my arm.

"Milan, thank you for all you've done," she said.

"I didn't do anything. I wish I could have—but I think he was—I think it was over even before you hired me."

She nodded. "I know," she said, "but you've been a good friend, and I won't forget it." Her blue eyes shone wetly. "Call

104

me, all right? Look, this is so terrible. I can't even think. . . . But I'd like to see you again."

"Okay," I said. Sometimes I'm a very stupid man.

"I mean—I'd like to see you. You probably think that's awful of me. Especially now. But you have such strength, Milan. I'm going to need your strength."

I didn't know what to say. I put my arms around her. She almost disappeared against my chest. Her shoulders shook for a moment, and then she squeezed me, took a deep breath, and composed herself. She smelled of Irish Spring.

I drove out the Shoreway to Euclid. By the time I got to Walter's house the dampness of the night before had dried on the pavement, although it still sparkled in the grass, catching the winter sun's weak rays. I figured Walter wouldn't be at work because it was Saturday—but then from what I'd been able to ascertain he didn't much go to work even on weekdays anymore.

I pushed the buzzer, and the light behind it blinked off and then on again. I waited so long that I was afraid no one was home, or that if they were they were opting not to answer. Finally Vera Paich opened the door. She was wearing a pair of jeans that bagged across the seat and a plain-wrap gray sweatshirt raveling at the sleeves. Along her left cheekbone was a smudged blue bruise she'd tried to camouflage with too much makeup for ten o'clock on a Saturday morning. When she saw me standing on her threshold her eyes got big and scared, and she darted a look over her shoulder. From the back of the house, probably the kitchen, I could hear the genial racket of Saturday morning TV cartoons, which explained why her little girl wasn't hanging on to her leg.

"Hello." She made it one syllable.

"Vera, is Walter home?"

"No," she said, too quickly.

I looked at my watch. "Are you sure?"

Her chin bounced up and down like a blue jay drinking from a birdbath, and she pulled the door closed a few inches as though she couldn't wait to shut it altogether. "Please," she whispered. "He's not here."

"Then why are you whispering?" She rolled her eyes, and she seemed to be grasping the edge of the door to keep from falling. I wondered where she'd gotten the new bruise on her face.

No, I didn't.

She was so pathetic, so entreating, and so anxious for me to go away I was ready to abandon ship, even though I would have bet the farm she was lying to me. Then Walter came out of the back of the house into the square little living room.

"What's the idea?" he said. He had on a pair of stained chinos and a T-shirt that looked as if he'd gotten it from the bottom of the laundry hamper. The stretched-out neckline sagged, and there were yellow stains under the arms. "You gonna keep bothering us all the time? Whattaya keep comin' around here for?" He shouldered Vera out of the way as if she were a coatrack instead of a person and loomed in the doorway with bunched fists. Vera backed off, pressing herself against the wall.

"I have to talk to you," I said. "Can I come in?"

"No," he said. "You got nothing to say to me."

"Believe me, I do."

A sneer put an S curve in his upper lip. "What?"

"It's about your grandfather."

"What he does is his business, I already told you. Now why don't you just beat it and leave us alone?" His chin jutted forward at an aggressive angle that just begged for an upper-cut.

I stuck my right hand into my pocket, as though it had a life of its own and had to be controlled. I'd been tactful and gentle with Danica and Tootsie, sparing them as much ugliness as I could. With Walter, I took a breath and just said it. "He's dead, Walter. Someone shot off the back of his head."

Vera Paich gasped and stifled a sob with her hand.

There was a moment when nobody moved, when we all looked like a posed photo taken on a stage set. Then Walter's whole body shook with a single tremor, as if there had been a tiny earthquake just where he was standing, and he let out a breath as if it were one of the last ten he had left.

"I'm sorry," I said.

Vera moaned, a high-pitched animal sound, and Walter's head snapped around. Every time he so much as looked at her she seemed to diminish in size. She skittered along the wall like a crab and disappeared into the rear of the house. Over the sound of the cartoons I heard the child, Constance, say something to her mother, and when Vera replied she sounded as if she was crying.

Walter seemed to be memorizing the middle button on my coat; he stared at it, his brow knitted, without really seeing it. Not wanting to intrude on his grief I waited a decent interval. Finally I said, *"Now* can I come in?"

He tore his gaze away from the button and focused on my face, if indeed his wild eyes were focused at all. Flecks of white saliva appeared at one corner of his mouth.

"No," he said.

"Walter, somebody shot your grandpa."

"I can't help that now."

I quietly moved across the threshold. "Maybe you can, Walter. Maybe if we talked—"

"No!" he said again, more forcefully this time, and tried to slam the door shut. I was too far inside, and he wound up slamming it against me. It hurt.

I reached out for a fistful of dirty T-shirt and pulled him close enough to smell the morning coffee on his breath. And cigarettes. And last night's rye. Maybe burglars had come in the night and stolen his toothbrush.

"You want to work on that temper of yours, Walter."

"Just get outta here, Milan."

"I will. But I'll be back when you're in a better mood," I said. "And I'll tell you this . . ."

The bloodshot whites of his eyes were showing all around the pupil, and I could feel him trembling, feel the rage inside him fighting to get out. But I was a lot bigger than he was and whatever he wanted to do to me, he was going to think more than twice before trying it.

"When I come back, if I see any more bruises on your wife, you're going to think you've been run over by a snow blower."

I tossed him away from me. There wasn't much to him, and he stumbled halfway across the room and hit an end table near the couch, having to grab the wall to keep from falling. He crouched there, and if looks could kill, my family would have been wearing black.

As I headed down the walk toward my car at the curb, I reflected that I could stand to work on my own temper a little.

Police mug shots are never flattering. They aren't meant to be. They're strictly utilitarian, like the picture on your driver's license or your ID badge from work, and the photographer never bothers to say "Smile!" or "Look over your shoulder at the camera and be sexy" or worries that the light makes your nose seem enormous. They simply want to capture on film the way you look for identification purposes. Period.

The mug shots Marko Meglich was showing me weren't too bad, however. Maybe it was because the subject himself wasn't bad, if you liked the swarthy, smarmy type. He was Central Casting's idea of a small-time mob hoodlum. Shown full front and in profile, the guy had an annoying self-possession that belied the numbers across his chest. His black hair was slicked straight back like Knicks coach Pat Riley's, and even though in police custody at the time the pictures were taken, he still radiated a heavy-lidded sensuality. His mouth was generous and full-lipped, twisted into a confident, knowing smile. The kind of smile you just itch to slap off.

"I picked this file up from the organized-crime guys this morning," Marko was saying. He leaned back in his executive chair and laced his fingers behind his head. Since it was a Saturday and officially his day off, he hadn't worn his usual three-piece suit in to headquarters but instead sported a pair of chinos, tasseled loafers, and a black and white and cobalt blue Irish cable-knit sweater.

Marko said, "The life and times of Nello Trinetti. Are

they kidding me with that name, or what? Nello Trinetti, for God's sake. They must've made it up."

I read from the first page of the file. " 'Age thirty-four. Known associate of the Scarpatti crime family.' " I looked up at Marko. "Cleveland is out of their territory. It's too far west."

He shrugged. "It's the jet age."

I put the photos back into the folder and replaced it on his desk. "I didn't sleep much last night and I've had a tough morning. Save me some reading."

"He's a freelancer. Small-time stuff, but kill a peddler or kill a president, it's still a pretty cold way to make a living. Nobody's ever been able to nail him down. Never had enough for an indictment. But NYPD says he's taken several contracts in Brooklyn and Queens. They know it, he knows they know it, and he laughs in their faces."

"What's he doing in town?"

"That's what I'd like to know. He's been here about two weeks, subletting an apartment in the Flats. Monday night he got into a slight altercation with some guy at the bar at The Jesters and the poor dumb son of a bitch filed charges against him. The preliminary hearing is in about an hour."

"On a Saturday?"

"You ever hear of criminals working a five-day week?"

I said, "I appreciate your showing me his picture and all, Marko, but next time find me a Kim Basinger look-alike."

He leaned forward suddenly and slapped a big, manicured hand on Nello Trinetti's picture. "Bogdan Zdrale," he said. "I like this guy for Bogdan Zdrale."

"What's a Brooklyn leg breaker got to do with Bogdan Zdrale?"

"Nothing that I know of. But the MO fits. According to New York, the ones they figure him for were done with a twenty-two at close range in the back of the head, execution-style. The time frame works out too."

"What's the motive?"

"I don't have one. Yet."

"Why would they import a New York button to take out a seventy-five-year-old man?"

"Who knows with those slimeballs? Maybe one of the New York guys owed someone in the D'Allessandro family here a favor. You know how the ginzos are about favors."

I looked away, suddenly uncomfortable. I know about favors. I have a recent history with the D'Allessandro family.

Giancarlo D'Allessandro has been on top of the heap in the Cleveland mob since anyone can remember. He's old now, old and sick, and he's turned most of the operation over to his nephew Victor Gaimari, an Ohio State alumnus who masquerades as a stockbroker, with offices in Terminal Tower and a secretary who truly believes her boss is legitimate.

Times have changed, and like any canny businessmen the mob changed with them. The days of cement overshoes and machine guns in violin cases only exist now in old Edward G. Robinson movies, and if they call a guy Scarface, it's usually because of an injury he got playing college football. Most contemporary hits are carried out against companies on paper around big conference tables by guys wearing Brooks Brothers suits who would never dream of owning a diamond pinkie ring, and the enforcers are bankers or lawyers. Punks like Nello Trinetti are anachronisms now, throwbacks to a bygone era, though their masters still keep them around for show, and for those rare occasions when wet work is a last resort.

The code, however, has remained the same. Respect, unswerving loyalty, the family above all, *omerta*—the code of silence—and a favor granted is a favor owed.

And I owed Giancarlo D'Allessandro a favor.

I've been back and forth with the mob a few times in recent years. I don't like them and they sure as hell don't like me, but I try to stay out of their way, and when I can't I deal with them as fairly as I would my car mechanic or the dry cleaners on the corner. They respect me for that, which is why I'm still walking around. They've had a couple of reasons to put me in the pond, but respect on both sides has kept me healthy.

Several months earlier Matt Baznik, one of my oldest friends, had needed me to get his young son out of more trouble than either of them knew what to do with. The kid had grown up in my living room, eaten at my table, played with Milan Junior and slept in his bed. I couldn't say no, and the only way I could help him was to find out a name, two little words on a piece of paper. And Giancarlo D'Allessandro was the only one I could turn to who knew where to get that name.

Victor Gaimari had given it to me in a sealed envelope—and made it clear that it was a favor. And since then I hadn't once closed my eyes at night without worrying that the next morning would be the day the marker was called in.

So I knew about owing the D'Allessandros a favor.

I took out a cigarette. I didn't want it, but lighting it would give me a few extra moments to get my thoughts together.

"I'm out of it," I said. "My job was to find Bogdan Zdrale. The ball's in your court now."

Marko shifted around in his chair, looking uncomfortable. "I can't. I have rules to follow."

"You're a cop investigating a murder. You've got every right."

He shook his head. "I have rules."

"What do you mean, you have rules? What is that, the Edict of Nantes?"

"I can't get in this Trinetti guy's face."

"Why not?"

"I've got no probable cause."

"A man is executed gangland style, and a known mob enforcer just happens to be in town. Sounds good to me."

"Me too. But the county prosecutor wouldn't touch it, and any judge worth his salt would chew me a new asshole. These scumbolinas have good lawyers."

"I don't know what *I* could do."

"Sure you do," he said. "Poke around."

"I've got a living to make."

"What if it was your grandpa?"

"My grandpa died in bed, as you well know."

"Jesus, Milan, I'm not saying make it your life's work.

Just give it a look, okay? If it's nothing then it's nothing. But at least we'll know."

I gnawed at my lower lip. It's an inescapable truism that friendships almost always end up being about using. It shouldn't be that way, but it is. Every relationship anyone has ever had in their life is based on some sort of quid pro quo. Marko and I couldn't remember a time when we didn't know each other, when we weren't friends. We'd played ball, gone to school, fought and worked together. And yet I rarely saw him anymore if there wasn't a case involved. I used him to get favors and information from the police department that I couldn't get on my own. Now he wanted to use me to poke through some dirty laundry that he couldn't touch himself. I didn't see any way I could tell him no.

I sighed. "Why in hell would the mob want to toast Bogdan Zdrale?"

"He may have been into the shys," Marko suggested.

I shook my head. "For what? He didn't gamble, he was too cheap. No drugs, no whores, he didn't even drink anymore. His biggest vices were cigarettes and coffee, and his house was paid off twenty years ago. You know how those old-time Slavs are, Marko. Your grandpa and mine. They'd rather sell their children to the Gypsies than owe anybody a nickel."

Marko drummed his fingers on Trinetti's picture as if he were playing a Bach fugue on it. "Zdrale gets dusted like it's a good old-fashioned mob hit—the only thing missing is a dead canary in his mouth. And this Nello clown here just happens to show up, making lounge lizard moves on the chicks down at Shooters and throwing his money around in The Jesters. You can tell me his being here at the same time an execution-style murder goes down is just a coincidence, but I don't believe in them."

"Neither do I," I said.

When I walked into the courtroom and sat down in the third row, one of the bailiffs asked me if I were a witness or a defendant. I explained that I was just an observer, and he gave me the withering look cops usually reserve for people who gawk at accident scenes.

The courtroom wasn't much like the ones you see on television. There was little feeling for the majesty of the law here. It more resembled the kind of room in which you apply for unemployment benefits. Institutional gray carpeting with lighter-gray walls, observer's seats that looked as if they'd been bought cut-rate from a failed movie theater in a suburban mall, and city, state, and national flags in stanchions anchored to the floor so no one would steal them. There was a telephone on the prosecutor's table, but none for the defense. Apparently they had to communicate with the rest of the world via jungle drums. There were enough microphones in the room for the governor to hold a press conference. The judge's bench was on a nine-inch riser, not high enough to intimidate anybody.

But the magistrate, Thurlow Wilford, would be intimidating no matter where he sat. He has skin the color of black coffee, a fringe of gray hair surrounding a gleaming pate, a gray mustache, and a physique only marginally fuller than when he played linebacker at Ohio State in the early sixties. He enunciates his words very precisely in a low baritone purr, and because he speaks so softly people tend to shut up and listen. He is highly respected around the city and state and held in great esteem by his fellow Democrats, and periodically rumors surface about his being appointed county prosecutor one of these days, although everyone who knows him expects that he'd turn it down were it offered. Because of nearsightedness, His Honor frowns a lot through his glasses just as a matter of course. When he actively works at frowning, he has a brow like a thundercloud.

Four people stood in front of his bench: the plaintiff, the defendant, and their attorneys. The plaintiff, whose name I found out later was Wade Kooby, was small and ginger-haired and ratlike; his jaw was puffed and discolored, and his right eye was swollen nearly shut. A large white plaster across the middle of his nose held the broken bones in place. Without the shoulder pads in his windowpane plaid jacket he would probably run about a hundred and twenty pounds.

The defendant was Nello Trinetti. Even if I hadn't recognized him from his mug shot, my first clue would have been the luminous gray suit and the matching pearl gray tie against a jet black silk shirt. Not what I would have worn to court to face an assault charge, but then that's me. He was one of those fortunate few who are better-looking than their photographs, and his slicked-back hair, capped teeth, and olive complexion probably held him in good stead with women. His chin was at a cocky angle and his shoulders pulled back so that the suit hung on him just so. Self-assurance is an attractive trait, but in Trinetti it crossed over the line to arrogance, bristling from him like the spikes of a blowfish. He looked like an extra in a Martin Scorcese film.

I recognized his lawyer, too. Tom Vangelis was one of the old-timers, and though somewhere in his mid sixties, his hair was still dark and full ánd his face unlined except for two deep creases at the corners of his mouth, which were probably from laughing at the justice system he was so often able to lick. There was never a whisper of criminal complicity about Vangelis, but he was on retainer to Giancarlo D'Allessandro and Victor Gaimari, along with several other Cleveland and Columbus wise guys, and he was damn good at what he did, which is why the D'Allessandro organization had thrived almost without official legal blemish for so many years.

As I sat there in the old theater seat, wishing I had some popcorn, Judge Wilford was saying, "You're charged with felonius assault, Mr., ah, Trinetti. You understand this is a preliminary hearing to determine whether there is enough evidence to submit the case to the grand jury, do you not?"

"I have an excuse, Your Honor," Trinetti answered.

Wilford sighed and lowered his large head onto his chest and glowered over his glasses without saying anything. Trinetti didn't seem in the least cowed.

"We look forward to your sharing it with us," Wilford said, and the proceedings began.

The battered plaintiff took the stand. He had a voice like chalk on a slate blackboard, and he spoke through still-puffy lips as the prosecutor asked him about the assault. Apparently on the Monday night in question, Kooby had been at The Jesters restaurant with a date. Trinetti had been there too, by himself, and had come on to the woman, at which Mr. Kooby took great offense. "He dropped an ice cube down my date's front, Your Honor!"

There were titters all over the courtroom, quickly silenced as Wilford looked around for their source. I felt like laughing too but knew the judge's reputation too well. Not only was Wade Kooby the kind of person other men took those kind of liberties with, but only a real schlemiel brings his date to The Jesters.

Words had apparently turned to blows and the result was Mr. Kooby's wrecked appearance. At least that was his side of it.

Then Tom Vangelis swung out from behind the defense table.

"Mr. Kooby," he said, "is the young woman—your date—here in court today?"

"No, she isn't."

"Why not?"

"I—wasn't able to contact her."

"You weren't?" Vangelis put down his yellow pad and clasped his hands behind his back like a Hasidic rabbi on his way to sabbath services. "Don't you know her phone number?"

Kooby looked around nervously.

"What's her name?"

"Sable."

"Sable?" Vangelis repeated, his eyebrows shooting up into his hairline. "What a lovely name, Mr. Kooby. Does she have a last one?"

"Uh . . ."

"Don't you know the last name of your date, Mr. Kooby?"

"Well . . . we just met."

"I see." Vangelis leaned against the railing of the jury

115

box. There were no jurors, but it was a gesture he'd perfected over the years and he would have hated not using it. "How did you and Sable meet, Mr. Kooby? Something romantic, like both running for the same cab in the rain?"

"Objection," the prosecutor snapped, not even bothering to get up.

"I'll allow the question," Thurlow Wilford said. "I'm kind of interested myself. But stuff a sock in your sarcasm, Mr. Vangelis."

"Sorry, Your Honor. Answer the question, please, Mr. Kooby."

"We, uh, met through a—a mutual friend."

"A blind date!" Vangelis said. He pushed himself off the jury railing and went back to his table, glancing once at his pad. "I suggest, Mr. Kooby, that the mutual friend was a phone operator at the Magic Moments Escort Service, and that Sable—" He glanced up at Wilford. "Sable Frost, Your Honor, or at least that's her working name; her real name is Sylvia Bornicki and she's employed by Magic Moments as a paid escort." He turned back to Kooby. "That Sable is a hooker you hired for the evening, for two hundred dollars plus other considerations."

"Irrelevant, Your Honor," the prosecutor said.

"I withdraw the question." Vangelis bowed in the general direction of the prosecution table.

He was good, Vangelis. Worth every nickel they paid him. Undoubtedly the owners of Magic Moment were associates of his, or at least he knew how to get to them. He'd done his homework. By the time he was finished with Wade Kooby the little man was nearly in tears, probably wishing he'd kept his mouth shut about the assault.

When Vangelis finally sat down, Wilford said, "What about this, Mr. Trinetti? Did you indeed strike the first blow?"

Trinetti stood up even though no one had asked him to. "This man insulted me with a racial epithet, Your Honor, and that's why I hit him. I'm sure you can relate to that, sir."

Light flashed off the judge's glasses, and his voice was

like thunder rumbling in the next county. "Don't jerk my chain, Mr. Trinetti. Did you hit him first or not?"

"Well, sir, I admit I dropped an ice cube down the lady's dress. It was pretty low-cut, you know. But it was a accident. And for that he called me a guinea," Trinetti said easily, clearly deeply wounded by the follies of others. "Only he used the F word. You know which one I mean, Judge, but I don't wanna say it here in front of everybody."

"The court appreciates your delicacy, Mr. Trinetti," Judge Wilford said. "Now let me understand this. You dropped an ice cube down the front of the dress of the plaintiff's companion, and then he used an ethnic slur?"

"Damn right!" Trinetti said, and then fluttered his eyelashes innocently. "Excuse me, Your Honor, I mean yes."

"Did he threaten you physically in any way?"

Trinetti looked over at poor scrawny Wade Kooby and laughed. It was one of the most distinctly unpleasant laughs I'd heard in a long time.

"Do I take that to mean no, Mr. Trinetti?"

"Yes, Your Honor. I mean no."

"And that's when you struck him?"

"Hey, I don't let nobody insult the Italian race."

Judge Wilford's massive chest rose and fell beneath his black judicial robe. "Your pride in your heritage is admirable indeed, Mr. Trinetti. But we just can't go around bashing in people's faces because they don't like our last names or the color of our skin. I find there is sufficient evidence to bind the defendant over to the Cuyahoga County grand jury. Bail to be set in the amount of three thousand dollars." He glanced at the defendant. "And Mr. Kooby, you would be well-advised to eliminate ethnic slurs from your vocabulary." A smile played at the corners of his eyes. "At least until you've ascertained just who it is you're talking to." The gavel crashed down on its block like the crack of doom.

"Now this is just the first step," I heard a plainclothes cop saying to Kooby on the way out. "You're going to have to go through this again before the grand jury, only then his lawyer is going to be even tougher. . . ."

117

If the decision shook Nello Trinetti's composure he was damn careful not to show it. He smiled up at the magistrate and shifted his shoulders under the expensive jacket, punched Vangelis in the arm by way of thanks, and walked out of the courtroom without even looking at his victim, thus depriving poor Mr. Kooby of the only positive left to him, the chance to gloat. If Kooby didn't withdraw his complaint before it ever got to the grand jury, Nello was supremely confident that Tom Vangelis would get him off.

So was I.

NINE

The Jesters is an old-line Cleveland eatery located right in the middle of the downtown area on a block-long dogleg of a street off East Ninth. At one time, just before and after World War II, the street was the city's hot spot, with girlie joints like the French Quarter, Mickey's Show Bar, and the Frolics Café, now long gone. The Jesters, on the more respectable side of the street, is the only survivor, surrounded now by cold marble and glass high-rise office buildings and frequented at lunchtime and happy hour by much the same crowd as hangs out in Gershwin's a few blocks away. They serve large portions of basic beef and potatoes, pouring generous drinks at the oval bar under the colored lights. But this was a Saturday night, and the brokers and bankers and middle managers were home in Shaker Heights or Rocky River, and the after-sundown crowd had taken over with a vengeance. I had to assume that everyone in attendance had made a special effort to be there, whether for the food, the uninspired piano music, or the ambience, which is pure Early Wise Guy. The place looks like a nightclub in a George Raft movie. I'm sure that if Raft ever visited Cleveland to plug a picture, he wound up at The Jesters.

You come to The Jesters to see and be seen, to impress people who think a necktie hand-painted with a Miami Beach seascape is the height of fashion and who wouldn't know a good Chardonnay if it bit them in the ass. Guys who wear their pants with knife-edge creases and call their bookies several times a day. Hot-eyed divorcees and thirtyish women from the typing pool looking for a little excitement, only to find people sitting around moaning how they'd missed the afternoon's exacta by a nose. The rhinestone-tie-tack crowd.

I spotted Nello Trinetti the minute I came in. He and his party had taken up residence at a banquette along the wall. He sat between two busty blonde women who wore their hair shoulder-length and bouffant, held stiffly in place by a ton of spray. One seemed poured into a red wool jersey dress through which her nipples poked like snub-nosed bullets, and the other was in form-fitting ice blue silk with a yard of cleavage showing.

The foursome was completed by one of Giancarlo D'Allessandro's soldiers, a low-level errand boy named Joey who had crossed my path a few times before to our mutual detriment. He was wearing sunglasses. He always wore sunglasses, day or night. It was his trademark. He thought they made him look cool. Truth is, they made him look like an asshole.

Joey was working hard on the blonde in red, but he was a scummy little punk with oily hair and acne, and neither of the women seemed remotely interested in what he had to say. They couldn't take their eyes off Trinetti. And though I couldn't see what was going on under the table, my guess was they couldn't take their hands off him either.

I slid onto a barstool where I could watch them and ordered a Stroh's. The bartender gave me the fish-eye, because this was not a beer-drinking crowd, but he served me with enough good grace to ensure a tip. The pianist on a platform behind the bar played Billy Joel. Billy Joel was losing decisively.

I had almost finished the beer before Joey spotted me, and his heavy black brows, which met over his nose, came down lower over his sunglasses. I smiled and waved, and he didn't wave back. Rude.

He leaned across the blonde in the red dress—not as simple as it sounds—and whispered something to Trinetti. My guess was that it was about me and that it wasn't compli-

mentary, but that might have been my own insecurity showing. I didn't think so, though. Trinetti listened, then looked up
and met my gaze. We stared at each other for about fifteen
seconds, and then he smiled broadly at me, showing his
dimples—at least, his mouth smiled. The rest of his face
didn't.

I rose and carried my glass over to the banquette. Even
with the shades, Joey looked as if he was about to cry.

"Hello there, Joey," I said.

If you really want to diminish someone, tack a "there" on
the end of your "hello." I really shouldn't have wasted it on
Joey—it was like attacking a mosquito with a Patriot missile.

"Who let you in here, Polack?" he said.

I made a mental note to buy Joey a map of Europe for
Christmas. "Aren't you going to introduce me to your
friends?" I asked.

He didn't answer. I guess he just forgot his manners.

"I don't think we've met. I'm Milan Jacovich," I said, and
stuck my hand out to Trinetti.

He looked at it for a few seconds like he was trying to
identify what it was, and then gave it a cold shake, no ma-
chismo, no test of strength. It was his way of telling me I
wasn't worth proving anything to. "Nello Trinetti," he said
dryly.

I turned to the blonde with the ice blue décolletage.
"Milan," I said.

"Brandy," she said, and then indicated her girlfriend as
though she wanted to make sure I knew she had Nello all
staked out for herself but that the other girl might be available.
"This is Tammy." I won a small bet I'd made with myself that
both their names ended with a y.

I turned back to Trinetti. "I don't think I've seen you
around."

"That'd be my guess, too, rosy cheeks," he said, allowing
himself another cool smile.

Rosy cheeks. Give me a break.

"May I join you? It's lonesome up at the bar."

He clucked his tongue. "Life sucks sometimes."

"Doesn't it?" I said, and sat down next to Brandy. She scooched closer to Trinetti to make room for me, but he didn't seem to enjoy it. The smile dimmed a bit.

"What's on your mind, rosy cheeks?"

"I'm just trying to show an out-of-towner how warm and friendly us Clevelanders are."

"You showed me, okay?" He had a way of waving his hand in front of his ear, fingers cupped and palms inward, like the queen. He had nice hands, small but artistic, with thin tapered fingers. The nails were manicured and buffed to a high gloss.

"And I wanted to tell you how impressed I was with you in court this morning. That was quite a performance."

"You were there, huh?" He beamed like a tailback pleased that I'd been in the stands to see his hundred-yards-rushing game.

I leaned closer to him, the perfume rising from between the white globes of Brandy's breasts making me dizzy. I was watching his eyes. Anybody can read another person's eyes; it just takes practice. I've had my share. "I'm a friend of Bogdan Zdrale's," I said.

His eyes didn't flicker, nothing moved. Maybe he was a good actor, to go with his movie star looks. "I'm glad for you," he said.

"I was wondering if you know him."

"Know him?" he said. "I can't even pronounce him." That made him laugh a lot, and it seemed to tickle Joey, too. Their merriment was way out of proportion to the joke—or to anything the Marx Brothers ever did, either, but they were getting lots of mileage out of Nello's witticism. His laugh was more of a snigger, probably cultivated from seeing Richard Widmark as Tommy Udo in *Kiss of Death* on the late show. Why not, they were both punks.

"We don't hang around with Polacks," Joey put in. It made him feel good saying "we," putting himself in Nello Trinetti's league. It wasn't exactly a major league, but then it probably was to Joey. Everything is relative.

Tammy gave him a playful slap on the arm. "Don't say that," she admonished him. "I'm part Polish myself."

Joey leered at her nipples. He'd obviously had a little too much to drink. "Which part?"

Tammy slapped his arm again.

"So who's this guy I'm s'posed to know?" Trinetti said. "What's his name again?"

"Bogdan Zdrale."

He shrugged. "Never heard of him. Why, he somebody important?"

"Not really. He didn't wear expensive suits—I don't think he even owned a suit. He was just an old man who died."

"Let me extend my sympathies."

"That's very nice of you," I said.

Trinetti wasn't smiling at all anymore. "Look, what's your act, rosy cheeks? I mean, I'm with some people here . . ."

He was good, Nello. If he was the guy that did Bogdan Zdrale, he was really good.

"Just paying my respects."

"You paid 'em, okay? Now don't push me. I don't push so good."

"Chill out, Nello. I'm not some shoe clerk you can slap around like Wade Kooby."

That one got his eyebrows up. It was nice to know I'd finally impressed him. "Then who are you?"

I stood up. "I'm a guy you don't fuck with, Nello. Because if you do, I'll eat your lunch."

He looked at me like I was a new life form. I ignored him and smiled at the two women. "A pleasure, ladies." Catching the eye of a passing cocktail waitress, I said, "Bring my friends here another round, please," and tossed two twenties onto the table. Then I leaned over to Nello and said, "The change is for the waitress. Keep your fingers off, rosy cheeks."

There is some truth to the accusation that Nello Trinetti had done absolutely nothing to me and that for no good reason I'd come after him with six-guns blazing. This is America and a man is presumed innocent until proven guilty, di-dah, di-dah, di-dah. But Nello was the kind of sleazy punk who wormed around legal loopholes, who sat back and laughed at the justice system our Founding Fathers so laboriously constructed and put into place, so I didn't feel much guilt.

Besides, I'd seen Wade Kooby in court, and Nello had busted up more than his face. He'd probably gotten a kick out of coming on to Kooby's date in front of him, humiliating him and figuratively cutting his balls off. Getting laid wouldn't be enough for Nello—someone else would have to get hurt along the way so Nello could exult in his own silly act of toughness and invincibility.

So I felt no regret for what I'd said to him. And perhaps, if he'd had anything to do with Bogdan Zdrale's death, I'd shaken him up enough to make him nervous. And when guys like Nello get nervous, they make mistakes.

I sauntered slowly toward the door. It was a long walk. I wasn't worried though. Nello Trinetti wasn't going to shoot me in the back.

Not even in The Jesters.

I hate those Sundays I don't get to spend with my sons. Not that I see that much of Milan Junior at all anymore. He has a busy schedule, between school, sports, and hanging around with his friends. Today they were going to check out the action at the Severance Center shopping mall and hassle the girls, who would pretend annoyance and giggle behind their hands. Much preferable to spending time with your old man. Stephen was just approaching that stage of maturity where he was ashamed to be seen with his father in public, but he'd been invited to somebody or other's birthday party, and even though according to the divorce agreement Lila and I had worked out it was my day to be with him I had to step aside gracefully. Custody and visitation arrangements cause much heated wrangling when a marriage is dissolved. Then suddenly the kids get old enough to make their own decisions and begin the rite of passage to adulthood and the legal mumbo jumbo whirls right down the drain. Let some judge try and tell a ten-year-old he has to miss a party to hang out with his old man.

So it was to be a lonely Sunday. Families often spend Sundays together. Couples were out doing fun things and holding hands. I wasn't part of a family anymore, and since breaking up with Mary several months earlier I wasn't part of a couple, either. I had heard through various sources that she was now seeing her boss, Steve Cirini, who was one of those patterned-suspenders guys with a power tie. Mary was a fast-lane business type, and I guess his life-style dovetailed neatly with hers, like two spoons front to back, better than mine ever did.

It didn't make it hurt any less, though.

The telephone sat on my desk like a mute rebuke. I ran my fingers over the buttons a few times as if I were reading Braille, until I realized there wasn't anyone I wanted to call. It was a depressing moment of truth.

There was always Auntie Branka. But if I called she'd invite me over to her house for dinner, and if I went she'd only make me eat her stuffed cabbage and ask me whatever happened to that nice Mary girl, and wasn't it time I thought about getting myself a wife again because it was no good being alone. That was too high a price to pay for gorging myself on *gibanica,* even the way Tetka Branka makes it. I couldn't have reached Ed Stahl if I wanted to; he guarded his weekends with an answering machine that screened all incoming calls. Sonja Kokol, my old school chum now turned psychologist, newly married and the proud owner of a brand new house in Mentor, was probably doing something romantic like checking the Sunday paper for sales on furniture. Marko Meglich spent most of his free time out with one of the interchangeable twenty-year-old bimbettes who helped him to forget, for the moment anyway, that he was a forty-year-old divorced cop. My banker buddy Rudy Dolsak was pretty much of a stay-at-home, unless his son was playing basketball at Cleveland State.

There was a time when Matt Baznik would have asked me over for dinner of a Sunday, but I had helped Matt's kid

125

Paulie out of a particularly sticky situation a while back, getting myself in trouble with the federal cops and nearly killed in the process, and while Matt and his wife Rita Marie were everlastingly grateful, there was a definite strain to the relationship now, an awkwardness that made them uncomfortable and me sad, and we hardly ever got in touch anymore.

No good deed goes unpunished.

I toyed briefly with the idea of calling Danica. She had, after all, asked me to. But two days after her grandfather's body had been discovered didn't seem like a propitious time to invite her to Sunday brunch, and I was sure she'd be busy with funeral plans and with consoling her mother and dealing with her own grief. Besides, I wasn't sure I wanted to.

I was attracted to her, there was no getting around that, and she'd come right out and told me she'd had a thing about me twenty years ago. I was a little gun-shy when it came to women. I come from the kind of solid European peasant stock that gets married for life; we take "for better or worse" pretty seriously. But my marriage had broken up anyway, leaving me practically reclusive when it came to a social life, and then after a year and a half that I thought had a future to it, Mary and I crashed and burned. I wasn't ready for any more draining and demanding involvements at the moment. I have the same physical needs and desires of most men my age, but Danica didn't seem the kind of woman I would take to bed once or twice and then lose her number, despite her boldness at confessing her long-ago crush, and I didn't think I was emotionally capable of anything much more than that. I didn't like it that way, didn't like myself for it, but we can't always choose the way we feel, and I had to play the hand I'd been dealt.

So I finished my morning coffee, cracked open a beer, and decided to do something productive. My apartment really didn't need to be thoroughly cleaned, but I had a few things that could keep me occupied if not very stimulated, industrial security jobs that I still hadn't completely closed, and after updating those I could clean out some files and then bring my bookkeeping up to date. When you work out of your home you're never really away from the office, even on a sad and solitary Sunday.

When the strident ringing of the telephone broke the silence it startled the hell out of me, but I snatched the receiver up eagerly like a drowning man reaching for a piece of flotsam on the surface of the sea.

I wasn't at such loose ends, though, that I was glad to hear the silky, high-pitched voice of Victor Gaimari. Life just doesn't get that lonely.

"Well, Milan," he said.

Victor Gaimari is the nephew and heir apparent of Don Giancarlo D'Allessandro, and the underboss of the Northeastern Ohio mob. He commutes to his downtown office from a baronial home on three acres in the suburb of Orange. One of our town's most eligible bachelors, if the society columns of the *Plain Dealer* are to be believed, he is seen at the theater and the symphony and upscale restaurants like Giovanni's and Morton's, with the beautiful daughters and ex-wives of some of our most prominent citizens. He had a VIP loge at the Stadium and never misses a Browns game, sits on the boards of several prominent local charities, is a three-handicap golfer and a regular on the local tennis courts. He sports a year-round Palm Beach tan, courtesy of a tanning salon, and a Cesar Romero mustache. He smiles a lot and talks down to you like Mister Rogers, and he runs the day-to-day workings of the state's organized crime, deferring to his uncle in only the most major policy decisions.

Everybody in town knows who and what he is, but the society types politely ignore it as if it were something he couldn't really help, like a wart on his nose or a cockeye or a nervous tic. He's a charmer, Victor, but underneath he's even more of a snake than his uncle. At least old Giancarlo is honest about what he is. Victor is a collar-ad phony.

"How are you, Victor?" I said. I didn't care how he was, but my mother raised me with manners, so I asked.

"I've been fighting a sinus condition all winter," he said. "It's very annoying, especially when the weather gets damp.

And I have to tell you, Milan, I'm a little bit troubled this morning."

I didn't need to ask why. Joey, the punk with the sunglasses who'd been at The Jesters with Nello Trinetti the night before, had probably been on the phone to Victor before early mass this morning.

"I'm sorry to hear that, Victor." Sure. The way I'm sorry when the Cincinnati Bengals lose, the way I'm sorry when a politician gets nailed for malfeasance in office, the way I'm sorry when the exterminator comes and massacres a nest of cockroaches under the kitchen sink. I always worry about Victor Gaimari's peace of mind; it's one of my big priorities.

"I think we should sit down and talk about it, don't you?" Victor said.

"Not much to talk about, as far as I can see."

His voice, which is usually whiney, took on a bit of grit. "I think there is." He cleared his throat. "After all, Milan, when you needed us a few months ago, we were there for you."

"You mean this is a command performance?"

"Not at all. I don't want this to be confrontational, although you and I seem to do that a lot. Let's see if we can keep this just a friendly exchange of information between gentlemen."

The "exchange of information" got my attention. Maybe there was something to be gained, although the thought of spending a Sunday with Victor didn't thrill me. As for the "gentlemen" part—well.

He said, "I know Sundays you always reserve for your sons, but—"

"I generally do, Victor, but not today."

"Good. Good for us, I mean. Then can we get together? I could come there, if that's convenient."

"I don't want to put you out, Victor," I said. "Why don't I come to see you?" I don't know what got into me. I guess I wanted to see how the other half lives. Or I wanted to break free from the confines of my apartment. Or maybe I just didn't want Victor Gaimari in my home.

"Outstanding!" Victor is such a goddamn yuppie. "Shall we say one o'clock?"

He was hopeless. "I will if you will, Victor."

Orange, which has always sounded to me as though it should be in California or Florida, is tucked away in the high-priced suburban hills and valleys to the far east of Cleveland, with nary an orange grove in sight. There isn't much to it—a civic center, school, and library off Chagrin Boulevard, and the rest is residential, big sprawling houses set well back from the street on lots of lushly wooded land. The kind of community you move into when you hit the Super Lotto jackpot on a good night.

Victor Gaimari was wearing a dazzling red and blue sweater, dark blue cashmere slacks, and tasseled black dress loafers over fuzzy blue knit socks. The outfit probably cost not quite as much as my car. He had a tumbler of reddish liquid in his hand with a celery stick jutting out of it like a spoon in a mug of coffee at a roadside diner. A knitted red coaster hugged the bottom of the glass.

"Milan, I appreciate your coming," he said, ushering me in. He uses my name a lot when he talks to me. We didn't shake hands. "Can I get you a bloody Mary?"

I shook my head. "Not right now, thanks."

He shrugged as if it were my loss. "I kind of make it a Sunday afternoon tradition whenever I'm home," he said. He led me through a large living room furnished expensively in traditional style and dominated by a gleaming ebony concert grand, which I was almost certain he didn't know how to play, and into a spacious sunroom toward the back of the house. Three of the walls had picture windows, and no other house or building spoiled the view through any of them of the broad expanse of woods thick with maple, oak, and buckeye trees, and rolling, dark green hills with occasional patches of snow that hadn't yet melted or been washed away by the February rains. The furniture was all rattan with light green and gold cushions and thick glass tops on the tables. A huge TV screen had been built into the one windowless wall, but it was turned off in favor of some opera music playing from large hidden speakers. Verdi, I think, but then he's the only Italian composer I know.

Victor waved me onto the sofa and seated himself on a big soft-looking chair, crossing his legs. "So what's going on, Milan? Joey Bonfiglia tells me you crashed his party last night."

"Joey doesn't lie. One of his few virtues."

"The Jesters isn't exactly your usual stomping grounds, is it?"

"It's a public place."

"It is that." He sighed. "I guess what I want to know is whether we have a problem here."

"That all depends."

He raised his perfectly sculpted eyebrows. "On?"

"What Nello Trinetti is doing in town."

He nodded, thinking about it. "Why do you care?"

"I might not care at all. You tell me."

"What if I said he was just on vacation?"

"I'd be very disappointed in you, Victor. I love this town as much as the next guy, but vacationing in Cleveland in February? Is he here for the wind surfing or just to work on his savage tan?"

He laughed. "You do have a way of cutting through the bullshit, don't you, Milan?" He uncrossed his legs and crossed them again the other way. "Suppose you tell me what your interest is, and then maybe I can help you out."

"A seventy-five-year-old man by the name of Bogdan Zdrale was found dead Friday night. Shot, execution-style. He'd been dead for a while, and the time of death seems to coincide with Mr. Trinetti's—vacation."

"I see," he said, emphasis on the *I*. "Who is this Bogdan—what is it?"

"Zdrale," I said, pronouncing it carefully, ZhdRAH-leh. "He's nobody. That's the point, Victor. He was the grandfather of a friend—a client, actually. A retired steelworker with a small pension who minded his own business. He didn't gamble or drink or cat around."

"At seventy-five, I'd be impressed if he did."

"The thing is," I said impatiently, "that from what I've been able to ascertain, he was harmless."

"To whom?"

"To everybody."

"So?"

"So I want to know who killed him."

"What makes you think it was Nello Trinetti?"

"I don't think anything, Victor. I'm asking."

He indicated a large cut-crystal ashtray on the table at my elbow. "If you want to smoke, Milan, it's all right. I don't smoke myself anymore, but it doesn't bother me when other people do."

Knowing that his uncle went through three packs a day, I could see why he'd grown used to it. One didn't tell old Giancarlo D'Allessandro to go outside and smoke. At least not twice. "That's all right," I said.

"Will you believe me if I tell you that I never heard of this Bogdan Zdrale?"

"If you tell me it's the truth."

His gaze was level. "It's the truth. For Christ's sake, Milan, we don't execute old men. Even if we wanted to, it'd be too much trouble."

"And would you want to?"

He shook his head gravely. "He had no connection that I know of with any of our people. That's the straight dope. You can take it to the bank."

"What's Trinetti doing here?"

"I'm not sure that's any of your business."

"I suppose it isn't. But I'm asking you anyway."

He took a sip of his bloody Mary and made a face at it. "You can't let these things sit," he said. "The ice melts and it tastes terrible." He set the drink down on the glass table in front of him, got up, and went over to the window. The many faces of Victor Gaimari. I'd seen him as respectable stockbroker, bachelor-about-town, and mobster. Country squire was a new one on me, but I had to admit that it fit him like a soft leather glove. "I put in some tulips and azalea in September. You'll have to come back later in the spring. This will be

131

beautiful in another six weeks, alive and green as far as the eye can see."

"Unlike Bogdan Zdrale."

He turned to face me. "You're like a terrier when you latch on to an idea, aren't you? Well, to set your mind at ease, we didn't send for Nello Trinetti. He's a New York punk. I've only met him once in my life, and I didn't like him. I keep trying to tell you that we don't do business that way anymore, but you just won't listen. I don't know why he's in Cleveland, but it has nothing to do with me—or with Mr. D'Allessandro."

"If he's not here for you, what was he doing with Joey Bonfiglia?"

"Joey Bonfiglia is an errand boy, as you very well know, Milan. He works for my uncle. Who he sees and what he does on his own time is none of my business. I imagine he's hanging out with Trinetti for the free drinks and because men like Nello seem to attract a certain kind of female that would appeal to Joey."

"Joey gets Nello's discards, huh?"

He allowed himself the whisper of a smile. "I imagine it's something like that."

"If Trinetti isn't working for you, why am I here? Why are you concerning yourself with what happened last night?"

"Because any time someone with an Italian surname gets into difficulty in this town, the finger gets pointed right here." He indicated his chest. "I don't like that. It's insulting. It's racist, not to put too fine a point on it, and I wanted to see to it that it didn't happen this time."

"And that's it? That's what you wanted to talk about? Political correctness?"

"That's it, Milan."

"Fair enough," I said. "But you spoke on the phone about exchanging information. I told you why I'm interested in Nello Trinetti, now you tell me why he's here."

"I told you, I don't *know* why he's here. But I give you my word, it wasn't Nello Trinetti, or any of our people, who hurt Bogdan Zdrale—whoever the hell he is."

"Was," I said.

TEN

It's often said that poor, truncated, unloved February is the sixteen weeks between the end of January and the first of March. Valentine's Day is only important if you're in the second grade or in love. Since they've compressed Washington's and Lincoln's birthdays into one forgettable three-day weekend, no one pays particular attention to them, except that it's a day off when the weather is too rotten to enjoy it. The extra day of Leap Year every fourth year most people feel would be more welcome in July. The midwestern winter climate is, of course, unrelentingly grim, producing a kind of cabin fever that makes tempers short and the days long, as even a trip to the market is weighed and considered against having to deal with the icy streets and drifting snow. And of course February marks the beginning of Lent, which in strongly Catholic industrial cities like Cleveland is taken very seriously, and the faithful all swear to give up things that it's too cold or nasty or depressing to do anyway.

But the main reason for the February malaise is the paucity of activity in the sports world. Football is a memory, and baseball, conjuring up the sun-dappled expanse of green outfield grass and the taste of cold beer, is still two months away—and for Indians fans, too painful to think about. The basketball season reaches its midpoint, at which the various NBA winners are usually as easy to predict as the tides. Talk of your favorite team takes a back seat to bitching about weather and politics and your boss, and the dedicated fan goes into hibernation as surely as the honey bear.

So in Janko's Tavern that Sunday afternoon there were no noisy games to enliven the dreariness of the day, no one spilling beer or popcorn in their cheering enthusiasm, no wagers being made across the bar, no arguments or second-guessing the coaches. No one was watching the television set; in its isolation above the bar it was playing a rerun of *Barnaby Jones*. As dated as the twenty-year-old show was, it was newer and fresher than the atmosphere in Janko's. Stale tobacco mist hovered about six feet off the ground, and newly applied disinfectant warred with the morning-after-a-Saturday-night smells of sweat and spilled beer. A middle-aged couple was having a quiet but intense marital spat down at one end of the bar, their heads wreathed in smoke. He was chewing a De Nobili cigar and wore a pair of bib overalls, a white T-shirt, and a finger-thick gold-plated chain around his neck; she wore a purple down vest over a long-sleeved man's undershirt. A solitary drinker hunched over a shot of bourbon and a Little King beer midway to the back, defeat and resignation in the slump of his shoulders. And Elmo Laketa sat in solitary mourning at his usual table between the two rest rooms, his mask around his neck and his oxygen tank beside him, a cigarette burning in the ashtray.

Janko had been leaning against the backbar casting a critical eye over a dog-eared copy of *Hustler*, but when I came in he shifted slightly and nodded at me over the magazine, one shaggy eyebrow arching in a question. He had no doubt heard the news about Bogdan Zdrale by now. I asked him to bring a couple of beers and made my way to the back.

"Hello, Mr. Laketa," I said.

He looked up at me with eyes like a burnt-out fire pit, and without saying anything waved me into the chair opposite his. I sat down and reached over to squeeze his meaty forearm. He turned his head away from my sympathy, his face scrunched up like a discarded newspaper, and he smacked his lips loudly.

Many of us experience the death of loved ones at a fairly

early age, when we lose our grandparents. As we get a bit older we come to understand that our parents will someday leave us too, that it is the natural order of things. And the world is full of widows and widowers who somehow adjust and regroup and go on. But to lose a friend of sixty years' standing can be insupportable, the loss holding up as it does a mirror to our own mortality. Laketa was a sick old man, and he was hurting.

"So, Jacovich," he said.

"So, Mr. Laketa." He was looking inside somewhere, beyond my reaching him, perhaps seeing a happier past, or more disturbing, a future as blank and bleak as a new sheet of paper. He was silent a long while. The death of Bogdan Zdrale was a back breaker.

"He's gone. Bogdan." It took a great effort for him to force the words out. They bubbled around inside his ravaged lungs.

"I'm very sorry."

He blinked rapidly and bobbed his head, taking no notice as the beers arrived.

Janko nudged me with his knee. "Take it easy," he said under his breath before he went back behind the bar.

Elmo Laketa studied the tabletop, which was marred by beer rings and cigarette burns and the gouges and scratches of thirty years. His stubby fingers traced the scars in the wood as if by touching them he could discern their stories. "Why, Jacovich?"

"I don't know," I said. "Some things you can't explain."

"He had a lousy life. Now he die lousy. Why?"

"I'd like to find out myself." I tasted my beer and set the glass back down. "Why do you say he had a lousy life, Mr. Laketa?"

He curled his lip, glaring up at me from under his fearsome eyebrows. "Life is lousy," he said, as though I should have known it. "For everybody, life lousy."

"But why for Bogdan, especially?"

His shoulders rose and fell, and I could hear the phlegm rattle in his chest. "Things happen, you know? Happen in your life. For him was the war. After war—never good again for Bogdan after war."

"What happened in the war?"

He picked at the leathery skin at the edge of his thumbnail. He'd obviously been at it for some time and had managed to make it bleed. "He was in camp, Bogdan."

"A POW camp?"

"Concentration camp!" he said angrily. "No POW—concentration camp. Banyitsa, near Belgrade. Two years. He change after that. After that, all was shit."

"What happened when he was in Banyitsa? Do you know?"

He shook his head sadly. "He never talk about it, Bogdan. But he change." He coughed once, violently, clearing his lungs. "Maybe just get old. Tired."

He seized the fresh beer bottle by the neck and put it to his lips, his Adam's apple bobbing as he swallowed. When he finally put the bottle down it was three quarters empty. He coughed, then sucked in some air.

"Tired of the shit, Jacovich." He waved his hand as if he was shooing away a fly. "Go away now. I'm tired too, you know?"

I knew.

When I got home it was getting dark and my head was buzzing. The war had been over for more than forty-five years; there had to be something else.

On my answering machine was a message from Danica Paich, telling me that her grandfather's funeral had been set for Tuesday morning. I made a note of it.

I fixed myself a packaged macaroni-and-cheese dinner and tried to ignore the cardboard taste, washing it down with Diet Coke. So much for Sunday dinner. In the end I threw most of it into the garbage and filled up on Triscuits. Something was itching at me, and I wasn't going to rest until I'd scratched it. I just had to figure out how.

After watching *60 Minutes* I dialed Ed Stahl's number. Ed knows everything and everyone in Cleveland and could probably point me in the right direction when no one else could.

I waited through twelve rings, my uneasiness growing incrementally after the fourth one. Ed, as a dedicated and aggressive journalist, always kept his machine on, even when he was home but didn't want to be bothered on his day off. It wasn't like him to cut himself off from the outside, even after a threatening phone call. All at once Sunday night didn't seem quite so boring and benign.

I switched off *Murder, She Wrote*. Ordinarily it was a pleasant enough diversion if you were willing to believe that a little old lady—or anyone else—can solve murders on a weekly basis, although if anyone could, it would probably be Angela Lansbury. I shrugged into my coat, wrapped a wool scarf around my neck, and went downstairs to fire up my car. The scarf was another gift from Mary. The memories just don't quit, do they?

I didn't like it that Ed was neither answering his phone nor recording his messages. It was only a five-minute drive to his place, and the traffic was light, most sane Clevelanders staying in on a chilly Sunday evening.

Ed's house was dark. No porch light, no garage light, no lights in the windows. That was another bad sign—he usually left a light on in front. I parked at the curb and made my way through the open gate to his overgrown front yard and up a flagstone path that was glistening in the heavy mist. A cold wind was blowing from the north, which presaged some snow for the morning.

I crossed the covered porch to the front door. It was heavy walnut inlaid with leaded glass, behind which were net curtains. I couldn't see any lights in the interior of the house, but I rang the doorbell anyway. It was a jangler and sounded loud and intrusive inside the house, like an alarm in an old fire station. I waited, then rang again. Finally I gave it a shave-and-a-haircut, and I sensed some movement inside this time. The curtains on the inside of the door moved a fraction of an inch, then went back to their original position.

Without the porch light I didn't figure he could see well enough to recognize me. "Ed?" I said loudly. "It's Milan."

The dead bolt clicked, and the door opened just enough to allow me to enter the square coatroom just inside. The door slammed shut again and Ed and I were nose to nose in the near-dark. He was wearing a pair of baggy cords, a faded yellow shirt, and a well-worn cardigan sweater, and his shoulders were hunched around his ears in tension.

"Ed, are you all right?"

"Shh. Come upstairs," was all he said.

He turned and I followed him up the heavy curving staircase to the second floor, hanging on to the polished wooden railing to keep from breaking my neck in the dark. He led the way down the upstairs hall to his study, a converted sun porch overlooking his back garden. The smell of his pipe tobacco in the small room made my nose prickle. The personal computer on the desk was turned on, the lit-up monitor providing the only light in the room, and the motor making an eerie whirring sound. Next to the computer keyboard was a tumbler half full of what I knew must be bourbon. I didn't notice any ice cubes.

He had drawn the heavy curtains across the windows. Ed often spoke of how he loved to sit up there and look out at the trees in the moonlight; closing the drapes against the view was uncharacteristic of him.

"Are you expecting an air raid?" I said.

"You carrying, Milan?"

I shook my head in the dark. "Just my Swiss Army knife. I don't wear a gun when I go to visit friends, Ed. What's going on here?"

"Bastards!" he said.

"What happened?"

"The bastards aren't kidding. I got another call this morning. Same thing, same voice, same bullshit threat."

I looked around the darkened room. "That's all?"

He shook his head. "I wish it was. I found a dead rat on my front porch this morning."

I gestured toward the covered windows. "Your garden is practically a jungle; there are rats all over."

"Yeah, well this one had his neck broken."

I tried to put the best face on it, even though the breath of dread was blowing on my neck. "Maybe a dog got it and left it there."

He started filling his pipe from a ceramic-ginger-jar humidor. "Did the dog get up on his hind legs and stuff it in my mailbox, too?"

"Jesus, Ed—"

"It was a message, with my name on it."

The hair on the back of my hands prickled. I knew he was right. "What'd you do with it?" I said.

"Why? You want to recycle it, give it to somebody else, like a Christmas fruitcake?"

He jammed the stem of the pipe between his teeth. "If they come," he said, "if the bastards come, I'm ready for them." He reached into the right-hand pocket of his cardigan and produced a .38 police special.

"Careful with that," I said, pushing the barrel off to the side before he shot my head off by accident. "You ever use one of those?"

"There's always a first time," he said.

"Put it away, Ed." He hesitated. "I'm not going to sit here while you wave it around like a flag on Veterans Day."

He stared at the weapon in his hand as if he didn't know how it had gotten there, and pushed it back into his sweater pocket, which was pulled out of shape by the weight of it. "They're not going to run me off, Milan," he said. He removed the pipe from his mouth to take a sip from the glass. "Who the hell do they think they're dealing with here? They aren't going to make me quit."

"Maybe if you just eased off for a few days, you—"

"Screw that!" Ed said, and pointed his pipe at the computer monitor. "That's how I ease off!" There was a ragged edge to his voice.

I leaned over to read it. Ed said, "Sit down. You might learn something."

I sat in his chair behind the desk, pushing the pillow he used for back support out of my way. Since there was no other light in the room, the amber words stood out in startling clarity.

SEEMS LIKE OLD TIMES
by
Ed Stahl

Back in the Roaring Twenties, they called it "Chicago-style," but it happened all over. Even in Cleveland. The punks and wise guys that made up the various organized-crime families during the Prohibition era walked tall, pushing the little guys around, intimidating businessmen and buying politicians and labor unions. Cocks of the walk, soldiers in an army of occupation without a flag.

Just a mention of certain names gave most honest, law-abiding people goose bumps. Al Capone, and don't dare look at his scar. Bugsy Siegel, and you'd better call him Benny, if you knew what was good for you—or better yet, Mr. Siegel. Charles Luciano, good old Charlie Lucky. Meyer Lansky. Dion O'Banion. Dutch Schultz. Jake Guzik, "the Greasy Thumb." They were big men in their time, because they spent freely and were always good for a laugh or a headline.

But scratch off the veneer, take away the long black limousines, the diamond pinkie rings, and they were just small-time punks who happened to be in the right place at the right time.

It worked for them for a while. People figured it was safer to stay out of their way, to pay up, to play ball. All the punks had to do was rattle their sabres and everyone fell into line. The name of the game was intimidation, and they were the major league players. Never mind the 1927 Yankees, this was the real Murderers Row.

Ed was holding a match to the tobacco in the bowl of his pipe, the flame flickering high and yellow, watching my face almost eagerly for a reaction to the column. I had to push the page-down key of the computer to read the rest of it.

Times changed, then. We all gained a measure of pride during the Second World War, and we realized that as a

nation and a people we were better than that. We weren't
going to let a bunch of jerks in shiny suits tell us what to do
and when to do it. So the organized-crime guys found other
fish to fry, went into less visible enterprises, and the era of the
celebrity gangsters ended.

Oh, they hung around, they managed to put their dirty
fingerprints on a lot of things, but Mr. and Mrs. Average never
heard about it, being busy making a living and raising their
kids and chasing the American Dream.

Some of the "boys" are still in Cleveland, of course, and
forgive me if that doesn't exactly come under the heading of
hard news. You read about them in this space from time to
time, and they touch your lives every day without your even
knowing it.

That's okay. Guys in black hats have to live, too. But it's
time they woke up to the nineties. The old big-shouldered,
side-of-the-mouth stuff doesn't work anymore. This is the Age
of Information, and ink-stained wretches like me earn our
paychecks by raking around in garbage and writing about
people like them.

I use the word "garbage" advisedly. There has been some
hanky-panky with the city's trash-hauling contract, as I wrote
a few days ago. Maybe you don't care, as long as the truck
comes by every week and carts off your refuse. But it's your
tax buck that's paying for it, and there are rules about that sort
of thing, rules that have been blithely ignored by Dosti & Son
and whoever it is at city hall that they have in their pockets.

It's business as usual, I suppose—except they forgot
Harry Truman's old axiom about staying out of the kitchen if
you can't stand the heat. They don't like what I wrote about
them, and they let me know it, in a pretty graphic way.

I wonder if the rat they left in my mailbox was one of
their relatives.

Okay, guys. Message received. Now here's one for you.
I'll continue doing my job, which is writing about things that
the people of this community need to know about, and I won't
be intimidated by your silly schoolyard threats. Bugsy and
Capone are gone. The good old days that weren't so good for
the rest of us are out of date. So are you, dead as the bron-
tosaurus.

And with just about the same brain capacity.

I leaned back in the chair and lit a Winston, noticing my hand wasn't as steady as it usually is. I said, "Ed, you can't run that."

"Watch me."

"Look, so far it's just been a couple of irritating phone calls and a dead rat in the mailbox. Just shut up about it for a week or so and they'll get tired of it and go away."

"And what am I supposed to do in the meantime?"

"You can start by spiking that column."

"Too late—I already sent it in. I've got a modem on the computer, y'know."

"Then call your editor and tell him you changed your mind. Write a column on how the salt they put on the street to melt the snow wrecked your best pair of sixty-nine-dollar Florsheims. Say something nice about the Gateway project, how much we need a new stadium and sports arena. Or say something bad about it and suggest they put the money into the schools. It doesn't matter."

"It does to me," he said, finishing off the drink and pouring himself another one. He didn't offer me any because he knew I prefer beer. Besides, this wasn't a social visit. "What are you doing here anyway?"

"I tried to call you and got concerned when your machine didn't answer."

He shrugged. "Thanks," he said, and lifted a silent toast to me. I didn't know how many he'd put away before I got there, but his speech was slurred; he sounded like a sloweddown phonograph record. I'd never known Ed to have more to drink than he could handle. And normally he could handle a lot. "Why were you calling?"

"To find out how you were."

"You lying shit," he said mildly, "you've never in your life just called to see how I am. You must've wanted to pick my brain about something."

"Skip it," I said, uncomfortable with the truth.

"I don't want to skip it. Business as usual. I'm not going to stop living because some punk likes to kill tree rats. What's on your mind?"

"Ed, it's not important. It can wait."

"If it could wait you would've called the paper in the morning. Come on, spill it."

I got up and went over to the window, pulled aside the curtains and peered out. The bare trees of February sent wispy fingers up into the night sky.

"Stay away from the windows!" His voice was ragged, filled with alarm.

"Ed . . ."

He didn't even look sheepish. "I know, rampant paranoia. If you got a dead rat in your morning mail you'd be jumpy, too."

I let the curtain fall back into place.

"Come on," he coaxed. "Tell me what you want. It'll be good for me, make me forget my troubles. Whattaya need?"

"I don't want to bother you with it."

"Bother me," he said. "My column's finished, and I don't have anything else to do."

I had misgivings. Grave ones. But I went ahead anyway. "Who do you know here in town that can tell me about concentration camps?"

"Concentration camps? You mean Nazi concentration camps?"

I nodded.

He combed his thinning hair with the fingers of his left hand; in his right he still held the drink. "There must be twenty thousand European Jews living in Cleveland who survived the Holocaust," he said. "Right here in the Heights, a lot of them. You see them on their way to temple on Saturday mornings with their grandkids in tow. To say nothing of all the literature you could find in the libraries."

"I know," I said. "I mean an expert. Someone who's made a study of it, has the whole picture."

"Holocaust studies aren't really my beat. But I seem to remember—wait a sec." He went to a file cabinet against the wall and got down an enormous Rolodex. "I'll have to turn on a light to do this."

"No one will see it through those blackout curtains," I said.

"You better hope not." He switched on a small brass piano lamp with what must have been a forty-watt bulb. During less stressful times he probably used it as a night light. I could see the lines of strain around his eyes and mouth. He held the Rolodex close to the lamp, squinting as he turned the wheel and the cards flipped by like an old-fashioned nickelodeon machine. After a few minutes he removed a card and held it at arm's length. He wasn't wearing his Clark Kent glasses.

"Here, try this guy," he said. "Jacob Bauch." He rhymed it with *ouch*.

"Who's he?"

"Jacob Bauch, Esquire. He's a downtown attorney with a very distinguished corporate practice."

I shook my head. "A corporate attorney. Sounds like a sweetheart."

"Don't be hasty. He does a lot of pro bono work, too. Mostly for the Jewish community, and sometimes for people that are suing the companies he's represented in the past. So we're talking about an attorney of very high integrity here."

"You're the only guy I know who could use 'attorney' and 'integrity' in the same sentence."

"Sure, he's made a lot of money, but he's given back, too. He's one of the good guys, Milan. Trust me."

"Was he in a camp?"

"He's got numbers on his arm."

"That doesn't make him an expert."

"I don't know about that," he said. "But he can be pretty relentless when it comes to war criminals. He was one of the earliest Nazi-hunters, and he's connected with the Simon Weisenthal Foundation, the Jewish Defense League, and a couple of other militant organizations I can't remember offhand. When the late Rabbi Meir Kahane came to Cleveland for a speech several years ago, he had dinner at the Bauchs'."

I shook my head. "I'm not sure this is the guy I want to talk to.

"If you want to know about concentration camps he's the best I can come up with."

I took the Rolodex card from Ed and copied the information into my notebook. Bauch's office was on Euclid Avenue near Playhouse Square. His home was on Roxboro, not too far from me in Cleveland Heights. "I'll give it a try," I said.

Ed put the card back and switched off the light. "Good," he said, "let me know if it's worth anything."

"Thanks, I will. In the meantime, where do you want me to sleep?"

He frowned. "Your own bed. What the hell kind of a question—"

"I'm staying here tonight."

"I don't want you to."

"I don't care what you want, I'm staying."

He snickered. "Is that what you usually do, invite yourself to spend the night? No wonder you never get laid."

I ignored the dig and started to take my coat off.

"Go home, will you, Milan? I'll be okay."

"Ed, I'm not going to leave you like this. Just point me to the guest room, or a couch or something."

He emptied his glass, almost tossing the whiskey down his throat. It made him cough once. "Are you going to baby-sit me for the rest of my life?"

"Not unless you offer me a beer," I said. "And not if you run that column."

"I have to."

"Why?"

"It'll do one of two things. Either let them know I'm not afraid of them and scare them back under their rock, or force their hand."

"Force their hand? Are you nuts?"

"No, but pretty soon I will be if I don't do something." He ran his hand over his face in exasperation. "Look at me— sitting here in the dark like a goddamn mole! I don't want to live like this."

"Ed," I said, pointing at the computer monitor, "if you print that tomorrow, there's some people may decide you don't want to live at all."

ELEVEN

I dislike not sleeping in my own bed. It's a peculiarity of mine, a holdover from childhood. I never saw the charm of sleeping over at another kid's place, because I couldn't get a good night's rest, worrying about the strange sounds and smells of a different house. And ghosts and monsters, of course, the ones who lived under the bed or in the closet or behind the dresser. We had them at my house, too, but at least the monsters who lurked in my closet were *my* monsters, and I learned at an early age to deal with them. I haven't changed, except maybe now I lie awake in strange beds wondering whether the sheets are clean.

On this particular night I also had Ed Stahl to be concerned about. His fear about someone being after him wasn't just paranoia, I was afraid, but thinking about it didn't help any, so I stopped worrying about going to sleep and just tried to relax and not stare at the ceiling in Ed's spare bedroom, and from time to time I drifted off. I was never completely under, though, and at six thirty in the morning when Ed banged on the door to tell me he was a working journalist and had to get going early, I was hardly rested and refreshed. My bones protested as I hauled myself out of the narrow guest bed; I was feeling my age, and that scared me worse than dead rats in the mailbox.

I've never been an early morning person, especially when I've slept badly, but compared to Ed I'm a day at the beach. He not only refused to converse, other than to grunt unintelligibly, but he wouldn't even make eye contact. He grew marginally more cheery after he'd had coffee, but drinking some didn't help me any. Ed makes it in an old-fashioned percolator, and it's the worst I've ever tasted, strong and bitter with a nauseating aftertaste. He was too grumpy to offer me a second cup, which was just as well.

Someone from the paper had been summoned to come and pick him up. It was barely a ten-minute drive from his house to the newspaper office on Superior Avenue, but under the circumstances he wisely chose not to take his own car. I could tell it was getting to him, though. I watched him go off with misgivings. He was right, I couldn't baby-sit him forever. Ed is one of the best friends I have, and not only was I fearful that something might happen to him, I was saddened by his own fright. He's a tough guy, one of the last of the press-card-in-the-hatband big-city reporters, and seeing him hiding in the dark with a gun in the pocket of his sweater, hearing him call someone to come and drive him to work because he was afraid to do it himself, was a shock to my own system, my sense of the proper order of things.

I got back to my own place before eight o'clock, glumly clearing the dirty dishes and cleaning up the cracker crumbs from the night before. I straightened up the kitchen and then cleaned myself up, showering and shaving in water as hot as I could stand it. Throwing on my old battered terry-cloth robe, I made myself some coffee; it wasn't great but after Ed's it was an epicurean delight. I'd picked up the morning paper on my way in, and I sat down at the kitchen table and opened it with trepidation. Maybe, I hoped, there had been some sort of computer glitch, maybe somehow the column hadn't gotten to the newspaper and they'd be forced to run a Value City sale ad where Ed's musings normally appear. No such luck. There it was:

SEEMS LIKE OLD TIMES
by
Ed Stahl

I didn't even look at it. After all, I'd read it.

I finished my coffee and went through the pockets of the coat I'd worn the night before for my notebook. When I found it I called the law offices of Jacob Bauch and made an appointment for later in the morning.

I don't know what possessed me to put on a suit. I'm not a suit kind of guy. I never even wear ties and sports jackets unless I have to. Maybe the formality of a blue suit was my own way of paying tribute to a man who'd been through the gates of hell. Or maybe corporate lawyers intimidate me.

Euclid Avenue is Cleveland's main drag, what State Street is to Chicago or Wilshire Boulevard is to Los Angeles. Once, nearly a century ago, a stretch of the avenue was known as Millionaires Row, and more recently it was the main corridor from downtown to the east side. But in the past few years it's fallen on lean times. They built the Galleria at Erieview a few blocks north, and the glittering Tower City shopping center below Terminal Tower, and one after the other the small retailers of Euclid Avenue have had to close their doors. Those that could afford the new downtown venues relocated there, and the others have either gone out of business altogether or moved out to the suburbs. Between Public Square and East Eighteenth Street there are a dozen vacant storefronts, and the recent renovations, repainting, and the resurgence of Playhouse Square and its glittering theaters hasn't done much for the small stores. There are a series of underground vaults that extend the basements beneath the city's sidewalks, which make the cost of any significant remodeling prohibitive. As a result, Euclid Avenue needs help.

The temperature was somewhere in the mid forties, and the sun was giving us a February surprise. Bauch's office was in a new building near Playhouse Square. The Renaissance is solid proof that someone is trying to do something for the avenue, a tiered, gold and black marble wedding cake which stood out from the drab old buildings that surround it like a black swan among scrawny chickens. I took the elevator up to the seventh floor.

The law firm of Bauch and Dellatorre occupied an end

suite. It was what I pictured a corporate attorney's office to be, showy, elegant, and up to date, while still remaining traditional. I opened the doors to find a small, attractive woman in her late thirties at the reception desk. She had a stack of files on the desk next to her, and the top one was open. She looked a little frazzled, but she still managed a warm smile when I came in. Her hair was dark and cut short, and a few strands of unretouched silver caught the light. She had enormous brown eyes that danced with energy and curiosity and an eagerness for whatever was going to come next.

She glanced down at an appointment calendar and then up at me. "Mr. Jacovich?" she said.

I admitted it.

"I'm Shushano Bauch. Have a seat, please. "Mr. Bauch will be just a few minutes."

I sat down in a comfortable upholstered chair against the wall.

"May I get you some coffee?" she said.

"No, thank you. Are you Mrs. Bauch?"

"Miss," she corrected. "He's my father."

"What was your first name again?"

She pronounced it carefully: "Shushano."

"That's a lovely name," I said. "I've never heard that before."

"It's the Hebrew word for rose." She blushed rather prettily. She seemed like a very nice woman.

"You work for your father full time?"

She indicated the stack of file folders. "I'm a full-fledged attorney here. But our regular receptionist is out today, so I have to fill in. The curse of being a junior partner."

"You'd think the boss's kid would get some special consideration."

She looked heavenward, smiling. "You don't know my father very well."

"I don't know him at all," I said.

"May I ask who referred you to us?"

"I don't exactly have a legal problem," I said. "I'm a private investigator." I gave her a card—the real one. "I need

150

some information, and Ed Stahl from the *Plain Dealer* suggested I contact Mr. Bauch."

"Information?"

I didn't quite know how to say it. "The Holocaust."

"Oh," she said. She put my card in the top drawer of her desk. "Well, you've probably come to the right place."

Jacob Bauch was in his late sixties, a short stocky man with an unruly tangle of white hair framing a round face that might have been cherubic except for the lines of chronic anger that hardened his mouth. He wore a three-piece gray wool suit with a subtle blue pinstripe, and across his vest stretched a gold chain. On the back of his head was a black, white, and blue knitted yarmulke affixed to his hair with two bobby pins. His eyes were big and brown and probing, and he had an operatic basso profundo voice with only bare traces of any accent.

"So if this man wasn't a Jew, why come to me?" he was saying. He sat leaning forward in his chair, resting his elbows on his enormous polished ebony desk. "Stahl must have told you that my expertise and my concerns are somewhat specialized."

"I was hoping that if you didn't have answers you could point me toward someone who does."

"Tsk," he said. "Waste of time."

Shushano Bauch was sitting in the second of two client's chairs across the desk from her father. In front of her on the corner of the desk was a switchplate with several buttons and red and green indicator lights. She had explained to me that they always recorded conversations with clients in the office but they wouldn't dream of doing so without asking permission. Knowing my voice was being preserved for posterity I had unconsciously lowered it a few tones.

"Maybe not, Dad," she said. "I think we ought to hear what Mr. Jacovich has to say."

Bauch shrugged with his whole body and leaned back in his leather executive throne, interlacing his fingers across his little paunch. He glanced at his daughter, and the fierce pride he took in her spilled out of his eyes. Then he turned his attention to me. "So say, Mr. Jacovich."

I cleared my throat so the recorder would pick up every golden syllable. "Bogdan Zdrale was in a camp called Banyitsa," I said. "Just outside Belgrade."

He nodded. "I know of it," he said. "I've made a lifelong study of the German operation in World War II, mainly to try to understand what could possibly have prompted such inhuman outrage on an international scale. I haven't figured it out yet."

He looked off at a point somewhere beyond my left shoulder for a while, and he was fifty years away from us. Finally Shushano looked at me with a silent plea for patience and said, "What about that camp, Dad?"

"There were two camps in the Belgrade suburbs, as I recall. The one they kept the Jews in was on the bank of the Sava River. They called it the Saymishte. That means fairgrounds, which is pretty ironic when you come to think about it. Banyitsa was for the goyim—non-Jews." He paused, composing himself for a story, reaching back into his vast store of World War II lore.

"The Banyitsa was run along the same lines as Dachau. The same . . . social structure, I suppose you'd call it. Which is to say it was a death camp. That's what it was for, nothing else." He forced out the last two words through his clenched teeth.

"Is that all you know about it?"

"I know that nearly seventy thousand Serbs died there."

Stunned, I sat back in my chair. I was finding it difficult to swallow, and almost unconsciously I massaged my Adam's apple with my fingers. "Seventy thousand?"

He smiled mirthlessly. "Seventy thousand people just in the one camp alone. That's more than the entire population of some cities. The numbers bother you? You're surprised? Study your history, young man, or else you're doomed to repeat it. Almost every Serb back then followed General Drazha Mihailovic, who organized the Chetnik Freedom Fighters. There weren't enough of them to really fight, in the traditional sense of an army in a war, but their job, as they saw it, was to sabotage in any way they could Hitler's war machine in Yugoslavia. By the way, they also saved a hell of a lot of American asses who were shot down over Yugoslavia, more than five hundred, so the story goes. As a result, the Nazis treated the Serbs nearly as savagely as they did the Jews. There just weren't as many of them, so you don't hear that much about it, but it was every bit as genocidal. The German high command issued very specific orders—to be as brutal and cruel as possible in Serbia. It was the only way they knew to discourage resistance. Public beheadings, mass drownings in icy rivers, wholesale shootings. Common graves as big as football fields. And it was just the tip of the iceberg. You've read of such things, surely?"

"Yes, sir," I said. "But I didn't realize it was that bad in Yugoslavia."

"Ah!" he said, and it was like a whip cracking. "All over Europe it was that bad. The Nazis didn't know the meaning of mercy, of pity. The Jews were their particular favorites, but there was enough sadism left over to go around." Jacob Bauch sighed. "Human life was pretty cheap in those days."

"There were survivors," I said. "Bogdan Zdrale for one. And you. You must have been tough."

"Toughness had nothing to do with it," he said. "They killed the tough ones first. You survived by being smart. Me, I was good at figures. Mathematics. I helped the Germans keep their books. They were scrupulous about record-keeping. How many pounds of human hair they harvested from the corpses, how many articles of clothing they stole, how much gold they extracted from the teeth of the dead." A smile played at one corner of his mouth. "They slaughtered nine million people, and the dumb bastards wrote it all down for posterity." Beneath the starched white cuff of his shirt I could see the crude tattoo on the inside of his wrist as he passed a hand in front of his eyes. I couldn't begin to imagine the pictures he was trying to wipe away.

I glanced over at Shushano Bauch. Her mouth was set in an anguished line and her eyes were shining. She was too young to have suffered what her father had, but she must have heard these stories or variations on them a thousand times before, and each time would have to bring new pain.

"So you had to be either smart, Mr. Jacovich, or corrupt," Bauch said.

"In what way corrupt?"

"The Germans had a remarkable talent," he said. "Well actually two, if you count their unbearably depressing music. But they had the uncanny knack of being able to turn people against one another. So if you were in a camp and you were willing to brutalize your own people, they just might let you live. They called those special pets of theirs *kapos*—you've heard the expression?"

"Yes, sir."

He stared at a point somewhere over my shoulder. "I think they enjoyed it, the Nazis. Killing wasn't enough. They enjoyed making human beings into animals that would brutalize their own. Their own families sometimes."

"There were those who would do that?"

"Of course," he said, and as he spoke his voice got higher, his breathing more shallow, and his words came faster. "The Holocaust literature is full of them. It's not so hard to understand if you had been there, Mr. Jacovich. The cruelty—the absolute barbarism—it's more than the human mind can comprehend. Slow starvation, disease, torture. Beatings—that was no big deal. The beatings were on a daily basis, and you didn't particularly have to do anything to earn one.

"Every day hundreds, thousands of people were put to death like cattle, brutally and without a shred of compassion. It got so that some would sell out their own mother for a crust of bread or a few shreds of rotten meat, or one more day of life." His lips compressed, almost disappeared into a hard, thin slash. "If you had a mother left to sell, that is. Most of us did not."

After a moment he took a deep breath and composed himself somewhat. "You understand, I speak only from my own experience. I was at Dachau for two years, and then towards the end, I managed to escape into the woods. By the time I was found the war was over. But from what others have told me, it was the same at all the camps."

"It was that way at Banyitsa?"

"I would suppose. So you needn't wonder why when I get wind of someone who was a war criminal, who was a torturer and a murderer, I go after him with all the resources at my command, which are considerable." He leaned forward in the chair again. "Some of the turncoats that they recruited, that they bribed with the chance of survival, these barbarians, they were repatriated. Many of them—they came to this country and have lived quiet, peaceful lives. These scum, these criminals . . ."

I rubbed the bridge of my nose, where a headache was starting. "Suppose you had run into one of them, over here after the war. What would you have done?"

He made a steeple of his hands in front of his face and looked at me over his fingers. "You've heard the motto 'Never again,' I assume?"

"Yes, sir."

His eyes turned to black marbles. "We mean it." His gaze didn't waver. "I would have killed him. I would have found some way and I would have killed him."

Shushano moved uneasily in her chair.

"And now?" I said. "Nearly fifty years later?"

Jacob Bauch didn't even think about it. "I would find some way to kill him," he said. "Even now."

"I'm going to lunch now. I'll get my coat and go down with you," Shushano Bauch said. We had just walked out of her father's private office into the reception room, and I was shaken to my toes. I knew that the attrition rate among Serbs during the Second World War was high, but I had no idea Hitler had embarked on that particular path of genocide.

She put on a gray tweed coat and wrapped a fuzzy wool scarf around her neck. "Are you okay?" she said.

I must have been looking green around the gills—I certainly felt green. I gave her a brave smile that must have turned out pretty wimpy. "I think so. That's pretty hard stuff to listen to. But I'll get over it."

We went out into the corridor. "Did it help?" she said, pushing the button to summon the elevator. "What he told you? Will it help with whatever it is you're doing?"

"I don't know. An old man is killed, and there isn't a single motive. Nothing wrong in his life. I thought if I went back far enough I could find something."

"Fifty years?"

"You never know," I said. The elevator door opened and we got in. "You said you're going to lunch?"

She nodded.

"Will you join me? I'd like to talk to you some more."

She leaned against the wall of the elevator and crossed her arms across her chest, swaying slightly with the movement of the car. "Is this lunch going to be business or personal?" She was smiling when she said it.

"What would you like it to be?"

"Objection! The witness is evading the question."

"Objection sustained. Okay, it's both."

The door opened and we walked out into the lobby. It's built in an octagonal shape in black and gray and salmon-colored marble with an eight-sided catwalk up above, all trimmed in smooth, gleaming brass.

"Is it that important to put a label on a simple lunch?" I asked.

"We live in a world of labels," Shushano said. "I don't usually date men who aren't Jewish. My father being the way he is, it's just easier not to."

"I didn't ask you to move in with me, just to have lunch."

We stood facing each other in the lobby, a small island in the river of pedestrian traffic that swirled around us. "Exception," she said.

"Noted."

There's a fancy Chinese restaurant, the Hunan, just off the Renaissance lobby, all done in black lacquer and lavender napery, but neither of us seemed inclined to go there, and the Hanna Deli just across the street has marvelous sandwiches but tends to be noisy at the noon hour. So we simply crossed Euclid and started walking west toward Public Square without any real destination.

The Sweetwater Café used to be the place to go for lunch around Playhouse Square, but it's gone now, forced out by the new construction and relocated to the Galleria, where it's now called Sweetwater's Café Sausalito and caters to upscale shoppers. Unless you want to dine at the counter of a coffee shop, this particular stretch of downtown Cleveland is not exactly Restaurant Row. I figured we'd probably end up at the Roxy, but for the moment it was just nice to walk along with a pretty woman and enjoy the unaccustomed and welcome winter sunshine.

"You'll have to forgive my father," she said after about a block. "I've been listening to his horror stories since I was old enough to talk, and it still spooks me. But once you get him started, I'm afraid he gets carried away."

"There's nothing to forgive," I said. "I'd get carried away too if I'd been through what he has."

"Sometimes it's difficult for him to make it through a whole day; the memories, the nightmares. A word—or sometimes not even that—and it triggers a rage or a depression. There are things that happen to people they can never get over."

"I'm sorry. I didn't mean to upset him."

"Those who were in the camps and managed to make it through really only have two choices. They can let it break them and live bitter and beaten until they die, or they can get mad and fight. My father is a fighter."

"How does he know who to fight?"

She had a pretty long stride for a short woman, but she broke it to glance sideways at me. "I'm not sure I understand the question, Mr. Jacovich."

I moved closer to her, so that our shoulders were almost touching as we walked. "Since this lunch is only half business, perhaps you could call me Milan."

"All right, Milan."

"And I'll call you Shushano."

She raised her eyebrows. "That was pretty good for a first try. But getting back to your question . . ."

"Oh. Yeah. Well, how does one go about . . . hunting those war criminals. Who knows about them? Where do you start?"

"There are people who have devoted their lives to it. For instance, in 1975 an Israeli journalist managed to get hold of a list of people who might possibly have collaborated with the Germans and sent it to the Mossad in Israel and to the INS here.

"And the list, how would a private citizen like your father lay his hands on something like that?"

She stopped smiling. "I'm going to take the Fifth on that one, Milan. My father is a very successful attorney, and very rich. He has a lot of important connections, not just here in Cleveland, but with Jewish and Zionist organizations all over the world. If he wants something badly enough . . ." She shrugged her shoulders.

I didn't say anything.

"Does that bother you?" she asked.

I nodded. "I have to admit that it does."

"Why?"

"It's vigilante justice," I said.

"That's a knee-jerk reaction, if you don't mind my saying so. Don't you believe those who committed one of the most heinous crimes in the history of civilization should be punished?"

"Of course I do," I said. "But I was a cop for a long time. I understand the way the law works, and I know that we can't all go around dispensing retribution wherever we think it will do the most good, or else we'll have anarchy. You're an attorney—so is your father. That must mean you respect the law."

"Law?" she said, almost scoffing at me. She lowered her head until her chin was almost touching her chest and she spoke so softly that I had to move closer to hear her. "In the middle of the night, my father was arrested, dragged to the train station, and herded onto a cattle car with his parents and his two sisters and about a thousand other people, jammed so tightly together that no one could sit or lie down. If someone fainted, or even died in transit, they just remained upright, because there was no room to fall. Their destination was Dachau—they didn't know what that meant then—and after they separated the men from the women and children, he never saw his family again." She spoke in a kind of singsong, as if this were a grade school recitation she'd committed to memory.

"He found their names in the records the Germans made him keep for them—the lists of the dead. He saw his friends, his neighbors, murdered, raped, mutilated, and starved, and then buried in a huge heap like so much compost. Where was the *law* to protect them? He lost his respect for the law in those Dachau years."

"Then why become a lawyer?"

"You can't beat the system until you learn how to use it, Milan. Now he works for justice. Law and justice are two entirely different propositions, you know." She cocked an eyebrow at me. "You disapprove."

"Not really"

"Sure you do. As they say, I guess you had to be there. Hell, it was all before I was born, and sometimes I don't understand it myself, so I don't expect you to. It isn't any skin off your nose. But don't tell me that if someone hurt a person you loved, you wouldn't go to the ends of the earth to bring whoever did it to justice, because I won't believe you."

"I probably would," I said. "That's why I'm not being judgmental. People are driven by different obsessions. With some of us it's money, good old-fashioned greed. With others, it's sex."

"Not all bad," she grinned.

"No, not all. Then there are the bottle babies and the druggies and the gamblers and the foodies and those who just plain lust for power."

"What's your point?"

"Any obsession can be dangerous, Shushano—a snake that eats its own tail."

We crossed East Ninth Street and headed for the Roxy, as I'd figured we would. The wind coming off the lake through the canyon of tall buildings whipped at my trenchcoat.

She frowned into the sunshine. "It hasn't hurt my father any."

"Not yet," I said. "But his obsession is hate, and hate hurts everyone. It doesn't matter who you hate. Germans, Jews, blacks, gays, women, Slovenians, fat people, the Pittsburgh Steelers—true hatred hurts, and it ultimately destroys both hater and hate-ee."

"And what's your obsession, Milan?"

I had to think about it. "I'm not sure. It sounds pretty pompous to say truth. That's a nebulous concept, when you get right down to it."

"It doesn't sound pompous at all. I think you're probably a very nice man, Milan."

"For a goyim?"

She laughed. "You mean a goy. 'Goyim' is plural."

I twirled an imaginary mustache. "Well, I'm a man of many faces."

We went into the big white granite slab that is the National City Bank building, all at once grateful to be in out of the breeze. The restaurant, an old downtown standby that has been refurbished and now caters to the upwardly mobile crowd, is below ground level, and as we started down, she held up her hand. "Before we go in, I'd like to request a five-minute recess."

"Why now?" I said. "I was just starting to feel like I was winning a few points."

"Because," she said, moving away from me down the hall, "defense counsel has to go to the john."

I watched her walk away. Her stride was decisive, with a sense of purpose. There is something deliciously sensuous about the sound of a woman in high heels walking across a hard tile floor, and I enjoyed the noise along with the view. She was attractive and sexy and smart, and almost as tough as her father.

She must have been hell on wheels in a courtroom.

As a taxpayer, I'm deeply appreciative of any measures the government institutes to cut costs. It's nice to know that the check I write every April is being handled with a certain amount of care. However, civil servants are only human—or so they tell me—and are not to be blamed if they occasionally go too far with their economy measures, as you know if you've ever tried to call a government agency. I spent fifteen minutes on the telephone with the offices of the Immigration and Naturalization Service in downtown Cleveland without ever speaking to a human being.

First I got a warm and sincere recorded voice that could've been your favorite uncle's, thanking me for calling what he archly referred to as "Ask Immigration," which sounds like a household hints column in a small-town newspaper. I was instructed to push the number one on my touchtone phone if I wanted to hear what they had to say in English. I didn't wait to see how many other choices there were.

Having made that first decision, I got to listen to the same pleasant male voice entreating me to be patient and listen to the second message all the way through, which turned out to be another invitation to push another button, depending on your particular problem. For instance, if I wanted information about passports and the proper forms to fill out, I was to press number one again. If you don't have a touch-tone phone, I guess you can't get out of the country.

Then I was told to press number two for "instructions on how to talk to an INS officer." That one really tempted me. I wonder if they tell you to sit up straight, speak clearly and concisely, and refer to the officer at all times as sir or madam. I didn't press two, however, because I was far too eager to learn what number three would bring me. A "menu," as it turned out.

The catch is—and you are informed of this up front— that you must select and listen to at least one recorded message on the subject of your choice before you are allowed to speak to a real live breathing and, one assumes, thinking person. This is high-tech manipulation at its worst, and in the mood I was in I refused to go for it. I didn't have all day. The system of computerized recording might save the federal government a lot of time and money, but it doesn't do much for the equally valuable time of the poor taxpayer trying to ask a simple question.

I hung up and called Marko Meglich. I had to go through several people to get to him, but at least they were alive.

"I understand you and Nello Trinetti got to know each other Saturday night," he said in a tone calculated to let me know he was really too busy to talk to me.

"Word travels fast. Yeah, I had a drink with him."

He chuckled. "When you do something, you go all the way, don't you? So?"

"He's strictly small-time."

"That's not exactly a hot news flash."

"I know. But he's a lamebrain; I don't think they'd give him anything more complicated to do than emptying an ashtray. We're wasting our time with him. We should be heading in another direction altogether."

I heard him suck in a breath, a sure sign he was annoyed. "You were the one said it looked like a mob killing."

"I changed my mind. If I were you, I'd get hold of every piece of paper I could that bears on Bogdan Zdrale's immigration to this country. His birth certificate, if they have it, his passport, his naturalization papers, and anything else you can put your hands on, especially anything regarding his war record."

"His war record?" Marko said, and I could hear the annoyance in his voice. "You mean from World War Two? Sure—while I'm at it you want me to dig up something on John Quincy Adams?"

Sarcasm has always been Marko's strong suit, but it tends to give me a pain in the ass. "Zdrale spent some time in a concentration camp. When you can't find a motive in the present, you have to look for one in the past."

I heard papers rustling. "So what am I supposed to do with these naturalization papers when I get them?"

"That depends on what they say."

"Damn it, Milan, don't be cryptic with me! I haven't got the time!"

"Listen, pal, you asked me to poke around on the Nello Trinetti thing because your badge wouldn't allow you to do it officially. Now I'm asking you to use that badge to cut some red tape, that's all."

"I don't even know what I'm looking for."

"I don't either, but I'd give special attention to his war record."

"What's World War Two got to do with Nello Trinetti?"

"Nothing," I said.

"Then what are you jerking my chain about?"

"About Zdrale. It's worth a call, anyway. I tried to get through to INS, but I figured you could avoid a lot of the crap by going through official channels."

"You don't know the federal bureaucracy, then. They don't give a damn who you are or what color your badge is; they take their own sweet time."

"Not if you call the FBI."

"It's not their table."

"It is if it has to do with war criminals."

That slowed him down a little. He said, "That's pretty heavy, Milan."

"*Possible* war criminals."

"I can't call in the Fibbies on a possible. The local cops and the feds aren't exactly lunch buddies. Remember that attempted bank heist on Lee Road when the FBI showed up unexpectedly and they and the Cleveland Heights police almost blew each other away?"

"What's it going to cost you to check?"

"My ass, maybe. Besides, World War Two was twenty-five years before Nello Trinetti was even born."

"I think Trinetti's clean for this one."

He snorted. Over the phone it was a singularly unpleasant sound. "And how did you come to that conclusion?"

There was no way out of telling him, and I braced myself for his withering scorn. "Because Victor Gaimari told me so."

He was incredulous. "You actually asked Victor Gaimari?"

"You know damn well that if there's a contract out in this town, Gaimari's going to know about it."

"Did you expect him to *admit* he'd ordered up a hit?"

"No," I said, "but he didn't bat an eye about it when I asked him, either."

There was a Jack Benny–length pause. Then he said, "Aw, Jesus, Milan. What are you, silly?"

TWELVE

Saint Theodosius Church styles itself in the Cleveland area yellow pages as "a landmark of the Apostolic Faith." It was the church used in the filming of *The Deer Hunter* several years before. The church is on the near west side, but the cemetery is several miles away, down in the city of Brooklyn; if you take Biddulph Road west across Ridge Road you run right into it. Many of the North Coast's Serbian families, and most other Clevelanders of the Eastern Orthodox faith, ultimately wind up here.

It looked a little desolate with the snow falling and everyone in dark clothing, like a black-and-white movie. The cemetery was flat and barren, with a few scrub pines and oak trees, and a large open area at the northeast corner—room to expand.

The rows of crosses with the three horizontals bisecting the vertical were of varying sizes, colors, and materials, and there were lots of large double and triple grave markers over family plots, with names like Krochmal and Trbovich and Varholick carved in the stone.

Some of the years of interment chiseled beneath the surnames postdated the Second World War by only a few years, leading me to believe that those at rest there had fled Europe because of Hitler to spend their last days in America, and I reflected how bitter it must be to have to spend eternity far from the country you loved.

There was an older section of the cemetery, too; the dates of passing were from the early part of the century, and on those the legends on the markers were mostly in the Cyrillic alphabet. A few graves were barren or choked with dried weeds, but most had been kept up in some fashion or another, and here and there a bouquet of artificial flowers had been placed at the base of a headstone, a startling splash of color in the drab landscape. Weeping granite angels stood sentry over neat mounds of earth covered by grass turned brown by the long winter, and there was one section reserved for the graves of children. Little bright blue windmills had been placed on a few of them; on one there were inexpensive plastic toys, bears and dogs and little cars to cheer the heavenly rest of a three-year-old boy who had died in 1952.

Many of the stones had photographs of the occupants affixed to them, people with strong, solid, often stern faces who had done a lot of living before making their final journey to Saint Theodosius. One I noticed had a photograph of an elderly couple before a many-tiered wedding cake, probably in celebration of their fortieth or fiftieth anniversary. On some of the double stones, most of which said FATHER and MOTHER, the dates of death indicated that one had survived the other for more than twenty lonely years.

As a Slovenian I was raised Catholic rather than in the Orthodox religion, but I still couldn't help wondering where I would wind up spending forever. Graveyards make even cockeyed optimists reflect on their own mortality, but here in this place where the old-fashioned concept of the family unit seems so strong, where soulmates for life had become side-by-side soulmates for eternity, it hit me hard that there would be no double headstone marked FATHER and MOTHER for me.

The sun had shouldered its way through the permanent February overcast and finally given up and stepped gracefully aside to make way for a Currier & Ives snowfall, the kind that swirled gently rather than pelted. The flakes were big and fat and feathery, clinging prettily to the skeletal branches of the trees and collecting on the backs and shoulders of those present, and it seemed I could almost discern their delicate crystalline patterns as they floated past my eyes to fall onto Bogdan Zdrale's casket. Already his wife's name, MARIJA, and the date of her death had been carved on one side of the double-width stone.

The priest was about forty years old, tall and broad with a wide face that looked like a peeled potato and a voice that could lull the most hopeless insomniac to slumber. He wore his funeral robes across his wide shoulders like a tablecloth, and the gold cross around his neck sparkled in the winter light. There were candles around the casket trying valiantly to stay lit in the snow, and the pungent smell of incense carried on the wind.

Tootsie Paich and Danica sat on metal folding chairs at the graveside, their eyes red and their faces swollen and puffy, twin portraits of grief. Next to Tootsie, Vera Paich sat looking cold and miserable and as frightened as usual. Beside Danica in another chair, Elmo Laketa stared straight ahead in his starched white shirt and nubby wool tie under his corduroy foul-weather jacket, hatless. Snowflakes clung to his hair and fierce eyebrows, and the ever-present oxygen tank was beside him at the ready. A thickly built woman in her late fifties stood next to him, her hand patting him almost idly on the shoulder, and I assumed she was his daughter Sophie. A man I didn't know was on the other side of her, his arm linked through hers, probably her husband.

Walter Paich stood behind his wife's chair, sullen and apparently hung over, a khaki parka covering his blue wedding-christening-funeral suit, and a cigarette jutting from between his second and third fingers. Pale-faced and hollow-eyed, his cheeks scraped raw from a fresh shave, he was the unhealthiest-looking human being I'd ever seen standing upright.

There were about fifty people at the interment, most of them septuagenarians, but a few wide-eyed children and impatient teenagers had showed up too, and Janko from the tavern, his hands deep in his pockets, pulling his dress-up coat tight around his volleyball belly. Not too far from him were Mr. and Mrs. Lazo Samarzic.

I stretched my back muscles under my overcoat. Several months earlier some clown had taken batting practice with a Louisville Slugger and used me for the ball, and I tended to stiffen up in cold weather. I spotted another familiar face; Joe Bradac looked nervously at me and moved closer to the cluster of people near him, his head bobbing a quick, birdlike hello. His nose was bright red—it remains so between November and April. I noticed Lila wasn't with him.

But the big surprise on the mourner's list, to me anyway, was John Hanratty. Spanish John looked as sharp as ever in a dark gray suit, flashing white shirt, and tastefully dark tie, a voluminous black leather trench coat belted tightly around his slim waist. He smiled a bit when I caught his eye, and then winked, his black eyelashes batting away the snowflakes. I moved over to stand next to him.

"What are you doing here?" I asked out of the side of my mouth.

"Paying my respects," he whispered. "Shhh."

The young priest went on about how Bogdan Zdrale had been a joy to his family and proceeded to name the members thereof, consulting a list on a three-by-five index card he'd carefully palmed. It was the standard eulogy delivered by a hired clergyman who hadn't the foggiest notion what the deceased had been like.

"You don't even know these people," I muttered to Spanish John.

He looked at me knowingly. "I know Danica," he said, and his condescension made me grit my teeth to keep from answering him. He had only met Danica when we'd gone to look at Bogdan Zdrale's abandoned van. But John always made friends quickly—especially when they were good-looking women.

Danica looked over briefly while the priest paused to check his notes and smiled a very small smile. I didn't know which of us it was for. I smiled back at her.

The casket was a dull-finish gray, blanketed with a wreath of roses and lilies-of-the-valley that looked peculiar with the light dusting of snow that covered the mourners. It was as if we were part of a living diorama that was slowly being frozen. Off to one side, lurking near a huge stone obelisk with NIZETICH carved on it in gothic letters, two cemetery employees dressed in work clothes waited with impatient uninterest until the ceremony was over, the mourners had dispersed, and they could get on with their labors.

"Did it ever occur to you that a funeral isn't the greatest place to make a move on someone?" I said to Spanish John.

He was all dewy-eyed innocence. "It isn't?" he said, which annoyed me sufficiently to move away from him and stand off by myself.

The priest finally wound down, having consumed enough time to make it look good, and all around us people were beginning to move about, stamping the snow off their shoe tops and brushing it off their shoulders before they moved forward to engulf the family with murmurs of sympathy, leaning over at awkward angles to speak to the seated Tootsie and Danica and then straightening to accept Walter Paich's dead-carp handshake. Spanish John waved a hand at me and limped over to the edge of the grave, quietly shouldering his way through the crowd until he was standing next to Danica. She looked up at him with brimming eyes.

I went over to Joe Bradac, typically on the fringes of the crowd and looking a bit like he had wandered into the wrong funeral. He didn't look glad to see me.

"Hiya, Milan," he said, putting on his gloves. His watery little eyes were darting around behind his glasses, looking for an escape route.

I didn't say anything else, and that made him even more uncomfortable. Not giving someone enough strokes is a sure way to get them twitchy.

"Hey," he finally said, "Danica told me you really worked hard for her. I appreciate it."

"You do, huh?" I said.

"Well, yeah."

"Where's Lila?"

"She's home," he said. "She doesn't really know the Paiches."

I nodded, letting the silence grow again, and Joe pulled off his right glove and held it in his left hand. He said, "It was nice of you to come today."

I looked over at the family. "How's Danica doing?"

"She's all right, I guess. But this busted her up pretty bad. She's been crying for three days straight. You know, having her grandpa killed like that . . ." All of a sudden he stopped talking and his mouth clamped shut. He looked away and put his glove back on. If he wasn't careful he was going to wear it out. He took a deep breath, and when he released it the vapor jetted out from between his lips into the cold air. "So, okay then. I'll see you around, Milan," he said.

My own hands were balled into fists and I wanted to smash them into his face, breaking his glasses and whatever else they could reach. I only nodded curtly at him and spun around on my heel and walked away. There are days when your timing is all off and life's little misdeals pile up on you like wet snow on your front walk; I was having one.

The ashes of my marriage were thoroughly cold, yet Lila had been my dear friend for more than half my life and was the mother of my sons, and despite our at times somewhat spiky relationship, some residual love still exists. You can't spend half your life with someone and suddenly stop caring about her as though a light switch has been flicked off.

I don't want to live with Lila anymore, nor she with me, but I would still lie down in front of a train to protect her, if it came to that. And I had the feeling that she was soon going to be in need of a certain kind of protection, if Joe Bradac had his way. He was sniffing around Danica Paich like a horny stray dog, and if Lila found out it would be a real gut shot for her. I hadn't been a world champion husband, I knew that, but I'd never cheated on her.

And Joe Bradac wouldn't, either—not if I had anything to say about it. And I'd make it my business to have a say.

"Jacovich."

I turned to see the Samarzics coming toward me, walking carefully through the fresh-fallen snow.

"Hello, Mr. Samarzic."

"You remember my wife Millie?" he said, presenting her to me like a birthday present.

"Sure. We didn't formally meet, but I saw you at the market," I said, taking her warm, rough hand in mine. "It's nice to see you again."

"Thank you. I only wish it were under better circumstances." She had a very nice smile and a kind, ruddy face.

Samarzic jerked his head back toward the grave. "A terrible thing, huh?"

"Yeah."

He sighed sadly. "There's animals out on the street now. They'll kill an old man for what's in his pockets for shit to put up their nose or shoot in their arm."

"Is that what you think happened?"

"Sure," he said, and put a protective arm around Millie as if a crazed junkie lurked behind every tombstone. "In that neighborhood, what else?"

I didn't answer.

He said, "Well, anyway, it's up to the cops to fumble around and do nothing now. You're out of it, huh?"

"How do you mean?"

He took out a pack of Winstons and offered me one. I shook my head. He stuck one in his mouth and lit it, cupping it in his hand against the falling snow. "The girl hired you to find her grandpa, you said. He's found, yes?"

"He's found, all right. But I'm not sure I'm out of it."

He frowned. "How come?"

I shrugged my shoulders, feeling a twinge in my back.

"You know what I think?" he said.

"What?"

"I think that you couldn't find the old man when you were s'posed to and it was a kick in the gut to your ego. So now you're going to run around doing the police's job and getting in the way."

"Lazo," Millie Samarzic chided.

"No, I got to tell the man what I think."

"Lazo, leave him alone."

"It's okay, Mrs. Samarzic," I said. "He might be right."

171

"Damn right I'm right, Jacovich."

"My only question is, why should you care?"

He glared at me, the set of his shoulders tense and aggressive. Then he relaxed. *"Jebem,"* he said, a very nasty Serbo-Croatian word. "What you expect from a Slovenian?"

He took his wife's arm and started toward Danica and Tootsie. Millie looked back over her shoulder at me and raised her eyebrows as if to say, what am I going to do with him? I smiled back. She seemed like a nice person, and a patient one; life with Lazo Samarzic couldn't be one long festival.

Spanish John was in the middle of the press of people paying respects, his arm around Danica, his palm at her elbow, looking concerned and protective and very much like he belonged there, and I noticed as the time wore on and the snowfall thickened that she leaned against him for support and warmth, occasionally looking up at him with gratitude or perhaps something more. At one point he caught my gaze and flashed his too white teeth at me over the heads of the mourners.

I wasn't sure why it bothered me so much. And I didn't have the time to think about it.

Although the formal service had ended several minutes before, Vera Paich still sat on the folding chair, her hands folded in her lap and her knees pressed tight together, hoping, I suppose, that no one would notice her or talk to her. The force that drove her seemed to be mere survival, the need to get through the day without anyone being mean to her. Her husband was standing as stiff as a winter birch, looking from one of his grandfather's mourners to another with a kind of sullen desperation. His nostrils flared like a horse's. Walter's years of being a nasty and unlovable bastard were coming home to roost; no one was talking to him, no one was giving him the sympathy and the strokes that were his due as a member of the deceased's immediate family. And he was dealing with it the way he dealt with everything in his life, with a kind of pent-up rage that was this day close to boiling and ready to spill out.

I thought about going over and expressing my sympathies but decided not to. The whole point of such an exercise is to lend succor and support, but I didn't like Walter Paich and he didn't like me, and though I may be guilty of a lot of things, hypocrisy is not one of them. So when his angry gaze touched me from about twenty feet away I simply nodded at him. But the look was cold enough to frost a margarita glass.

I went over to his mother and took her hand.

"Oh, Milan," she said, and sniffled. Her nose was running from the cold as well as from crying, and she dabbed at it with a wadded-up pink tissue that was about ready to retire.

"I'm very sorry, Mrs. Paich."

"I know," she said. "It's just so hard to understand. He had such a hard life, my father. Full of fear, full of anger." She drew in a ragged breath and looked over her shoulder at the gray coffin, resting on the straps that would soon lower it into the open grave.

"I'm going to do what I can to find out who's responsible for this," I said.

Alarm darkened her brow. "Ah, no, Milan. Leave him rest, why don't you? He's peaceful now."

"Yes," I agreed. "He's peaceful."

I put my cheek against hers briefly and squeezed her hand, then gave way to the next person in line, who would undoubtedly murmur the same inane words of reassurance and give her the same sort of nonhug and feel their duty had been done.

I looked around. Janko was standing somewhat apart from everyone else, looking out of place and forlorn. After all, he wasn't exactly a friend of the family's—he was a saloon-keeper who had baby-sat old Bogdan Zdrale when no one else wanted to bother with him, and he probably didn't know what to say to the Paiches or they to him. I moved around the grave and shook his hand.

"Hello, Stroh's-no-glass," he said, relieved that someone was finally talking to him.

"You remembered."

"Told you." He ran a hand over his head. "Poor Bogdan, huh?"

"Who'd want to do something like that, Janko? He was a customer of yours, a friend. Would you know?"

"Ay-yi-yi, what are you, still at it? Let it go. The man's in the ground, for God's sake."

"Why does everybody want me to back away?"

"I dunno. Maybe old Bogdan had some secrets that are better off being left secret."

I felt a quick rush. "Like?"

"I don't know *like*." He was flirting with surliness. "Everybody's got secrets. Don't you?"

"A few."

"There ya go, then. Or maybe it's just time to bury the dead and take care of all of us who are left."

"That's what I think, too. There's a killer walking around somewhere, and that's a danger to everybody."

He considered it, actually working his jaw while chewing it over in his mind. Then he squinched up his mouth in what passed for a smile and punched my arm in camaraderie. "Well, I wish you luck then, Stroh's-no-glass," he said, and he walked away.

Secrets.

My stock in trade. Stirring other people's ashes, uncovering the secrets they keep hidden in the bottom drawers of their lives. I tried to tell myself that it was a necessary job, that I helped people and every once in a while set aright things that had been very, very wrong. But it's a lousy job most of the time, and each time I dig up somebody else's dirt, I get a little dirtier myself, a little more diminished, a little less whole. Each nasty little secret takes away a part of me, chips away at my humanity. By the time I finished with Bogdan Zdrale and Nello Trinetti and Ed Stahl and Joe Bradac, I hoped there would be enough left of me to bury when the time came.

As I stood in the middle of the aftermath of an old man's funeral, life turned into one of those nightmares you don't ever believe can happen to you. All conversation suddenly halted, leaving a ghostly silence. Every head turned in my direction, every eye was on me. Some were curious, some frowned their disapproval, and a few, despite the solemnity of the occasion, were laughing openly at my obvious discomfort.

My beeper had gone off.

THIRTEEN

If he hadn't thought it was important, Ed Stahl never would have called me in the middle of a workday, and I wouldn't have felt like such an idiot at Saint Theodosius cemetery, surrounded by grieving people while from the vicinity of my belt emitted a series of self-important electronic burps and beeps. Ed spends most of his time running down news sources and banging out copy, not calling his poker-playing buddies to chat. So when he asked me to meet him at the Headliner I agreed at once, even though I was cold and wet and depressed from the funeral and wanted nothing more than to go home, change into a pair of sweats, switch on some jazz on WCPN, and stay in my chrysalis until spring.

The Headliner Café is one of Cleveland's more cherished legends. It's housed in a faded yellow brick building on the corner of Superior and Seventeenth Street, one block west of the *Plain Dealer* offices. It's the natural mecca for the reporters and rewrite guys who come in at five o'clock in the afternoon and sit bitching about their editors at one end of the rectangular bar. The other end of the bar is usually occupied by Teamsters who have wandered over from nearby construction jobs or from their local a few blocks away on Chester Avenue. Some of them still wore their hard hats or had them on the bar next to their cigarette packs and boilermakers. Like the newspaper people opposite them, almost all of them were smoking. The place is paneled in an inexpensive pine and has an acoustical ceiling and an ornate rotating fan, and there is an old-fashioned cash register behind the bar, which resembles the one on *Cheers.* Along one wall hand-painted reproductions of family crests clash strangely with the laminated front pages of the *Plain Dealer* and the old Cleveland *Press,* headlines trumpeting such memorable events as TRIBE WINS! and JAPS SURRENDER.

A dining room hides behind a partition, but none of the in group ever sets foot in there, since the Headliner's culinary specialty seems to be anything with canary yellow gravy on it. Once in a while, especially during lunch hour, you'll see some woman in the place, but otherwise it's the classic men's bar, full of smoke and boasting and overly loud talk. The Headliner's busiest day of the year is Election Day; after the victory parties wind down, even the TV reporters wander in and pretend that they're real journalists, sitting around and drinking until far into the wee hours for no apparent reason. The fact that there is no place to park within several blocks deters no one.

The bartender, a good-looking young guy with long black curls, is one of the owners. The café has been in his family for three generations; they lived in an apartment upstairs until the building was reduced to one story back in the sixties. He likes to boast that he was conceived on this corner.

As befits a bylined, prize-winning writer whose photograph appears atop his column each day, Ed holds court in one of the red leatherette booths by the window, usually the one in the corner. But on this particular day he was sitting halfway down the bar, his back to the old-style pinball machine and his eye on both the entrance and the window looking out onto Superior Avenue. The old Wild Bill Hickok syndrome: don't turn your back on the door. Ed wasn't taking any chances. He was puffing furiously at his pipe when I sat down on the adjoining stool. At his left hand was a portable tape recorder; at his right was a half-gone Jim Beam on the rocks. An ashtray overflowed with mounds of ashes.

"Ever since this shit started I've been recording all my phone calls," he said without preamble. "I'm not at such an advanced state of senility that I've gone completely stupid."

"You got another call?"

He looked around to make sure there was no one within earshot, then shoved the tape recorder across the table at me and pushed the play button. He had the volume turned low, and I had to lean forward to hear.

First the susurrous rush of audio presence, a blip, and then, *"Stahl here."* His voice was clipped, professional, and in the background I heard the sounds of the city room.

"Sweets to the sweet, asshole," another voice said. It sounded like a young man, throaty, almost sensuous.

"Who is this?"

"Sweets to the sweet," it said again. *"Dead rats to a dead rat."*

There was a click as the connection was broken—it sounded as if someone had depressed the button rather than putting down a receiver—then only the sound of Ed's breathing. Finally he said, *"Shit,"* and the recording ended.

He turned off the machine and cocked an eyebrow at me.

"Someone's trying to do a number on your head, Ed."

He grimaced. "Whattaya mean, trying?"

"Why don't you stop being a stubborn idiot and call Mark Meglich?" I said.

"And tell him what? That somebody's saying mean things to me on the phone? That homicide should send a team out and never rest until the brutal murderers of that rat are brought to justice?" He finished his drink and signaled for another one. Nobody seemed to care if I wanted anything or not.

"What are you going to do?"

"Go right to the source," he said. "I'm going to go talk to Jimmy Dosti."

"Ed, that's nuts!"

"Fuck it! What's to worry? He's not going to blow me away in broad daylight."

"You're just going to make things worse."

"I'm living in a state of siege. I keep all the lights off, whenever the old house creaks or moans I pee in my pants, and my nanny comes to pick me up and take me to work every morning. How much worse can they get?"

The bartender came with the drink and Ed snatched it from him before he could set it on the bar. "Listen, Milan, I'm an investigative reporter. I pay for my groceries writing about things that sometimes get people upset. I didn't get that little Pulitzer loving cup for ripping the lid off corruption at the home and garden show. I write what needs to be written. And once I start getting scared and thinking about who's going to come after me every time I sit down to do my column, I might as well hang it up and start doing tasteful little watercolors that nobody wants to buy, because I'll be no goddamn good to anyone as a journalist. You know as well as I do that Jimmy Sweets is the one putting the heat on, and I want a stop put to it, because right now I can't even function anymore, not as a journalist and not as a human being. Now that's it!"

He gulped down about an ounce of whiskey, enough to make him grimace in pain. Ed has an ulcer, and his drinking doesn't do it any good. When he hits the Jim Beam that hard he usually gets pretty sick.

"I don't like getting pushed around," he said.

"The only one that's been pushed around is the rat," I said. "And you've gotten two stupid phone calls. So what? You probably get crank calls and letters all the time anyway."

"Don't try to talk me out of it," he warned.

"I'd be a pretty lousy friend if I didn't."

He sighed. "It isn't going to do any good, so save your breath. I wanted to tell you, so in case anything happens to me somebody will know where I was going and maybe they can nail the bastards."

He looked so fierce, his thinning hair disheveled, his eyes angrily peering through his thick Clark Kent glasses, and his wool necktie askew. And so vulnerable. "What if I talk to him?" I said.

"Who?"

"Dosti. I'm used to dealing with guys like that."

"I don't need anyone fighting my battles for me."

"You need somebody to do your thinking for you, Ed.

You won't let anybody help you, and now you're going to go out there and bend over for him so he can kick your ass. Nobody's talking about fighting your battles, but Dosti wants a piece of you, and if you do a John Wayne number and tweak his nose in his place of business, he's going to help himself. But me he's not mad at—as far as I know."

"He might *get* mad."

"That's okay," I said. "I'm bigger than he is."

"Everybody's bigger than he is, the little shit."

"So what's the problem? Come on, Ed. You talk about being able to function; do it, do what you do—write your column. And let me do what I do. You know damn well it makes sense."

"How'm I supposed to live with it if anything happens to you?"

"Nothing's going to happen to me. If the mob was going to have me dusted they'd have done it long ago. This could be the beginning of a dialogue that might eventually lead to peace."

He started to laugh. "A dialogue? You're starting to sound like a journalist."

"I've been hanging around you too much. How about it? You go back to the office and browbeat a copyboy and let me do my thing."

He bit down so hard on his pipestem I thought it would crack between his teeth. Finally he nodded agreement. He didn't want to, but he did.

"So that's settled. I'll go see Jimmy Sweets. Call it taking a little pressure off."

Ed tossed back the rest of his drink. "Call it squeezing a pimple," he said.

The near west side is a neighborhood in transition; it has been for thirty years. Many of the European families that settled there in the aftermath of World War II have moved to the south side, now, and a large Hispanic population has moved in. It's still an immigrant neighborhood but it's taken on a new flavor. Puerto Rican churches and bodegas line Lorain Avenue, although it's still possible to get a great hot dog or klobasa sandwich in a stand-up lunchroom not much bigger than most people's closets.

Dosti & Son was headquartered in a flat-roofed structure of dirty red brick, the type built in the fifties, with louvered windows and metal-framed glass doors that clashed with the facade of the building. I parked in a paved front lot that could accommodate about twelve private cars. Around the back was a huge parking area for the garbage trucks, plus a smaller maintenance yard, all surrounded by a twelve-foot cyclone fence with concertina wire stretched across the top. I hoped the employee benefits were good, because something had to make up for a working atmosphere that resembled a federal prison.

The woman at the desk was in her fifties and had inexplicably dyed her hair the color of straw and then sprayed it so heavily that the individual strands were gummed together.

"Help you?" she said as if she didn't want to. She curled her lip back and bared her teeth when she talked, like a bad actress in a low-budget vampire movie.

"I'd like to see Mr. Dosti," I said.

"Junior or Senior?"

"Senior."

"And your name is?"

I handed her one of my legitimate cards, which she regarded in a contemptuous manner. She held it between two fingers and said, "May I tell Mr. Dosti what this is in regard to?"

I hoped Dosti would be pleasant to me, because his receptionist made me long to put my fist through a wall. "Tell him it's about Ed Stahl."

Her lips pursed. She rose and went to a door, punched a code onto a keypad fastened to the doorframe at eye-level like an electronic mezuzah, and disappeared, leaving me to cool my heels in the reception area. A coffee table from a 1950s furnished apartment held a tattered back issue of *Life* with a picture of General Norman Schwarzkopf on the cover, which will give you an idea of the last time anyone updated the reading matter. There was a cracked Naugahyde sofa, a limp dieffenbachia teetered on a metal plant stand in the corner where it might get the weak light coming through the glass outer door, and on the paneled walls were several framed color photographs of gleaming green garbage trucks. I'd have to ask Dosti for the name of his decorator.

In a few moments the woman came back, cheeks flushed through her too-thick powder. "This way," she said, holding the door open for me.

We went down a long corridor, industrial cream-colored paint on the walls, linoleum the color of dried blood on the floor, and buzzing fluorescent lights on the ceiling, past offices occupied by frowning guys in white shirts and inexpensive ties with telephones growing out of their ears, a supply room, a Xerox room, and a small kitchen with a sink, coffee maker, and microwave oven. Coming toward us a young woman in a too tight skirt and three-inch heels carried a thin manila folder and chewed worriedly on her lower lip. She didn't smile or acknowledge either of us as she clattered by.

At the end of the hall was an open door, and my faithful guide handed me through it into a large room with paneling much more elegant than that in the reception area, a large oak desk that gleamed under its coat of polish, and a large color TV that was tuned to *Oprah* with the volume off. James Dosti, Senior, sat behind the big desk like a cigar-smoking Italian Buddha. I recognized him from the occasional newspaper photo, the infamous Jimmy Sweets—a tough, square fireplug of a man with beetling brows like hairy awnings over piggy brown eyes and a nose that had been broken and badly reset. He was playing with my card, turning it over between his fat fingers. On his desk was an apothecary jar filled with the kind of jelly beans Ronald Reagan was so fond of; Dosti's penchant for them had given him his nickname.

Standing off to one side was a man about thirty years younger than Dosti, but with the same build, minus the excess bulk, and the same simian features. He stood about five foot four, with arms at least half that long. I would have bet dinner he was James Dosti, Junior. He wore a pinched expression I was sure was perpetual, like a man with chronic lower back pain. If his father was called Jimmy Sweets, perhaps the guys in the back room referred to James the younger as Jimmy Sour, although not to his face. He should have sued the city of Cleveland for building the sidewalks so close to his ass.

Behind the desk was an enormous blowup of a city map, punctured with multicolored pins and flags at strategic locations. It was the only decoration in the room, but admittedly an improvement over the framed garbage truck photos in the reception area.

"Jimmy Dosti," the old man said, the words issuing from around his half-smoked cigar. He cocked his head toward the younger man and said, "This's Jim Junior."

I nodded at both of them, since neither made any effort to shake hands. Nobody asked me to sit down, either, but I did anyway, in an uncomfortable chair on the other side of the desk.

"Don't get too cozy," Jimmy Sweets said, "because you aren't staying long. What can I do for you?"

"I'm a friend of Ed Stahl's—"

"That shows bad judgment right there," Junior interrupted me.

"Stahl is a fucking big mouth," the older man said. "I don't like him and I don't like people who like him. He accuses me in print without getting his facts right. I don't like that. Makes me look bad."

"He's got a Pulitzer prize that says he always has his facts right."

"You can put it in your ass, the Pulitzer prize." He looked at my card once more and flipped it onto the desk. "What's Milan Security?"

"I do industrial security work," I said.

"We got our own. We don't need any."

"I'm not selling any."

"I know your name, Jacovich," Sweets said. "Know your reputation."

"Should I be flattered?"

"No. You're a real boil on the ass to some people I know. What do you want?"

"To talk about this little feud between you and Ed Stahl."

"So?"

"Ed's a reporter."

"Huh?"

"They pay him to write what he writes. There's nothing personal in it."

"The cocksucker calls me a crook in the papers and you tell me it's nothing personal?" His eyes bulged with outrage. "He named names, for Christ's sake! You don't name *names.*"

He looked wildly around the room for a moment as though from one of the corners answers to the great and profound questions of the universe might issue forth. Then he rummaged through his top drawer and pulled out the two columns Ed had written about him and threw them across the desk at me. "Here, read," he said. "Names. Ed Stahl don't like Italians. He never writes anything good about Italians, only bad stuff. He put down Frank Sinatra once, even. All the time he takes shots at me, he takes shots at Frank Celebrezze, he even takes shots at Ernie Accorsi."

Celebrezze is a well-known Ohio politician and Accorsi heads up the Cleveland Browns' front office. I said, "Every journalist in town takes shots at them sometimes, Mr. Dosti. It's got nothing to do with their being Italian. They understand why, too: they're public figures. It comes with the territory."

"Territory," he mumbled. "I'll tell you about territory." Rolling his chair away from the desk, he reached up and slapped a meaty paw against the city map on the wall. "This is *my* territory. We been serving this town for a long time now. Built this business from nothing, and if we hadda bust a couple a heads to do it, well tough shit, you know? We do a good job, we know our business. Nobody has no complaints about the trash pickup, nobody bitches about the landfill, we run it nice and clean, according to the government whatchacallems."

"Federal guidelines," Junior offered.

"Right, right. No toxic waste, we're goddamn careful about that. All put in proper containers. We make a buck, the city gets its garbage hauled off, and everybody's smiling. Why'd Ed Stahl have to call names?"

"It's his job."

"This is ours," put in Junior.

"I know," I said, "but there's a right way to do it and a wrong way."

Jimmy Sweets was getting red in the face, his bull neck bulging over his tight collar. "Who says it's wrong? Stahl?"

"The law."

"Don't make me laugh," he said. "I don't think there's one guy doing business in this city that's a hundred percent legit. All the saints are dead, you understand what I'm talking about? You shave a little here, you add a little there, you skooch the numbers around until they read the way you want them. That's how it's done." He took the now dead cigar out of his mouth and put it in an ashtray; with his fingers he picked some loose leaves of tobacco off his tongue. "I still don't know why you're here, Jacovich. Whattaya want?"

"I'm just the messenger. Ed Stahl wants to call a truce."

Junior sniggered, and his father silenced him with a look. It was the patented hard-guy look, and even though it was directed at his son, I was sure Jimmy Dosti had done it for my benefit. "A truce?" he said. "You tell Stahl to shut his damn mouth. *That's* a truce!"

I said, "Ed has lots of things he can write about. More important things. He would have stopped after that one column if you hadn't started throwing your weight around."

The little eyes almost disappeared within their buttresses of flesh. "What are you talking about?"

"We all three know what I'm talking about, Mr. Dosti. Intimidation. Threats. Anonymous phone calls and dead rats in the mailbox."

Jimmy Sweets shoved a new cigar into his face and lit it with a wooden match he took from his top middle drawer. The smacking noises he made with his lips were like pistol shots. He said to Junior, "What's this guy, nuts? Talking about dead rats."

"He's nuts," Junior affirmed. "Talking about dead rats."

I tried not to cough as the cigar smoke drifted across the desk from Dosti to me like smoke from a cannon that's just been fired. "I'm asking you in a nice way, Mr. Dosti. Ed's had his say and you've had yours, and now it's time to move on. Let it die a natural death and there won't be any more trouble."

He leaned forward and put his hands flat on the top of the desk, elbows out, the long cigar jutting out from between his teeth. He looked like a belligerent gibbon. "Are you threatening me, Jacovich? Who the fuck are you, anyway? Nobody threatens me, I don't care if you *are* asshole buddies with Vic Gaimari. You don't come in here and make threats to me, or they'll haul you outta here in a trash barrel, I swear to Christ."

"I came to make peace, Mr. Dosti. To try, anyway."

"Try again," he growled. "Ed Stahl minds his own business." He pointed a finger at me like a gun. "And you mind yours. That's how you make peace." He swiveled his chair around behind the desk so he was facing his son. "See to it that this guy gets off the property," he said. "I'm sick of looking at his ugly face."

The younger man took a few steps toward me and I stood up, towering about seven inches above him. Sometimes my size is intimidating enough to keep me out of trouble. "Don't even think about putting your hand on me, Jim Junior," I said.

I stood outside in the cold, feeling the disapproving eyes of the receptionist boring into me through the glass, and buttoned my coat up to the neck against what had become a serious wind. It was still snowing, and it had turned into a wet, heavy snow, the kind that sticks to the pavement. I wrapped my scarf around my neck, pulled on my gloves, and started across the lot to my car, stepping carefully to avoid slipping on a patch of ice. I reached into my pocket with gloved fingers for my car keys; I keep them on a chain with the Swiss Army knife Milan Junior gave me for Christmas one year. Two men in work clothes were hurrying around from the rear of the building and coming toward me, purpose in their stride. I sighed. I recognized the walk, that aggressive set of the shoulders, from every B Western I had ever seen. This was to be the showdown at sunrise in the middle of a dusty cow-town street.

"Hey!" one of them said. "Hey, you!" He was almost my height, and I could see that under the blue coveralls and the fur-lined parka he wore over them he was built like a concrete slab. The guy behind him was only slightly smaller. He was wearing a blue Cavs cap and had a three-day stubble and a peculiarly loose lower lip. He probably drooled a lot when he ate soup. He didn't have a jacket. *Chooch* was stitched over his breast pocket in red yarn.

"You parked in my space," the first one said. I couldn't help noticing the monkey wrench sticking out of the side pocket of the coveralls. "This here's my parking space and I come driving in and you're in it."

I looked around. There was no indication that the space was reserved. Unlike Deming Steel, there wasn't even a number. I'd been careful about that—I knew what a terrible offense it was to park in a numbered space. "I didn't see any sign."

"There isn't any sign," he said. "Everybody knows this is my space. I been here seven years, this has always been my space. I don't need no sign."

Chooch, the loose-lipped guy, was edging around to the other side of me. They were trying to surround me. About as subtle as a high school marching band.

I said, "Well, maybe you do need a sign, because I didn't know it was your space. I've never been here before."

"That ain't an excuse! Because of you I hadda park clear out back."

I don't even know why I was talking to them. We all knew what the scenario was to be, who had orchestrated it, and what was supposed to happen. I guess that small part of me that has evolved a half step higher than a wild dog was trying to negotiate out of a preordained and inevitable fight.

"Sorry," I said. "I'll just pull out and you can have your space back."

"Too late," he said. "I hadda walk all the way around here from the back in the snow."

"I said I was sorry, bud."

"Sorry doesn't help my walking around in the fucking snow," he said. He telegraphed the swing, tensing his shoulders, sucking in a breath and bulging out his eyes before he looped his arm overhead, the monkey wrench all at once in his fist. Instinctively I moved toward him, which took me out of the clutches of Chooch behind me, who'd made an ineffectual grab for my arms. I ducked under the bigger man's arm, and when the wrench whistled by my ear I grabbed his wrist and twisted, turning back into him and jamming his elbow into my side. His own momentum carried him past me and snapped his wrist with the sound of a tree branch cracking off under the weight of the snow. I felt the bone break in my hands, and my stomach lurched, but I didn't let go. The wrench hit the pavement, the snow on the ground muffling what might have been a loud clatter.

Still using his own body weight against him, I turned again, using my hip for ballast, and he hurtled to his knees, letting out a scream that could be heard in Rocky River. I sensed Chooch coming at me from behind again, and I started around, but my feet slipped in the wet snow and I lost my balance as he thundered into my back. He rammed a fist into my kidneys, and then he reached around me, his fingers clawing at my face, at my eyes.

I tucked my chin into my chest and bent forward, pushing Chooch away from me with my butt. Straightening up quickly, I thrust the point of my elbow right into his loose lips. I turned all the way around and lashed the closed Swiss Army knife on the other end of my keychain across the bridge of his nose, and he lurched and fell back over the front fender of my car, his hands up to his face, bleeding from the slash on his nose and from his broken mouth, spitting out a front tooth.

The guy with the parking space was still on his knees, his face white with pain and shock and his right hand pressed between his thighs, and he kept repeating a bad word over and over, rocking back and forth as though in prayer. I bent down and put my mouth close to his ear.

"Tell Jimmy Sweets if he wants to try again, it's going to take more than a couple of fat clowns like you."

I nudged him aside with my knee and he fell over like one more sack of garbage in the Dosti & Sons catalogue. Through his pain he looked up at me with a hatred that made his eyes sparkle.

I opened the car door. He was still down there when I started the engine. Chooch, who'd been lying face up over the fender like a guy trying to catch a few quick rays, jumped away as if he'd caught fire and stumbled over the cement block that kept careless parkers from driving into the cyclone fence. He sat down hard, his fingers scrabbling at his mouth where his lost tooth used to be, and the two of them watched me with a kind of stunned wonderment as I drove up the driveway and out onto the street, my all-weather tires biting into the slushy snow.

FOURTEEN

I don't get over to the west side very much; no east sider does. It's like crossing an international border, except you don't have to get your passport stamped. In effect Cleveland is two cities separated by a river, much like Buda and Pest, and except for downtown, which is considered neutral territory by both factions, east siders and west siders pretty much stick to their own bailiwicks, especially since they shut down the Main Avenue Bridge for a year to repair it. Yet today I had twice crossed the Cuyahoga from east to west.

One of my favorite restaurants in town is on the west side. Johnny's Bar was remodeled a few years ago, spruced up from the workingman's tavern it had been, and now the subdued and elegant decor matches the terrific food. Johnny's is always jumping, even at six o'clock on a snowy Tuesday evening, and it usually draws the best-dressed crowd in town.

Since I was on the wrong side of the river anyway and it was dinnertime, I decided to stop in for one of their great veal dishes. I considered it carefully before deciding to have my dinner there; Johnny's is one of the places Mary and I had gone to a lot, and I didn't want to spend the evening stirring up feelings that would engender self-pity. The day so far, with Bogdan's funeral and Ed Stahl and the fun and games at Dosti & Sons, had been a real lemon, and I didn't need any more angst at the moment. However, the food at Johnny's is good enough to bury bad memories as well as a sore kidney.

I sat at the bar and had a drink and chatted with Billy, one of the owners, and then moved to a table in the rear corner of the dining room to eat. I ordered one of the evening specials, a stuffed veal chop with a cognac sauce reduction that could make a strong man weep, and it made me glad I'd come. But I still recalled those evenings here with Mary, romantic dinners bursting with the magic of anticipation, and it wasn't lost on me that I was the only one in the room who wasn't with a date, wife, or companion. All the diners, from the fledgling lawyers in their twenties to the good solid three-piece-suit types over fifty, seemed to be paired up. I was getting used to a solitary existence again, just as I had after Lila and I had decided to end our marriage, but there was still the dull and constant pain of loneliness, one that kind of gets you in the heart. Except for Marko and most of my Wednesday night poker buddies, almost all my friends are married.

I was also upset by what I was going to have to report to Ed. I went over my meeting with the Dostis in my mind and couldn't really fault myself for any sins of omission or commission, but the fact remained that I'd blown it for Ed and made what might be a dangerous enemy.

I had a brandy after dinner, which helped to ease the ache from Chooch's lucky punch. Then I went across the street to the church parking lot where Johnny's customers leave their cars at night and started home.

Driving was slow in the falling snow as I headed over the river to the east side and up to the Heights. It was the kind of wet, heavy snow that would cause a lot of wrenched backs when householders tried to shovel their driveways in the morning, and the temperature was cold enough to turn it quickly to ice, causing driving conditions that are nightmarish even for the careful motorist. Clevelanders are crazy drivers sometimes, making arbitrary lane changes and turning without signaling, but nobody really drives at excessive speeds, even when it isn't slippery, because of the proliferation of potholes in the street; you hit one of those babies going fifty miles an hour and you'll be picking up the pieces of your transmission with a broom and a dustpan.

As I came over the rise of Cedar Hill, a car parked across the street from the Nighttown Restaurant fired up its engine and pulled out into the traffic behind me. I didn't think anything of it—it's a public street, after all—until I made a left turn onto the side street where the entrance to my parking lot is and the car followed. Close behind.

I didn't know who was tailing me, or why, but I didn't much like it. If I pulled into the parking area behind my apartment building and he came in after me, I'd be hemmed in and out of options, and I try not to put myself in spots like that. I had to make a quick decision.

I drove up the street past my driveway and turned right on Euclid Heights Boulevard, a broad street with a grassy median strip where the city has planted hundreds of new trees. I was still keeping to a leisurely pace, but with one eye firmly on my rearview mirror. I headed east, my tires crunching over the salt laid down by the city trucks to melt the ice, past the blocks of substantial old homes and brick apartment buildings that defined the neighborhood, and up to Coventry, where I was stopped by a red light. My new friend showed no sign of going away but hung one car-length in back of me. It could have been coincidental, he might have just been going in that direction, but I had a gut feeling that he had been waiting for me a block from my apartment and that he was going to stick with me. I decided to find out for sure.

I crossed Coventry and continued eastward past the elementary school, crossing Superior Avenue and driving under the natural arch of overhanging branches of oak and catalpa, past the churchlike clapboard building that was the first school in Cleveland Heights, now boarded up because it's too historic to raze and no one knows what else to do with it. I turned right at Lee Road, then made a quick left on Hyde Park Avenue, whose colorful houses back onto Cain Park on the south side of the street. At the end of the block I turned right onto Compton and then quickly left on Blanche, and when the other car stayed close I was sure it was me he was after.

I got to the traffic light at Taylor and stopped. The traffic lights above the intersection were bouncing crazily around in the wind. I reached into the glove compartment for the .38 police special I always keep there. When I carry a gun on my person it's a .357 Magnum, but that one was in its usual place in my top desk drawer, since it hadn't occurred to me to wear a weapon to a funeral. I was glad I had the backup in the car. I pulled off my right glove, shoved the .38 into my coat pocket, and stepped out into the street as my little shadow came up the block behind me. I was either going to make him talk to me or run; however it turned out I figured I'd be ahead of the game.

I think that seeing me standing in the street shook him up, because he slowed for a second, hesitating. Then he gunned his motor and the car hurtled toward me, its headlights piercing the lacy curtain of falling snow.

I could feel my stomach tighten up. I didn't have a lot of maneuverability, but I jumped up into the air and over the fender of my own car as he roared past me, his front fender brushing the skirts of my coat and kicking up a wave of wet slush that caught me across the shins and immediately filled my shoes. It was the deep snow that saved me; with the street as slippery as it was he just couldn't get close enough to me to make it count.

He hit his brakes once more, and I thought that he might back up and try again. I took the .38 out of my pocket and slipped my finger through the trigger guard. But he changed his mind, revved up again, and went careening around the corner onto Taylor Road in defiance of the traffic sign that said NO TURN ON RED. I was hoping there'd be a Cleveland Heights cop around to see it—they invariably are when *I* do something like that—but no such luck.

He headed south on Taylor at about sixty miles an hour, kicking up twin wakes of slush behind him. He was traveling too fast for the weather conditions, and he skidded on the icy pavement, and sideswiped a parked car with that sickening crunch of metal and the sound of shattering glass the urban driver hears in his nightmares. He didn't even stop, just righted his wheels, backed up a bit for traction, and tore off into the night, bouncing noisily over a pothole as he went.

Whoever owned the car he hit wasn't going to be too happy about it.

It was snowing too hard to get a good look at the driver or even to read the license plate. I could only tell it was a tan Ford sedan, model year somewhere in the mid eighties. I thought about following him but gave the idea up quickly; it was no night for a car chase.

I got into my Sunbird, leaned back against the seat, and lit a Winston with a hand that was shaking more than I care to admit. Despite the cold my shirt was drenched with sweat. And I was mad as hell. Being followed was bad enough; nearly getting run over was something else. I'd have to have another talk with Jimmy Sweets, a serious one this time, someplace where he didn't have the luxury of having oversize slobs with monkey wrenches a phone call away.

I drove back home watchfully, almost in slow motion, through the freezing slush, the .38 on the seat beside me. Apparently my friend in the Ford was going home, too, to lick his wounds and call it a night.

"Do you realize how long it's been since I've been in your apartment, Milan? Nearly two years."

I poured Marko Meglich a mug of coffee and the third one of the morning for myself. "That long?"

He took the mug from me. "I hate that. I miss you, Milan, no lie. We had some pretty good times together, didn't we? Jesus, twenty-five years since the old football days at St. Clair High—that's a hell of a long time to know somebody. We ought to see more of each other." He waved a hand at the manila folder he'd brought for me and put on my desk. "Not like this—not professionally, talking about killers and punks and crap like that. I mean doing fun stuff together like we used to. Go to a ball game or something."

"We have different lives now, that's all. You've got your job—and your twenty-year-olds."

Marko's insistence on dating postadolescent tanning-booth bunnies is a sore spot. Not that I give a damn, but *he* felt awkward about it every time I'd run into him somewhere with one of his teased-hair babies. Not awkward enough to stop, though.

My little dig made him color slightly. "And you've got ESPN," he said. "I don't understand you. The biggest event in your life is some obscure basketball game like Charlotte against Miami, and it's televised. You build your week around it. Jesus!" He shook his head. "I had high hopes for you, Milan, when Mary was still around. You were such a pill after your divorce, and then Mary came along and I thought you were coming back to the land of the living. But now you're turning into the old hermit of Cedar Hill again. You gotta start getting out some more, have a little fun. Don't you ever have the urge to touch something soft? Listen, if you want me to introduce you to somebody . . ."

"Thanks. But when I go out with a woman I insist that she's old enough to remember that Paul McCartney used to be in a band before Wings."

"You're too picky, that's the trouble with you. You won't sleep with a woman unless she has the body of Kim Basinger, the brains of Eleanor Roosevelt, and a face like some old painting of the Blessed Mother. And besides that, you have to be in love with her first."

"Not necessarily. But unlike some people I could mention, I do kind of like to know her last name."

He shrugged. "Use it or lose it," he said.

It was just before eight in the morning, too early to trade banter or insults. Marko had dropped by on his way to work, dressed in his usual three-piece suit, charcoal gray today, with a green and black tie, and I had thrown on a Kent State sweatshirt and a pair of cords that should have been in the laundry basket. He preened his mustache, catching his reflection in the window and turning to admire his profile, and I ran my hand over my unshaven chin; there were more differences between us than the women we fancied.

"You're hopeless," he sighed. "But if you want to waste your life dating Mother Hand and her five lovely daughters there's nothing I can do about it. Even so, I wish we saw more of each other. Remember the old days—you and Lila, me and

Dara, going out to dinner? We were . . . comfortable together. We all knew each other since we were kids. There were always things to talk about, little private jokes we all had." He looked around my front room, his eyes sad as a basset puppy's. "Now you're living here alone, I'm downtown by myself in a condo, our wives have gone on with other interests, other guys. Christ, how does it all fall apart, Milan? What happens to people?"

"It's called life, Marko."

"Yeah—and it sucks."

"Consider the alternative. You've been a cop too long. You're getting cynical."

He looked genuinely unhappy for a moment, too awash in sudden and unaccustomed nostalgia to even care that I'd called him by his old name. He and I had our differences, but he'd been a good friend for as long as I could remember, and seeing him feeling sorry for himself was upsetting me. I said, "Tell you what. Baseball season'll be here before you know it. The Indians, opening day. You and me. You bug out of work and we'll go, sit by first base like we always used to. Only now we're old enough to drink beer."

He brightened considerably, lost in those innocent youthful days that memory sanitizes into an idyll. "We used to cut out of school and go to the first game every year. I remember one time, about ten thirty in the morning on opening day, you put your head down on your desk, and when the teacher asked you what was the matter you said you had a headache and she let you go home, and we wound up at the game. The Yankees, wasn't it?"

"We were thirteen. What a memory you've got."

"I remember the good things," he said sadly. He sipped from his mug and then put it down on the desk with a clatter and picked up the folder. He straightened his back a little and composed his face into a professional frown, chin set firm and brows knit. The subject was about to be changed.

"This is all I was able to come up with on Bogdan Zdrale's immigration and naturalization. If anyone finds out I made you a copy, my ass is grass. You owe me on this one, buddy. I just about had to promise the guy at INS my first-born child to get this."

"You don't have a first-born child."

He gave me his patented sly grin. "Yeah, but the INS guy doesn't know that."

I took the folder and started to open it, and Marko said, "Let me save you a little time. The guy was a corporal in the army during World War Two, spent two years in a German prison camp, was liberated in 1945, and applied for refugee status. He came over here in 1946, settled on the east side of Cleveland, and went to work for Deming Steel. His final citizenship papers are in here too. He always paid his taxes and kept his nose clean." He tapped the top of the folder. "Pretty dull reading."

"I'm most interested in the prison camp." I opened the folder and shuffled through the papers until I found what I was looking for—a photostat of a prison ID card with Zdrale's picture on it. A man in his late twenties, thin and haggard with haunted eyes that had seen too much of despair. "It's in German," I complained.

Marko took the folder from me and pulled out another sheet of paper, a U.S. government form, filled out in the careful, cramped, cursive writing of a petty federal bureaucrat. "This is the loose translation," he said.

Bogdan Zdrale had been taken prisoner by the Germans near Belgrade in September of 1943 and transported to Banyitsa prison on October 3 of the same year. Apparently because of his skills as a machinist he'd been assigned the task of making sure that the electric generators and the camp's motor vehicles, the trucks and jeeps and the commandant's staff car were in running order at all times. From what Jacob Bauch had told me of his own experience in the camps it's probably what had kept Zdrale alive when so many of his fellow Serbs were dying.

I looked through the rest of the papers. There was a copy of his passport, confirmation of his ocean journey from Trieste to New York in 1947, his alien registration number, and a copy of his naturalization papers. There were also several letters from Elmo Laketa and from a Parma couple named Rade and Nena Stanich who vouched for Zdrale's character and that of his wife so that they'd be allowed to enter the country. He had apparently lived with them for a few months before his Deming Steel job enabled him to first rent the little house in Slavic Town and then eventually buy it. I jotted down the Stanich's address. The testimonial had been written forty-six years ago, but people who came from the old country in those days tended to stay put, and there was an off chance I'd still be able to find them.

"This is all ancient history," Marko said. "You're wasting your time."

"I don't see the police department wrapping this one up very neatly."

"Look, when a guy is found shot to death in that neighborhood it only means one thing."

"Are you telling me that a seventy-five-year-old Serb was driving around trying to buy crack and the deal went sour? And that the crack dealer then drove his van clear out to Wickliffe and dumped it, wiping his prints off everything in the process?"

"I'm just saying that trying to track down somebody with a gun and a motive down there is like looking for a yuppie on Public Square. There are so many you wouldn't know where to start. The case is still open—it's a homicide, we'll keep it open forever if we have to—but there are other priorities."

I leveled a finger at him. "You asked me in on this, Marko. Are you telling me to get out now?"

He put up both hands in front of him like a politician trying to quiet a crowd on the courthouse steps. "I asked you to check out Nello Trinetti, and I still think you might be better off chasing that angle down."

"Actually," I said, rubbing the sore place over my kidney, "I might be better off watching my own ass."

"Why?"

I told him about Ed Stahl and the Dostis, and about my night visitor in the tan Ford. He heard me out, concern creasing his forehead, and then he said, "Ed's right about one thing."

"What's that?"

"There's not much the police can do. We don't have the manpower to put anyone on Ed, you know that. We can't trace the phone threats back to Jimmy Sweets, and the last time I looked there's nothing in the criminal statutes about killing rats. In fact, most people would call it a public service."

"Is it a public service to send two goons after me in the parking lot?"

"You'll never prove it was Dosti behind it. I can have the two guys picked up, but the worst we can do is charge the two of them with assault. And when the jury sees one guy with his wrist in a cast and the other one whistling through an empty space where his teeth used to be, the DA's gonna have a fine old time getting much more than a judicial finger-shake."

"How about the one who tried to run me over last night?"

"There are probably ten thousand tan Fords registered in the county. Give me an ID or a license number, and I'll have him in irons in time for the six o'clock news."

"You're not real concerned about it, are you?"

Marko pushed aside his suit jacket and put his hands in his pants pockets, a gesture more patrician than I think he intended. "Sure I'm concerned. You're my oldest friend. And Ed's a good writer and he does good things for the community, even though he is a boil on the ass sometimes. But my hands are tied until we can either positively identify the person making the threats or an actual crime is committed."

"So you can only protect him after he's dead?" I said as we went to the door.

Marko sighed and put on his overcoat. "Give me a break, okay? I'm just a poor civil servant."

I fingered the velvet collar of his chesterfield. "Not so poor, I'd say."

In a sudden and uncharacteristic moment of sentiment, Marko put his arms around me and hugged me to him. I don't think we'd hugged since our last college football game. "I'm serious about getting together, Milan. I miss your company. I miss the old days."

"Me, too," I said, meaning it. "We'll do it."

He started out the door, turned, and pointed a pistol-like finger at the folder containing the life and times of Bogdan Zdrale. "You never saw that. And when you finish with it— burn it."

The Heights Health Club on Mayfield Road is usually pretty crowded early in the morning, when many of its members come for a workout or just a warm soak before beginning their day's labors. I had called Jacob Bauch at home and Shushano had told me he'd already left and that a dip in the Jacuzzi was part of his daily routine.

I normally avoid health clubs. All during my football years my preoccupation with my own body had bored the hell out of me, and now that I no longer have to weigh in each afternoon the whole concept of focusing all my thoughts and energies on a workout seems a waste of time. I read all the articles about how important an exercise program is, but like so many other health-oriented theories these days, that could change at any time, and a six-year study by some obscure university somewhere will be published saying that regular exercise is bad for you and makes your hangnails fester.

I'm also lazy.

But there was no getting out of this, I supposed, so I took my dusty gym bag from the back of a closet, packed it with all the necessities, and drove over to Mayfield Road. I went into the club, paid my guest fee, and resisted the blandishments of the muscle-bound young man at the desk who wanted to give me a guided tour of the place and design a special workout program just for me.

I put on my swimming trunks in the locker room, noting sadly that there was just a bit more flesh hanging over the waistband than the last time I'd had them on more than a year before. I looped the locker key around my neck by its plastic thong, slipped on my rubber flip-flop sandals, threw my towel over my shoulder, and went out onto the gym floor.

Public workout facilities have come a long way from the days of the liniment-smelling YMCA gyms, maybe because they've gone co-ed. If you've been in one health club, you've been in all of them; they only vary now by degrees of pretentiousness. The Heights was somewhere in the middle, not so elegant as to scare off the working class but carpeted and mirrored, with incandescent overhead lights designed to be kind to those past twenty. Despite being located in Cleveland Heights, a racially mixed community, almost all of the faces were white.

The Muzak system was playing a stringed instrumental version of a Barry Manilow song, if such a thing is imaginable. Several people were pedaling furiously on the stationary bikes near the locker room doors, rushing hellbent to nowhere, some of them with the *Plain Dealer, The Wall Street Journal,* or a paperback novel propped on the handlebars. Over in one corner were the iron-pumpers, a bunch of guys in their late thirties who were losing their hair and trying to make up for it by developing their upper bodies; most wore shirts and tank tops and one even had a wide leather weight belt. A few women in designer leotard outfits were daintily lifting the five-pound dumbbells, one of them obviously more concerned with how she looked while doing it than with any health benefits that might result.

I went past the Nautilus machines and into the large, echoing room where the swimming pool, sauna, and Jacuzzi sent vapors of eucalyptus and chlorine-scented steam toward the high vaulted ceiling. One hardy soul, a middle-aged woman, was doing laps in the pool, goggles over her eyes and pink plastic plugs in her nose. Several other women, mostly older and heavier, sat in one-piece black suits on the edges of the tile dangling their toes in the water.

In the octagonal whirlpool bath six elderly men stood waist-deep, breasts sagging and loose skin on the undersides of their arms flapping, their grizzled gray chest hair darkened by the hot water. They were engaging in friendly discourse, with big gestures and rising voices to drive home their points. They probably never used any of the other facilities, the weights or the machines or, God help us, the aerobics class scheduled for later that morning. In the old country they would have sat around playing *pishe-payshe* in a little café near the synagogue. But now the health club Pool of Philosophy had taken its place as a community center for old-timers to meet and swap stories and ideas.

Jacob Bauch was one of them.

I took off my sandals, draped my towel over a bench, and stepped gingerly into the steaming pool, feeling the currents from the strategically placed jets beneath the surface swirling around my thighs. Bauch didn't notice me until I moved through the hip-deep water to stand next to him. There was a lot of scar tissue on his arms and back; old scars, long healed on the surface but, I knew, festering inside.

He squinted up at me. "Well, well. The detective. What's your name again?"

"Milan Jacovich," I said.

"Uh-huh. It's nice to see you so early in the morning. I can't believe you suddenly had an urge to develop a more perfect body, so I'll have to assume you're here because you want to see me."

"You've got me," I said.

"How'd you track me down? Shushano? She was quite taken with you, you know."

"I hope that doesn't bother you."

"Certainly it bothers me," he said without rancor, apparently unconcerned that every other man in the pool was hanging on each word. "If Jews start to intermarry with non-Jews, pretty soon there won't *be* any more Jews. Read your Old Testament, read your history books. We've survived the Philistines and the Egyptians and the Romans and the Turks and the Cossacks and the Nazis and the Arabs, and now we're facing our greatest challenge—the liberalism of the twentieth century. We're so interested in convincing everyone people are all the same that it's threatening to destroy that culture and those traditions we've fought for two thousand years to preserve. So yes, it bothers me, and I'm warning you right now that I'll take considerable pains to sabotage anything that the two of you might have in mind." He gave me a sly look. "You didn't come here to ask for Shushano's hand or anything foolish like that?"

"Not after just one lunch," I said. "I think you're jumping the gun a little, Mr. Bauch."

He waved a hand at me. "Thank God for small favors. Then it must be more of the Banyitsa business, yes?"

"I'm afraid so," I said.

One of the other old men came slowly across the pool to stand next to him, giving me a suspicious look. Around his neck was a thick gold chain with a *chai* dangling from it. "Jack? Who's this?"

"One of my daughter's suitors," he answered.

"Oboy!" the old man said, looking askance at me. "Oboy!" He shook his head as he moved off again. I was embarrassed, but in a good way, if you know what I mean.

"So," Bauch said, "you want to pick my poor old brain some more."

"If you'll let me."

He sighed, put-upon. "A man can't even take a hot soak and a *schvitz* in peace these days."

"If this isn't a good time . . ."

"Stay, stay," he said, "you're already wet. And if I chase you off, Shushano will be mad at me. She thinks you're a nice guy."

"That's generous of her."

"I don't know how generous. I've been called a lot of things in my day, from dirty Yid to brilliant lawyer, but nobody *ever* said I was a nice guy. I think I like it that way." He held the waistband of his swim trunks away from his body so the water could get in, breathing through his mouth in pleasure. "Tell me what's on your mind."

I squatted down until the hot water came up around my shoulders, letting one of the jets pound my sore kidney. It felt good, therapeutic, and all at once I was glad I had come. "You told me that there's an extensive network of Jews in this country involved in ferreting out Nazi war criminals," I said.

"Groups like the Jewish Defense League and the Weisenthal Foundation."

"It's no secret."

"Are there networks like that of non-Jews?"

"What, Nazi-hunters? Hard to say now. Most of the countries that suffered most under Hitler were swallowed up in the Eastern bloc after the war. Hungary, Yugoslavia, Poland; it's not an easy thing organizing for revenge when you've just exchanged one boot heel on your neck for another one. In one way the Jews were lucky—we got Israel." He splashed water on his face. "After two thousand years of persecution, we were entitled to a little luck, no?"

"Absolutely," I said. "But I was thinking more of here in the United States."

He thought about it, his brown eyes quick and bright. "I don't know of any formal, organized movement. After the war ended and the refugees came, everyone was busy putting their lives back in order—what was left of their lives—and adjusting to a new country. Getting a job, learning the language, letting the wounds heal. There were some who went Nazi-hunting, sure, some Poles in Detroit that I remember, and some Slavs in Wisconsin. But it was mostly on their own. What do you think, they took a pledge, paid dues, and had monthly meetings where they sang the club song?"

"I don't know," I said. "That's why I'm asking you."

I noticed that two of the men who had been in the pool had climbed out, and the ones remaining had moved over to the other side, giving us a modicum of privacy.

Bauch said, "It's hard now to prove a man was a Nazi, after so many years. The memory goes, mostly because there are things most people prefer not to remember. It's one man's word against another. And the American system of justice isn't structured to deal with war criminals anymore. Nuremberg was a long time ago. Now the only thing you can do with one if you find him is press for extradition to Israel for a trial and hope for the best, and that takes years. Years." He cupped his hands and splashed water on his chest and shoulders.

"You'll pardon my French, but it's a big pain in the ass—if you're going to do it through legal channels."

"And if you're not?"

He sat down on the ledge that ran along the side of the pool, beneath the surface, the water coming up to his chin. "Your questions give me a headache, Mr. Jacovich."

"I was thinking perhaps of some Slavic group, Mr. Bauch."

"What, like the Serb National Foundation?"

"Well, not exactly. An organization that's a little more militant."

He nodded. "There's the Chetniks, of course. That's a centuries-old Serbian underground organization that started during the war of liberation from the Turks. In more modern times they used the name for the resistance fighters, the partisans who fought the Germans under Mihailovic." He chuckled. "A bunch of tough *momsers,* they were. Mountain fighters. A warrior breed."

"Are they active here in America?"

"Well, you can't look them up in the yellow pages under Militant Serbs. But I imagine if you pushed hard enough you'd find some of them, or their children. What's going on over there in Yugoslavia right now, the Bosnians and the Croatians and the Slovenes all wanting their independence, don't be surprised if you hear from the Chetniks again."

He closed his eyes, luxuriating in the warmth, but his forehead was furrowed with thought. Finally he said, "Are you thinking that this old man, the one who got killed—what was his name?"

"Bogdan Zdrale."

"Yes. He was a soldier during the war? And he was in Banyitsa?"

I nodded.

"And you're thinking maybe he was one of these Chetniks, that he might have seen someone right here in Cleveland, someone from the camps who had collaborated with the Nazis, who had committed war crimes? And maybe somebody killed him to keep him quiet?"

"I have to explore it, certainly. It's a possibility."

He breathed deeply, rubbing his hand across his face. "There's another possibility, too, Mr. Jacovich, one you ought to at least think about."

"What's that, Mr. Bauch?"

He stood up again, the water pouring off his body, and looked right at me. "That maybe this Bogdan Zdrale of yours was killed because *he* was the war criminal."

FIFTEEN

Mitchell Stanich was a middle-management guy, a regional sales manager with a small machine-tool manufacturing firm in Cleveland. I'd tracked him down with the invaluable assistance of my friend Renee who works at the hall of records downtown. There was a price tag for her help, of course—life is full of price tags. With Renee it's carefully perusing the latest photos of her grandson, with Renee waiting, hands on hips, while I make the proper appreciative noises. I had hoped when the little boy had outgrown infancy the flood of snapshots would ebb, but it was not to be. I think she takes pictures of the kid every weekend of his life.

After every photo had been examined and clucked over, we had spent a long afternoon together in the stacks of the public records, which lay bare the secrets of anyone in the area who has ever bought a house, applied for a driver's license, been born, gotten married, or died. We were researching the life and times of Rade and Nena Stanich, finally discovering that Rade had died in 1968 and Nena five years later. Their only son Mitchell, born in 1949, had kept their modest house in Parma for a few years after they were gone and then sold it to buy another, which turned out to be a large well-kept brick Georgian in a then new development in Parma Heights, when he'd married in 1977.

I sat in Mitch Stanich's pleasant living room sipping the beer his wife had supplied me with before she disappeared upstairs to put the kids to bed. There were two of them, a boy and a girl, dark-haired and bright-eyed, between six and ten years old, with their Serbian heritage written all over their flower faces. Their father, sitting opposite me on an ottoman, was a pleasant-looking man of medium height, broad-shouldered and running more to chunky than fat, with curly, jet black hair going silver at the temples and thin at the crown, a heavy but neatly trimmed mustache, and the open, friendly smile of the born salesman. The Mitch Stanich family could have posed for a Norman Rockwell magazine cover.

He'd been fairly puzzled and not terribly receptive when I called him at dinnertime and asked if I could talk to him that evening, but when I explained that it had to do with the man who'd been found shot on the east side several days before, he'd agreed to see me after dinner, eager to be of any help if he could.

"I read about the murder in the paper," he said, "and I was shocked. Who wouldn't be? An old man, couldn't hurt anyone. He deserved a more peaceful death. Violence like that is so . . . senseless. I guess it's a sign of the times, but it doesn't make it any easier to swallow." He looked up at the ceiling as though he could see through it to his children's bedroom. "You have any kids?"

"Two boys."

He shook his large head from side to side. "Then you know what it's like. When you have kids it just gives you the jimjams to think you're living in the middle of that kind of thing." He shrugged and took a pull of his own Stroh's. "We can't hide our families in a cave, I guess, so we just grit our teeth and hope for the best."

"Mitch"—we'd immediately gotten on a first-name basis; he was that kind of a guy—"when you read the news on Saturday, did Bogdan Zdrale's name mean anything to you?"

"No," he said, a vertical crease bisecting his eyebrows, "other than I recognized it as being Serb. That's probably the only reason I paid any attention to it at all. I mostly avoid news stories about murders and things. Although sometimes it's hard—dead bodies aren't exactly a novelty in certain parts of this city."

"You didn't know him, then? You don't remember him as being a friend of your parents?"

He thought for a long time. "No," he said. "It's a fairly unusual name, and I think I'd recall if I'd ever heard it before. It's possible the folks knew him back when I was a little kid, or maybe even before I was born, but I don't think they could have been close friends. I can't remember anyone by that name coming to the house for dinner or anything. Why? Should it have rung a bell?"

"Your parents sponsored Bogdan Zdrale's coming to America."

He looked surprised. "They did?"

"They vouched for his good character on his immigration papers, along with another man named Elmo Laketa. Do you know him?"

"Elmo Laketa? No, that doesn't sound familiar either."

I was more than a little bit at sea. I hadn't expected a dead end here, of all places. "When did your parents arrive in this country?"

"Right after the war. Late 1945, I think." His smile got a bit wider. "I didn't come along for a few years yet."

"You'd think that if they knew Zdrale well enough to sponsor him, they'd have seen a lot of him when he got here."

He sat forward on the ottoman, his elbows on his thighs. "That's not necessarily so," he said. "My father was a very loving, concerned man, and he had committed himself to helping others. He did very well over here; worked in a foundry until he'd saved enough money to buy it. And after he started making the bucks—I'm not talking big money here, but we were always comfortable—he was very active in civic affairs, in the church, things like that. And he was always more than generous with other Serbs, especially JC families."

"JC?"

"Just come," he explained. "From the old country. I guess he felt the U.S.A. had been good to him and this was his way of giving back."

"You mean he might have sponsored Bogdan Zdrale without even knowing him personally?"

Mitch Stanich shrugged his broad shoulders. "He might've been a friend of a friend of a friend and gotten involved that way. He was passionately interested in the welfare of the Serbian immigrants. My father was one of a whole group of Serbs in Cleveland, well into the fifties, that tried to bring displaced people over here to start a new life. Sometimes they even paid the immigrants' way. So if my father did sponsor this Bogdan Zdrale in some way without even knowing him, it wouldn't surprise me."

"Your father was from Belgrade, originally?"

"Right. But so were thousands of others. It's hard to say whether he knew this man in the old country or not. Maybe he brought him over so he could work in our foundry."

"I don't think so," I said. "First of all, Zdrale came over before your father owned the foundry. And from what I've been able to find out, his only American job was with Deming Steel."

He sat back, his hands flat on his hams. "Oh. Well, it was an idea, anyway. I wish I could be of more help, Milan, but I don't personally know of any connection between him and my parents."

"Was your father in the service during the war?"

"He was with Mihailovic," he said proudly. "Except he didn't see much action, unfortunately. He was captured by the Germans, early in 1942, if I remember the family stories."

I inadvertently squeezed the beer can so tight my thumb made a dent in it, and the beer gurgled inside. I put it down on the coffee table, feeling adrenaline course through me. "Prisoner of war?"

Mitch pressed his lips together. "We knew it happened, but he never talked about it. Well, only once that I can remember, when I was a kid and I asked him. But otherwise he never talked about it, never even mentioned it, and my mother didn't either. I can understand why. Four years," he breathed softly. "Can you imagine it?"

I could imagine it, all right. I imagined it so well that I

didn't need to ask where Rade Stanich had spent those years of captivity.

But I did anyway.

"Thanks for letting me come by so late," I said as Danica Paich stood aside so I could enter. It wasn't really all that late, just past nine o'clock, but social evenings usually start earlier.

"That's all right, Milan, you're always welcome." She looked tired, dark circles beneath her blue eyes giving them a melancholy cast. She had on a pair of tight jeans and a sweater, very different from the business clothes I was used to seeing her wear. "Would you like something to drink?"

"No thanks. I won't stay long."

We sat down in her living room. It was a little two-story house, with white aluminum siding and black trim, just off Lake Shore Boulevard. The tiny living room was barely able to contain the little love seat and matching easy chair upholstered in a tropical print, a small bookcase, and an entertainment center with a TV, VCR, and sound system. Red and green lights were dancing and bubbling for no discernible reason, and the radio was tuned to what the media people refer to as a light rock station. To me, light rock is an oxymoron; if it's rock it isn't light, and if it's light it isn't rock.

"I just had a few things I wanted to check out with you," I said.

She ran her tongue over her lips. "There's no need for you to do this anymore," she said. "I hired you to find my grandfather. Now that— Well, your job is finished."

"That depends on how you look at it," I said. "I'm on my own hook now; I don't expect you to pay me for this."

"I'm not worried about the money."

"Don't you want to know what happened?"

"Of course. But you shouldn't have to waste your time. The police are involved now. They'll get to the bottom of it if they can."

"The police think it was a drug deal gone bad."

I heard a sharp little gasp, and angry red spots appeared on her cheeks. "I never heard of anything so absurd."

"Me neither. That's why I'm still asking questions."

She took a deep breath, her breasts straining against her blue and white sweater, and exhaled noisily. "You don't have to."

"I want to. Danica, did you ever hear your grandfather mention a man named Rade Stanich?"

"No," she said flatly.

"Or Nena Stanich? They weren't friends of the family?"

She shook her head. "Why?"

I told her about Zdrale's immigration documents.

"Milan, I wasn't even born yet!" She sounded exasperated.

"I know," I said. "I'm just asking."

"Well then, the answer is no, I never heard of them."

"Do you suppose your mother has?"

Her shoulders lifted and fell. "You'd have to ask her."

"Would you?" I said. "Ask her?"

"Now?"

I nodded. She glanced at her watch and shrugged. Then she got up from her chair, frowning, and went into the kitchen, where a bright yellow cordless phone rested on the counter. She picked it up, extended the antenna, and punched out seven numbers.

"What was that name again?" she called out to me.

"Stanich," I said, and then spelled it. "Rade Stanich and his wife Nena."

"Stanich," she repeated. She listened for a moment and then said, "Mama?" Another pause, and then she rattled off several sentences in Serbo-Croatian. I did pick up the names Rade and Nena Stanich, but that's all I could understand. The conversation lasted about three minutes, and then Danica hung up the phone and came back into the living room.

"Mama never heard of them either. Why don't you talk to them?"

"They've both been dead a long time," I said. "But it's possible your grandpa knew Stanich in the prison camp."

"I told you, he never talked about that. Never once. I suppose it was very painful for him to remember. If my mother hadn't told me about it, I never would have known what he did in the war. What does that have to do with anything, anyway?"

"I'm looking for a motive. If it wasn't a drug deal—and I'm as positive as you are that it wasn't—there had to be a reason for your grandfather's dying that way."

"Random violence," she said. "Crime in the streets."

"That's too easy. There's no reason I've been able to find that your grandfather would be in the neighborhood where he was killed. So I'm figuring that somebody brought him there."

She sat on the arm of the love seat. "You think it had something to do with the war?"

I nodded. "Or with that camp."

"Thousands of people went through that camp."

"Right. But only a few survived. Your grandfather was one, and Rade Stanich was another."

"That was such a long time ago, Milan."

"A war is always a huge event in the lives of everyone involved," I said. "And prison camp even more so. A trauma like that can breed hatred, and hatred lasts a long time."

"Not Grandpa, believe me. He didn't want to hear about it. It just didn't interest him. He didn't belong to any Serbian clubs or organizations, he had no axes to grind, no agenda. He never voted in his life. I never knew him to pick up a newspaper, not even for the sports results. When the Serbs started fighting for independence last year he probably wasn't even aware of it."

"But he hung out with other Serbs, including when he went on his little trips."

"Old men, all of them. I doubt they traded war stories. He didn't have very good English, he never bothered to learn, and I suppose it was a comfort to him to be able to talk to people in his own tongue. A little peace, that's all he ever wanted. He was a simple, uncomplicated man. He came to Cleveland after the war and he worked at his job and took care of his family. He minded his own business."

I tried to smile but I could feel it freezing on my face.

"The unspoken end to that sentence is, I think, that I should go and do likewise."

There was a light sheen of perspiration on her forehead, and she pushed a stray lock of hair back from her eyes. "Milan, you've been wonderful, and I'm really very grateful to you. But it's time now to put this behind us. It's been terrible for Mama and me."

"And for Walter," I said.

She waited just a beat, like a glitch on a videotape. "And Walter too, certainly."

The phone rang. She threw me an apologetic look and went into the kitchen to answer it.

"Hello," she said, and then "oh, hi," her voice becoming softer, more melodious, more intimate. Almost a purr. "Hang on a minute."

She came out into the living room holding the telephone, her hand over the mouthpiece. "Milan, will you excuse me for just a second?"

"Sure."

She took the phone upstairs with her, and I heard a door close.

I wondered who she was talking to. Whoever it might be was treated to a more flirtatious tone of voice than Danica's mother had been. I sat there for a time, feeling intrusive and out of place, and finally I stood up and wandered around for lack of anything else to do, looking at the pictures on the wall, small floral prints in inexpensive frames. I scanned the titles in the bookcase, and found Judith Krantz, Susan Isaacs and Jean M. Auel represented, as well as several books on computers and business management, a volume of photographs of rural Ohio, Leo Buscaglia's *Loving*, and several of those pop psychology self-help tomes aimed at single women that have proliferated on the bookshelves in the past few years like rabbits on aphrodisiacs. Her carefully filed audiotapes were of the same ilk as the radio station she had playing, Billy Joel and Phil Collins and Wilson Phillips and George Benson. There were a few compact disks too; rapid-fire technology is rendering our entire existences obsolete.

I wished now I'd accepted her offer of a drink, just so I'd have something to do. You can spend just so much time reading book spines and tape labels before it becomes voyeurism. Could I infer from her reading material that she had trouble in her relationships with men or had a bad self-image that held her back in her career? Did her music of choice reflect a rather bland romantic bent, without fire or passion, or did it mean she simply bought the pop stuff everyone else was buying and had no firm tastes of her own? The easy conclusions were making me uncomfortable, so I went back to sit on the love seat and wait for her.

After about five minutes she came down the stairs; I noticed she hadn't brought the phone with her. Her cheeks were flushed and her eyes were shining; she seemed to have shed five years or so up on the second floor.

"Sorry," she said with a toss of her hair. "I'm going to have to cut this short now."

It must have been quite a phone call. "That's okay, I was just about through anyway." I got to my feet awkwardly.

"I didn't mean to be snappy with you just now, Milan. I want to put this behind me. What happened is too horrible to think about, so I think the best thing to do is just put it out of my mind."

"If that's what you want."

"It is, and I know it's what my mother wants too. We're simple people. We can't deal with it right now."

I nodded, but I wasn't going to put it out of my mind. I was in too far to quit now; that's just the way I am. Call it stubborn, or call it protecting what had become an emotional investment, but I was in the Bogdan Zdrale case until it was closed, one way or the other.

"I just don't want to talk about—bad things anymore," she said, walking me to the front door. "But that doesn't mean I want you out of my life. Not at all. You've been a good friend—more than a good friend. I hope you'll call me sometime."

"I will," I said.

"Promise?"

"Promise."

I leaned down to kiss her cheek. She turned her face to mine, put her hand on the back of my head, knotted her fingers in my hair, and pulled me toward her, taking my lower lip between her teeth and running her tongue over it while she nipped, mashing her pelvis into mine. I was too shocked to kiss back. She finally turned me loose, and I straightened up, feeling flustered and dumb.

"Please call," she said, her mouth slack and sensuous. "I mean it, Milan."

I guess she did.

And then I was out on the sidewalk again, disturbed in more ways than one. I was having trouble figuring out Danica and her mixed messages.

And I was also wondering why if Rade and Nena Stanich had cared enough about Bogdan Zdrale to sponsor his immigration to the United States and even possibly pay his way, their family and his had never even heard of each other.

Sixteen

It was seven o'clock in the morning, with the temperature around fifty and a gray drizzle washing away the snows of the past few days, which would make walking and driving a little easier but had a deleterious effect on the disposition. It probably isn't meteorologically accurate, but emotionally a sunny day of twenty degrees is a lot warmer than a wet gray day of fifty.

The damp chill penetrated the metal womb of my car. I'd heard on TV that when you're cold you're supposed to relax your shoulders instead of hunching them up as most people do, and I tried it. It didn't work. I wrapped my fingers around a cardboard cup of coffee purchased at the local convenience store along with a Super Lotto ticket for the Wednesday evening drawing. I was hoping the ticket was more of a winner than the coffee, but I needed it for warmth while I sat waiting in front of the residence of James Dosti, Senior. He lived in upper-middle-class comfort in a pleasant-looking ivy-covered Tudor with a twin gabled roof and leaded windows in the community of Seven Hills, a suburb a few miles south of downtown.

It wasn't the lavishly lawned, fortresslike gangster compound that you've seen in Francis Ford Coppola movies, but a nice, moderately expensive house built atop a rise with a gently sloping lawn and a paved driveway, not as elegant as crushed oyster shell but a lot easier to shovel on snowy days.

There were no hard-looking guys in bad suits strolling the grounds with one hand conspicuously in their jacket pockets, no armored limos with dark windows, and the only alarm system was a fairly simple residential model that could be purchased for under two thousand dollars, not much different than the kind a business executive or restaurant owner or an orthodontist might have protecting his home from burglars. No snarling attack dogs, no surveillance video cameras endlessly sweeping back and forth, no electric-eye beams. Leave that sort of ostentation to the crime bosses of New York and Los Angeles and Las Vegas; it just isn't Cleveland's style, even among the wise guys.

Then again, Jimmy Sweets was not Don Vito Corleone. He wasn't even Giancarlo D'Allessandro, when you come right down to it. He was just an opportunistic, cigar-smoking Italian leg buster with a good head for business who happened to be well connected. He liked palling around with big boys like his cousins D'Allessandro and Victor Gaimari; slurping pasta with them in their favorite restaurants made him feel important and protected, like part of the family. And while he kept hitters like Chooch and his buddy around the business office just in case of emergency, he wasn't nearly high enough on the outfit's depth chart to rate twenty-four-hour guards and fancy surveillance cameras outside his house.

The lack of heavy security enabled me to park just down the street from his driveway without attracting his attention. Even so, I knew I was on borrowed time; in an affluent area like this one in Seven Hills a low-priced car like mine can't park on the street with its driver on board for too long without making somebody curious.

Quite a few of the householders were already leaving for work, early for people who clocked in at eight thirty or nine. From the general tone of the neighborhood I got the idea that lots of them were small business entrepreneurs, very comfortable without being rich. In any case the big American-made sedans kept coming every few minutes, which at least gave

220

me something to look at besides the still facade of Jimmy Sweets's house.

I already had plenty to think about. Bogdan Zdrale and his connection with the long-dead Rade and Nena Stanich, if that meant anything at all, Ed Stahl and his troubles with Sweets, Walter Paich and his domestic difficulties, and Danica sucking on my lower lip and doing bumps and grinds against me even as she shooed me out the door to prepare for the arrival, I assumed, of a lover.

I knew I was biting off too much—and not getting paid for any of it. What Danica had said was true, that her grandfather's death was now a police matter and none of my business anymore. But once I start something, I can't rest well until it's finished. I need closure. Loose ends make me nervous; they're also damaging to my self-confidence and self-esteem. I couldn't let any of it go just yet, not until I got a lot of answers to questions that were eating a hole in my gut.

Ed Stahl's troubles with James Dosti and his crew had nothing to do with me either, except that Ed was my friend, and for friends I always go the limit if I have to. If it meant getting the guys with the bent noses mad at me, so be it— they've been mad at me so often in recent years it's becoming a way of life.

Except now it was more personal than that; I don't like being followed in the middle of the night and I don't like inept attempts to run me over in the snow, and I'd come here to Dosti's home, away from Chooch and his other hard-asses at the office, to tell him so.

At about seven twenty the white garage door at the top of the driveway went up like the front curtain in a Broadway theater, and a cream-colored Cadillac Sedan de Ville glided out, its windshield wipers on slow to combat the relentless drizzle. It paused at the top of the rise for about a minute as the driver hit his remote button, closing the garage door behind him. I couldn't identify him from my vantage point, but I could make an educated guess.

I put the coffee cup into the plastic drink holder over the

hump of the drive shaft in my car and turned the ignition key, and the car coughed into life.

When the Caddy started down the driveway I pulled up to block the exit with my car. Now I could see that it was indeed Dosti senior behind the wheel, and when he saw my car in his way his face contorted in rage. He stomped his brakes and honked at me, leaning on the horn. There's nothing as angry-sounding or shocking to the nervous system as a car horn on a quiet street.

Leaving my motor running, I got out and went around to the driver's side of his car. He recognized me, and his face went one shade purpler under his sunlamp tan. He pushed a button and his window slid noiselessly open.

"Either you're the stupidest fuck that God ever put on this earth," he said, "or you got the balls of a brass monkey. Get your car out of the way."

"In a minute, Mr. Dosti. There are things we need to discuss."

"Huh?"

"We have to talk."

"I got nothing to say to you."

"Then I'll talk and you listen."

He was so angry his eyes almost disappeared into deep pockets of wrinkles. "You can't block the drive like that."

"Call a cop," I said.

The muscles at the hinge in his jaw bunched up like a clump of grapes, and his right hand moved to the lapel of his coat. I let my own coat fall open to show him the butt of my .357 in the holster under my arm. "Don't be dumb, Mr. Dosti. We're both packing, so let's not do a Dodge City number trying to prove who's tougher."

He started to get out of the car, but I blocked the door with the bulk of my body and pushed it shut again, virtually trapping him inside. He looked around wildly as if he didn't believe it was happening to him—to Jimmy Sweets.

"You're toast, Jacovich," he gargled finally, gripping the wheel with both hands, his knuckles turning white. "You're ancient history, you understand me?"

222

"That's what I want to talk to you about."

Uncertainty flickered across his mean, piggy face. "Huh?" he said stupidly.

"What's the idea of having me followed?"

"Huh?" It seemed to be his favorite word.

"The guy in the tan Ford night before last who tried to run me down."

"I don't know nothing about it."

"Sure. You're just an innocent lamb."

"You're nuts. Nobody was trying to run you over."

"I'm not that nuts Mr. Dosti—I know when I'm being followed. After our conversation at your office I went home, and he was waiting near where I live. I spotted him and tried to evade him, but he chased me around Cleveland Heights for about five minutes and then when I got out he tried to run me down, and if the street hadn't been so icy he would have. Don't you think you're overreacting just a little bit?"

He stared straight ahead for a second, composing his thoughts, and then he glared up at me. "You got the wrong man, Jacovich. If I wanted you iced, you'd be iced by now, and I wouldn't send no asshole in no tan Ford that'd miss. And you can tell that to your newspaper buddy, too. When I want him, he's mine—and he will be unless he shuts his fucking mouth."

"You trying to tell me you didn't send Chooch and his buddy after me when I came to see you the other day?"

He tossed his head like a pouty six-year-old. "Those two? Sure I did. But I told 'em to just mess you around some, to let you know it ain't healthy to bother me anymore. They wasn't gonna kill you, f'crissake. Whattaya think, right in my own parking lot? You dumb-ass."

I closed my coat and flipped up my collar to keep the rain from going down my neck. What he was saying made sense. "And you had nothing to do with the guy in the Ford?"

He took a cigar from a leather pouch on the seat beside him and stuck it between his teeth. They probably went for three dollars apiece. "That's not my style," he said.

I stood there with my hands in my pockets, feeling

dumber than I had in a long while. Jimmy Sweets was a minor league Mafioso, and I had no doubt he was behind the threats to Ed Stahl. But for some peculiar reason I believed him about the guy in the tan Ford.

"If he wasn't yours, whose was he?"

He lit the cigar, and clouds of malodorous blue smoke drifted out the car window. "How'm I s'posed to know who else you've pissed off? A slob like you, Jacovich, he makes enemies wherever he goes. I can name ten guys'd like to put a lily in your hand—and you don't haul your ass out of here in two seconds, I might have you done just for the fun of it. But whoever it was tried to run you down, he didn't come from me, all right?" His voice rose to a hoarse roar, like a lion a mile upriver from a hunting camp. "Now move your fuckin' piece of shit outta my driveway!"

Lazo Samarzic blew on his hands to warm them, even though we were inside the big building at the West Side Market. He'd been out in the produce shed since first light with his wife and his brother Mirko, listening to the rain, which had gotten steadily harder, punish the roof over his head, and even though he wasn't particularly glad to see me I think he was grateful for the respite. Rain doesn't keep the regular shoppers away from the market, and he'd been busy.

"Rade Stanich," he repeated. "Never heard of him. Why, I'm supposed to?"

"He knew Zdrale."

His thick eyebrows danced. "Lotsa people knew Zdrale that don't know me and vice-a-verse." He looked around at the milling customers as if all of them might have known Zdrale.

"And Stanich's name doesn't mean anything to you?"

He thought about it again for a while, then shook his head resolutely. "This may be a surprise to you, but there's about a million people come from Serbia that I never met. I'm just a guy trying to make a living, trying to help out people from my homeland." He gave me a sly wink. "Like you. You help people too."

"When I get paid for it."

"That's what I don't get," he said. "You said you're not making money for this no more. What are you bothering about it for?"

"Call it curiosity," I said. We were standing against a wall drinking black coffee from one of the concessionaires at the market. It tasted of the cardboard cup it came in, but it was still better than the coffee they served at the convenience store near Jimmy Dosti's house.

"Curiosity can get you hurt."

"Is that a threat?"

I didn't think that was particularly funny, but it got a laugh out of him. "You hang around with the wrong kind of people, Jacovich. That was a whatchamacallit, a friendly piece of advice, not a warning. Nobody's threatening you here. Look, I was born just after the war started. By the time I knew enough not to crap in my pants, it was all over. I don't remember any of that shit, you understand? The war, prison camps, the killing—it had nothing to do with me."

"You're a Serb. It had everything to do with you. You must have had family . . . "

The lines at the corners of his mouth deepened. "My family," he said pointedly, "is my wife. My daughters. My brother. My friends. Everything else is for the history books."

"You're a pretty big man in the Serbian community here. They come to you for help and advice—that tells me something about you."

He finished his coffee and pushed himself away from the wall, crumpling up the cup. "All you need to know about me is that I knew Bogdan Zdrale to say hello to and that's all," he said, throwing the cup into a trash receptacle. "A nice old man, kind of quiet, I don't think we had what you'd call a conversation twice in our lives."

"When he was missing everyone was after me to find him," I said. "Now that he's dead, people are stonewalling. What's going on?"

"Stonewalling." He shook his head sadly. "That's a bullshit word—where you hear it, on the six o'clock news? The world's a hard place," he said. "Hard even to survive. Every day is a fight, a struggle up the hill pushing the rock. So that's why we have funerals. We need them. Gives a chance for us to say good-bye to the dead, do our tears. And then we have to take care of the living. The living are more important, no?"

"So as long as Zdrale's dead anyway, it's not important who killed him? Is that it?"

He put an arm around my shoulders; there was the clean smell of fresh produce about him, mixed with cigarette smoke and his own masculine odor. He spoke to me softly and slowly, as though I were a not very bright child. "Picture it, Jacovich. An old man, sometimes a little bit out of it in the mental department. Driving around, he gets confused. He winds up in a neighborhood nobody in their right mind would go into. He's lost, he gets out of the car and walks around on the streets until some animal out there finds him, robs him, and kills him. It's that easy. Sad, yes, but easy. Now you come. You come around and ask people questions, make people feel bad, keep the bad memories alive. Walter and Danica and their mother, they need a little peace, a little time to grieve alone and then to heal. I think you should back away. You seem like too smart a guy to keep pissing into the wind."

"I don't see it that way."

He looked at me levelly for a moment with flat lizard eyes. I couldn't tell what he was thinking, but it was a challenge. We did the staring contest for quite a while, and then he started moving away, back toward the produce shed where he'd left his family to tend their business. "That's too bad, then," he said.

I watched him go, a big strong man walking with a heavy rolling gait, confident and aggressive. The shiver that went through me had nothing to do with the cold, rainy day.

When I got back home I shuffled through my mail, but there was nothing interesting. A few bills and a few ads, as impersonal as the message in a fortune cookie. Letter writing is an art lost to this generation of Americans—unless you count Ed McMahon's cheerful bimonthly epistles.

I called Ed Stahl at the paper to report on my talk with Jimmy Sweets, but he was busy running down another story and sounded cranky, angry with me for disturbing him. Ed's reputation for toughness and irascibility was on the line, and I think he wanted everyone to believe the whole situation with the Dostis wasn't bothering him much—at least that was the public face he put on it. Of course no one else had seen him huddled in the dark with a murdered rat in his garbage can and a loaded gun in his pocket.

I heated up a can of black bean soup for lunch, put in a dollop of sour cream and sprinkled it with dill weed, and ate it with several slices of buttered pumpernickel bread, washing it down with a Diet Pepsi—it was a bit too early in the day for a beer. After I washed the dishes and the soup pan I transferred the notes I'd taken in the past few days from my pocket notebook to three-by-five cards and moved them around on the top of my desk for a while, until finally something made sense. There was a note on one of the cards that was something I should have checked out right away but hadn't. At the time it hadn't seemed important, but now it was jumping up off the card at me. Either I was doing too many things at once or I was getting careless in my old age. I picked up the phone and punched the ten-digit number.

The deputy chief of police of West Allis, Wisconsin, was named Phil Miller, and his voice coming through the line sounded as if he had a severe cold. I introduced myself, used Mark Meglich's name as a reference, and asked him some questions.

"I appreciate your taking the time to talk to me, Chief," I said.

"Hell, it keeps me in the office and out of the weather. What's it like out in Cleveland? For three days we've been up to our asses in snow here, and it's not showing any signs of quitting, either."

"Cold and rainy."

"That's not as bad as three feet of snow," he said, snorting to clear his sinuses. I think he was perversely pleased that his weather was worse than ours. "Snow you got to shovel. I shoveled off my driveway this morning, and now I think I'm coming down with the flu."

"Chief Miller, about the Malinkovich shooting . . ."

"Yeah," he said. "Sure I remember it—four years ago, in the summertime. This is a little town; we don't have many homicides here, so it's not something I'm likely to forget. Especially like that, shot in the head and dumped in the park like a sack of garbage."

"Shot in the head?"

"One time. Clean as a whistle."

That had resonance. But then again, if you're going to shoot somebody, one bullet in the head is the best way to go—economical and efficient. It certainly wasn't any proof that the two crimes were linked. I said, "Lieutenant Meglich mentioned that one of your investigators talked to a guy from Cleveland by the name of Lazo Samarzic."

"We talked to a lot of people. Like I say, this is a pretty quiet town most of the time. Murder makes us nervous. Yeah, Samarzic. He'd been here to visit Malinkovich about a week before the shooting, according to Malinkovich's son, so we checked him out. Sent one of our guys all the way to Cleveland. Of course, we cleared it with your police department first—didn't want to step on any toes. Christ, try justifying the expenses for that kind of trip when the city council's crawling all over us about the budget!"

"How about Samarzic? Obviously he checked out or you would have taken further action."

"Right. I don't think there was anything to it. Mele Malinkovich had a farm just inside the city limits. He ran a few dairy cows—if you've got a couple acres everybody in Wisconsin runs cows. You'd think it was a state law, you know? But mainly it was a truck farm, sweet corn, for the most part, and Samarzic's a greengrocer, so it made a certain amount of sense. It was a business trip, that's all. Besides, Samarzic had alibis up the wazoo, and we couldn't break them."

"You haven't closed the case yet?"

"No, we haven't closed the case yet," he said, an edge to his voice. "It's a homicide—they're like a Seven-Eleven store, they never close. We don't have the facilities of a big-city department here. We asked the Milwaukee PD for some help, but it wasn't their jurisdiction, and they frankly weren't all that interested, so they sent one of their guys out on temporary duty, and he dicked around for a week or so and then kind of faded away. And since it was four years ago, it's not exactly one of our heavy priorities, if you know what I mean."

"Tell me about Malinkovich."

"I don't remember that much about him. Like I said, he was a small farmer. Seventy years old or thereabouts. I can look it up for you exactly if it's important."

"I don't think so. What else?"

"He was a widower, wife'd been dead about eight years. Two grown sons; one worked the farm with him, the other one's a foreman in a meat-packing plant in Milwaukee."

"The sons inherit?"

"Yeah, but BFD. The farm kept them in groceries but not a hell of a lot more, if you're thinking he was killed for an inheritance."

"Malinkovich have enemies?"

"Everybody has enemies someplace, unless they're a little plaster saint. Wait a second." He paused to blow his nose, twice. The first blow was violent, the second more restrained. "Sorry," he gasped. "God, I hate winter. You ever hear anything so crazy as a guy who hates cold weather living in Wisconsin? I'm gonna retire to Southern California, if I could ever get used to Monday Night Football starting at six o'-clock."

I chuckled. I didn't think it was funny but the laugh was expected of me, and I wanted him to keep talking.

"You remember anything else about the Malinkovich case," I asked.

"Now wait, there was one thing," Miller said. I could almost hear the wheels turning. "We tried to run it down, but we kept smacking into the bricks at every turn, so finally we decided it wasn't worth pursuing."

"What was it?"

"Well, I've got no hard evidence," Miller said. "I mean, he didn't have a party card or anything, no swastikas flying from the front porch. But from what I could find out, from the people he hung out with and the newspapers he subscribed to and the reading material he had around his house, Malinkovich seemed to be some sort of Nazi."

SEVENTEEN

I sat on a high stool at my kitchen counter, drinking cinnamon-laced coffee from a white mug festooned with little red hearts. I call it my kitchen out of force of habit, but it isn't really mine anymore. I continue to think of it as such, though, maybe because I still make the mortgage payments on the house it's in, which is still listed in the telephone directory under my name, and my two sons still live there. It hasn't really changed much since I moved out. The same delicious smells of stew cooking, the same light green curtains with the white dots, the same Sparkletts dispenser in the corner, the same collection of wild-looking potted plants. Some of the plants were taller and more lush, and there were new notes and photos of the boys, who were also taller, affixed to the refrigerator door with orange magnets that looked like little Cleveland Browns helmets.

Lila Coso Jacovich, my former wife, had changed more than the kitchen. She'd lost some weight, for one thing, and it made her seem more fragile, almost brittle. Her hair had always been shoulder length, softening the sharp planes of her face, but now she wore it shorter and, I suppose, more in current fashion. But the pixie cut aged her, emphasizing the lines around her pretty mouth. It seemed to me she didn't smile as much as she used to, although that could've been my imagination—or maybe she wasn't smiling because my being there in the house we had lived in together and that now she shared with Joe Bradac always caused her some degree of discomfort.

"I don't really know what you want me to tell you, Milan," she was saying in the put-upon tone that I'd grown to know so well during the waning years of our marriage. "Just because I'm Serbian doesn't make me an expert on the culture. You know my parents never bothered with it that much."

"Yes, but your uncle Toma does."

"Maybe you should talk to him, then."

"Lila, I'm not going to stay long, if that's what's worrying you."

Her eyes flashed like the blue steel of a handgun. "I'm not *worried*," she said, laying into the word like a quiz show host trying to help out a stupid contestant. "I just have things to do."

"All right, I'll make it quick. Are there any militant Serbian organizations here in Cleveland?"

"Militant about what, for heaven's sake?"

"I don't know," I said. "Let's say about crimes against Serbs and Serbia."

She put the palms of her hands at the small of her back, a sure indication she was becoming exasperated with me. "What kind of crimes, Milan? Honestly, when you get mysterious like this I don't know what you're—"

"Something that might have happened during the war, or maybe afterward, during the Tito years."

"That's ancient history," she said.

"Not to everybody."

"Well, naturally there are people who aren't going to forget things like that."

"The Chetniks?"

She frowned, her brows knitting together over the bridge of her nose. "The Chetniks? I haven't heard of them being around. Not for fifty years. And not in Cleveland. But the church declared 1991 as the fiftieth anniversary of what they called the Year of the Genocide, so there are lots of people who remember. And are still angry." She allowed herself a small smile, but it turned out fake, like laughing at the minister's corny joke. "You know us Serbs—we can be pretty feisty sometimes."

"I'm not talking about feisty, Lila, I'm talking about murder."

Some of the color left her cheeks, and she put her hand to her mouth and chewed absently on a red-tipped fingernail. The polish Lila had usually worn when we were married had been more of a muddy brownish-pink that I'd frankly never liked. That I never told her I didn't care for her shade of nail polish was pretty much the way the entire marriage had gone toward the end. Two people who couldn't or wouldn't communicate. The red polish was another sign of change.

"I certainly don't know anything about that, Milan. Are you talking about Walter Paich's grandfather getting killed? Is this where all these questions are leading?"

"Joe tell you about that?"

"He said Walter asked him for help when his grandfather was still only missing, and that he'd recommended you."

I stood up, putting my coffee down on the pink-tiled counter a little harder than I'd meant to. *Walter* asked *Joe* for help? I opened my mouth and then shut it again—and not a moment too soon.

"Did I say something wrong?" Lila asked.

I recovered nicely, I hoped. "No, no."

"My God, you nearly jumped out of your skin." She laughed nervously, then turned around and busied herself at the sink, stacking dishes. "Since they found the old man, I'd think your part of it would be finished."

"That seems to be the popular misconception," I said. "Lila, do you know Lazo Samarzic?"

"Not personally, no."

"But you know who he is?"

She crossed her arms across her breasts. "Everybody knows Mr. Samarzic."

Mr. Samarzic. There are people in this world whose very essence demands a title before their names, even when they're not in the room. Imagine saying, "Hiya, Hank," to

Henry Kissinger. Or "How's it shakin', Sandy?" to Sandra Day O'Connor.

"How well do you know Mr. Samarzic?"

"Well, I certainly know who he is. I've nodded to him across the room a few times. He's kind of the mayor-at-large of the Serbian community on the east side."

"Who elected him?"

"Nobody elected him! Some people are just natural-born leaders, and Mr. Samarzic just found himself as a kind of father figure to a lot of the old-country Serbs here, that's all. People come to him with their troubles, with their problems, and he helps to solve them if he can."

"What kind of problems?"

"All kinds," she said, leaning against the counter and looking down her nose at me in that way she has. "He's a kind, caring man. If you lose your job he'll try to get it back for you, or help you get another one, or make sure your family has enough to eat until you find one yourself. If you get in trouble with the law he tries to get you a good lawyer, or raises your bail. If you have an argument with your neighbor or somebody's hassling you—"

"Hassling you about what?"

"Oh, all sorts of things!" she said, losing patience. "You know exactly what I'm talking about. Why do you always make such a big deal—?"

"And what does he get out of all this?" I said. "Your Mr. Samarzic?"

The question seemed to surprise her. "Well, he—nothing, I guess. I mean, nobody pays him money. He gets respect."

"But you don't know him personally?"

"I said no, Milan. I just see him and hear about him, that's all. My goodness!"

"You suppose Joe knows him?"

At the mention of her consort's name her face became a blank mask, devoid of expression, which I knew from long experience indicates gathering thunderheads on the emotional horizon. "I wouldn't know," she said. She sneaked a look at the clock above the sink. It was a few minutes before four.

"I'm going," I said, anxious to get out of her way before the storm broke. I went out of the kitchen and through the dining room to the front door, Lila following. "Tell the boys I'll see them Sunday. And tell Joe—"

Her eyes narrowed dangerously. "What?" she snapped.

"Nothing," I said. "I'll tell him myself."

I went down the front walk and started up the street to my car. I certainly would tell Joe Bradac a few things. *Walter* asked *him!* The lying, wimpy little . . .

I stopped as I saw my younger son Stephen coming down the block with two other boys, swinging his backpack from one hand.

I love both my sons very much. Milan Junior is halfway to being an adult now, with his own concerns, his own agenda. I am very proud of his scholastic and athletic accomplishments, proud of the young man he is becoming, and being with him fills me up with love and warm feeling. But when I see Stephen, a little part of the world glows with his inner sunshine. Stephen will still cuddle and giggle, still wrestle on the floor with me. He's still my little boy.

He glanced up and saw me and broke into a broad smile, and he gathered his feet under him as if to start running toward me. Then he realized where he was and who he was with and he stumbled slightly as his whole body stiffened and his manner changed. He looked quickly away from me, and his walk down the street became more loose-limbed and studiedly casual, the ultimate in ten-year-old cool.

The three of them were almost past me.

"Hi, Stephen," I said.

He barely glanced at me. "Hey, old pal," he answered out of the side of his mouth, burlesquing it, a W. C. Fields voice with a Charlie Chaplin walk. "Whattaya say there, old buddy, old pal?" And he gave his backpack a twirl.

I got the picture. Guys his age don't kiss their fathers in front of the other members of their tribe—they barely acknowledge that they *have* fathers, as if they were the only ones so encumbered and it was somehow shameful and embarrassing. It didn't make his rejection of me any easier to take, but I understood it, the need to keep face. I had probably done the same thing to my own father. And it probably hurt him, too, only now he wasn't around anymore for me to make it up to him. Sometimes I think the twentieth century is the most difficult and painful era man has had to survive since the days of the Black Plague.

I watched the pack of boy-children go by, whispering to themselves, the other two dark-haired and gangly, Stephen blond and compact. When they were about twenty feet beyond me Stephen turned his head very quickly to look back at me. A small smile curled up the corner of his rosebud mouth, and with his free hand still down at his side he gave me a surreptitious little wave, being careful that his friends didn't see it. I grinned back, returned the wave, and got into my car.

The sky, dark with the rain clouds, was rapidly losing whatever of the day's light was left as I pulled into the lot of police headquarters at Twenty-first and Payne. Every time I look at the building I remember signing in on the roster, and I feel as though I'm wearing a coat that's too heavy around the shoulders. I have little nostalgia for the years I spent there in a blue uniform. It's not that police work hadn't appealed to me; despite the many frustrations of watching the guilty beat the judicial system, of seeing a perp you'd spent a month setting up and running down walk out of court on a technicality with a wave and a smirk, there were satisfactions, too. It was good knowing that you were contributing something to society, to keeping shaky order in a world that is increasingly out of kilter. It was the internal politics that finally got to me, the apple-polishing, ass-kissing crap that had nothing to do with keeping the streets safe and the bad guys at bay.

I'd left the department and gone civilian for several reasons, one being that I don't like bosses. All my life I've had to do things the way somebody else wanted—my father, my football coaches, the officers in the army, and finally my supervisors on the force. I figured it was time for me to start doing things my own way for a change, so I'd handed in my badge and opened Milan Security, a one-man industrial security operation, and reveled in the luxury of calling my own shots. I make a decent living now, but at the startup being a small-business owner had cost me some money and some financial security, and in the end it had cost me a marriage, too.

It took me a while to get over that. My book says you get married forever, raise your kids, enjoy your grandchildren, and know that there is one person in your life—your mate, your other half—whose unswerving priority is your happiness and well-being, just as hers is yours. The fact that my marriage had not exactly been a comfort to me in its last sputtering years didn't matter; right was right, and I was willing to make adjustments. Lila was not. So it was she who finally pulled the plug, and in retrospect I suppose she was the smart one. Losing her hurt me for a long time; losing the daily companionship of my children and the chance to watch them grow still hurts, every minute of every day.

Marko Meglich wasn't in his office, so I used the free time to duck into the men's room on the second floor. Spanish John Hanratty was standing in front of the sink, carefully combing his hair before the mirror as if getting ready for an appearance on *Top Cops*. If John spent as much time being a good cop as he did on his personal appearance, he'd probably have made lieutenant years ago.

"Milan, how ya doin'?" he said, his toothpaste-ad smile brightening up the dimly lit washroom. "You find out who did Danica's granpappy yet? I saw her last night, and I can tell she's still bothered by it."

I just looked at him, and then moved to one of the urinals. "Funny subject for pillow talk."

"This was this morning." I didn't really see where that was deserving of an answer, so I didn't make any. "Hey, come on," John said, "don't be like that. She's a nice kid and we have fun together. We're both single, consenting adults, right? Lighten up."

"This is about as light as I get, John."

"You're just bummed out because you had eyes in that direction yourself, right? The old green-eyed monster. Listen, you shoulda said something. I woulda passed."

"The last time you passed was in Pop Warner Football when you were fifteen years old." I flushed the urinal and went past him to the sink to wash my hands.

He grinned, causing his dimples to show. It was supposed to be charmingly roguish, but if so it was lost on me. At least John was no hypocrite—he enjoyed his reputation as a womanizer, even flaunted it. I guess the rewards he got from his activities outweighed the scorn he surely received from most people. In this age of sexual caution and raised male consciousness Spanish John was the rakehell, daredevil dicer-with-death. All he needed to complete the picture was a flowing white scarf and a single-engine plane that didn't look like it could carry the mail over the mountains.

"Hey," he said, "don't be so goddamn judgmental, all right? Listen, we never know what's gonna happen to us, Milan, so we take things when and where we find them. I could get hit by a truck tomorrow. Look at the leg here. That redneck aims a couple inches higher and I'm singing soprano. Life is meant to be lived."

He moved closer so I could see him in the mirror next to me. He lowered his voice, even though there was no one else in the men's room. "Danica's quite a girl. Got a few head problems, but that just makes it more interesting."

As usual, the liquid soap dispenser was empty. "What kind of problems?"

He came as close to frowning as I'd ever seen him. "She's a little screwed up. I never met anybody that needed approval so bad. Male approval, I mean. She soaks it up like a sponge. She's a very insecure little girl under all the professional success and all." He winked at me. "But it makes her work that much harder to be loved, if you get my drift. And I'm sure not gonna complain about that."

I turned and flicked the excess water from my hands into his face. It was the only way I could think of to express the disdain I was feeling. He blinked a few times, startled, and moved back out of range. "Hey, come on, man. I mean, I really like the chick."

"So much that you discuss how good she is in bed in a men's toilet," I said.

He stuck his jaw out, on the defensive. "Christ, Milan, you're such a bluenose. No wonder you quit the force—a bunch of guys scratching their balls and saying hell and damn all the time. It must've made you crazy."

I took a few paper towels out of the dispenser and dried my hands with them. I was going to wad them up and throw them at him when I finished, but they would have just wound up on the floor and become the janitor's problem.

"We're not talking about the Blessed Mother," John went on. "I mean, she's been across the street a couple of times."

"Save it for the locker room, John, all right? I'm really not that interested," I said, disposing of the towels and starting for the door.

"Hey, don't worry about soiling her reputation or anything," he called after me, sensing that he'd gone too far, that he had ruptured the fabric of our friendship without even knowing it. "She's been with a lots of guys, she admitted that to me the first night. Her own brother, for Christ's sake."

I somehow managed to miss the door handle, and I just stood there with my back to John, my hand groping, trying to force my lunch back down my throat.

"I mean, he used to force her and everything, when she was about twelve, but I guess she must've liked it because since then it's been all her own idea. Milan? Hey, Milan, where you going?"

I stood in the parking lot resting my hip against the fender of my Sunbird, the fortress-like headquarters building dark and threatening against the sky. The icy mist felt good on my flushed face, but it wasn't doing much for the constricted feeling in my throat. I felt like I'd swallowed a gym sock. Incest was something you read about in the paper that happens out there someplace, not close to you. It certainly explained Danica's driving ambition to succeed in business, her flirtatiousness with me and Spanish John and even with Joe Bradac, her desperate need for attention from men, to prove her worth and keep proving it. Every case of her sort that I've read about has stressed the terrible blow to a child's self-esteem that comes with sexual victimization. My heart ached for her.

And it was no wonder, I thought, that Walter Paich made my skin crawl every time I was near him, no wonder that his mother and sister did their best to pretend he didn't exist. I looked down and realized my fists were clenched and made a concentrated effort to relax them. It wasn't any of my business; as much as I wanted to charge over to Walter's house and pound him into the floor, I realized it would not only be inappropriate but probably wouldn't be appreciated by the maiden whose honor I would be avenging. Danica had probably stuffed all that down into the depths of her psyche, just the way she wanted to bury her grandfather's murder.

As for Spanish John, he was right. He and Danica were both unattached and adult enough to know what they were doing, and it wasn't anything worse than I'd done many times in my life. It had nothing to do with me. It would be a while, though, because of his big mouth, his inexcusable violation of Danica's privacy, before I'd be able to sit down at a poker table with him again.

I stood there filling my lungs with damp air until the blood stopped pounding in my head and I was able to relax a little and remember what I'd come for.

I went back inside and climbed the stairs to Marko Meglich's office. Wherever he'd been fifteen minutes earlier, he was back now, barking orders into the telephone. An electric heater made the small room more stuffy than toasty. He waved me into his visitor's chair.

I waited a few minutes until he had finished chewing out his subordinate—I assume it was a subordinate, or he wouldn't have been talking that way. He slammed down the phone and said, "You look like they dug you up three days ago."

"Nice to see you, too."

He held up a traffic-cop hand. "I hope you're not going to lay any shit on me today, Milan, because I don't need any right now. You better be here to tell me you've hooked up Nello Trinetti to the Zdrale case."

"I haven't even looked in that direction. Gaimari told me he didn't know anything about Bogdan Zdrale or why Trinetti's here, and I believe him."

"God damn it, I told you—"

"Listen," I said with some heat, "I'm the guy who left his buzzer on the desk and walked out of here years ago, remember? I don't work for you anymore. Don't talk to me like I'm the hired help."

He glared at me for a second, his cheeks flaming, and then he looked away and scrabbled nervously at his mustache with his fingers. He's only been wearing it for a few years and every once in a while he feels the need to check and see that it's still there under his nose. "Sorry," he said. "This's been a bitch kitty of a day." He jerked his head at the telephone. "A single mother in Tremont just beat her four-year-old kid to death with a broom handle for spilling his chocolate milk on the carpet. Jesus."

"I'm sorry too, Mark. It hasn't been one of my best days either."

He squared off some of the papers on his desk so that they lined up perfectly with the edge. Everybody knows you can't solve a homicide when your papers aren't straight. "In that case I have another little problem," he said. "I need another one—I don't have enough."

"What's your other little problem?"

"I don't like things I can't explain. And I don't like out-of-town shooters in my town. It makes me look bad, and that makes me nervous. And when I get nervous I get mean. If Trinetti didn't come to Cleveland to take out Bogdan Zdrale, what's he doing here?"

I shrugged. "Like I said, I don't carry a badge anymore."

"Don't remind me, damn you." He pulled a pack of

Camels from his top drawer and lit one. "So if you can't help me on Nello Trinetti, what do you want?"

"Maybe I *can* help you with Trinetti."

He leaned forward eagerly. "How?"

"I'm not sure yet. I've got an idea, though. But I want something in exchange."

He puffed angrily on his cigarette. "What?"

"Another favor."

His shoulders slumped. "What is it this time?"

I reached over and took a piece of paper from the memo pad on his desk and scribbled a name on it. "You think that pal of yours at immigration would be interested in your second-born child?"

EIGHTEEN

You can't park on the street downtown. Like all older cities of the East and Midwest, Cleveland was laid out before the modern era when everybody and his brother owns an automobile and drives it everywhere, and its streets are too narrow to accommodate both traffic and cars parked at the curb. As a result, I had to leave my car in the eight-story garage next to The Jesters and, miserable in the icy mist, conduct my little stakeout on the sidewalk across the street, walking up and down from one end of the block to the other. The neon lights of the restaurant looked cheery and inviting and warm, and I kept moving, less because of the temperature than to avoid attracting the attention of a patrolling cop who just might wonder why I was holding up the wall of an office building at one o'clock in the morning.

I'd taken a chance and stuck my head in the front door of the restaurant when I'd first arrived, to make sure Nello Trinetti was there. He didn't see me, but I saw him; he was at the same booth, tapping his fingers on the tablecloth in time with the piano player's inept Neil Diamond medley, his garish diamond ring catching the colored lights overhead and throwing them back. This time he was without Joey, which surprised me. Punks like Nello are like nuns—they rarely go out by themselves. He was talking to a woman who was neither Tammy nor Brandy. She sported a blond beehive and a form-hugging dress in a shiny rust color. I guess Nello had a favorite type. I decided to wait for them outside.

The piano player came out at about one fifteen with one of the cocktail waitresses. They both had the just-freed attitude of convicts on parole day; the piano player even stopped and took a deep hit of the cold night, as though he'd been breathing prison air for twenty years. Then they went quickly down the street, probably off to the kind of after-hours joint found in every cosmopolitan city where bartenders and musicians go to unwind after a long evening of dealing with drunks and losers who are down to their last ten dollars, sick and sullen with alcohol and enraged because they haven't scored, and who take it out on whoever's handy. Those who work in saloons earn their money.

Nello and his new friend emerged about ten minutes later, heading to the parking garage where I'd left my car. He was wearing a belted camel's hair coat about two sizes too big for him. It looked like it belonged to his father. She had a short leather jacket with a fake fur collar.

I strolled up the ramp about fifty feet behind them, trying to be unobtrusive, and stopped to conceal myself behind a concrete pillar as they reached a three-year-old white Plymouth Duster. She scribbled something on a cocktail napkin and handed it to him, explaining something to him in great detail, hand gestures and all. I supposed she was giving him directions to her place. Then she unlocked the car door and turned to give him a good-bye kiss. It was the kind of kiss usually reserved for private moments behind closed doors, all open mouths and tongues. He slipped one hand inside her jacket and massaged her buttocks with the other, squeezing them as if he were shopping for melons, and their bodies ground together for a few minutes while I shifted from one foot to the other trying to stay warm. Finally they broke apart, gasping for air, mouths wet and eyes shiny with lust. She leaned up and licked his ear, got into her car with a flash of stockinged thigh, backed out, and drove down the ramp past me. He watched her go and then headed farther up into the structure.

On the second level from the top he stopped at a blue Mercury Sable, which I assumed was a rental car, since I've never known any private party who actually owned one. I walked up behind him as he fished in his pants pocket for his keys.

"Hello, Nello."

He jumped, flattening himself against the car.

"Just leave your hand in your pocket there for a minute while we talk."

He relaxed when he saw who it was. I don't know who he was expecting, but at least he knew I wasn't a hired assassin from a rival crime family. I imagine it's tough for guys like Nello, jumping at shadows and searching the faces of strangers. Occupational hazard.

"Hey, rosy cheeks," he said, breathing relief. "You following me, huh?"

"That's right."

"You get off that way, spying on people? I bet you almost creamed your pants when I was feeling her up. You wanna come back to her place with me and watch while I put it to her?"

"I'll make a deal with you, Nello. You try not to piss me off too badly and I'll try not to mess up your pretty face."

He smirked, squaring his shoulders. "You talk pretty tough for a minimum-wage chump. Can you back it up?"

I held open my coat so he could see the piece. "How bad do you want to find out?"

He started to take his hand out of his pocket. "Watch the hand," I said.

He sighed and shoved it deeper into his pocket, jingling his loose change. The body language was casual, but his eyes snapped in fury. He wanted a piece of me, now, and so badly he could almost taste the blood. He leaned against the fender. "What's on your mind, rosy cheeks? You still trying to find out who snuffed the old guy? What was his name?"

"That's not important anymore."

"Make it snappy, then," he said. "I don't want that hot little cooze to cool off while I stand here beating my gums with you. I already blew fifteen bucks on her drinks."

"The last of the big spenders, huh?"

He dipped his head modestly, giving me a crooked grin. "Okay, how's this for snappy? Ed Stahl."

His face changed in a way it hadn't when I'd talked to him about Bogdan Zdrale, an almost imperceptible widening of the pupils of his eyes, and his tongue darted out to moisten his lips. "Who?"

"You're the one in a hurry to get laid, Nello, so let's not waste each other's time. I know Jimmy Sweets brought you to town because of what Ed Stahl wrote about him in the paper. I should have figured that out days ago, but I was too busy worrying about my client. Are you planning to kill him, or are you just supposed to scare him off?"

"What's it to you?"

"It's something to me; that's all you need to know."

"Jeez, first it's some old fart I never heard of, and now it's this Stahl guy. What else are you gonna try and pin on me? J.F.K.?" He sounded aggrieved, put-upon, a poor soul.

"I imagine I could pin quite a bit on you if I really put my mind to it, but I don't have the time. I believe what you told me about the old guy the other night; this is a new conversation. You're not here on vacation, and nobody else in the D'Allessandro family knows why you're in town, so it only makes sense that somebody else sent for you. I'll lay you eight to five it's Jimmy Dosti, and that means he's put out a contract on Ed Stahl."

"So?"

"Where'd you get the idea for the rat in the mailbox? You must've stayed awake all night thinking that one up."

He shrugged his shoulders. At least he didn't deny it. He got points for that.

"Lay off if you know what's good for you, Nello. The cops know you're in town, and if you so much as go near Ed Stahl again, or call him on the phone, you'll spend a long time wishing you hadn't."

"My lawyer don't like that kind of talk."

"Your lawyer's not here."

"You still got no proof, rosy cheeks."

"I don't need proof. I'm not a cop. So I'm telling you if

anything happens to Ed Stahl, even so much as a case of nerves, I'm going to put you in the hospital with tubes sticking out of places you didn't even know you had. And then I'll come after Jimmy Sweets. You can tell him that."

"I will," he said quietly. "Make book on it."

"That's if Mr. D'Allessandro doesn't get the both of you first. I'll be on the phone with Victor Gaimari first thing in the morning to let him know the little games you and Jimmy have been playing. You can tell that to Jimmy, too. They take a dim view of outside talent coming into town and making noises without their okay." I couldn't quite hide my own smile. "It shows a lack of respect."

He lost a little of his color, and his smirk turned into a sneer of false bravado. Jimmy Sweets was one thing; Giancarlo D'Allessandro was quite another. Respect was right up there on their priority list with eating and sleeping and breathing, and both Dosti and Trinetti had committed an egregious breach of etiquette by mounting a campaign of terror against Ed Stahl without first getting permission from the don, permission that would have been unlikely in coming; the mob keeps their hands off newspaper reporters as a matter of policy.

"If I were you," I said, "I'd go back to New York in the morning and forget all about Cleveland."

"I forgot about Cleveland five minutes after I got off the plane." He gave me a nasty, crooked little smile. I wanted to erase it with my knuckles, but I used what little restraint I had left. "You lousy small-change pissant. Are you rousting me out of town?"

"Put it any way you want," I said. "You've been told."

"Yeah? Well, tough shit, because I got a grand jury hearing next week."

"Make sure you're healthy enough to show up for it."

"You all through bullshitting now? Because I've got someone to see."

"Wouldn't want to keep the lady waiting, Nello. Just remember what I said."

"I'll remember," he said. There was a fleck of white spittle on his lower lip. "Jimmy Sweets'll remember, too."

"Fair enough." I turned and started to walk away, gambling that he wasn't going to shoot me in the back in such a public place. It wasn't his style. Guys like him prefer working close up; it's the only way to go with a small-caliber weapon like they usually favor. Which meant he also needed the advantage of surprise.

"Hey, rosy cheeks!" he called after me. "Okay if I take my hand out of my pocket now?"

"Sure," I said, without turning around. "Nice and slow. But watch what you do with it—your little friend would hate it if all your fingers were broken."

I sat low in my own car on the third level until I saw Nello's blue Sable screech down the ramp past me. I couldn't get a look at his face, but I'm sure he wasn't happy. The poor bastard was caught in a three-way squeeze. He probably wasn't all that afraid of me, although I'm sure he knew I wasn't kidding when I said I would personally avenge Ed Stahl if anything happened to him. But he'd turned to stone when I'd mentioned that D'Allessandro and Gaimari weren't going to like his coming to town on his own hook to hassle Ed Stahl—or worse. Those were guys people in Nello's circles didn't want to make angry. And yet if he went back to Jimmy Sweets and said he was backing off—and survived to tell about it—he'd be marked an inept failure at best, and when the word got back to New York that he hadn't been able to fulfill his contract, he'd be relegated to running errands to the corner for ice cream cones.

It'd be good for him. Build his character.

I was mad at myself. I should have put Nello's arrival in town together with the threats against Ed from the beginning, but since Marko had hooked him into the Bogdan Zdrale killing, I'd been pointed in the wrong direction. Besides, the mob usually doesn't terrorize with threatening phone calls and dead rats. They just do it. I had to assume that Nello

248

Trinetti had a few little kinks of his own when it came to doing his job.

My eyelids were getting heavy—two A.M. is somewhat past my bedtime. I waited about three minutes until I was sure Nello had left the premises, then backed my own car out of its space and drove slowly down the ramp and out onto East Ninth Street. Like most big cities, Cleveland's downtown streets are more or less deserted at that hour of the morning, except for the people of the dark—the hookers and pushers and the homeless huddled in doorways with their precious stash of shopping bags for a pillow. But then again, so are her other streets. Cleveland is not a nighttime kind of place.

My tires hissed against the dampness on the pavement as I made my way up to the Heights, but the temperature had risen to the low forties, so there was little danger of ice. I was glad about that. I'd been up for more than twenty hours and I was in no condition to be fighting the steering wheel and skidding on the hill.

As I was putting my key into the lock of my apartment door, the lights went out—but it turned out to be the heavy blanket that was thrown over my head, suffocating me, and the glancing blow on the back of the head with what felt like a crowbar or steel pipe.

Pain exploded behind my eyes, spreading like a spider-web crack in a windshield. I struggled to breathe through the heavy fabric, and I could smell the damp wool of the blanket, stale bologna sandwiches, and dust and motor oil and a sweetish scent that seemed familiar but that I couldn't place. I staggered forward, struggling to free my hands, but someone big and strong had wrapped his arms around me from in front and was holding them close to my sides, and the blanket fast over my head, while someone else gave me another shot with the pipe, this time catching me high across the shoulders, which hurt more than the one to my head because this one connected directly, knocking the wind out of me. I didn't have the breath to groan in agony.

I fell against the wall, taking the guy holding on along with me, and our feet danced a frenzied gavotte as we scuffled for a solid foothold on the worn carpet while the hitter moved around us, apparently looking for a good angle.

I felt the beginnings of panic in my chest, fluttering against my ribs like the wings of a wild bird who has somehow wandered into the living room. I've been punched around before, more than I care to remember, but I was always able to see. The blanket was a good touch, I had to give them that. I was disoriented and giddy from the claustrophobic smothering, and I wasn't even sure how many of them there were—two at the very least—and because I couldn't see them, I couldn't brace myself for the next blow. It came, as I knew it would, this time along the side of my face, almost taking my ear with it. Temple gongs went off inside my head.

I rammed my knee up between the legs of the guy holding me, but missed the mark. He grunted nonetheless; a hard knee in the thigh is no fun, either, and his grip loosened about a quarter of an inch, just enough that I was able to wriggle one arm free. I couldn't do much with it, though, hampered as it was by the blanket. I hunched my shoulders against the next hit, and when it landed the pain almost put me under, searing across the back of my neck.

With my right hand I clawed frantically at my coat, trying to get to the .357 under my left arm. Whoever was holding me was almost as big as I am, strong and burly, and he had me in a bear hug. I butted my head forward against the stifling wool, and I think I caught him in the face, because he cursed and loosened his grip another smidge.

My fingers found the butt of the pistol, welcome as the touch of a lover. I scrabbled at it to free it from the holster, meanwhile kicking my foot out and connecting with the shinbone of the guy whose arms were still wrapped around me in a crushing embrace. I'm a big man and I wear heavy shoes—it must have hurt him a lot.

We lurched away from the wall, with me trying desperately to keep my balance. I knew if I ever went down under the blanket and the weight of my dancing partner I might never get up again. I was hyperventilating, desperately trying to maintain control, and had to will myself to keep my wits about me. If I went over the edge, I'd be lost.

With much effort I was able to work the Magnum loose from its holster. My assailant was still squeezing me tight and I couldn't move my hand to where I wanted it. I tried to keep him busy thinking about the toe of my shoe knifing into his shinbone again and finally was able to get the muzzle of the pistol pointed upward and away from me. I squeezed the trigger.

The explosion, magnified under the heavy material, deafened me, and powder burns scorched my chest. The man who was holding me screamed, and the viselike arms around my body went slack. But before I could pull the blanket away from my face something crashed into the back of my cranium, and an ocean of black ink engulfed me and covered up my head. I went down, feeling the coarse carpet of the hallway under my hands, and for the life of me, I couldn't think of a single good reason to try to get up again.

I was vaguely aware of the sound of running, running away from me, that peculiar sound of feet going down the stairs, like little boys tumbling to the table for pizza. It was nice that they were going away—then it would be quiet and I could sleep peacefully. After a few seconds I heard a door in the hallway opening.

"Milan?" came a voice from far away.

I rolled over onto my side. It only took me about eight days. I managed to get the blanket off my head and sucked in huge quantities of oxygen in the mistaken hope that it would clear away the little black tadpoles doing the breaststroke in front of my eyes.

"My God, what happened?" It was my across-the-hall octogenarian neighbor, Mr. Maltz—I recognized his voice. I flopped over onto my back like a dying carp and managed to get my eyelids open even though there were twenty-pound weights holding each of them shut. Mr. Maltz was standing in his doorway, holding the lapels of his flannel bathrobe together at his throat. On his feet were white cotton socks and old-fashioned carpet slippers.

"What was that, a gunshot? I look through the peephole and I see you on the floor. You're shot, Milan?"

"Police," I croaked. "Call the police."

And then I pulled the blanket up to my chin and went to sleep.

As I mentioned, it was way past my bedtime.

NINETEEN

"Milan, you're acting like a goddamn jerk!"

Dr. Ben Sorkin was pulling my eyelid back with his thumb and shining a light into my pupil, and his mouth was set in an angry line. Ben was another old friend. We'd met at Kent State, and when he opened his private practice—Cleveland still has several members of that vanishing medical breed, the general practitioner—Lila and I had used him as our family doctor. He'd taken care of our boys' measles and chicken pox as well as their childhood cuts and bruises. Lately I'd been coming to him for my cuts and bruises too. So when the squad car had arrived at my apartment at three A.M. after being summoned by an agitated Mr. Maltz, I'd resisted going to the nearest emergency hospital and demanded to be taken to Ben's house just off Coventry in Cleveland Heights, where he got out of bed without disturbing his wife, threw on a jogging suit, and came downstairs to examine me in his kitchen. But it wasn't being awakened in the middle of the night that was pissing him off.

"I want you in a hospital!" he snarled. "Give me twenty-four hours, that's all. For observation."

"There's nothing to observe, Ben. They didn't even break the skin."

"You're concussed, for God's sake."

"I've been concussed before," I said. Indeed the incredible headache behind my eyes felt familiar. I thought of

Muhammad Ali, that once magnificent hunk of humanity, and lots of other fighters not as good as he at dodging punches, who had taken a few too many shots to the head and now had trouble remembering their home address, and wondered just how close I was cutting it. Maybe I needed to find another line of work.

Ben snapped off his slim little flashlight, and I blinked the black dots away. He sat down at his kitchen table across from Lieutenant Mark Meglich, who had watched the entire examination with a sour expression on his unshaven and sleepy-eyed face.

"Macho man," Dr. Sorkin said. "You've got all the maturity of a six-year-old. You think you're invincible to everything but Kryptonite."

"Maybe I am," I said. "I just took a couple to the head with what felt like a crowbar and we're sitting here discussing it." I touched the lump at the back of my skull with fingers that trembled a bit. "But the bastard didn't hit nearly as hard as that offensive guard for Indiana that time. What was his name, Marko? The one with the elbows?"

My former football compadre shrugged his shoulders. "I only learned the names of the running backs—they were the guys that hit me."

Ben put his fingers on my pulse, looking at his watch. "What are you now, Milan? Forty-two, forty-three?"

"Forty. Don't rush me, Ben."

He shook his head like a disapproving Sunday school teacher. "The big four-oh. You want to see forty-one? You treat your body like shit. You smoke, you drink too much beer, you don't get enough sleep, and I'll bet your cholesterol count is triple your IQ from all that sausage crap you eat."

"Watch it," Marko said. "To a Slovenian that's an ethnic slur."

"You're not a kid anymore, Milan. You have to start taking care of yourself. The body doesn't heal the way it did when we were in college. You belong in a hospital where we can keep an eye on you, but you want me to let you go out and run around with a concussion. You have a death wish, is that it? Think of your kids if you won't think of yourself. Little Stephen standing by your coffin with tears in his eyes . . ."

That upset me, as he knew it would, and as a defense I started to laugh. "Talk about guilt trips!"

He smiled in spite of himself. "It's genetic—my mother used to do it to me. Come on, Milan, I mean it. I need you in University Hospital until at least tomorrow morning. We'll take X rays, maybe a CAT scan."

"Can't do it, Ben."

He turned to Marko. "Arrest him, will you?"

"I wish I could, but being a pain in the ass isn't a crime," Marko said.

"He's got a mushy spot in his head—he needs to be watched."

I hate it when people talk about me as if I weren't there. "Gentlemen, could we just cut through the crap here? I'm going to live, Ben, just to spite you. Give me something to make it not hurt so much and I'll get out of your hair."

He sighed, and began scribbling something on a prescription pad. "When you conk out driving sixty on the Shoreway and take five or six innocent citizens into the rail with you, remember old Dr. Ben told you so." I hoped the pharmacist would be able to decipher his writing better than I could, or I might wind up with birth control pills. "What're you trying to prove, Milan?"

"Nothing."

"Then why are you like this?"

"Because two goons tried to kill me and I want to find out who they are before they try again."

"Why don't you leave that to us?" Marko said.

"Us the police, you mean? Because the only clue you have is a smelly old blanket that anyone with ten bucks could buy at J C Penney. And with all the other crap going down around here, you'd get around to it right behind busting eight-year-olds for boosting candy bars out of the corner market."

Ben said, "You're not being fair to Mark."

"Poor Mark," I said.

"You're not being fair to me, either. I'm your doctor, for God's sake, why can't you just once listen to—"

"You finished writing that prescription?"

He glared at me, and then slumped down in the kitchen chair. "Take two of these every six hours," he said. He ripped the sheet off his pad, annoyance stiffening the set of his shoulders, mumbling something about a hard-headed Slovenian son of a bitch. I couldn't imagine who he meant. I folded the prescription and put it in my shirt pocket.

"I'm bringing Nello Trinetti in," Marko said.

"For what? He had nothing to do with this."

"What makes you so sure?"

"The mob doesn't do things this way."

"What way?" Ben said.

"Throw a blanket over a guy's head and try to bash his brains out. They like things cleaner—a bullet behind the ear and dump the stiff in a culvert. No muss, no fuss. It's a question of style."

Ben turned his face away. "I don't want to hear any of this."

"Ben's right, Milan. Come on, I'll drive you home and tuck you in." He ran a hand over his whiskers. "Maybe I'll tie you down while I'm at it."

"You're a kinky bastard, aren't you?" I said. I stood up, fighting off a wave of dizziness that almost knocked me off my feet. "Thanks, Ben. Don't worry, I'll be fine. Send me a bill, okay?"

He rose too, shoving his fists into the pockets of his warm-up jacket. "It'll be a tax write-off for me—I'll be very surprised if you live long enough to pay it."

The barest traces of light smudged the eastern sky as Mark and I went out to his car at the curb. The tree lawn was wet and squishy under my feet, kind of the way my head felt. I looked at my watch. It was twenty minutes to seven. The rain had stopped, and if I correctly remembered the forecast I'd heard on the car radio earlier that night, it was going to be a partly sunny day and perhaps everything would dry off.

Already it had warmed up a few degrees, but it was still several months until shirt-sleeve weather.

Marko fumbled for his car keys. "If not Trinetti, then who?"

"That's the Final Jeopardy response," I said. I leaned on the door handle to steady myself while he slid in, reached over, and unlocked the passenger door. I got in and put my head back against the headrest.

"Let me worry about it, why don't you? You need to stay off your feet a few days, no kidding. You look like Banquo's ghost." He fired up the engine, gunning it to get it warm in a hurry.

"If I don't find out who those guys were, I'm going to *be* Banquo's ghost."

"You sure you put a bullet in one of them?"

"I think so. But they both ran away under their own power." I put my hand over my eyes, and the touch of my cold fingers felt good.

"He'll need to get that slug taken care of, and when he does, it'll have to be reported."

"You're pretty naive for a guy with a gold shield. He'll probably dig it out himself with a kitchen knife."

"Give us some credit, okay? We'll find them."

"*I'll* find them," I said. "Or else they'll find me. Either way."

"Jesus, you need a keeper, you know that? Ben's right, you haven't got the sense God gave a cranberry."

I closed my eyes against the thrumming in my head. "Did you get that stuff from immigration I wanted?"

"You only asked me this afternoon!" he exploded, putting the car in gear. "What am I, a magician?"

"Marko the Magnificent." I sighed, and it came out ragged. I was in worse shape than I wanted to admit. "Cut me a little slack, all right?"

"Sometimes it seems like cutting you slack is what I do for a living," he said. On the short drive from Ben's house to my apartment he probably said some other things, too, but

257

you couldn't prove it by me. I'd closed my eyes and gone inside for the duration.

I paced the floor of my den, glancing occasionally at the inanities of *Good Morning America* on the tube. I never watched the show, but Ben Sorkin had told me not to go to sleep, so I tried to pretend that the vapid young actor plugging his new movie was the most fascinating person in the world and to stay awake and be interested in the clip he'd brought with him. It didn't make me want to rush out and see the movie. I wanted some coffee but I didn't think I could keep it down, so I gulped a bunch of Advil with a little water and hoped that would dull the edge of the pain until the drugstore opened and I could get my prescription filled.

Mostly I replayed the attack over and over on the VCR inside my head, and the memory of the claustrophobia, the desperate attempts to take a deep breath through the smelly, suffocating blanket, made my palms sweat. Two men. Bumbling, ineffectual, clumsy, but the one who held me had been big and strong—and was probably walking around with a bullet in him. They weren't particularly good at what they were trying to do; when I fired the gun they both cut and ran. This was no hired hit. This was amateur night.

Something nagged at me, and it wasn't the headache. I was missing something somewhere, I knew it. It was in the back of my brain behind the bruises. I tried to bring it to the front, but without success.

At nine o'clock I walked unsteadily across the street to the drugstore and waited while they filled the prescription. There were eight pills, white and cylindrical, and they smelled like stale spit, but half an hour after I took two of them as directed, the blinding headache had subsided to a bare essence, which was good enough for me to sit at my desk and get some bookkeeping done. It's the part of self-employment that I hate, and doing it while I felt as lousy as I did seemed almost like a penance for not heeding the advice of my doctor and checking into University Hospital for a work-up.

Just after I took my second set of pills, Marko rang my doorbell. He had a brown paper bag in one hand and a manila envelope in the other.

"How do you feel?" he said.

"Brand new. What's in the bag?"

"Soup," he said. "I stopped at Corky and Lenny's and got you some chicken soup and some macaroni salad. I figured if I left it up to you, you'd fry up some klobasa and onions, and I don't think that'd do you much good."

I grunted a graceless thank you, took the bag from him, and went into the kitchen and put it on the counter.

"Aren't you going to eat it?"

"Right this minute?"

"You probably haven't eaten all day. You need to keep up your strength. Go ahead, have some, it's still hot."

"I'll bet Boy Scouts help you across the street, Marko." I pointed at the envelope. "Is that for me too?"

"You're the most hardheaded bastard I've ever—"

"And a good thing, too." I took the envelope from him and tore it open.

"Same deal as on the other one," he said. "You never got this from me."

It was the same kind of Immigration and Naturalization Service file he'd gotten for me on Bogdan Zdrale. This one was for Rade Stanich. I sat down at the Formica-topped table in the kitchen and began thumbing the pages. "Sorry there's no coffee. Grab yourself a beer if you want."

He took a Stroh's from the refrigerator and popped it open. "Find what you're looking for?"

"Give me a minute."

"You're really pale," he said, sitting down across from me.

"That's the third time in the last two days you've told me how lousy I look. Be quiet, will you?"

He sat there sulking over his beer while I examined the contents of the file folder. After a few minutes I flipped through the papers again, faster this time, and Marko noticed my agitation and leaned forward, resting his forearms on the table. "Find something?"

"It's what I didn't find. There's nothing here about Rade Stanich's internment in the Banyitsa camp."

"So maybe he wasn't there."

"His son says he was." I held the file up like exhibit A. "Are you sure this is all of it?"

"The guy said he faxed me the file. Why would he leave something out? Unless two papers stuck together by accident or something."

I shook my head, and the pain inside bounced around like a Ping-Pong ball in a Lotto machine. "That'd be one of those pesky coincidences again. Listen, these documents are on file here in the Cleveland office?"

"Right, out on the west side."

"How easy is it to get to them?"

"That depends on who you are."

"What does that mean?"

"You have to have a good reason," he said. "If you're just a nosy parker—or a pushy private investigator—they keep them buttoned up pretty tight. But if they're your own records, or those of a member of your family, you can get access to them without too much trouble."

"Can you take them home with you?"

He shrugged. "Not if I know the federal government you can't. This country runs on its paper. But I guess you could make copies."

"So if those were my papers, or my father's, let's say, I could go in there and take a look at them?"

"I suppose."

"Would there be somebody hanging over my shoulder while I did?"

He finished his beer and took the empty over to the wastebasket. "What are you getting at?"

"If there was something in those records that I didn't want anyone to know about, what would stop me from taking it out of the file and putting it in my pocket?"

"That's against the law."

"Oh, right," I said. "That's why your desk is two feet high with your caseload, because no one ever breaks the law. Is there a way I can find out if anyone, Rade Stanich or anyone in his family, had been in to examine his papers?"

"I don't know," he said. "If it was lately, I suppose there'd be a record. On a computer someplace. But Stanich came to America in 1945. Any number of people could have poked around in this file in the last forty-eight years. It'd probably take another forty-eight to trace it." He sat back down. "You want to tell me what you've got? Or what you think you've got?"

It hurt my head to think, but I didn't have much choice. "Bogdan Zdrale was in Banyitsa during the war, and according to his son, so was Stanich. He was one of Zdrale's sponsors to come to this country, but no one in either family can remember ever hearing of the other, which strikes me as odd, to say the least. And now there's no record of Stanich ever having been in Banyitsa."

"So? What does that prove about who killed Zdrale?"

I massaged the ache across my shoulders and sighed. "At the moment," I said, "not a damn thing."

TWENTY

When I had stayed awake as long as I could, long enough to convince myself that it was safe to close my eyes and rest without conking out permanently, and after a lot more pacing and an absolute overdose on daytime television—Geraldo was doing convicted sex offenders—I slept fourteen hours, from six thirty at night until eight thirty the next morning. I woke up with a mild headache, sore and achy in the neck and shoulders, but compared to the way I'd felt when I went to sleep it was a Hawaiian holiday. I took two more of Ben's magic pain pills and then stood under a shower almost too hot to bear, letting it pound on me in all the painful places. I threw on some sweats and I drank a whole pot of coffee and two glasses of grapefruit juice. Despite my long fast I didn't feel like eating anything.

Putting the last of the coffee at my elbow on a little individual electric warmer Mary had bought me, I sat down at my desk. It's where I do my best thinking. The kitchen is for eating, the den is for reading and relaxing, but my desk in the front room somehow puts me in a thoughtful and analytical frame of mind. And I had some heavy thinking to do.

Whoever had wanted to make me guest of honor at a terminal blanket party hadn't been sent by Jimmy Sweets, I was almost positive of that. Sweets probably didn't think I was worth the trouble. What I'd said to Trinetti about the D'Allessandro people being unhappy with unauthorized hits in their town was true, and Dosti was smart enough to know that if he took me out he'd have a lot more questions to answer when Victor Gaimari did the asking. Chooch and his friend had screwed up once trying to mess with me, and Dosti wouldn't have trusted them a second time. For the heavy stuff he obviously imported out-of-town talent anyway, guys like Nello Trinetti, who wouldn't have had the time to go get a pal from someplace and wait for me in my dark hallway with a blanket and a crowbar. And errand boys like Nello don't do wet work on their own hook. The people who pay their salaries don't like it. No, it was strictly an amateur job, sloppily planned and badly executed.

What amateurs were mad at me?

I massaged the back of my neck as best I could, wishing I had a loving someone there to do it for me.

I sat and stared at the index cards on my desktop, a yellow pad in front of me on which I doodled a little stick-figure gallows, a habit of mine since childhood. No hanged men, just empty gallows, nooses waiting. My mother thought it was morbid, and it got on my father's nerves, but they never thought to send me to a shrink to find out why I was preoccupied with hanging. That isn't the Slovenian way—and they were probably right.

When I'd filled up the sheet with the gruesome little things I tore it off, wadded it up, and missed the wastebasket. Basketball has never been my game. I didn't want to risk bringing on a dizzy spell by bending down, so I left the crumpled-up paper on the floor while I thought some more.

Finally things started to make a little bit of sense to me. I learned a long time ago that Sherlock Holmes was right: when all probable solutions are eliminated, whatever is left, no matter how improbable, has to be the right answer.

I cleaned and oiled my .357 Magnum while I mulled over what I was going to do. Then I changed out of my sweats and into a pair of jeans and a turtleneck, strapped my holster under my arm, put on my coat, and went out to make the drive across town.

It was a mild day, what the weather reporters on television call "partly sunny," and there were a few mourners who had come out to Saint Theodosius cemetery to stand in silent contemplation before the final resting places of their loved ones, but the place was so big that they were hardly aware of me as I wound my way between the rows of markers. One old man looked up as I passed him, but since my features were as Slavic as his he must have thought I belonged there and paid me little more attention. The newly turned earth over Bogdan Zdrale's grave smelled of spring, but that wasn't what I was looking for. I wasn't sure what I *was* looking for, or what I hoped to find. Maybe another piece to the puzzle.

What I wound up with was a missing piece. Or a missing grave. But it helped.

After about fifteen minutes of wandering I found a weathered granite headstone on the far side of the cemetery from where Bogdan and his wife were buried. The carving was both in Cyrillic and Roman script:

Mira Samarzic
1914–1952
Mother

It isn't an uncommon name; it could have been another Samarzic family, I suppose. But I didn't think so. From the dates on the stone, Mira Samarzic could easily have been the mother of Lazo and Mirko. And with all the family plots in the cemetery, I couldn't help wondering where Father might be buried. Perhaps he was still alive, but if, as was customary, his wife had been a woman somewhat younger than himself, he would be an extremely old man now. Not impossible, but highly improbable. And if he were indeed deceased, why wasn't he buried next to his wife?

Probably because he'd died somewhere else.

I walked back to my car, working my neck muscles to keep them from stiffening up again, and sat there for a while with the window open, smoking a cigarette and thinking. Then I pulled out slowly onto Biddulph Road, hung a left, and headed back downtown.

The West Side Market was more crowded than on my last two visits, maybe because of the break in the weather. Lots of old ladies pulling metal shopping carts behind them, younger women with net or plastic bags bulging with meats and fruits and vegetables and all talking at once, their voices blending into a low rumble under the roof of the produce shed. I had to shoulder my way through the crush to get to the Samarzic Brothers stall.

Lazo Samarzic and his wife were in their usual places. Several shoppers were examining the merchandise, and the bins were only half full; it had been a good day for them. When Samarzic looked up and saw me his entire body stiffened, and he seemed to grow taller as I watched, his face settling into a mask of anger. Mrs. Samarzic glanced quickly away, busying herself rearranging tomatoes in the bin. Her face was pinched and pale.

"Hello, Mr. Samarzic."

"What do you want?"

"That's no way to talk to a customer."

"You're no customer," he said. "Don't waste my time. I got no time to waste. I'm running a business."

"Okay, then, how about a head of lettuce and some mushrooms?"

He waved a hand at the rows of merchants on either side of us. "Get it someplace else. I'm sick of talking to you. You keep coming around, asking dumb questions. You get on my nerves."

An elderly woman with a plastic shopping bag looped over her arm came up and started squeezing tomatoes, and Samarzic's wife moved over to her, frowning a little more with each squeeze.

"Nice tomatoes, yes?" Mrs. Samarzic said.

"I want a nice ripe one," the old woman told her, chin whiskers bristling.

"A little shorthanded today, aren't you?" I said. "Where's your brother, Mr. Samarzic?"

His wife looked over at him, fooling nervously with her

collar. His cheeks flamed; even his ears were bright red. "What's that your business?"

"Since he visited me the other night I thought I'd return the favor."

And then the color went away as if someone had opened a spigot and drained all the blood from him. His eyelids fluttered. "What visit?" he said, but his voice quivered all at once, and he coughed the frog out of his throat and gripped the edge of the bin with both hands. "What are you, crazy? My brother don't even know you. Leave us alone, Jacovich. There's nothing here for you but trouble."

I headed back over the Lorain-Carnegie Bridge, for the moment driving against the traffic, having confirmed a suspicion. As soon as I hit downtown I'd be in the beginning of the rush hour, or as we sometimes call it in Cleveland, the rush minute. The public radio station plays pretty good jazz all day long, but I listened to it as background music, thinking about things. As they used to say in school, what did we learn today?

Not much. A few of scraps of conjecture that wouldn't even hold up in small-claims court.

One: Lazo Samarzic's father died in Serbia, some time prior to 1952, or else he would have been buried at Saint Theodosius cemetery next to his wife.

Maybe.

Two: Mirko Samarzic hadn't come to work at the family business with his brother today because he was nursing a gunshot wound that I put in him when he'd thrown a blanket over my head and tried to kill me.

Maybe.

Three: When you go for two days without eating anything except pain pills you start feeling very light-headed and weak.

A definite yes on that one.

I went home and parked my car where I was supposed to—Deming Steel isn't the only one with assigned parking spaces—but instead of going up to my apartment I walked across the street to the Mad Greek on Cedar and had a bowl of soup and a sandwich. I can't even remember what kind, but that wasn't their fault. I just wanted to get something into my stomach, fast, to keep from passing out. The service was quick and efficient or I might have eaten my napkin.

I stopped off at the apartment for a quick check of my answering machine. Lila had called but said it was nothing important and to call back tomorrow. There was a message from Shushano Bauch too, saying she was just wondering how I was coming along, and that perked up my evening a bit. I didn't think I'd tell either of them that someone had tried to kill me.

It was a little after seven when I arrived at Danica Paich's house. Danica's being home on a Friday night was a long shot, I knew, but her lights were on. I just hoped she didn't have any company.

I was lucky. She was alone, but she looked very hassled and pinch-faced when she opened the door. She was still in her business clothes, and she had chewed most of her lipstick off.

"I can't see you now," she said, a little out of breath. "It's a family emergency."

"What's wrong?"

She shook her head, unwilling to talk about it. "You'll have to go."

"I only need to ask you a few questions about Walter. It won't take but a minute."

"Walter!" she croaked. "I don't even want to hear that son of a bitch's name! He's the problem."

"Maybe I can help."

She filled her lungs and held the breath for a moment, then let it out, stepping aside for me to enter. "I don't think so," she said as I went by her. She closed the door and came into the living room. "Vera's on her way over here with the baby to spend the night. Walter beat her up again."

"I'm sorry," I said through gritted teeth. "There's no excuse for that."

"There's no excuse for anything he does," she said bitterly. "And he's been getting away with it for years."

"You hate him very much, don't you?"

She was flying around the room picking up magazines and wiping dust off the occasional tables with the side of her hand, but my question stopped her in mid flight. She stared at me. "I have every reason to."

"Then tell me something; how well does Walter know Lazo Samarzic?"

"Milan, she'll be here any minute and I have to get the extra bedroom ready. I can't be bothered with that crap now. Please!" She picked up her coat from where she'd tossed it onto the sofa and hung it in the closet near the front door.

"It could be important, Danica."

"Not to me."

"To everyone."

"Why?"

"I'm not sure yet. Just answer my question, won't you?"

She shut the closet door and turned to lean against it, her hands behind her back. "I told you I don't know much about Walter or how he lives his life. But he's a born follower, Walter. He never had an original idea in his life, unless it was nasty. He talks about Mr. Samarzic all the time—follows him around like a puppy hoping to be tossed a bone."

A shiver ran through me. It might have been the headache, but I didn't think so. "What kind of bone?"

"Who knows? Maybe he just wants to feel like a big shot. God knows he isn't one anyplace else."

I heard a car pull up into the driveway outside. Danica rushed to open the door. Vera Paich was coming up the walk, holding the baby and two large plastic carryalls that mothers always use to lug around all the mysterious paraphernalia that seems to be absolutely necessary to the care of infants and toddlers. Her left eye **was** swollen half shut and red-turning-purple, and her lower lip was split and puffy. A dark bruise shadowed her jawline, and there was a caking of dried blood around one nostril. And everything on her face that wasn't bruised or cut was red and misshapen from crying.

I've been worked over by professionals and wound up not looking as bad as that.

The baby, Constance, was blissfully unaware in sleep, her chubby cheek and little flower mouth pushed out of shape where it pressed against her mother's shoulder.

"Oh, Vera," Danica said.

"Take the baby, take the baby," Vera gasped, and Danica lifted the child from the mother's shoulder to her own. Vera stumbled past her into the living room and stood leaning on the end of the sofa for support.

"I'm not takin' it no more," she wailed. "I'm not goin' back there. No more! I mean it this time." I realized it was the longest speech I'd ever heard her make.

Danica pressed her cheek against Constance's face. "What happened, Vera?"

"He's just drunk again, whattaya think? He's been drinkin' all day. He got up mean, he went out drinkin' this afternoon and then he comes home and drinks some more. He always hits me when he gets like that. It don't matter if I did anything wrong or not."

"What was he mean about?" I said.

She jerked around nervously when I spoke. It was the first indication that she'd even noticed I was there. "Huh?"

"Did it have anything to do with Lazo Samarzic?"

"Milan!" Danica said. "Now stop it! This isn't the time." She went to Vera and put her free arm around her. "Vera, you haven't done anything wrong! Walter just likes to make other people feel bad about themselves—he's always been like that. Come on, honey, let's put the baby down and get you settled."

They went up the stairs together, Vera leading the way and alternating between sobs and muttered threats. Danica threw me a murderous glance over the top of the baby's blonde head before disappearing onto the second floor. I took off my coat and sat down on the sofa, listening to them move around above me, their voices low so as not to wake the sleeping child.

Wife and sister, two victims of the same sour, twisted man. Walter Paich was one of the world's classic losers, a guy not smart or strong or fair of face, who lived by tiptoeing around the edges of his own life. His failure as a human being had made him a toady and lickspittle to those who he perceived as more worthy than himself. That's a pretty bad self-image, and it so emasculated him that the only time he could feel the weight of his own scrotum was when he was bullying people who couldn't fight back.

I looked up at the ceiling as Vera's voice rose to a mournful wail. I hoped she meant what she said, that she'd never return for more abuse, both for her own sake and for the little girl's as well, but I wasn't optimistic. We all have patterns, and no matter how painful or destructive they seem, they are always of our own choosing. It takes a stronger resolve than Vera was ever likely to possess to break out of your bad pattern and nurse yourself back to emotional and spiritual health. So chances were she would go back to Walter, history would repeat itself—as is its wont—and someday he'd injure her or the baby seriously. Or kill them.

I nearly jumped out of my skin when the doorbell rang. Vera's keening grew louder, and I heard Danica speaking softly, soothing her. She came halfway down the stairs, crouching down so we could see each other.

"Milan! If that's Walter, don't let him in! Please."

I opened my mouth to say something, but nothing came out. I hadn't signed on as guardian of the gates, and as much as I disliked Walter Paich, I didn't want to get into the middle of a domestic dispute. Outraged husbands and wives were more dangerous and unpredictable than bank robbers, and Spanish John Hanratty had a permanent kink in his knee to prove it.

She raised her eyes to the second floor. "She'll get hysterical if you let him in. Please, Milan!" And then she ran back up the stairs to the crying Vera.

I stood up awkwardly, crossed the room, and opened the front door.

"Milan! What are you doing here?"

Joe Bradac. He was surprised to see me, to say the least.

Joe Bradac, all dressed up for a Friday night in a sports jacket and tie under his usual blue parka, a single rose wrapped in cellophane in his hand.

Joe Bradac at Danica's house.

Joe Bradac without Lila.

"That's the question of the evening," I said.

His fingers fluttered up to the knot in his tie over which his prominent Adam's apple hung like a promontory on the face of a mountain, and he stretched his neck as if to free it from the constriction of his unaccustomed buttoned collar. He looked like a kid coming to pick his date up for the junior prom, except that instead of a clear plastic box with an orchid he carried the rose.

His thick-lensed glasses had slipped down the bridge of his prominent nose, and he pushed them back up with one finger. "Uh," he said.

That's the thing about him. He always knows just the right thing to say, Joe.

"Uh, well, I knew Danica was having a bad time—on account of her grandfather, y' know—and I was in the neighborhood anyhow and I thought—well, I wondered how she was doin' and all, and I thought . . ."

We were still standing in the doorway, him outside and me inside. I stepped over the threshold and pulled the door to behind me, taking care that I didn't lock myself out.

"You better go home, Joe."

He blinked. He always blinked a lot. Another of his endearing qualities. "Well, yeah. I mean, I just stopped by. I'd kind of like to say hello to Danica, pay my respects. . . . " He waved the rose like a symphony orchestra conductor, not knowing what else to do with it.

"Go home, Joe. Now."

"Uh." He didn't move. Maybe he was just paralyzed by fear; the way I was feeling, he had every reason to be.

"If you go now, I won't say anything to Lila, and you won't wind up with your balls in her pocket." I moved closer to him so he had to look up at me. "Or in mine," I added.

He licked his dry lips. "Uh," he said again. His Adam's apple was working overtime and made his voice quaver. "All respect, Milan, but you got no right telling me what to do about this. It's not your business anymore, you know?"

"That's what you think. Lila and I might be divorced, and she might be living with you now, but I still care about her more than anybody else in the world, her and the boys. And if anybody hurt her I'd break their goddamn back. You understand me, Joe? I wouldn't care if I was married again or she was married again or what. Anybody that hurts her, they have to deal with me."

He backed up, almost falling off the step, and he waved his arms for a second to keep from going down. "Well, sure, Milan, I know how you—listen, you got this all wrong here, though. Danica's just a friend. I told you already. I just wanted to see how she was getting along."

"Fine. She's getting along fine. Good night, Joe. Have fun smelling your rose."

He never took his eyes off me as he backed up along the walkway like a courtier leaving the presence of the king of Siam.

"Joe?" I said. "You don't come back here. I don't ever want to hear you came back here."

Making a superhuman effort not to slam it, I went inside and closed the door. I stood leaning against it, breathing hard. Anger was working my chest like a bellows.

After a few minutes Danica came back down, looking tired and drawn.

"Was that Walter?"

"No. It was Joe Bradac."

She paused at the foot of the stairs, her hand on the newel post. We just looked at each other.

"I sent him home," I said. "And he probably won't be back."

"You had no right."

"Yes I did, Danica."

She came into the room and sat down on the sofa. "Don't judge me, Milan. I can't handle that in my life right now."

"You've already got John Hanratty," I said, "and you're flirting with me. You don't need someone else's man."

She examined the ragged edge of a fingernail. "You don't know everything about what I need."

"I know more than you think. You're a beautiful woman with a good head on her shoulders and a responsible job. You have everything going for you, if you'd only realize it. You don't need constant validation to prove to yourself that you're worth something. The past is past—you told me that once. Let it die. Start believing in yourself. Start having some respect for yourself."

"You missed your calling, Milan; you should have been a priest. Or one of those people who go around giving motivational seminars." She slumped against the cushions. "I want you to go home now. Leave me alone, leave my family alone. I'm grateful to you, for what you tried to do, but I want it to be over—starting right now."

"I'll leave," I said. "But it isn't that easy anymore."

I got out of there so quickly that I didn't take the time to put on my coat. I had stopped on the walkway and started to shrug it over my shoulders when I saw the car parked in the driveway. It was the one Vera Paich had arrived in.

A tan Ford sedan with a crumpled bumper and a smashed-in right front headlight.

TWENTY-ONE

My anger at Joe Bradac had dried up and blown away by the time I got home, perhaps because I now had other things to think about that were more important. Things that had to do with life or death. Maybe mine. Joe never knew how lucky he was.

It was inconceivable to me that Vera Paich had tried to run me over in the snow the other night, but it was the Paich family car that had been used, and if we could exonerate baby Constance out of hand because her little legs were too short to reach the pedals, it wasn't too much of a leap of the imagination to suppose that it had been Walter behind the wheel. Trying to figure out why was harder.

But I managed.

I thought about calling Marko, but I still didn't have anything to tell him except who had driven the Ford. Still thinking about it, I had just gone to get a beer out of the refrigerator when the telephone rang. I picked up the wall phone in the kitchen.

"Are you one of those people who don't return their messages?" Shushano Bauch said. "I figured you for a classier guy than that."

"Sorry," I said, "but I've been busy."

She must have picked up on the strain in my voice, kind of like Kirk Douglas in *Gunfight at the O.K. Corral.* "Are you all right?"

"Sure," I said, putting the cold beer bottle to the lump on the back of my head. "Why?"

"Because you haven't called me in the last few days, and frankly I was disappointed. I'd expected you to."

"Oh," I said. That was the level of my witty repartee at the moment. Oh.

"Didn't you want to? I kind of got the idea you did."

"I wanted to very much. I thought about it a lot. But I don't think your father would like it if we went out."

"Then don't go out with my father. I'm a grown woman, and I pick my own friends and lovers. I'm not talking about anything heavy, and if it ever got that way I suppose I'd be the one to back off. Because of my father. But I still think you're damn attractive, in a rugged, football-player kind of way, and what's more important, you seem like a nice, decent person. A caring person. I don't meet too many of those in courtrooms wearing three-piece suits. So I guess this is my way of telling you that I'd like to get to know you better, and if you'd like to have dinner sometime, or go to a movie, feel free to call."

I sat down at the kitchen table with the receiver between my chin and shoulder and I twisted the cap off the beer bottle. "Okay," I said.

"You sound tentative about it."

"No, I'm not, but . . . "

"If you're worrying about Dad tapping his foot at the front door if you bring me home one minute past ten o'clock, don't. I don't have to check in with my parents every hour on the hour."

There was a chirp in the receiver that I knew to be my call-waiting signal. I hate those damn things almost as much as beepers.

"You've got another call," she said, "so I'll let you go. But let me hear from you, Milan."

"I will. I promise."

"You're a fool if you don't," she said.

And she was right.

I depressed the button on the phone and let it up again to receive the incoming call.

"Yes?"

"Jacovich?"

"This is Milan Jacovich."

"Samarzic."

I sat up a little straighter. "What can I do for you, Mr. Samarzic?"

"We have to talk, you and me."

"I think we do too."

He hesitated. "I don't talk over the phone."

"You want to get together in the morning?"

"What's wrong with now?"

I looked at the kitchen clock. "It's almost eleven."

"So? Tomorrow's Saturday. You'll sleep in."

"Why don't you come over here then?"

"No," he said. "Meet me."

"When and where?"

"In about two hours," he said. "Heritage Park."

The Flats is the name by which those parcels of downtown riverfront land located along both banks of the Cuyahoga just before it meets Lake Erie have been known since the city's earliest days. At one time there were barren stretches of mud and weeds there, then warehouses and light industry took over. Sometime in the early eighties a group of enterprising Clevelanders gave the neighborhood a massive face-lift, turning the Flats into the restaurant-nightclub center of northern Ohio. The east bank was developed first, and for a time anyone who was anyone under the age of forty hung out down there on the weekends. You were sure to meet someone you knew on a Saturday night if you hit enough bars. Certainly you'd meet someone you'd like to know.

Lately the developers have turned their attention to the area across the river, converting an old electrical generator station on the west bank into a cavernous fun palace for the well-heeled young called, fittingly, the Powerhouse, with a sports bar, a banquet hall, and the ubiquitous T.G.I. Friday restaurant. It's all part of the sprawling Nautica Entertainment Complex which also houses watering holes like Coconuts,

Shooter's, and Café Costanzi along with a parking lot the size of Vermont and a cluster of the kinds of itsy-poo shops that only sell items no one in the world really needs and in which tourists love to leave their money. A lot of the nighttime action has crossed the river now, and the east bank of the Flats has become a bit tattered and dowdy, victim of the ever fickle loyalties of the in crowd.

And now they're talking about building a marina and commercial center on Whiskey Island just a bit upriver; where once big-bellied men had strained and sweated hauling iron ore, now other big-bellied men would lounge on the decks of their power boats and clink ice cubes in their sour-mash highballs, make deals, and trade invitations to see Browns games from their VIP boxes.

Cuyahoga is an Indian word meaning "crooked river," and the waterway lives up to its name in the Flats. It's been dredged and rechanneled in places, but its muddy green water still meanders all over the place. Lorenzo Carter was Cleveland's first permanent resident; he built a cabin on the riverbank about four hundred feet from where Moses Cleaveland first landed and gave his name to the city, losing an *a* somewhere along the line. The cabin is still there, on Merwin Street, in a vest-pocket patch of territory now called Heritage Park, and Mr. Carter's cabin is open for inspection during the summer.

It isn't really a park at all. There's a patch of grass with a couple of dogwood trees that flower in the spring and a plaque marking the burial spot of a time capsule celebrating the centennial of organized labor, to be opened in the year 2088 when none of us will be around to care. The rest is a broad wooden deck built out over the edge of the river, with a couple of modern lampposts and some big square wooden blocks that serve as benches, and a walkway leading down to the cabin. Across the river is the old River Fire Station, now converted into a union headquarters. The smell of the river is strong here where it takes one of its hairpin curves, and flows under the red-painted swing bridge at the end of Center

Street, the only such bridge in Ohio, which cheerfully swings open clockwise when a boat has to get through.

I pulled my car into an unpaved lot and waited. There were a few other cars parked there, probably belonging to the folks who'd walked under the east arch of the Detroit Superior Bridge to get to the Flat Iron Café. But most of the Friday night revelers were across the water at Nautica, and it was quiet where I was, with the huge bridge looming over me and the downtown skyline behind me, Terminal Tower lit up brightly against the dark cloudy sky and the muddy Cuyahoga lapping quietly at the rocks and pilings lining the bank.

After a few minutes I got out of the car, leaving it unlocked, and walked past the grassy plot and out onto the deck. I stood looking down into the murky water running by, hearing the traffic rumbling on the bridge over my head, and finally sat down on one of the wooden blocks facing the parking lot. This way if anyone was going to attack me from behind, he'd have to have goggles and swim fins and a tank of air.

I puffed on a cigarette while I waited, feeling the damp cold in every bone. Maybe Ben was right—I wasn't a kid any longer, and I didn't take good enough care of myself. Here I was, recovering from a concussion in the middle of a winter night, smoking a cigarette out by the river waiting for a man I thought might be a killer. Most guys my age would be home watching a late movie on TV or reading a book or probably asleep.

He was seven minutes late. His headlights blinded me for a second as he pulled into the parking lot about twenty feet from my car, and then it was dark again. I saw the dome light flash on and off as he opened the door and got out. He was alone, but I kept my hand in my coat pocket, touching the grip of the .357, which I'd brought along for the occasion. It felt cold to the touch, even in my pocket. Maybe that's where they got the expression "cold comfort."

He stood there for a moment, a large silhouette in the dark. He took a long time looking around, although I was sure he'd seen me pinned in the glare of his lights when he drove up. Then he started slowly down the walkway, his hands in the pockets of his wool jacket, his head down, a cigarette dangling from the corner of his mouth. His heavy work shoes clunked as he stepped out onto the decking.

When he got a few feet away from me, he took one last drag on the cigarette and threw it into the river. "Jacovich."

I stood up and ground out my own smoked-down butt. "Mr. Samarzic."

He shook his head sadly. "This is shit, you know. It's all shit. We shouldn't be on different sides, you and me. We should be working together. We got the same concerns. We share things—a heritage."

"That may be the first time in history a Serb ever said that to a Slovenian," I observed.

"Don't be like that. You know what I mean. We're both Slavs. Roots, I'm talking about, that go back two, three hundred years."

A gust of wind came whistling down the channel from the lake, and I shuffled my feet to keep the blood circulating. "If we're going to reminisce about our grandfathers, could we go someplace warm and do it?"

Instead he went and sat down on the wooden block. I had no choice but to sit down again next to him, if only to get out of the breeze.

"Your people, Jacovich; where they from? Ljubljana?"

I nodded.

"My people from Belgrade. My mother came over here to America after the war. My father died there."

"In the war?"

He lit another cigarette, the yellow flare of his lighter turning his face into a fright mask, all angles and shadows. "In prison," he said. "German prison."

"Banyitsa?"

He didn't look at me. "That's right." The smoke came out of his nostrils in twin streams and dissipated almost immediately in the cold air. "You ever lose somebody, Jacovich? I mean, have somebody taken away from you?"

"Not in the way you're talking about."

"That he died in the camp, it killed my mother. Not right away, but in her heart she died with him. Finally a few years after we come over here and settled, she just gave up and stopped caring. We buried her in St. Theodosius, just like Bogdan Zdrale. So the Nazis, see, it's like they took both my parents. I grew up on my own, just an aunt to take care of me. But I remembered my papa—a big, strong man he was, and so proud to be a Serb. He was like a leader of the people back in the old country. Not a big-shot politician, but more like a . . . friend. You fight over a goat with your neighbor, you go see Samarzic. Somebody owe you money and can't pay? Samarzic, he'd help you work it out. A good man, my papa."

He tugged the bill of his tweed cap farther down over his eyes. "Your papa still alive, Jacovich?"

"No."

"But you remember, right?"

"I remember."

"Sure. So I decided to be strong like him. To honor him, his memory. Take care of other people. And I do, just like my father. You ask anybody who knows me."

"I have asked them. And they've all told me. The Cleveland connection."

"Huh?"

"Nothing. Go on."

It took him a moment to get his thoughts back on track. "So then, I try to be a good man like him, like my father. But always I remember, you know? I remember the Nazis."

"It was fifty years ago, Mr. Samarzic."

"Okay, so it was. But I wanted to do something." He put both hands in front of him, fingers curled and palms up, as if he were weighing two honeydew melons. "Not do nothing, I couldn't stand that. I wanted to avenge my father and my mother for what happened when I was just a little kid. I started asking around, I started writing letters to people, looking for something to do to take the pain away, the anger. There are people here—Serbs, I mean—who never forget what the Nazis did to them, who carry hate around with them all these years. Me, I don't hate the Germans no more. It was war, it was

281

us fighting for our country. Our lives. But I find out a few things. I find out there were Serbs from Banyitsa who were traitors, who turned on their own people. One, I find out, lived in West Allis, Wisconsin."

"Mele Malinkovich?"

His head whipped around toward me, eyes snapping. Then he smiled a little. "You're pretty good at your job, huh?"

"I'm pretty good."

We sat in silence for some moments. He just kept looking at me, the little crooked smile never wavering. He was probably wondering what else I knew. Finally he looked away again, hunching forward and putting his hands between his knees.

"Yes, I find out about this Malinkovich. He was with the army, just like my father, with General Mihailovic, and when he got captured and they put him in the Banyitsa, he turned traitor. He volunteered. He was like a—a trusty, no? Like a guard. Guarding his own people, beating his own people with whips and sticks. Killing his own people."

"How did you find out about him?"

"For the last ten years or so it was—how you say it when you think about it and you think about it, all the time?"

"An obsession?"

"Okay, yeah. So all those years I was talking to people, other Serbs all over the country. Malinkovich, when I get his name—it don't matter how—I go see him. He was a farmer; I pretend I want to buy from him. We talk, we talk a lot of bullshit, we drink zelavka together, and I lie to him. Pretend I'm just like him, like he was about the Nazis. I tell him I hate weakness in people, whether it's Jewish weakness or Serb weakness. I have all the right things to say, yes, Jacovich?"

"All the right things, Mr. Samarzic."

"And then he tell me about the camp, how he survived in the camp, and how now he hated the Jews and the blacks. He even take me into his basement there and show me his Nazi flag—his filth! I see that and I want to vomit, you understand, inside I'm on fire. But I don't let on—I pretend like that's such a good thing, to have a filthy goddamn swastika in your basement."

He shuddered, and I don't think it was from the cold. "So we make a deal for some corn, some other stuff, and I leave," he said, sniffing, and wiped his face with his hand. "But I go back again a few weeks later, and this time we're old pals, yes? I take him out, get him drunk in the town there, and when we go out to my car to take him home, he's leaning against me, too drunk to stand up straight, and he's singing me a little song about how we're gonna kill all the niggers and the Jews. So I take my gun and shoot him in the fucking head, and leave him there in the park for the rats and the crows." He turned and looked at me, his eyes cold as river stones. "For my papa. For my mama and my papa, you understand?"

I stayed quiet.

"It was a debt, Jacovich. Someone hurts one of mine, I hurt them. I always pay my debts."

I shifted my weight on the wooden block, feeling the cold wood through my pants. Samarzic pulled himself to his feet and walked a few steps to the heavy chain that was supposed to keep people from falling into the water and stared down the channel to where the east bank restaurants and clubs were clustered.

"Then six months ago—maybe seven—I hear that right here in Cleveland there is another man—another Serb, God damn it—who was at Banyitsa, who collaborated with the Nazis against his own people. I made it my business to find out who he was." He snorted again, hawked, and spat into the river. "Then I find out it was someone I knew."

I stood up and went to stand by him. "Bogdan Zdrale?"

"It made me sick."

"Sick enough to execute an old man?"

"My father never had the chance to be an old man," he said.

"How could you be so sure it was Zdrale?"

"Nobody lived through the Banyitsa unless they played catch with the Nazis."

"Played ball," I said.

"What?"

"Played ball, not catch."

"What's the difference?

"There are different ways of cooperating, Mr. Samarzic. It's called survival."

"Shit," he said. "That's all shit."

Neither one of us spoke for about a minute. Then I said, "Why are you telling me this?"

"So you'll understand."

"What?"

"That when someone hurts one of mine, I pay my debts." He moved a few steps away from me, away from the river- bank, and then turned to me. His face was a dark thunderhead of anger. "Mirko," he said. "My brother Mirko—he died today. Bled to death. Somebody shot him."

"I'm sorry, Mr. Samarzic."

"You're sorry," he said in a voice like grinding gears, and all at once he ran at me, hitting me in the chest with all his considerable weight. I was too surprised to stop him, and the impact knocked me off my feet, but I was able to wrap my arms around him and pull him backward with me. The chain caught me across the legs, and even holding on to him, I lost my balance; together we tumbled over the chain and down the incline into the Cuyahoga, bouncing against the rocks and chunks of metal and granite that line the bank. I hit my left elbow and it immediately went numb.

The riverbed slopes up there at Heritage Park, and the water isn't more than three feet deep, but we both hit shoul- ders first, and I gulped in a lungful of air just before the freezing water rose up over my head. Samarzic and I had a death grip on each other, but he had landed on top, and his weight was crushing me, forcing the air out of my chest.

I squeezed my eyes shut and tightened my bear hug around his middle. It didn't seem to faze him any, so I loos- ened my grip to bang away at his rib cage with my fist, butting at his face with my forehead. We rolled around on the bottom for a while like two dolphins mating, and the mud was a smothering cloud as it churned around us. Our efforts took us down a slight incline to where the water was a foot or so deeper. After a moment his hold on me loosened, probably because of the freezing water, and I was able to thrash out from under him.

I rose up like a sputtering Venus in the waist-deep water, the brackish smell of the river permeating my clothes, hair, and nostrils. I wiped the water out of my face just in time to see him come at me again. I tried to sidestep him, but my feet lost their purchase in the mucky bottom, and he hit me a glancing blow with his shoulder. Barely ducking a round-house right, I stumbled away. I couldn't get out of the way of the left hook, though—it came too fast, catching me on the cheekbone, snapping my head back.

You really do see stars when you're hit in the head. All the pain from my earlier concussion came roaring back over me, and I swayed dizzily, trying to focus my eyes. He buried a fist in my midsection, doubling me over, and then punched me in the side of the head.

The icy water engulfed me again, and this time I hadn't had the chance to take a deep breath first. I clawed at the mud, my legs pumping furiously as I tried to regain my footing, and the river poured into my nose and mouth, viscous enough to chew. Finally getting my feet under me, I heaved myself up into the biting cold air. He stood about five feet away from me, and he had a little nickel-plated .22 in his right hand. The same caliber as the gun that had fired a bullet into Bogdan Zdrale. It was pointing at the middle of my chest.

He was dripping, shivering with cold, but the gun remained steady.

"Your brother was trying to kill me to keep me from finding out who killed Zdrale," I said, gasping and coughing, colder than I'd ever been in my life. "So I shot him, without even being able to see who he was. Now you're going to shoot me. When does the killing stop, Mr. Samarzic?"

"When all the enemies of my people are dead," he said.

"The police know about Malinkovich. If you kill me now it'll just make it worse for you."

"Proof, Jacovich. They need proof. This is America." He

closed one eye, aiming carefully. "I told you to stay out of it, Jacovich. Now it's too late."

I watched, water-logged and helpless, as his finger slowly tightened. But rolling around in the mud with it is no way to treat a gun, and apparently some foreign matter had jammed the barrel, because when he tried to pull the trigger there was an orange flash and a muffled explosion, like someone popping a paper Coke cup with his heel at a ballgame, and the little .22 blew up in his hand.

The smell of burning flesh joined the others around us while his screams bounced off the supports of the bridge over our heads and echoed away off down the river.

Twenty-two

Even before going back to police headquarters to tell Lieutenant Meglich how I'd spent my Friday evening, I got a preventive tetanus shot at the hospital—Lazo Samarzic did too, probably a megadose, because he was the one with most of his hand missing. The Cuyahoga River hasn't caught fire in almost twenty-five years, but it isn't exactly an Alpine spring. I'd swallowed a good bit of it, and the doctor at the emergency room gave me something for that.

Marko didn't keep me very long. It was the quiet hours, the black hole between the night and the dawn, and he probably had one of his string of twenty-year-old girl-toys at home waiting for him—it was a Friday night, after all. And my story was a very simple one. Ugly but simple.

Lazo Samarzic was obsessed with the German slaughter of the Serbian people during the Second World War, and with his own father's death in particular, and had spent much of his adult life hunting down those who were responsible. After years of investigation and the expenditure of quite a lot of money, his first victim had been Mele Malinkovich, who had worked for the Nazis as a guard in return for staying alive at Banyitsa prison just outside Belgrade. I was sure that back in West Allis, Phil Miller was going to feel a lot better, cold or no cold, when Marko called him in the morning and closed a long-standing murder case.

Samarzic's second execution had been of Bogdan Zdrale,

and when I'd gotten too close to finding that out, he'd tried to make me the third. When I blindly shot my assailant through the blanket I had no way of knowing it was his brother Mirko. From what the police had been able to pry out of Lazo at the hospital, he and his friends had tried to doctor the wound themselves so it wouldn't be reported to the police, but poor Mirko had died two days later.

I promised Mark I'd fill in some of the cracks in the story when I felt better. All I wanted to do was get clean and get some rest; I was sick and tired in the most literal sense. One of the graveyard-shift cops had to drive me back down to the Flats to pick up my car, and by the time I got home, showered the river crud off my body and out of my hair, and fell asleep, it was just after six.

By nine I was awakened, almost thrown out of bed, by horrendous stomach cramps, my intestines knotted like a kid's shoelace. The Curse of the Cuyahoga had struck, and I'm not sure the chalky white liquid the doctor had given me was any help, but then I don't know how sick I would have been without it. I spent the next three hours in agonizing pain, voiding my system in the most violent fashion, alternately worrying that I was going to die and that I wasn't. When it was over I just fell back on my bed, drenched in sweat but shivering anyway. I wrapped up in the quilted spread and floated in and out of a troubled sleep, drained and aching and dehydrated. I was running a temperature, and my throat was sore, too, but I didn't know if that was the result of throwing up so much or if I'd caught cold from my baptism in the river. At some point my head began to clear a bit, and I lay staring up at the ceiling, too messed up to do much of anything else.

And that gave me some time to think, to roll it all around inside my aching head. To put it together.

At four o'clock the fever broke, and I was able to stagger to the phone to call Danica. Marko had already been by to tell her they had made an arrest, and although she was shocked and shaken that Lazo Samarzic had killed her grandfather in cold blood, she was certainly relieved that it was over, that there was finally an answer. Bogdan could rest now, and somehow she and her mother could get on with their lives, she said.

That only made me feel worse, because I knew what I had to do. I asked if Vera and the baby were still there, and she sighed and said yes. Apparently Vera was still making noises as if she really meant it about not going back to her husband. Danica was probably wondering how she was ever going to get rid of her.

I took another shower, downed two of my headache pills, my dysentery medicine, a timed-release cold capsule, and a big slug of something cherry-tasting to soothe my sore throat, feeling worse than at any time in recent memory. Then I put on a pair of tan cords, two sweatshirts, and the overcoat I usually reserve for dress-up occasions, my everyday coat being soaked with river water. I wrapped a wool scarf around my neck and drove out to Lake Shore Boulevard in Euclid.

Walter Paich opened the door about two inches, enough to stick his nose through and say, "Get away from here, Milan."

I hit the door with what little strength I had left and it blasted open, sending Walter careening backwards through his living room. He crashed over the coffee table, upending it and scattering the contents of a brimming ashtray, and wound up half on the sofa and half on the floor, eyes alternately flashing fear and hatred, like a strobe light.

I shut the door behind me. A big suitcase and a bulging garment bag were on the floor near the entrance to the kitchen, and an open overnighter was nearby.

"Going somewhere, Walter?"

"What's it to you?"

"You planning on telling your wife you're leaving?"

"Whattaya want, Milan? You can't come busting in here like you own the place."

"I just did," I said. "You're in bad trouble. How bad depends on how nice you talk to me."

He wriggled all the way up onto the sofa.

"You tried to run me down in the street the other night, didn't you?" He flapped his lips like a goldfish. "Don't bother

289

to deny it, I know it was your car and I can prove it if I have to. You're kind of a dumb schmuck, aren't you, Walter? Using your own car. Who told you to? Lazo Samarzic? Or was it your idea?"

His mouth was a sullen arch over his chin, but since it was his normal expression I wasn't sure how much of it was meant just for me. "And then you and Mirko Samarzic came to my apartment and threw a blanket over me and tried to bash my brains out. Don't deny that, either. The smell of baby powder was all over that blanket—you probably keep it in the car all the time. I've run into dumb punks in my lifetime, Walter, but you belong in Guinness."

He didn't answer me. He pulled himself to his feet, rubbing his elbow where he'd hit it on his way over the coffee table.

"You're pathetic, you know that? Chasing around after Samarzic, taking off from work and running his errands, doing his dirty work, risking your job and your marriage just so he'd like you because nobody else ever has. In a way I admire you, Walter. Your loyalty to your heritage—the old Cleveland connection, huh? But it's a little skewed, isn't it? You wipe Samarzic's ass and you hate yourself so much for it that you come home and beat up on your wife. What do you see when you look in the mirror? Anything at all?"

"Mind your own business."

"It is my business when somebody tries to ice me, Walter. Are you that desperate for Samarzic's approval?" I looked again at the luggage. "Unless you had other reasons. What are you running away from?"

His lower lip was quivering, but I wasn't about to quit. I was on a roll now, scenting fear and wanting to move in for the kill. Baiting Walter Paich had somehow become a blood sport to me, and I wasn't going to ease off until I'd torn him down, layer by layer, peeled his skin off to reveal the pus beneath. I wasn't liking myself for it, but I could no more have stopped voluntarily than one can will himself to stop breathing.

"You've been a sad, frightened little man all your life,"

I went on, advancing toward him, adrenaline racing through me and making me giddy, "victimizing people weaker than you like your wife and your sister. Raping and torturing a little girl was just your speed when you were a kid, and now terrorizing your wife until she isn't even a person anymore but only a frightened and abused animal. You've broken her because it's the only thing that could make a miserable piece of shit like you feel like a man. You feel good about yourself when you're hitting her, Walter? She's just a little bit of a thing, but I'll bet you feel like some sort of tough guy when you make her lip bleed, don't you?"

His normally pasty skin had turned the color of a dirty bedsheet, and he pulled at the neck of his T-shirt as if he was having trouble getting enough air into his lungs.

"But now the shoe's on the other foot, isn't it? Now there's something that's scaring you big-time, making you run like a rabbit in front of a forest fire. What are you scared of, Walter? Maybe a real murder rap?"

I'd pushed too hard, I guess. My genuine rage combined with my weakened physical condition had clouded my judgment, and the suddenness with which he launched himself over the fallen coffee table at me took me almost unawares. But as in all other things, Walter Paich was a clumsy oaf, and by the time he reached me I was ready for him. I threw one punch, a left that cracked into the side of his chin, sending lightning bolts of pain up my arm to my damaged elbow. He flew backwards across the room again and landed in an awkward pile on his suitcases.

"You killed your own grandfather, didn't you?" I said, advancing on him and standing over him, an avenging angel. I didn't want to be here. "Didn't you, Walter?"

He looked up at me and tried to refocus his vision, a string of saliva dripping down his chin like melted cheese on a pizza. The whites of his eyes showed all around the pupils. "It was Samarzic," he croaked in a voice like dried leaves. "I swear to God. It wasn't me."

"Maybe you didn't pull the trigger, but you were the one who brought him to the place where he died. He wouldn't have gone there on his own, or because Samarzic told him to. You're the only one who does whatever Lazo Samarzic says because you think it gives you the balls that you don't have otherwise. Did you stand there and watch him do it, Walter? Make an old man kneel down in the filth and pump a round into the back of his head? Or did he send you off to Wickliffe to wipe down the van and leave it, because you're too much of a pussy even to watch?"

All of a sudden he rolled over on his side, his hand scrabbling frantically in the open traveling bag. When he brought it out, there was a gun in it, a Saturday night special you could score from a kid on the street for thirty dollars. Walter wouldn't have known how to go first class if you'd bought him a ticket.

"Are you going to shoot me now? I don't think so. You don't have the guts to do your own killing. And even if you did, they'll track you down. You can't run anyplace far enough. You don't even have a car, you poor dumb bastard. What are you going to do, take the Rapid?"

He was breathing hard, his skinny chest expanding and falling. "My grandfather was a traitor!"

"Your grandfather was no more a traitor than you are," I said.

"What do you know?"

I felt feverish again, my head was pounding, and my throat was as raw as a wound. I kept my eye on the opening at the end of the muzzle, which was wavering obscenely as he tried to coordinate himself. For all my aches and pains, he was a lot more rocky than I was. "Your grandfather came over here after the war under the sponsorship of Elmo Laketa and a man named Rade Stanich. Did you know that?"

His mouth hung slack. We were in intellectual waters that were way too deep for Walter Paich.

"But yet your family never heard of Rade Stanich, never saw him, even though he lived right over in Parma, a half hour's drive from your grandfather's house. So why the sponsorship? They were both in Banyitsa together, two of probably only a handful of Serbs that survived. But there's no record in

292

Rade Stanich's immigration papers that he was ever in a prison camp, because somebody—maybe Stanich himself—removed it a long time ago. Bogdan Zdrale made it through the death camp because of his skill with machines. The Germans needed him. But Rade Stanich survived because he cuddled up to the Nazis. It was Stanich that was the camp guard, not your grandfather, and because of his guilt, he spent the rest of his life trying to make up for it. He agreed to bring your grandfather to America in exchange for his keeping his mouth shut."

"You're a liar!" Walter said, but there wasn't much conviction in it. The gun wasn't pointing at me anymore, it was aimed off to the side. Walter was no longer paying attention.

"Am I? Why do you think your grandfather was such a sad and angry man all his life? Because he'd compromised his principles and kept silent about a terrible crime so he could come here and make a new life for his family. It was a hell of a sacrifice, Walter, but he did it for your grandmother and your mother—and for you. But Lazo Samarzic found out he was in Banyitsa and jumped to an ugly conclusion, because he was so full of bitterness and hate that he couldn't even think straight. And so he told you to somehow get your grandfather down under that viaduct on East Thirty-seventh Street, and because you're such a pitiful excuse for a man and needed so badly for Samarzic to like you and let you hang around him, you did it."

I swallowed twice to soothe the fire in my throat. "Your grandfather made it through Banyitsa because he was tough, and skilled with motors. But you were so anxious for Lazo Samarzic to like you that you plugged into Samarzic's sickness and hatred—and wound up killing an innocent old man."

He let his gun hand fall to his side. His jaw hung open and his tongue flickered in and out of his mouth like a blind lizard's. He stared at a spot on the floor, only he wasn't seeing it. He was seeing something else, and I was glad I didn't have to see it too. It was a place where nightmares live.

I regarded him with more contempt than I've ever felt for

anyone. "You've poisoned everyone you've ever touched, Walter. Your mother and your sister and your wife and your grandfather. You are one sick, sorry son of a bitch.

"My big regret about this," I said, "is what it's going to do to your mother. But I don't suppose you care about that. You don't care about anyone. It must be a pretty empty feeling." I turned and went to the door. "As soon as Lazo Samarzic feels well enough to talk, he's going to hang you on a cross to try and save his own ass."

I took a deep breath, tightening my stomach muscles to still the fluttering wings inside me. "I'm going to give you a break you don't deserve, Walter—for your mother's sake. I'm going to let you go to the police before they come looking for you. It'll go easier with you that way. Otherwise they're going to strap you into the chair and fry your worthless ass."

I opened the door and went outside. The cold air hit me like an oncoming train, and I shivered and tucked my muffler in around my coat collar to keep the wind away. In my mouth was the taste of copper. I worked up as much saliva as I could and spit into the grass, then started down the cracked walkway to the street.

I was just getting into my car when I heard the shot.